4

CKLE
REET

PEAK

D0492320

An *Abacus* Book

First published in Great Britain by Fourth Estate Limited 1988
Published in Abacus by Sphere Books Ltd 1991
Copyright © David Peak 1988

Typeset by Ⱥ Tek Art Ltd
Addiscombe, Croydon, Surrey

Printed and bound in Great Britain by
The Guernsey Press

ISBN 03491 0174 4

Sphere Books Ltd
A Division of
Macdonald & Co (Publishers) Ltd
Orbit House, 1 New Fetter Lane, London EC4A 1AR

A Member of Maxwell Macmillan Pergamon Publishing Corporation

The characters in this novel exist
or have existed. The cities, streets,
cafes and rooms can be visited. All
of the events described have
happened at some time or in one
way or another.

The Narrator, however, is a
figment of imagination and bears
no resemblance to anyone living,
dead, or otherwise.

The Courtyard

Kate tiptoed through the splendid archway just now carrying a bag of writing paper in her left hand. Though she wished to make an impact on the world, she couldn't bear to disturb it too soon. Most of the visitors, tourists and what have you were doing fine without her, thank you very much. She's always been inclined towards self-deprecation, so you can imagine the care she took when asking snoozers if such-and-such a bench-space was unoccupied. In the shadowed corner to the side of the Abbey she chanced upon a damp bench waiting green and lonely. Taking it, she lay the sheets of paper on her lap and began to write her diary. In many ways it's a requiem mass for you, J. She's been promising herself this pleasure since you fucked off and failed to return. In the meantime, fiction and what she's seen of reality haven't revealed whether she loves you, or you her, or not, but my goodness she's heard some sweet rumours.

It's a beautiful day, J. See them hurrying to and fro, breathtaken at the history of this familiar city, yet creating no significant history for themselves. Cold and damp in the shadows, though. Cold and damp. Something in her shakes as she works on this second paragraph and worries in advance what she'll say in the third. It wouldn't do to guess the conclusion and state now that she loves you still, but bits and pieces of her, infamous shreds and patches, hope for this to be so. It's taken quite some time to get cracking on a diary because there's no particular starting point and there can be

1

no end. This courtyard will do for one, though there's no telling what will do for the other. Lives overlap. They struggle free and soon it's as if they've always been; and death, though it tries its hardest, ends nothing at all.

If all this seems of no consequence so soon, J, it's because God, poor soul, hasn't quite made it as an author. His plots, if plots they are, drift aimlessly from one thing to another and it's often the case that whole pages, chapters, volumes even, pass by with little to justify them. Kate would love to create the story God has failed to provide, but doubts if she can. However, perhaps you'll sense that these words are the keenest expression of her disappointment.

She watches now as a young man in jeans shakes hands with a silver-haired gentleman then leads him out of the courtyard towards the busy street. Only then does the young man dare to turn and wink at her. Men: they can be crazy at times. From the back he's a bit like you, J, but not enough to deserve a wink in return. So Kate wriggles her bum and settles down, eager for change but with no place to go; still a little angry and lonely, ears pricked for those lyrics of romance. She manages to make you appear for a moment. You're the same, of course, and you end up kissing her, telling her everything's fine. Then you are gone. A ghost too considerate by far. Here we see a pair of dark blue men on stepladders struggling with the restored sign of 'The Golden Lion' as gusts of wind sneak in from the street sweeping dry leaves and abandoned lager cans across the flagstones. Kate yawns then sings to herself. It's an old love-song cynics would probably find amusing. Still it's one hell of a day, wild with pastel romeos and those long noble speeches she didn't get round to while you were with her; the late autumn's nipped and ragged with babies screaming for milk from breasts or bottles. Perhaps Miss Austen hung around this very place between masterpieces, resplendent in her eighteenth-century costume. Kate sees her now, wreathed in grins at the subsequent fuss which has been made. Even the dead like to be famous and Kate works towards such a state by writing and smoking too much. Unhappy doctors in oak surgeries everywhere have shaken heads and voiced this stern opinion. 'My dear, you'll get cancer and be dead at fifty-five.' 'Oh! As long as that, doctor?' She rolls and licks and lights, then pulls smoke into her lungs. Beginning like this is the worst thing of all. There's rarely any purpose to it. See how the groups of crazy people stroll to and from the Abbey, queue at the tea-rooms, gaze up at the golden tower, or take photos of the mumbling pump-room and its clockwork commissionaire.

A few yards from her toes a traffic warden seduces a nervous police officer. The warden's tall with a clipped moustache and an off-centre cap. He tells the officer how gorgeous she's looking today. The officer blushes, rocks from one comfy shoe to another and fiddles with her black lapels. Strings of pigeons swoop for crumbs. Bells ring. Punch thumps the stuffing out of an alligator or crocodile. It's something o'clock in the city as Kate takes a deep breath and decides to do wonders with her life. She imagines unfamiliarity, sexual recklessness, strong, sympathetic fingers in moonlight, bites on the neck, romantic excursions through the lapping backstreets of Venice; then conjures up one or two misleading storylines she might include in her diary only to be dissuaded by a critical wink from Mr Anthony Burgess who chances by on his way to the tea-rooms. At least she thinks it's him; she imagines one so rare and talented has few lookalikes.

'You're in a mess, Kate,' she says to herself. Quite simply. No fuss. A mess. A pieman pulls up to the kerb in a white van, turns off the engine and wipes his brow. The delivery of pasties and pork-pies can be hard work however light the advertised pastry. Pigeons which have been pecking around Kate's shoes suddenly flutter across to a blue-rinsed woman rustling a paper bag. The pieman hoists the tray of wares onto his shoulder, veers through the archway and heads for the snack bar, swerving to avoid a bright yellow sweeper being tugged across the courtyard by his broom.

And sure, beginning in any shape or form's tougher than you think; something to spend wide-eyed nights and sleepy days trying to solve. In the far corner, for example, hidden from the sunshine too, a tall, white-faced harlequin pulls three balls from a canvas bag and begins to juggle, lifting his legs in attitudes of mime at regular intervals. Meanwhile, the sweeper tips his hat to Kate as she moves her feet. She nods to him. He's cock-a-hoop and overcomes the power of his broom in a kind of bloodless coup. From the outset it's important to seduce rather than overwhelm with unlikelihoods, but can she help it if a Chinese flautist at the railings dries his lips with the back of his hand then swoons into another melody, causing the rugged man of letters – who's just inches from the tea-rooms by now – to stop in his tracks and look back? He's fond of this particular piece of music and maybe Kate is too. She bites into one of her salmon-paste sandwiches and bemoans her loneliness.

In dreams you come once more, J, taking my hand, examining it for a moment then pulling me to my feet. I'm too hot to care. You're being a dad again, brushing apple-strudel crumbs from my jeans, sliding the white chair back under the table, sweeping cigarette ash out of the gratuity saucer. As I bend down to adjust my jeans you take a photo of me, then, convinced you have captured Charm itself, lead me to the Abbey. You're whistling – as well as you're able – 'Scarborough Fair'. People watching us nudge each other because we remind them of something they'd half forgotten. It's one of those heartbeat summers which happened just moments ago. Inside the Abbey doorway you drop a pound into a large glass case a quarter full of money, then hug me. You're always hugging me, trying to let me know I'm the finest thing for miles. Passing through a second doorway we come into the Abbey itself and wander the length of the inside walls chuckling over memorial stones. You like the dead a lot and show your gratitude by pecking at my ear or allowing those keen fingers to stray up my spine.

In the semi-gloom among candle tears and the moan of an old organ we tiptoe from moment to moment, holding hands, pretending to be serious, glancing at one another over and over, driven to whispers by the pursed lips and shaking head

4

of a Christian young churchman in black and white whose job it is to deceive the bereaved or squeak severely along the aisles breastfeeding hymnbooks.

Now the flautist empties the contents of a checked cap into his pocket, packs up his instrument and leaves the courtyard. Kate's lonely for J. She can feel him licking, tickling her skin. She wants him there to point things out to her, make them real, dismiss all this fucking fantasy. Maybe he could slip from the past, join her at this bench, lean forward, touch her hair, squeeze his hand over hers in a warm conspiracy. She rolls one more cigarette to take his place, inhales as deeply as she can without coughing. She has no idea whether he's been to the courtyard himself, chosen the same bench, thrown his own crumbs to the pigeons; but she likes to think he has. Maybe he's standing before an almighty block of stone praying for the skills of a sculptor. This is a famous, memorable place. The harlequin's a regular.

Home

Derek's playing badminton at the sports centre with a friend
from the antique trade called Tom or Ron and has been out
of the house for an hour or so. Kate can now go Doo Lally
Tap in the comfort of her shed. Tom or Ron arrives almost
every week in his battered Transit, revving the engine and
repeatedly peeping his horn to irritate Miss Wintle next door.
Like the other one or two friends Derek has, Tom or Ron's
under strict instructions not to enter our marital home lest he
should grow overly familiar, sniggle back in the daytime, then
fulfil Derek's worst nightmare by hauling me up the wooden
hill to Bedfordshire.

So far tonight I've cut my toenails, fiddled with a dishcloth
in the kitchen, eaten half an apple and watched the first
glittering five minutes or so of the Miss Vagina contest in which
unattractive women from Berkshire claimed to love scuba-
diving and the novels of Marcel Proust. The compère was a
vaguely familiar man in a dinner suit whose charm involved
the invention of many tempestuous puns; don't tell a soul, J,
but it's often the case that a man with fastened hair and a stripe
down his trousers has hardly any brain but seems to enjoy a
good income as a result. Oh Kate, there are moments when I
love you without end. Come put down this tea and kiss me, for
goodness' sake. The vaginas slunk slinked one by one down a
flight of blue stairs and pointed to that Mr Morley fellow who
smiled too often and had celebrities either side of him who
wrote on bits of paper. In the audience women in sequins

6

raised fingers to red mouths at the thrill of the puns while pro-chemical-warfare males whooped and wolfed in the American way.

During the adverts I switched off, cut a piece of cheese and read another page of *The Well of Loneliness*. Have you read it? Catherine recommended it as 'the most poignant' book she's ever come across, yet it's endlessly depressing me. After a few sentences one ends up gazing at the sideboard or squeezing one's own thigh. The Introduction's been written by someone from Oxford who talks at length about lesbians and claims that timid women have been known to pass the novel on to their friends as a way of expressing hidden feelings.

Next to jogging and sexual intercourse, badminton is Derek's most regular pastime. Though he excuses it as a Relaxation Activity, he comes home after each session anxious, mildly intoxicated and resentful at having lost, clamping to his sides a pair of those unhygienic underarms advertised on television. He loves to make a song and dance about the great strength and agility required to play such a visually innocuous game and must explain the consequent ache in his thighs. 'Just feel how stiff this bit is,' he says, clutching the arm of the sofa and holding out his leg. Vaguely satisfied with my squeeze he then stoops ceremoniously to peck hello on my hair.

Right now I'm in my shed, J, should you ever come across these pages and wish to know. I dream you will and dream you won't. After all this time I still have the small fan heater and the anglepoise lamp I borrowed from your room and my husband has kindly allowed me to use his extension cable. Don't be disturbed by the term 'husband', incidentally. It means less than you think. His golf clubs are standing in the corner beside my table and, though he rarely plays, each iron is regularly washed in warm soapy water. The woods and driver have woollen poodle heads knitted by his dear mother from an unspecified number of unpicked jumble-sale cardigans for a birthday several years ago. Other than the clubs and my ornaments, the shed is full of junk – various rusting garden tools; one or two grimy engine parts retained for an emergency

7

on the Morris Traveller we don't own any more; the fraying remnants of a green carpet; three half-empty tins of white emulsion he bought at a car-boot sale and a damp cardboard box marked DEREK in blue felt-tip piled high with mildewed school-books. I can see 'Religious Knowledge. D. Rookson (Rooky) 3A.' Below this neat print the name Gwendoline is inscribed in flowery letters. Lucky creature will never know what charms have eluded her.

Beside me I have a stained Victorian inkwell, a china kingfisher I picked up from a secondhand shop last week, a tiny wooden lighthouse with 'Tenby' written round the top and a thermometer glued to the side, a pair of chalk dogs curled into a ball as a paperweight and a piece of that old bridge you loved so much. The weather in Tenby's fine for the time of year, by the way. Mentioning you so much is like casting a fly onto the river hoping to catch the same salmon twice and it seems that this and other witticisms are born of a brain going haywire. The kingfisher's hand-painted and stands in a clump of broken reeds.

And don't weep, but my famous ragged cloth parrot has an inkstain on the beak.

I don't think I'd give anyone *The Well of Loneliness*, least of all a woman I was in love with. Introductions to classic novels frequently get me down. There's always someone dead keen to give the game away before you've set foot in the first chapter; and then they wind up by explaining the subtle implications they've unearthed or invented in case we're too dim to understand. If ever I have the chance to write an Introduction – say to *Moby-Dick* or something – it'll say, 'Well, here's another book then.'

We're dancing, J. You're so excited you just don't know what to do with yourself. Some nostalgia junky has put 'In the Summertime' on the turntable. Next to us there's a middle-aged man with a Conservative bum and baggy brown trousers shaking his hands and waggling his knees for all he's worth. His steel-rimmed spectacles sparkle in the roving spotlights. You're reminded of an old friend from school days who looked just the same and who had an unacceptable passion for John Wayne movies. By keeping your eye on the dancing man and bringing into play your powers of perception, you have it all figured out that he works as an accountant with the Bradford and Bingley Building Society; is married to a barren Domestos representative from Winchester called Carlene; loves to watch the Angling Highlights on television while tucking into Payne's Poppets and invariably volunteers to run the human fruit-machine stall at the Historical Society's Summer Fete.

Moments later you've forgotten all about him and squeeze your head against mine. A woman at the bar screams and spills her drink because she's been goosed by a tipsy Country and Western fan. 'I think maybe we ought to make love when we get home,' you whisper, brushing your hand on my hair. We ought to make love. Pushing back your collar I kiss and bite your shoulder. You squeeze your middle against me as I touch your thigh with a single finger. We're all shivers. Now it's something by Nina Simone. Your shirt's damp with sweat. We've ceased to wonder at the lunacy of your movements while you're dancing. Later we'll sneak through the back door of the club, climb the railings at the side of the road then hurry through the tall grass towards the river.

A Bit Later

Catherine rang a little while ago. She's been having a bad evening what with her aching feet and unexpected raps on the door by a radiant pair of Jehovah's Witnesses. The male was just like Clark Kent, she said. Dark blue hair. Spectacles. American legs. Tightly packed suit. Teeth. With him was a small woman who spent the duration of the brief interview picking loose paint from the door frame. Then there was a nibble of guilt on Catherine's part for wishing them both goodnight just as Clark was offering her Eternities on earth and the glory of butterflies, beaming children, unpolluted rivers teeming with fish, and presumably, painless dentistry. Once the pair had moved next door she wasn't able to rest. Her head became fiddly and overwrought. She asked me if I'd like to go out with her for a few hours on Thursday night so she'd have something to look forward to, then proceeded to tell me in great detail about the tall man in green who marched up to her desk at the library this morning and asked her if she'd consider going with him to a concert by the Bournemouth Symphony Orchestra next week, given that his poor wife had recently passed on after a long, violent struggle with Hunting-don's Chorea. She said 'No' because Mrs Scarfe, the inorgasmic Chief Librarian, had been making life hell for her since nine o'clock and, besides, the man in green had three books under his arm which she quietly objected to – a thick piece of popular psychology called *Ways to Defeat Undue Hesitation*, a well-thumbed collection of extracts from the *Daily Telegraph*, and something else like *Origami for the Nimble-Fingered Enthusiast*.

Meanwhile Derek arrived back from the sports centre. He mumbled greetings, waved at the window to Tom or Ron – who couldn't leave the vicinity without a further string of peeps – then threw his racquet to the sofa and collapsed beside it with an ornamental groan. I turned from the phone. Smiled. He raised his eyebrows in irritable enquiry. Who was I wasting valuable time and money talking to now? He limped into the kitchen, returned with a beer, groaned a second time, rolled the cold can across his forehead, sat down, snapped open the newspaper, mumbled 'Fucking Lebanon' and crossed his thick legs. The words 'Whose legs are these?' ran through my head. He was wearing tremendous shorts. I noticed how curly the hairs were on the front of his thighs and how unlikely it would have been that Keats, turning a blind eye to Grecian urns, would have immortalised them in verse. It was quite frightening. The sole of his right training shoe was covered in scuff marks and waggled in time with imagined grievances.

Overhearing the gist of this business of the Bournemouth Symphony Orchestra he began to chuckle behind his newspaper. The days when he had such things to bother him were well and truly over. This was the *Guardian* and these Rambos with bullet slings were the Hizbollah. Don't get the impression his chuckles came out of the blue, J; he'd worked them all out beforehand in the kitchen.

Tuesday 5.02am

Unlike popular heroines, Kate yawns, scratches the tip of her nose, rolls the first of many cigarettes, then stares with some intensity at a piece of bread dropped by a bird onto the greenhouse roof. Which Human Being last took a bite at that, she asks, still in a madness of slumber. She sips tea. Feels the weight of her breasts beneath this fine shirt. His shirt. J's shirt. Maybe he taps the shed window, creeps through the door and links his arms around her neck or maybe she's wasting time on a bench down by the river when he comes unexpectedly round the corner of a hawthorn bush, hands in pockets. Maybe not. Life has no plot. Seagulls sweep back to sea. A pair of reflected herons pose at the water's edge. The world charms her and fucks her up. J says, Look, it's not that I can't live without you, but things aren't colourful anymore. My rainbows are absolutely grey. None of this Richard of York Gave Battle In Vain business. I walk here and there but I'm lost all the same.

J, you're crazy, she says, but he doesn't mind. That's how he likes to be. He enjoys rapping on the door of madness. It's low tide. The great river has become a small stream. Muddy water rolls and slurps over grey rocks. She must keep re-lighting her cigarette.

A bird now serenades the darkness a few yards from the shed. Kate didn't know birds sang so early at this time of year. She hasn't a clue what type of bird it is because she's never been a great one for ornithology – she hardly ever stalks the water meadows with binoculars and a Sherlock Holmes hat.

Perhaps it's a nightingale. Another opportunity to mention you, Mr Keats, but I don't think I will because you're beginning to sound a bit commonplace – a piece of our heritage referred to so often, it begins to fade away. Like Kellogg's Frosties. We can't go bothering about your poems too much when we have a succession of madpersons for leaders, spies in the tops of our apple trees with telescopes and raincoats and Danish Bacon juggernauts on the dual-carriageway. Nevertheless (Oh what a fine brown word) I've had a dream that one day I'll come across an anthology of modern poems in a backstreet bookshop or a bookstreet backshop that'll suit me down to the ground. The anthology will be called *Nightingale Memories*. I'll carry it with me in a leather bag, dipping into it on street corners and in cafés and what have you when I'm feeling down in the mouth or when warships loom.

Couldn't sleep. Derek's dreams involved perspiration and the necessity of kicking me to death. Then I started thinking about Mr Micawber. He's one of the characters who crop up when I'm most pissed off with my husband. Other nights it's Ishmael or poor old Sarah Woodruff. As soon as I remembered Micawber, I felt warmer somehow, comforted, secure; though being Mr Micawber from Mr Micawber's point of view must have been pretty unspectacular – dreams refusing to come true, constant poverty, wealth and opportunity hanging from unattainable futures. Odd how we're thrilled to bits by the lives of those who never quite make it. If Micawber had pulled himself together early in the book and bought say, a Scandinavian fitted kitchen for Mrs Micawber, he'd have bored us to death.

J comes through the park holding his coat together with one hand and guarding himself against the driving rain with a large black umbrella clutched in the other. He's on his way to visit me though I'm not in. I'm beneath the beech trees without my duffle, imagining for a moment I'm going to live happily ever after. Thinking himself alone, J bites his lower lip. His strides have become totally aquatic. I want to run after him but my legs won't work. It would be nice if he knocked at my door

13

now and then and there was no reply. He's too used to the sound of cock-a-hoop shoes springing up the stairs. The rain gathers in the leaves and falls as large droplets which thump against my shirt. There he goes. J. Another mess disguised as a modern man; the tall, romantic focus of all my attention. I came here to see if it was still possible for me to be myself. My stomach turns. I've been trying to quench a kind of fire which wriggles and tickles and tickles inside me; perhaps I'll die. For a long time Kate thought Burl Ives was simply Orson Welles breaking into song during the second bottle of sherry. J reaches the park gate in the way only he can, looks left and right, then steps into the road. There are moments of rain and winter when love can be the most unbearable thing; when you welcome it with open arms while praying it will go away. I dream about him all the time and wake with his voice in my ears, the tickle of his fingers on my cheek or his breath on my breast. His are the whispers which haunt my sleep. If, through circumstance or preoccupation with other things, his ghost is threatened, it soon comes to reassert itself. In the bed-dark I'm guilty. Derek's an ugly cuckoo usurping my nest.

Listen. The traffic builds up, driving an unwelcome wedge between what has been night and what will be day. Neon globes scattered around the old people's flats stain the mist which hangs against my window. I'm woken by the hubble of the kettle and open my eyes to see J making coffee and biting into a Garibaldi biscuit. My old blue dressing gown is hooked over his shoulders. He yawns the yawn of a man who's fucked too much, then strikes a pose in the mirror to see if his stomach is flat. It isn't, unless he breathes in, and yet the rest of him is so thin. A naked man is really daft unless you're in love with him. He pads to the curtains for a peep at daylight, finishes his biscuit then makes the coffee. Thinking music might tempt me to do it all over again, he puts on Joan Armatrading, breathes in and comes to wake me.

In half an hour Derek will hop through the front door ready to begin his morning exercise, pausing only to wonder what I'm doing out here when for so long it's been his prerogative

to get up first. As usua[...]
two, then handspring o[...]
imaginary neighbours who [...]
wear and nymphomania. By th[...]
cottage in the glen he'll have [...]
conclusion I'm having an affair. [...]
behaving so erratically of late. Heart in [...]
up Mariner's Drive to the old church, then [...]
alley into the lane leading to the Downs. Pum[...]

he'll run on the spot for a minute or
ver the gate for the benefit of
ay have both see-through night-
time he reaches the thatched
rroneously arrived at the
o *that's* why she's been
his mouth, he'll jog on
ut through the dark
s flashing.

d the television.
g how Bernard
so unlike – in
ginate. 'I think,'
eat into a press
and squeeze it all together.' Kate said a prayer for living
turkeys everywhere. Derek watched her anxiously. If she
looked in his direction for too long, he'd raise his eyebrows and
smile at her without opening his mouth. It's the expression he
wears when he loathes everyone including himself. Then he
turned his attention to the obstinately blank screen. The
television has replaced the wedding ring as the token of our
marriage. He yawned, rose, approached the set with great
caution and pulled the plug from the socket.

'This is the very first thing you should do in a case like this,'
he said. 'Televisions are dangerous if you don't know how to
proceed.' The plug having flopped to the floor, he stepped
back a yard or so and brought to bear all he understood of
electrical engineering.

'Could be the tube,' he said, 'in which case we're buggered.'

The room bristled. He went into the kitchen to search for a
screwdriver, humming in the way husbands do when they've
suddenly been given a problem to solve. A few minutes later
Miss Wintle came round wearing pink slippers and a new
Rousseau pinny to complain that our early morning activities
were disturbing her – Derek closing the door as he sets off; the

thunder of shoes against grass as I cross the lawn to the shed. Being of Cockney extraction, an instinctive wish to break into the Lambeth Walk lingered in the fur of her slippers as she explained that she'd been a light sleeper since the Cuban Missile Crisis and that the slightest sound could induce unbearable Stress. Kate was on the point of prescribing Valium for this old fusspot when Derek arrived in the background and waggled his white hands to keep me quiet. He must retain the respect he's built up in the community. Having listened to Miss Wintle's complaints, he promised to take immediate action and wished her (goodness how could he?) 'Bonsoir'.

Life's so small sometimes. A brisk wind drags raindrops across the shed window, breaking up the harvest moons of neon. A pensioner in one of the flats across the way boils something in a saucepan, prodding whatever it is now and then with a knife while her husband strokes the ginger cat sleeping in his arms.

Oh J, I'm not particularly fond of these cold nights. Darkness falls too soon. Dreams of summer are tales made up by children. Dead leaves papier-mâché the orange pavements. Wet tarmac on the dual-carriageway is ripped to shreds by countless tyres. The gloom's deepened by old ladies pulling fat shopping trolleys with squeaky wheels, the yap and howl of distant dogs and the mauve knock on scores of doors by the Cancer Booklet man.

Occasionally Derek feels compelled to beat back wild animals or drive a roaring chariot round a crowded colosseum, but, finding these natural instincts increasingly difficult to satisfy in the modern world, he comes to the shed to twist my arm and push it almost to the nape of my neck, then charms me with poems while ripping at my breasts with his fingernails.

Kate's Tuesday In Brief

8.22am.   Stubbed her toe on the fridge door. Husband collapsed in mirth.

8.29am.   A circular in the post insisted that the Whole Rookson Household would be Delighted to watch as a New Car rolled up to the drive they don't have. All they had to do was return their Lucky Numbers and maybe buy a set of records; something like 'The Golden Sounds of Pearl Carr and Teddy Johnson' or was it Pearl Johnson and Teddy Carr?

8.42am.   Husband late for work due to lack of clean underpants. Dog from Mrs Thrupp's came to nose through rubbish sacks as it does every week and was chased, as usual, by Derek, now fully dressed having discovered a pair of swimming trunks to wear.

8.47am.   Husband out of breath. Enquires of his wife why she isn't like every other woman in the country with regard to the washing of clothes.

10.07am. Kate struck by the thought that every house in the western world must have a jam jar in the cupboard with various numbers of stiff paintbrushes poking from it.

11.24am. Sunny interval.

12.01pm. Newsflash: There are tailbacks on the Wells Road due to an overturned chicken lorry.

12.44pm. That nice Mr Gorbachev popped up to offer further cuts in nuclear weapons.

18

12.56pm.   Kate discovered a copy of 'Those Bangkok Teen-agers' in her husband's depleted underwear drawer.

2.32pm.   A small pink man with a dark moustache, posh car, knock-knees and worn leather briefcase came to the door, shook Kate's hand, patted Mrs Thrupp's dog in error, grinned and introduced himself as Dennis J. Curlington. He most certainly hadn't come round to sell insurance, he insisted, but had she given any thought to what might happen if her husband suddenly took ill and died?

2.35pm.   Mrs Thrupp complained to the dustmen about the volume and content of their songs.

2.38pm.   Dennis repeated the finer points of the monthly payment, high growth, family package as an old man in blue overalls wandered through the background clanking a large spade.

3.00pm.   The News Headlines. Mr Reagan's nose was once again causing concern throughout the world though various doctors explained to various microphones that the general condition of the nose wasn't as dangerous as they had at first hoped.

4.02pm.   Anonymous phone call:
             Man: (breathing heavily) Look, love, I'd like to tear off your clothes, tie you to the bed with thick rope then suckle your cunt.
             Kate: (lighting cigarette) Oh really? Come straight round.

7.36pm. Now Kate's comfy in her shed, dreaming as rain prickles against the greenhouse roof. Perhaps there's a case for complaint in her narrowness of mind, the superficiality of her vision and the images of lunacy which ravish her consciousness. Surely she can't exist; she wouldn't make it from one day to the next let alone through a lifetime towards the lullaby of a tomb. Clocks tick. Birds bark. The mentally unstable friend of a friend performs a quickstep to the silent music of Joe Loss outside a Pizzeria in Princess Street. At car-boot sales there are dozens of angry pot-bellied dealers on the lookout for Rupert

19

annuals; so's Kate because she'd love to live in Nutwood where everything rhymes.

She's hoping to dream tonight. Sometimes it's all she has – this imagination of sleep, a little bit of tossing and turning, a sense of wonder as the familiar shapes of a grey bedroom reorganise themselves into something strange, unexplored.

J stoops down to take a jar of plum jam. For this week's thrill, he's determined not to pay for it so we must sneak past the Indian with the bobble hat and slip through the door. Then we wander home through autumn. Leaves are plucked from the trees by a cool wind. We love the coloured walls, the sound of birdsong, an old stick woman wearing green who creaks in the opposite direction sniffing the streets like a cautious rabbit, the insistent tweet of the pelican lights we press but don't use. At home we abandon the jam and lie side by side on the bed. He's naked and so am I. He begins to say something but is driven to silence by unbearable syntax. We love Tom Waits, the dance of candlelight, the greens, reds and golds of my painted plaster mantlepiece. In the end he mumbles that he loves me but adds quickly that the word 'love' is just some sickening shorthand for the truth.

Wednesday 5.15am

So softly, and with the perfume of love on her lips, Kate slipped from the warm double bed and tiptoed to the window where a sea of restless moonlight waited to illuminate her nightgown and the slim white body beneath. On the battlements far below her window stood the Count, his red cloak flapping in the wind. Kate's breasts heaved. She was about to wave delicate fingers when a deep voice from the bed spoke her name, making her jump. The Count leapt from the battlements into darkness as Kate turned to unravel the gloom in which her husband lay, curled in blankets. On the floor beside the bed she could just make out the glistening outlines of his armour and war-damaged shield. He called her for a second time. She stepped fearfully across the rug, her hands clasped. From a glen beyond the castle walls a nightingale sang. Derek's fine head loomed into the shadows before her.

'What are you doing out of bed already?' he said, chest hairs poking through his British Home Stores pyjamas.

She explained she'd been lured from sleep to the window by the glorious choirs of destiny. Her husband smacked his lips, sniffed in disgust, then reached for his bottle of nasal decongestant.

'What's this?' he asked. 'Getting post menstrual tension now are we?'

'Oh prithee, piss off, Sire,' said Kate to herself.

And now the blood's thumping in my ears. The rain starts and stops again and a cat's stalking across the shed roof. I came here with such enthusiasm this morning but energy has been lost between the idea and the turning of the key.

I'm reminded of the Gower Coast for no reason at all. There should be one by all accounts but this simply isn't the case. Last year's holiday. Derek wouldn't have anything to do with me because I spent so much time playing in the water on one of those large black inner tubes. Young men hooted. I waggled myself into the sea then waited for the biggest wave to roll and topple me through the surf. I could see Derek flat and unhappy on his maroon towel between two rocks, a flask of coffee and a pack of ham sandwiches by his side. I couldn't help calling out. I was having so much fun. The inner tube dipped, bobbed and rolled with the tide; fingers of water tickled my legs and chest, cooling me down.

Derek ignored me. He was pondering to himself the rights and wrongs of removing one's bikini top in public and so stayed on the towel for the whole day except on the two occasions he went in search of unseen rocks to have a secret wee. Each time he came back he pretended to yawn or peered out to sea like a lovesick matelot, but fooled no-one. Young girls nudged each other and whispered, 'He's been for a piss!' On his second return he was followed by a stream of Japanese men who splashed and giggled round the headland, each dressed in a grey suit and a pair of Samurai sandals, each squinting from rocks to beach to sky, taking photos, holding their arms wide in homage to absent gods. They sneaked along the sand within two yards of Derek who'd lain down again, thick and spectacular in his brief yellow trunks. A young boy, caring nothing for applause, ran naked from his mum's striped umbrella into the sea. The men laughed, clapped in Japanese, took more photos. For safety's sake Derek's hands left the sand and cupped over his groin. Behind him two lovelies in loose black bikinis played catch with a bright beachball, smiling one to the other and pointing at him with pale fingers. I was rolled to the sand by a wave, stood in my semi-nakedness and pushed back my hair. A particularly wicked Jap immediately raised his Pentax. Derek rolled up his towel and walked away.

22

My legs are wide for times gone by. The rain's clearing away leaving grey brushstrokes against a pale blue sky. Come, he whispered over and over. Come. I came, he gurgled and fell beside me. Blue with grey brushstrokes and the last of the roses; a bird; two birds and the fizz of traffic. No light or life coming from the old people's flats yet. Usually the tenants rise around seven-thirty, gawping through the windows for a minute or two as if surprised to find themselves still here. Surprised or dismayed. At this moment they sleep in rows punctuated by bricks and plaster, dreaming of those monochrome seasides, the wooden piers, the bored clipclop of a promenade donkey, the flickering striptease of naughty chambermaids; dreaming of a time loved ones billowed in an Easterly clutching beehives of candyfloss.

Last February one of the old boys tumbled down and died outside our gate. A crowd of people from Oak Leaze – who've also been tempted at one time or another by the dream of a new car rolling up the drives they don't have – gathered around the body whispering condolences to ignorant widows. Miss Wintle was running down her garden path waggling a Second World War first-aid manual and shouting 'Give him air'. Eventually an angry constable and a young doctor arrived, whereupon neighbours were ushered indoors to drool through their windows. Mrs Thrupp had known all along the old man didn't have long to go because she'd often seen it in his eyes. It was Sunday. Derek couldn't go jogging till they'd removed the body and only then with a sham and respectful lack of speed. Around here they call the flats 'the Departure Lounge' from which flights are regular but unscheduled and always in a single direction. Waiting passengers are given a comfy room, a vase, a bunch of fabric roses, reliable underfloor heating, a picture window overlooking the field at the back and a weak daylight to stir them gently in the mornings. Soon those mornings come to an end and a line of sleek limousines roll up to the drives they don't have either.

I'd love to die – though maybe not today – in a place which has had a lot of me in it, say J's room on a Saturday night. Just

23

like in those old movies about love on the dole, we're usually laughing as we fall through the door hugging our special chow meins. He fetches the plates and forks, unwraps the greasy cartons and tips them out, giving me an extra forkful of noodles in the hope I'll proclaim him a hero. Then we curl up on the sofa to watch the play of the gasfire on the mantelpiece. Tom Waits is Downtown, growling love songs with blue fingers in a crowded bar. A painted broad and an off-duty taxi driver smooch beneath a slow-moving fan. J has that look in his eyes. He's eating with one hand and playing in my lap with the other. We abandon the food half-way through and start to fool around. Tom runs skinny hands along the keyboard as we roll to the floor midst grease and strips of pork to make love. Sometimes we say fuck; other times we're dreamy as anything.

A Walk

It's a day for dying. She aches for J and invents a kind of history for herself. The hedgerows are thick with berries and birdsong. Oh yes, we came here one insubstantial day of woollen cloud and an unbearable sky. Now there's a big word for such a little girl: insubstantial. Later on she might say it again but for now it wouldn't do to have more than one 'insubstantial' in the first paragraph. See how mad I've become, J, since life's been an exercise in patience?

She steps from the road onto the mud track and sniffs at death. It blows in the wind which lifts dead leaves from the fields and scatters them across sky-crazy pools of rainwater. As ever the beech trees sweep the ridge and tumble down the hill towards the stream. They haven't changed, holding onto their glory with ease; motionless except for the rhythmic movement offered to their upper branches by the breeze and, as she likes to see it, haughty, solemn, contented, looking down on the flamboyant, more easily spent creatures who wander amongst them. And here's the gate where he took me in his arms and told me he didn't mind whether he was in a wood or in the backstreets of Cairo as long as he was with me; a gate crawling with ghosts.

The beeches thin to make way for a fir plantation. The air becomes dark and heavily scented, the path beige and silent, cushioned by dead needles. She loves to creep into the haunted shadows and imagine the comfort of a more natural tomb. Oh she has prayed and hungered for it sometimes, mark my words. Here, of course, love took a sorry turn as he lowered the zip on his jeans and asked to be eaten. For a moment, on her knees in the perfumed gloom, she lost sight of his poetry. He came into the liquid reaches of her mouth, but wasn't sure how to thank her other than by taking her wet fingertips and helping her to her feet. She spat him out as romantically as she could. Red and damp he hushed her with a finger to his lips and listened for imaginary crackles in the fern.

She doesn't see a soul. The wind blows. She sings 'Where do you go to my lovely, when you're alone in your bed'. Autumn birds chirrup because she likes the word. A path winds into secrecy less significantly than she'll remember it. She's heard of both the past and the present tense but is blowed if she can be bothered to sort them out. The past is, she whispers.

Coming out of the firs she climbs a gate and walks onto the naked headland. For a moment she's struck by the beauty of the Monument which stands at its crown. To the left, a long way down, brown and green fields sprawl into a distance hemmed by the silver river and pale blue hills of Wales. She pretends to swoon. At this particular water-trough he became a bit of a dad, wrapping an arm round her shoulders and pointing out the faint undulations of a hill-fort. The leap between a penis in the mouth and a fondness for those iron-age bastards required an aspirin, but she hadn't any in her bag. She heard tales of ditches and ramparts instead and nodded with ancient gratitude. The mud on her knees was drying. Later, in response to witticisms from a passing farmer, she claimed to have been praying to the Lord.

She springs around the Monument, a bit of an Isadora, trailing fingers over the coarse limestone walls, waiting for something to happen. Several more of the surrounding railings have been ripped out by vandals and now stand at angles in the grass. Cloud squeezes itself in an effort to rain. A tractor growls along the edge of the hill pursued by a swell of seagulls. She's fucking unhappy and unhappy fucking. At the north corner of the Monument the Rotary Club has erected a large block of stones with an inset metal plaque showing the distances to various cities and landmarks. Paris is way over there; J's in the opposite direction. It starts to rain. She tries to find pleasure in it as a genius should, and shelters in the small porch, sitting on a stone seat at the side, watching as the rain pats across the grass. Here he scratched her name with a penknife. Kate. 'Though not a vandal by nature,' he said, 'I'll make an exception in this case.' A freshening wind forces its way through the window-diamonds high above, howls down the spiral staircase then tries to escape by pushing against the door.

It was summer, of course, and the door was unlocked, allowing solitary Belgians to shuffle up and down. He held my hand and led me up the stone steps, spooking me as the fancy took him by hooting like an owl or pretending to be a stranger with vicious intentions. On the high balcony we leaned one against the other, looking out at the bloated countryside, hardly daring to say a word. He turned to me, winked, slithered a secret hand between my legs and squeezed me, making me wet. I slipped to my knees once more, but this time with the giggles. He grinned, expecting me to read his mind. He was fat with satisfaction that I wouldn't be able to look at the Monument again without remembering him. Pulling out a cigarette instead, he rubbed himself hard against the railings. I've heard Claire Rayner say something to the effect that a man can have an erection at the simple movements of a bus and perhaps this is a fact for which she has cause to be grateful, but I could tell J was disturbed. The Devil was in him. 'I'd quite like to do it again,' he said, 'but since this Monument has been erected to the memory of such a devout man, perhaps it would be best to refrain.'

Kate offered silent thanks to William Tyndale.

The rain dies. Clouds slide away behind sheaves of fir trees. The sun comes out. It's a sentimental afternoon, the kind which takes you by surprise, brings an unfashionable lump to your throat. She'd love to climb to the narrow ledge above the doorway but she's worried at how a fellow rambler might react to a woman aloft on Tyndale's Monument. A potential suicide, perhaps; a female turned crazy with those premenstrual blues. Certainly not a child compelled to climb on high and wag her raggedy shoes in the damp sunshine. Call the authorities, fetch a ladder, phone the next of kin.

She leaves the Monument, scrambles across the old quarry and comes out onto the track which cuts a diagonal swath through beech trees on its way to the village. This was one of his favourite places. From the track he threw himself down the bank, squealing through dust and leaf-mould like a child. At the bottom he climbed to his feet, brushed the dust from his jeans and laughed to himself. Calling, she threw a handful of twigs at him. Cigarette smoke was making him squint. She sees him just so: snapped, like a photograph. He's looking up at her, half afraid.

Following the track upwards to the gate she then discovers an unfamiliar path winding down the side of the hill. The damp banks are threaded with roots from the trees above, undermined by various animal holes, riddled with dead and dying things. She hums something by Dire Straits; wipes sweat from Mark Knopfler's brow. He whispers, 'Thanks, Baby, this one's for you,' and launches into 'Romeo and Juliet'. Hedgehogs fuck. Or maybe not. She has no idea whether they fuck or not. Can passion override the problem of spines? Write to Mr Attenborough. At the bottom of the hill she takes off her coat and sits on a moss-covered rock. She's listening, waiting, in the way abandoned lovers tend to do. The longer her history becomes, the more unlikely it seems. If you're reading this, J, drop me a line. I'd like an expert opinion on this history business. Each daydream is thicker than the last.

More water falls from the trees, patting and splashing on the bushes and brambles. Kate's lonely and beautiful. The kind of wood-nymph men dream of coming across when she's no longer there. Sometimes loving or the dream of a love gone wrong can woo you on the outer rim of madness; can tune you into the soft exhalations of a dying wood, the perfume of its decay.

Deep in the tangle of roots and shadows, she has dreams

which will haunt her again and again.

I've reached the part in *The Well of Loneliness* where Stephen shoots her horse and buries it at the foot of the hedge. The first time they jumped the hedge together, the horse was young; she was enthusiastic, confident, less afraid. Though books don't often stir me to any great extent, I was close to tears as the shot rang out and the old horse fell to the ground. Maybe it was just me. A book can have all kinds of effects according to what mood the reader's in. Look through the *The Well of Loneliness* when you've just been fucked to bits and it'll probably be an absolute scream.

Thursday

Thick scented fog streaked with frost. A dead daddy-long-legs hangs from an old web in the corner. Kate shivers, remembers being bitten by her husband. Perhaps this nightingale stands on the rim of Miss Wintle's pre-cast concrete birdbath. The melody's crystal clear. I've tired feet and nothing more. One word. Then another. Thump. The shed's cold yet fragrant and gentle to me. Ging Gang Gooley Gooley, or perhaps it's not Gooley at all. Those scouts. What a scream. Today she's a woman of few words. And those that emerge are rubbish. Madness. Lunacy. Gunk. I've been waiting in silence for an awesome passion to reach me. It hasn't. I'm bored and fucked to death with it all. Once bitten. Twice bitten. Dear Mr Eliot, thank you so much for your typescript of *The Wasteland* which I read with great interest whilst eating an orange. All I can suggest is that you return to your banking career forthwith, yours etc. Come, Kate. Pull yourself together. Put down exactly what you feel. Do the old mental fandango. The sentences grow shorter, which is a good thing except for those with an addiction to flowing prose. An earth twists. Huckleberry Hound makes no appearance in this journal except here. J sleeps somewhere other than with me. Grinning unconsciously perhaps at conquests yet to come. Women! Those naturally terrified creatures. Hating the men they love. Late last night I looked at the photos we took. I've held onto them all this time. How could I throw them away when they're all I have left of the facts? Can gawping at colour images or writing down mere versions of the past be classed as infidelity? If so, please don't condemn me, God; not that you're into condemning. I think maybe you reserve that practice for pinstripes on high speed trains heading home to Berkshire; not that you exist, either. We made you up some time ago in an effort to render living less pointless. No doubt dying will be unquestionably dark, dank and disappointing. Oh yes! The photographs. Well, they're mostly of me: a faint distant me standing, sitting or larking around in front of all manner of otherwise meaningless landmarks and tourist attractions. As far as I remember, J only kept one for himself. I'm balancing on my right leg at the end of the quay in bright sunshine. The water's colourful, like a Monet at his best; it's wriggled with sky and the soft echo of tall buildings. On my left the Greenpeace ship is at its moorings. Just after the photo was taken a rescuer of whales called 'Ahoy!' and waved her blue cap. It was the day of the water carnival. Behind J there rolled and flashed a small funfair where you could shoot a rubber Mrs Thatcher and win a coconut. Both sides of the harbour were thick with visitors. At two o'clock a man was wrapped in a straitjacket and some strong chain and was hoisted a hundred feet into the air by a crane. The idea was for him to escape before the rope holding him – which had been set alight – burnt through. He managed it just in time and everyone was bored to death. J wouldn't watch. He didn't want to be one of the crowd. As the tension mounted he went to buy a toffee apple. The tannoy announced that the man would try another escape at four. The sound of people not clapping ran round the harbour.

And I only have one of J. He's standing in the snow by an uneven grey wall, his left hand squeezed to his stomach with the cold, his right holding the scarf I bought for him. He wanted to be a survivor of inclement conditions so it was always difficult getting him to wrap up properly. Above the wall there's the branch of an apple tree and behind that, the steep black and white gable of a large house. To his left a woman in fur-lined boots is about to crush a plume of snow lying untouched in the gutter. Fur boots. Fir cone. How wonderful

31

it is that we're able to justify the same pronunciation for words spelt differently. Around a telegraph pole in the right foreground dogs have pissed, splashing the snow yellow. On J's neck, there's a purple bite he loves to display. In sexual abandon one's activities can border on cannibalism. He's having one or two tussles with happiness on a winter's day. Having glimpsed contentment he's not sure how to behave. His throat's red. I must have been over enthusiastic when I shaved him that morning during Joan Armatrading. He was both naked and embarrassed. There were certain things about being a man he couldn't bear.

In the afternoon we pull his sledge to the park. It's been one of those plump, self-satisfied snowfalls. The sky's an unbroken sheet of slate grey till a heavy mist comes down joining snow and sky together. The long dreary branches of the cedar are laden almost to breaking point. J's humming 'Oliver's Army' because he's not sure of the words. He's wearing a red tee-shirt and a thin jumper to teach the bastards a lesson. 'Oliver's Army' becomes 'Sultans of Swing' without ceremony as he winks at me and adopts a kind of nostalgia for the present. On a bank at the side of the bowling green a parade of hopping anoraks and fluorescent plastic coats wait their turn to come hollering through the snow. A series of adult lips puff into stiffened gloves. J has fun in the way one imagines F.R. Leavis and his dear wife Queenie may have done. A smile here, a brief 'Huh!' there, but mostly lines and theories disturbing the brow. He likes to take his public pleasures under duress. Over and over I drag the sledge up the bank to enjoy the few exhilarating moments of slipping down again. Between rides the more conscientious discuss the Middle East or the pork they had for lunch. The collective breath of the small crowd hangs in the air as a white, intangible reminder of times which may or may not have gone by. Following each of my turns, J wants to take me aside to discuss love. Maybe he's spotted a muscular bank clerk making eyes at me. The slope becomes packed and creamy. A man in a poncho with remnants of nutroast in his moustache thinks the afternoon is mind-blowing. J must keep kissing my ear to show everyone I'm his. A fair-haired toddler called Amy cries and has to be picked up by her crazy-looking dad each time slim mum slips into the mist. Dad says, 'Oh you are a silly bag of penguins, my girl.' Amy laughs while crying. Dad will buy her some Munchies if she's good. J scowls and, if it were physically possible, would love to turn up his nose. He has a dislike for the charming but unproductive worlds built up in fatherhood. Or maybe he's jealous. Who can tell? Eventually he tries the sledge for himself but comes back up the slope dismissing the experience as ludicrous.

Later, worn out, hungry and sickened with the snow, we tramp back to his place for toast, drawing the curtains to put the whiteness away. The season is one of cold breath and icicles. The city's shrouded in a silence broken only by the occasional flump of snow into snow. As the light begins to fade I leave J sleeping and return to the park on my own. The earth has taken on an impenetrable disguise; only a few railings and the dark edges of trees remain of what used to be. I'm trying to get my breath back after an hour of intimacy and music. I can taste him. Here and there the last of the children make reluctant snowballs. This gluttony of winter reminds me of something I can't identify: a word, a moment, a tune in the head. Silent people plough home pink and disappointed, pulling sledges behind them or hugging tin trays and plastic sacks. Kate takes a bench which has expanded, become grotesque. For a while after an act of love one feeds off silly dreams and waits for a consequence. She has a stomach-ache through it all. For some reason stepping aside to remember him is as important as being in his bed. The chill wind pricks her face. One day she's going to gather each dream and moment together and celebrate them all. Snow compacts under her bum. Cute bum with his fingerprints. People stare. She'd like to apologise to them, saying 'I'm awfully sorry. I was just trying my hardest to be *here*.' J has woken to her absence and comes looking for her, in a panic at first as he scoots up and down the road but then with a relaxed smile on his face as he spots her. In many ways he ruins the imaginary version she's been having of him. He's too unlike himself. He stands beside her looking this way and that hoping to catch sight of whatever attraction has proven finer than his arms. He offers tea and biscuits. Scrabble. A side or two of something by Joni Mitchell. Then he takes her hand and kisses each finger in turn.

His room's musty but pleasantly so, reminding a girl of the unspecific olden days when things were easier on the brain. The unwieldy houseplants are covered in dust and generally neglected. He says he must dampen a tissue with milk and wipe over the leaves when he has a moment. On the wall hang a pair of faded tapestries he's picked up, both showing stags in a Scottish woodland. The rugs covering the lino are threadbare. He's living in a shrine to both himself and to the various mild obsessions he's developed, tickling himself pink each time he comes through his own door. The room means a great deal to him. He talks of the spiritual excitement he experienced on first seeing it and, hours later, talks of it again. There are at least a dozen Victorian photo albums he's bought from secondhand shops with the intention of storing Time. The albums are filled with young men in light trousers and dark top hats standing to attention by balloon-backed dining chairs or sepia pennyfarthings; plump women wreathed in layers of heavy clothing, most of them bearing a close resemblance to the elderly Queen Victoria; ugly children in sailor suits; dancing dogs with ruffled collars; old men in drab coats scowling outside overcrowded hardware shops; busy streets full of grey trams. A favourite of J's is the muscular man with a long moustache and a black striped swimming costume who has one foot up on a chair and clenches his fist towards the camera.

'It interests me that this poor chap is long dead now,' he says.

'Perhaps it interests him too,' says Kate.

Behind the television stands an unused easel. Recently he's bought a large pad and a box of pastels in case he should want to create a picture one day. Since childhood he's had an affinity with the world of Art but no talent. In his formative years he had what he calls a 'crush' on Renoir. But, once again, it's the Renoir posed by photographers, rather than the real thing. He'd love heroes to lack mucous membranes and be free of the need to bathe.

In small piles around the walls sit dozens of Edwardian books with brightly coloured covers, most of them Sunday School prizes for dead people. By the gas fire stands an old, cracked, hand-painted jardinière, home to an undernourished aspidistra. And at the back of the room, tucked into the semi-darkness but dominating our imaginations, an ancient mahogany bed with buoyant spring base and elegantly turned corner-posts waits for us both.

We come through the door and warm ourselves up. He's faintly jealous of this need I have to be alone from time to time. Then he undresses and I undress. We toss a coin to decide who'll make the tea. He loses. I jump onto the bed. He does his best to make the tea with his back to me. I'm lying on the bed with my legs thrown open because that's the way I feel. There is something quite exquisite about nakedness in front of another person even though that person may be walking sideways on his way to the bed with a tray of tea. I'm not thinking about Michael Heseltine nor he of me. You have to be in a serious fringe-flicking mood to think of Michael Heseltine and this isn't one of them. J gives me my tea then breaks down in a moment of insecurity.

'I'm too thin for all this, for God's sake,' he says. 'Just look! Bones here. Spots here. How can you possibly enjoy me?'

I shrug my shoulders, put the tea on the chair and lie beside him. He hugs me close, his arms linked through my legs and round to the small of my back. I squeeze my thighs together and roll my breast to his mouth. Although I'm still not thinking of Mr Heseltine, I'm not thinking of him somewhat less than I was before. J removes his lips and watches the ceiling, inventing a coldness for me so he can rub me from head to toe, warm me up again.

We make love. Fuck. I scream. A tenant raps on the wall. Sunday afternoon should be free of such basic entertainment.

We can hear the commentary of an indoor bowling contest. J laughs. Closing my eyes with his fingertips he pads across the room to play Elgar, then conjures up some chocolate buttons which he places all over my body. My goodness, he's going to suckle them up one by one. Meanwhile Elgar celebrates spring. J's face lights up. He's squeezing a chocolate button into me and then will do his best to retrieve it with his tongue, though he's not going to explain why because that would ruin it. Suddenly it's winter. Elgar's going crazy. J's eating me to bits. He must find the button without resorting to fingers, though priests may frown on the exercise. I'm singing Tra La to myself. J's having the time of his life.

Friday 5.22am

Kate carefully avoids a number of slugs on her way to the shed, having spent the early part of the night being ravished by one of their kind. She's covered in fuckbites, her shoulders particularly, ruined for weeks to come. Compelled to tread lightly due to a soreness between her pretty legs, she remembers the ceremony before a woeful congregation in which a Derek with new shoes whispered 'With my body I thee worship'. Just hours ago he worshipped her from extraordinary angles, muffling protests with one hand, her arms with another and now she's unable to imagine how she'll cope with the day. She looks at the moon and almost falls over with vertigo, or is it tiredness of the soul? He pushed and pushed till satisfaction came in howls of anguish and perspiration, forgetting her role in all this to a large degree. Now she has nothing to look forward to other than this difficult business of being alive as the key turns in the shed door and Miss Wintle's bedroom light clicks on in sympathy. You might not believe this, J, but this morning you slipped through the bedroom door looking coy as could be, fiddling one set of fingers against the other then coming to my bedside, kneeling on the floor, slipping your hand beneath the blankets to hold mine. I curled and slept since dreams of you are the great narcotic. In both my body and soul, if you'll forgive such poetry, there lingers an unquenchable absence terrifying in its simplicity, dogmatic in its refusal to be flushed away. Derek said 'I'm going to rip your cunt apart,' having learnt at great cost how to woo a girl. So, in the darkness of morning she calls herself Kate for a

37

laugh, examines the dew-laden cobweb which hangs outside her window, dreams of the Immoral – not that she'd be able to list what the Immoral involves – it's simply that the morality of Oak Leaze seems infinitely dangerous, characterised by resentment, hatred and awesome dreams. Though it's a step in the right direction, there are no satisfactory sins in entering a shed each day. Though some may grumble or call her a fool, it all dies down in the end. Each strand of cobweb is parallel to the next, yet works its way towards the centre. The fan heater clicks on and off according to the temperature, giving the impression that mankind is terribly clever. Her tea's run out already. Maybe she'll receive a complimentary letter from Mr Bragg this morning, though he's probably not known for his correspondence with absolute strangers, however pale and delicate they may be. Previously one's husband grasped the principle weapon of his sex and pushed it between her lips, mistaking the tears in her eyes for joy. 'Oh let's fuck to your gullet,' he cried while these neat little houses ran this way and that, each with its own fenced garden, each with its number, each with its windows made to look faintly Tudor with strips of adhesive lead.

Moreover, she suspects that her husband rents adult videos and keeps them a secret. By the time she came home from her outing with Catherine last night, he was lounging on the sofa in his dressing gown, his body covered in baby oil. Oh he tried to deny it, but she'd spotted a certain glistening about the feet and wrists the moment she walked in. On the television was an innocent documentary about Venezuelan clay turning. He smiled. Stood. Clapped his hands. Kissed her on the lips. Made her a cup of tea. Asked her if she'd had a nice time with Catherine. Plumped her favourite cushion. Took the cup from her when she'd finished. Swilled it out. Kissed her again. Sighed. Twiddled his thumbs.

He'd missed her. Did she know what great legs she had? Would she like a hot water bottle? Perhaps for Christmas he'd buy her some Toulouse Lautrec underwear he'd seen advertised. Wouldn't that be nice?

It remains a mystery to Kate how her husband's legs can be

the stuff of nightmares of one moment and something quite fine to be sucked and bitten the next. Nature has played some wistful tricks on Girlkind. In this sticky game of trying to work out if you're in love with a man or not, forget the racing of your heart or a tendency to slurp too many Babychams: Love is when, in the morning, you don't regret having bitten his legs the night before.

Catherine's voice lures me through the twisting, lamp-hung cobbled streets from the riverside to the city centre which as usual shakes with countless shoes, splashes and sparkles with fountains the colour of neon, waltzes to the melodies of thread-bare buskers, rattles into the tins of the poor. Ungroomed hooligans, stick-waving spinsters, lovers and stale unbitten couples mill among the steamed-up hamburger bars having poured from various places of entertainment. We look around, Catherine and I. This feels good. I'll say it again. We look around, Catherine and I. Hippies finger each other's hair on the wall by the statue of Neptune; posh, rubber-mouthed students from the University warble in the middle of the road trying to out-prick each other by sidestepping cars; discredited professors sweep long fingers through silver hair awaiting trial on charges concerning unclothed Italian minors and an instamatic camera; elderly ex-piano teachers with a thing about Grieg have a night out on the town before going in for hip-replacement operations; young female painters with shrill voices and golden hair return home from inspirational trips to Barcelona, lugging fat suitcases covered in customs stickers and longing for a love other than the one they've found; gay men lean provocatively against the theatre walls carrying copies of *Good Housekeeping* and a single narcissus; gay women drag a flaming effigy of Edwina Currie along the gutter and chant death songs; those of a heterosexual persuasion check themselves in the clock-shop window while a tipsy hermaphrodite, unsure whether to commit himself to love, kisses his own shoulder then slaps himself across the face. From exclusive restaurants come cautious middle-aged politicians looking this way and that before leading dark fifty-pounds-an-hour women to a double-parked limousine; athletes with other people's hearts jog through the illuminated landscape to test them out. Here a solemn young man writes unsigned poems to the memory of a beautiful girl he once saw gathering daisies on a college green; there, a French woman scans the crowd for the only boy she's ever known who didn't boss her around and who always took the trouble to bring both roses and croissants to her bedside each day at dawn. But soft! Policemen with truncheons wait for a black man to drop a sweet wrapper so they can beat him up, unaware that in the doorway of the 'Los Luggage' travel agency a peckish Shi'ite Militiaman, here to lead a Holy War against the West, takes time out to enjoy an Imperialist half-pound garlic mayonnaiseburger. Close by, on cold steps once tramped upon by silent monks, an unkempt but provocative flower-seller, redundant for the winter, strums a guitar and whispers lyrics by Simon and Garfunkel, ignoring the howls of a starving dog who's rooting through the litter bin. On the corner of Denmark Street a police riot van, its engine ticking over, prepares to assist should any black man, having fouled the world with his sweet wrapper, resist the opportunity to be officially mugged. The only black man in the vicinity, mean-while, dances without music along the busy pavement wearing his Rasta hat and dreaming of Desmond Dekker, accidentally bumping into a bored trouser salesman who flicks at his braces and waits for his computer date who'll never show up despite being electronically perfect. A potential suicide uses the pelican lights to cross the road then hurries towards the suspension bridge as another, failed, suicide returns, having decided that Mr Lawson, sixty-four pounds a week, *Sun* Bingo and the squalid smile of Mr Archer are marginally preferable to the fatal injury of the approaching here's a plaintive cry – a baby strap-ped to the back of a low-breasted vegetarian wants its milk. Cars growl bonnet to boot; a bright-lipped girl in a tight leather suit chats to an off-duty bus-conductor with a bandaged head and, as if to render the evening supreme, a light-footed miracle named Catherine laughs, twists around and ruffles her closest friend's hair.

'You are a fool,' she says, stooping to pick up ten pence

someone has dropped. She then tells tales out of school of sudden loves, knickers on the bedpost, shameful slices of toast in the morning. A sleek white car rolls slowly along the road, its nearside tyres squashing leaves and rubbish in the gutter. One of a line of hooligans who've been jigging on the YMCA wall points to Catherine and shouts, 'Christ, Harry, I'd fuck that one stupid.' She ignores him, takes my hand and leads me across the road.

'And how's sex with you, my dear?' she asks. 'Don't you sometimes feel that all this copulation is simply not enough?' She lets go of my hand and lies her arm around my shoulder. I open my mouth to reply. 'Of course you do,' she continues.

The night's wild. We turn right into Christmas Steps and count them as we go down, pausing every few yards to peer through the green swirling windows of the squat trinket and jewellery shops. Dozens of splendid Victorians clatter up and down in their fancy dress. I'm glad of the cold and glad of life though I can't tell anyone why. Catherine's being ridiculous in the nicest way, wearing the night like a baggy jumper, playing silly games with my caution, my sense of resignation. I want J very badly, but keep it to myself. Catherine spots a ring she'd like. Maybe we'll bump into Dickens as he pants up the steps on his way for drinks. Catherine's a city girl and blends in nicely wherever she goes. She's approached three times by drunken double-glazing salesmen whose wives have become next to nothing in a short space of time. She tells them, of course, that there's nothing so tedious as the clean-shaven potential executive. They giggle, throw up at her feet or punch the ancient walls.

Like a love song, we pass 'The Silver Lining'. I remember J at a table in the far corner, pink from ear to ear, letting his coffee go cold because he doesn't want to get the froth on his lips. There's a naturalness about us as if we've been together a long time. He's relating a solemn, truncated autobiography, clearing the way for what's to come; making out with that natural fiction of his how all connections, moments, loss and subtle redirection have led him inexorably to this café, this winter, my hand. With

41

an apostle spoon he makes shapes in the sugar; long fingers dance on the table then rise to squeeze through his hair.

He's still in the café as Catherine and I tiptoe down the steps. Christmas already shows its embarrassed face through the shop windows in the form of tinsel trees and apathetic fairy lights. Catherine recalls a book of old photographs of the city and describes grey-gabled buildings, children in stiff trousers and yawning shoes, the masts of wooden ships gathered in the dock and poking above these very rooftops. 'Just over there,' she says, pointing to the right, 'ran Pickle Street.' She loves the name to death. We both agree we'd quite like to live in Pickle Street; number 4, perhaps, next to the barber's.

And then J again, standing in the cold this time, taking the scarf from his pocket as I move closer to him, wrapping it round my neck. The sky above domes dark and infinite. We saunter – for that's the only way to describe our movement – all the way to my place, on the verge of holding hands but not daring. At the gate he kisses me on the mouth then makes some remark about the universe to shield his excitement. He wants to be mature. I'm humming and tapping my left toe on the pavement. He squeezes his hands into his pockets, rattles the coins within then winks at me and walks off down the pavement, waving just before he turns the corner and fades away. The moon's covered in astronauts' footprints. A dog howls. I wait at the gate wondering whether to run after him – J, not the dog – because there's really no need for him to go home. From the park comes a damp palm of laughter. although such things are usually reserved for ridiculous books. Someone's having a semi-rural fuck, or is my imagination too concerned with fucks altogether? A boy goes home leaving a girl at her gate and a dozen living-room lights sneer at her through the dark. In my room the stillness is profound. I go to bed with my clothes on and read two pages of a *Dictionary of Quotations*. Perhaps he'll knock. In my duffel-coat I'm too warm altogether but there's nothing like a full set of clothing to keep one's terror at bay. I have the impression, J, that you curl up in embarrassment each time I say 'one's' but every now and again it's unavoidable in a diary. Ask Samuel.

Saturday 6.18am

Kate woken by a series of unconscious confessions from Derek and the tip of his somnambulant erection poking into her back. Men are such dogged creatures, even as they sleep. She squeezed herself against him for a laugh; 'Ho Ho' or something like that, not that she made a sound or dreamed repulsive dreams. An owl hooted from the Hundred Acre Wood. Mr Whatsit from number 3 started up his jelly-mould taxi and drove to the railway station to pick up people who wanted to go to a part of the city where, fortunately, other people were waiting to be taken to the railway station. Tigger gave up Bouncing at Rabbit as a bad idea and began to Fuck Kanga instead, who was much amused, promising him additional malt extract sandwiches in the afterglow. Derek shunted against Kate as though an electric current were being passed through his groin, proving that his kind of sex is simply a physiological response to a female stimulus. His legs were curly horrors again. As she slid away his arm flopped over her and his lips smacked. She felt it was quite urgent she should get out of bed. Besides, there was a tang of excitement about her throat. It was something to do with coming out here. Clear the garden tools from your shed, Sisters, and write it all down. Do away with this tomfoolery – keyless wedlock, high-fibre toast, a phone bill followed by another phone bill. Greasy toes.

Though Kate writes her requiem mass, she wouldn't like to classify it too strictly in case later generations criticise her tendency to deviate. Pepys would undoubtedly sneer at the content and, unlike Virginia Woolf, she doesn't have constant groups of gorgeous people coming round for lunch on a green verandah. Hers is a fucked-up life; an unstructured succession of day upon day, a howl of worries whose bite proves worse. Sometimes she loves and wishes to remember it, sometimes it's Monday and the world begins to piss down, the headlines weary, dreary; the fields kissed by low-lying clouds; the hall covered in circulars; the stairs shaking with the thick footfalls of a thick and witless husband ready for the scrape of a razor, the snap of underpants and dabs of this and that. Cats cry. Bulbs swell out of sight. The tide come in, goes out, comes in. As far as possible she wants to remember it all, excluding, of course, blinks of the eyes, certain natural but undignified functions; any post-orgasmic cheer experienced by the husband of the Premier; the carbohydrate content of sliced loaves; the opening hours of the local Spar; the reproductive cycle of common houseplants, dragonflies or married couples; the comings and goings of Mrs Thrupp as she hoovers gossip through flared nostrils; Derek's shoe size; the benefits of low cholesterol margarine and the frequency with which Mrs Thrupp's husband Colin slams the garden gate on his way to work at the Council's Highway Maintenance Depot.

Dear Quentin, though you probably don't exist, I address myself to you this morning because I've the feeling J's not listening – up to his eyes in a stranger's thigh, no doubt. We need someone else to confide in now and then, someone invented who'll make greater efforts to endure our lunacy. I imagine you're say, thirty-eight years old. To date you've been quite a whizzo at your career and to celebrate this fact you've been made to purchase a new Axminster for the lounge. While pulling up the old carpet you find that these pages have been scattered across the floorboards by the previous occupant as an underlay. 'Darling. Oh Darling,' you call out to your wife Jane who's busy in the Tulip kitchen preparing a Dover sole, 'you're not going to believe this. I've just found dozens of written-on pages under this carpet.'

Jane doesn't care a bit. Besides, she's preparing haddock in reality, thus proving the requiem wrong. For the moment, Quentin, you abandon this tedious business of home improvement, snuggle up in a bare corner, spend half an hour putting me into numerical order and then, wooed somewhat by the perfume of grilled haddock, begin to read. Your enthusiasm doesn't last too long. Too weary for dark blue men on stepladders, the ghost of Jane Austen and a certain lack of chronology, you tuck the pages into the teak alcove and return to the matter at hand, promising yourself another crack at them later on. Will this promise be fulfilled? Probably not. After haddock you'll tune in to the shipping forecast to see how things are going in or on good old Dogger Bank, then, creeping to bed, will peel off Jane's clothes in a game you've invented in which you try to pretend she's someone you've never met before; after all, you're absolutely sick to the back teeth of the sight of her face; for years you've watched her trim her toenails, run a Bic razor down her legs in the bath and queue in Boots for a new Mum rollette. Subsequent to this difficult intercourse, poor Jane, with a predictability which drives you crazy, will curl against you to whisper sweet dissatisfactions while you, being male, enthuse for adventure — some day you'll pack in your godawful job and row singlehandedly and blindfolded across the Pacific, dropping by at remote islands to search for traces of Gauguin or to rest while primitive teenager natives dive naked into blue lagoons. In the marital dark you may resent the fact that your wages turn so miraculously into tiers of pine shelving, co-ordinated kitchen utensils, sets of Utrillo tablemats, sturdy chipboard coffee tables or unopened sets of mah jong.

In the morning you may pick me up once more, conquer the beginning at last but come a cropper again and again over this Mr Burgess or his lookalike. You skip him, but soon realise by the movements within your dressing gown that Doing It the night before has been like a drug to an addict inasmuch as the one fix has made you want to Do It again. Though not liking me much so far, you make a sincere apology, return me to the alcove (under 'The Handy Home Doctor'), make coffee for

Jane, sit on the bed stroking her hair, so she knows what's afoot, kiss her ears, move insidiously from upright to horizontal, pushing your slippers off at the same time, wonder how on earth you've failed to notice the warmth and magic of her body till now, whisper fictions at her Roman nose then shuffle over her for the second fuck in twelve hours. This time the opened floodgates of sentiment allow cosy images of visits to garden centres, the construction of flagstone patios or week-long tours to the vineyards of Normandy.

However one may describe what Kate writes, she's lonely and worn out on a Saturday morning which suddenly comes alive with the sun though fingers of mist still wriggle among the trees at the riverside. A frozen-fish lorry shudders to a halt by a phone box on the dual-carriageway. Miss Wintle sings 'My Old Man's a Dustman' at her kitchen sink but stops at the sound of breaking china. 'Well stone me Arthur,' she says to her imaginary husband, 'that was your favourite plate.'

A surfeit of wet dreams has made Derek late getting up: he'll miss his Jog. Female devotees of curly thighs who line his usual route with hankies and pockets of rice to toss will be sorely disappointed. In his head and in his shop he's determined to be a significant man. But he'll only linger at the rim of poverty and die unsung, not a fan letter or sonnet to his name. Later Kate will take the scenic route to the supermarket, hum along with Max Bygraves, run her fingers over tins of alphabet spaghetti, tempt herself with plastic bottles of Imagination Foam Bath then buy the ingredients of her husband's Saturday Night Treat. Pork Chops. Mushrooms. Fried Onions. Chips. At nine tonight he'll yawn, express opinions on the low-quality of the television programmes he's been glued to for three hours, have a bath, scamper naked up the stairs to rummage for a fresh towel, lightly talc his groin and feet, spray his underarms then slip into bed with 'Book-keeping for the Small Businessman,' soon falling fast asleep, replenishing his vitality for possible intercourse on the morrow.

The Well of Loneliness is beginning to annoy me. Stephen always has enough money. More than enough. She doesn't have to put Life aside in order to go to the launderette; doesn't need to abandon her writing for half an hour while she pops over to Mrs Thrupp's with two week's money for the Little-woods bedside lamp she's bought. She's surrounded by people poorer than her who'll gladly undertake all basic tasks which would otherwise disrupt the run of her fabulous plot.

Bored. A hand between the legs under the desk. A pen twiddling. J's right at the back of the reference library. My shoes squeak over the wooden floors. A dozen lovers of Lenin look up from thick books. I'm holding tomato sandwiches and an expanded polystyrene cup of Brazilian coffee which has traces of vegetable soup on top thanks to a malfunctioning vending machine. We're supposed to be reading books about D.H. Lawrence, but within the hour we're walking down to the river wishing the bastard hadn't been so vain. Our *Women in Love*'s lie at the bottom of a plastic bag beneath a large packet of digestive biscuits and a box of tea-bags. The surface of the river is a mirror melted here and there by the breasts of swans. A man in a bowler hat bumps into us and begs our pardon. J's arm is tight around my shoulders, making it difficult to walk. Truant boys fish.

'And he does tend to say the same things over and over,' says J, breaking the mirror by throwing in a stone. A favourite topic among passers-by is this remarkable warmth for the time of year and J notes that the seasons do seem to have slipped to the right somewhat. He's very beautiful somehow, especially since he sees so much to make him smile. In the derelict boatyard we put down the bag, look at one another too enthusiastically, and embrace.

'Wow,' says J, 'I can feel it coming on again.'

There's glass under my shoes and dreams or memories of a large, decaying house in the country. The smell of leaves and greens and shadows and dark mossy corners defeats me. Maybe I'll lie down and simply roll through the grass, chew buttercups, howl at the sun. A bell sounds to indicate the opening of the swing bridge. For some inaccessible reason which will bother him for weeks to come, J goes to the edge of the quay and drops his *Women in Love* into the water.

'There,' he says, coming back to me with a grin. 'Bollocks to the lot of it.'

We embrace again but this time he squeezes his hand down the back of my jeans. We hear the roar of ships' engines. It's the *Balmoral* heading for Ilfracombe with another row of sightseers clinging to the railings.

'The touch of your bum is just magic,' he says. Having run out of ideas standing still, we wander in the direction of a mobile hot-dog van. From the ruins of a lime tree a bird sings. The hot-dog man's called Arthur and is having a bad day. Envisaging Doom, he presents us with an extra sausage. J's thrilled. He knew in his bones that the world was on the mend though the two o'clock news, rattling from Arthur's transistor radio, tries to tell a different story. Those creepy Lebanese gunmen have been at it again. J must take a bite of my hot-dog, me a bite of his.

Golden Lion

In deepest green shadow beneath the railway arches a bewhiskered man holding a tray of shoelaces offers a pair to Kate, but she only smiles and comes into the sun again, turning left at the undertaker's then beginning the climb to the top of a steep hill. Here, long ago, travellers halted their caravans on the bank above a vigorous stream which is hidden now between ranks of stout Victorian houses. If she could see it, she suspects it would be cluttered with bicycle frames, car tyres, Caribbean fruit-drink cans, tumble dryers even.

'You're a bit too crazy and a bit too romantic for your own good,' he says, though these days he's just a dream, a voice in the wind. The top of the hill flashes green and yellow beneath a canopy of trees. From a tunnel nearby comes the same railway line, crossed at Kate's favourite thinking-place by an uneven bridge whose parapets are flowers of wrought iron painted magnolia with a varnished wooden rail above. She reaches it and waits. Around her, the rustle of paper fanned by cold air from the tunnel, the rustle of leaves, the rustle of old men's newspapers in the small playground. Children squabble over turns on the slide while mums on benches share marital secrets and roar with laughter. She waits a little longer. It seems he may come along at any time.

'Nay, Madam, I know not seems,' he laughs, holding out his arms as if to balance on a wire. He hasn't yet discovered the piece of choc-ice on his chin.

She's been waiting for as long as she can remember and

though things happen in the meantime, none of them will influence her. Chance is continually dished up to those not requiring it. A watched pot never boils. A monumental ache is no guarantee of satisfaction though one might twiddle one's fingers or breathe in too deeply. He doesn't come. An ice-cream van rings from street to street with a chip-pan Italian at the wheel. She moves on. Crosses the road from the other side of the bridge then slips by the garage into the jaws of Blueberry Road. On the left, further rows of houses; on the right, a tumbledown wall which follows the railway line. Above this wall, on looped telephone wires, evening birds gather to loop and sing.

She laughs at the steering wheels in parked cars. Suddenly they're the most ridiculous things. Ordinary human beings sit behind them then seek their way through piles of brick and concrete. There were certain words at school, too. Everyone at Kate's table in the dining hall fell about during treacle tart saying 'Quince' over and over. Examining the homes on the left she then imagines the families living there. Gardens faint with flowerbeds, lichen-covered reproduction Venus de Milos, disproportionate rockeries, dry birdbaths, angling gnomes. Here we must picture the charm of weekends; blood-relatives spilling through open front doors; babies left to dribble on the step; admiring mums making daisy chains of dreams with lined fingers; dependable dads deep in the garden greenery; forgotten aunts pissed as parrots in chrysanthemum hats.

Somehow dusk comes. Now she'd like to be with him. Most of all she'd like to be with him in the kind of mood which leads her to pretend she's not particularly bothered whether she's with him or not. Instead the road moves on another half mile or so, keeping itself to itself, shrugging with parked cars. The lights have started to glow red. Approached by a stranger she wears the disguise of a girl going somewhere fine, looking up only when the danger's past at the jagged horizon where the cut-outs of a city rise. She waits and walks simultaneously. One day she'll read books because she wants to read books, make love, whisper nothings-at-all because she wants to whisper nothings, make love. One day she'll walk and have somewhere to go other than back again. This aimlessness will come to an end and she'll hardly think of him at all unless it's simply to giggle over the foibles of the past. She skips. Words like 'foibles' don't suit her. She's stolen it from some other character, having found an unruly gap in her sentence. He'll come round the corner with a loaf tucked under his arm, stop in front of her, say 'Hello there', and gaze at her forehead. It's a sure sign of love, gazing at foreheads. She's read it in a book by Desmond Morris or one of those other persons who make a dubious living by gawping at the antics of chimpanzees.

'And how are you keeping these days?' he'll ask. J, not Desmond Morris. One couldn't imagine Mr Morris asking such a question; he'd know by the way you were swinging your legs exactly how you were keeping.

'Oh, you know. The years roll by,' she'll reply, hating the diplomacy which breaks out between broken-up couples. 'And how are you?'

He'll look at the pavement, turn pink, shuffle his shoes.

'Actually I've married someone called Tara-Louise from British Telecom,' he'll confess.

She reaches the junction. A small crowd has gathered round an old lady who's just fallen bum first onto the pavement outside the shop allowing several Jaffa oranges and a tin of Batchelor's condensed soup to roll into the gutter. There are sufficient people to assist, so I needn't interfere – students of literature, zoologists, members of the flying squad, Johnny Morris, ex shot-putters in black underwear, four football fans, a black and tan collie cross, an unhappy priest. And I'm in love with the shop itself; its piles of milk crates, the black and white awning, the warm rows of tea-bags. The windows are covered in postcards. She skirts round the crowd to read them, having had fantastic dreams that one day there will be a message for her – 'It was all a mistake. Come quick. J.'

Two cards in particular catch her eye on this darkening night. The first, written in red, describes a slender young man aged twenty-five, interested in country pursuits, nocturnal

51

swimming, Samuel Beckett, German wines, Arachnida, The Spinners and philately, who's searching for a young woman, similar. Someone has written on the window in felt-tip, 'Philately will get you nowhere'. The second card explains how you can have a massage in your own home beneath the fingers of a most attractive brunette whose photo is attached. 'Thorough and experienced' she calls herself. She's also offering assisted showers in inverted commas.

In the fragrant dusk it often feels as if Kate will live forever, wandering, searching, stroking the passing walls, being scruffy and untalented, her shoes squeezing across the cambered tarmac. I'm ill, a child, a genius – call it what you like. She remembers those old photos once more. A little over there to the right a small stone cottage with a thatched roof stood among a copse of elms. The narrow lane leading to it had been churned up by cartwheels. At the cottage door an elderly man with a clay pipe and straw hat was holding on to the reins of a ragged work-horse. The lane then moved on to disappear among trees, hedgerows, the setting sun. Maybe the ghost of the man remains and she passes through him on her way to nowhere.

At the launderette – formerly the courtyard of a monastery – she waits again. Here his shirt turned pink. During the day a dark woman with nylon shoes helps students to fold their sheets, glad to pick out the ones missing their mum. Kate leans against the window and peers inside, sensing the warmth on her skin. The washers sit on plastic chairs, humming, remembering, working on crossword puzzles or the Introduction to a little something by Charlotte Bronte. The tubs rock back and forth. The dryers tumble with colour. She looks from one person to another – from the bronchial young man in jeans to the anxious woman in Walt Disney slippers and silken scarf. She calls it 'Watching the Waiters' – though by 'Waiters' she doesn't mean skinny Italians in dusty black who bring your melon or your smoked mackerel pâté. She means the tired people who watch and don't watch; who stand now and then to yawn or to slip sneaking fingers round the rim of the soap dispenser; who pout towards their washing as it mumbles with foam behind the cloudy glass eye.

Across the road and down a little vandals gather for their weekly conference outside 'The Milking Stool', holding glasses of lager and supporting themselves by squeezing one boot against the wall. Now J's having a whale of a time in the arms of painted infidels she's never even heard of. Stars creep out. The moon swings. Glenn Miller strikes up. Mickey Rooney mounts an orange box and pecks Judy Garland on those unbelievable lips. Somewhere over the rainbow there's peace of mind, James Stewart, spring lambs and clowns with shaving-foam eyebrows. The road fills with nights out. From a darkened alley on the left comes a backwoods villain in dirty cream corduroys which reach an undistinguished, overly flared conclusion three inches above brown cowboy boots. His teeth are long, crooked and green. He's on probation for eating children. Hear him growl as he clumps across the road then slips into another alley beside the florists. This could be a tumour; pressure on those creative cells driving the earth haywire. In the ironmonger's doorway someone vaguely familiar is trying to sell the last of his evening papers. Almost short enough to be called a dwarf, he shouts 'Banker in Panties Scandal' to a bored world then squints at it through myopic spectacles. The vandals crack jokes about his immense wellingtons and the state of his Hebridean cap.

Kate's reflection hangs in the butcher's window. During opening hours a man in a bloodstained white coat can be seen dodging slit lambs to reach the bacon carver. Each evening he creates a brief message on the display tiles with strips of plastic parsley. The first Kate ever noticed was 'Love's a Golden Lion'.

Eden Grove

Dripping with blood and mucus I'm shunted from my gently rocking world into dad's uncertain hands. As if to fathom out exactly what I am, he holds me upside down for a moment, slaps my bum and places me on a patch of wet eiderdown between mum's legs. He's seen it in films, this slapping business, but I won't cry, preferring to listen to mum's dreadful sobbing and her broken condemnation of the midwife who came just an hour ago to put their minds at rest. I wasn't due, she said. Mum lies crucified on the bloodied sheets. Dad pulls and snaps each of his fingers in turn.

We're in the midnight gloom of a council house which stands in the middle of a cheap estate roamed by mad dogs and stick-throwing children – ours certainly isn't one of those breath-taking landscapes with acres of trees and tumbling white clouds through which smugglers stalk while spotty girls with round glasses and pigtails have Ripping Larks. There's simply a tragic Aunty who comes round too often, a glass partition between the kitchen and the front room which rattles during rows and a brown utility sideboard crammed with chalk ornaments. People visit. I have various relations' noses but the eyes of my mum. Others Coo Coo or Tickly Wickly Wick, squeezing my belly with fat fingers. After a few drinks dad becomes a bit of a peacock. He was the first to touch the mess, the first to examine it from top to toe, the first to proclaim it almost perfect. Mum's exhausted. Dad pops me into a Moses basket and drinks from mum's gorged breasts. For several days she reels in pain and surprise. Her ugliness has become irresistible to him.

I refuse to give my verdict on the birth for several years. We continue to live in Eden Grove, a very long grey road with many grey trees, some rusting black cars, a lonesome lollipop lady whom boys keep telling to fuck off and many many fly-covered seashells of dogmess standing proud of the cracked pavement. Each of the forty-five lampposts has a yellow stain and a spray of grey grass at its base. We own a shed but no cat. Aunty appears in grim pinafores carrying fairy cakes and bags of pineapple cubes. She's much older than mum because, so she says, their own mum was a harlot. Old sprout stems shiver in the vegetable patch all winter. Dad builds a greenhouse I later break by throwing fallen apples for a dare. Every front garden has its own privet hedge. In autumn I find hundreds of dewy cobwebs clinging to them. I collect the webs with a forked stick. The spiders drop to the pavement and the idea is to crunch them before they reach the safety of the cracks. Mum has a nasty boil and must treat it with a special cream designed to suck out the pus. At the end of each privet hedge is a wooden gate painted to match the colour of the house it belongs to. The paint becomes so flaky you can make maps in it with your fingernails. Behind every gate is a ragged square of grass. Five doors down Mrs Furlong has collected dozens of smooth pebbles during outings to Chesil Beach, painted them in bright primary colours and arrange them around her piece of grass to spell GREETINGS EVERYBO.

The houses are pink then green, pink then green, with either cherry or dark green front doors, though there's something amiss with the Jacksons' place over the road which started out pink but has gradually turned a dirty grey with long black streaks hanging down the walls from broken guttering. Mum says the Jacksons are Yobbos, especially the eldest boy who keeps weeing in our hedge. The leaves along the bottom are beginning to turn brown. Dad chases him with a broom but it makes no difference; the lout just loves pissing in the open. Mr Jackson keeps his broken-down green lorry round the

55

corner outside someone else's house. It has a long wooden back with eight empty vegetable crates piled against the cab. The tyres are flat. On the right-hand door it used to say 'Jacksy's Fruit and Veg' but vandals have painted it over.

This is a market-garden town, I suppose. In season lorries full of peas, beans or asparagus trundle through the grey streets. Bells ring on Sundays. Scowling rentmen tap from door to door being screamed at. On Saturday mornings the monkey-puzzle churchyards flutter with windblown petals of confetti, small tombstone dogs stroked by toddlers in blue and gin-pickled priests who link fine fingers and giggle with the bride. Neighbours complain of this and that in accents which make each sentence sound like a question. Other, unholy, dogs yap, piss and fuck in the road while dads with no shirts run out to throw buckets of water over them. Grandmothers stumble home from the wool shop jeered at by boys hanging from the undernourished lime trees. Husbands who no longer get on with their wives have a *Parade* delivered inside their *Daily Sketch*, giving paper boys the chance to flick through the coloured pages in the shadow of the electricity station. Some people live in the corners of their windows, keeping tabs on situations; others linger in twos or threes around the lamp-posts telling jokes and rolling cigarettes.

In the mornings Mr Jackson slides into view at the kitchen window, a pair of black braces stretching over a string vest. With thick hands he grips the sink, waits several minutes, then snaps forward to throw up. Mum says its the drink. Mrs Jackson usually appears at an upstairs window in a pink nightie and green curlers, a duster in her hand. She gazes out at the weather then jerks her eyebrows. Soon the road will be raised from its slumber by her eldest boy scrapping with his brother in the back bedroom. My dad's downstairs eating egg and fried bread while mum wraps his sandwiches. Mr Jackson throws up a second time just to make sure, wipes dribbles from his lips with a Hogmanay tea-towel then reaches for a tumbler and the tin of Andrews.

Dad loves to tease mum. He sands down a piece of wood,

paints 'The Manger' on it in gothic lettering, varnishes it, then screws it to the wall by the front door. He doesn't like God very much and wants to niggle mum who likes Him quite a bit. God's in her head and in her understanding. If it rains dad peeps through the curtains saying 'God's pissing again!' Mum tells him it's one of the deadliest sins, making fun of the Lord. 'You'll see,' she says.

Crouching on the cupboard in my bedroom, I listen to the grumbles of old men or watch as stooped mums haul screaming kids through the wind. Sometimes I can smell cakes baking or hear the Rag and Bone man ringing his bell. If you can scratch together enough old clothes he'll give you a goldfish in a plastic bag or a balloon on a stick, but mum usually makes out that we're wearing rags already, so she can't spare anything.

On Mondays Mrs Jackson stands at the same sink digging her hands into domes of soapy sheets, a bright yellow scarf knotted over her curlers. Occasionally she becomes quite still and gazes out at the warm Indian Ocean from a hot sandy beach where natives wander from millionaire to millionaire with glasses of champagne on silver trays. At dinnertime her husband pops home to eat, slumping through the gate wearing his blue vegetable coat. Stolen apples make his pockets lumpy. He's whistling. Once inside he pours himself a pint of India Pale and settles down at the table. Mrs Jackson shouts at him in silence. He thumps the table.

Monday's boiling day. Whole gardens turn white and soon flap in the wind. For lunch we have bubble and squeak with a slice of cold Yorkshire pudding. Mum's in a bad mood because Dad once promised her a cottage in the country. She won't let me leave the table till I've finished every scrap then spooned my way through a leathery bowl of rice pudding. There's plenty of kids in India who'd give their right arm for a meal like this. The kitchen sink is stained with tea. We can just hear the crackle of our next-door neighbour's lungs above the sound of 'Workers' Playtime'.

After bubble and squeak I go back to my room. The walls

57

are covered in the Three Bears except for the damp patch round the fireplace which dad has left unpapered. Every few feet the Three Bears gaze into their porridge bowls while Goldilocks looks on through a pink window. The fields are scattered with blue trees and tiny bastard rabbits. Nothing happens afterwards. The same moment goes right round the room. Baby Bear's chair is in pieces on the floor but no-one's noticed it yet and probably never will. At one point Mummy Bear has a photo of our dead grandmother hanging from her bum. In the middle of the grey ceiling is a hole without its cover leading to the loft. Dad says demons will slip through the hole at night if I make a fuss about going to bed. Sometimes he comes upstairs and moves around my room, his hands scraping the walls. I'm half asleep. In the mornings he tells me it was a ghost and that if I ever hear it again I must keep dead quiet and close my eyes.

Grandfather stays with us for a few months but then a blood vessel bursts in his head and he whisks off to have a bit of slap and tickle with those naked angels. His chin's always covered in spit and lumps of dried egg. His shabby clothes and bowler hat remind him of the old days when he could saw through a log in seconds and spent many summer afternoons chasing country girls through the hayloft. A watch chain hangs across a black stomach. The stomach fills up, fills up, fit to burst. There's always a racing paper poking from his pocket. At night he says long prayers with no clothes on. On my way to the toilet I can see his enormous bum and dark hairy arms through the gap in his bedroom door. He dies in the middle of a prayer but no-one notices for a long time thinking his head lying flat on the eiderdown is a signal of extra holiness. After his death mum puts his bowler hat on the wardrobe but takes it down every now and again to have a chat if dad's getting on her wick or the ironing has reached breaking point.

After work dad scuffs up the hall in his tartan slippers then crawls into the front room on all fours pretending to be a dog. Reaching my chair, he growls, shakes his head, then pounces, poking his paws up my jumper. In all his born days he's never seen such a tickly girl, he says. The paws become hands. Mum comes to the partition and wipes her pastry fingers in her pinny.

Woollen gloves dangle from the arms of my duffel-coat on bits of elastic. It's a grey coat with peg buttons which won't do up when my hands are cold. Mum makes me wear it when we go shopping. Sometimes I see old crisp bags slithering up the pavement. Dad's favourite saying is 'Step on a crack and you won't come back'.

Woolworth's is the biggest shop. Inside the left-hand door are dozens of trays filled to the brim with all kinds of sweets. If Aunty comes with us for the company she has a quarter of rum and butters and perhaps some Pontefract cakes to keep her regular. The floor's made of wood. Mum drags me away from the sweets to the household section where there are shiny metal buckets, bags of Brillo pads, packets of Lux, tiny bags of blue which are supposed to make your sheets whiter and lumps of green soap with a baby carved on the side. Dozens of other mums clump up and down the aisles staring at the shelves or stooping to clout wriggling children. Most mums look slightly better than your own. If you take hold of one of the new floor mops and shake it, the tickly white dust goes everywhere.

Of course it's December here in the city, though there's no telling when I'll be rescued from your floorboards, Quentin. You could be reaching for the last shreds of summer or plodding home through another damp autumn unable to figure out your dreams. Maybe you're sick of the day's unending tedium and hum away your nights creating fictions of the young ladies you loved but failed to pursue.

Sunday 5.40am

So tired even J's suffocating beneath a blanket of cloud, slumber cloud. Rooks cackle from the tops of poplars, perhaps they don't. The monotonous breeze of sleep slips through the gorge watched by dead monks who are said to roam the cliffs. This tea is beautiful. Thank you, Mr Tips. I mentioned to J I'd be thinking of him as I fell against the pillow last night because Derek was so concerned with the state of his athlete's feet and the patches of damp which have appeared in the spare bedroom. But I didn't. Think of him, I mean. You know how it is, you keep poking at your memories but they dip out of sight each time. Sometimes I'm enamoured of him and the sticky bed imprisons me. Winter's really here. The darkness is audacious without him. Make a note of that sentence, J, it's sure to shiver your timbers. Before very long Kate has finished her first cup of tea and must go to the kitchen for a second. The night's being chewed by a ravenous moon. Miss Wintle's already up and about, on her patio throwing crumbs and breaking wind and I say, There you go, Kate, vandalising your dreams with farce. So tired, my eyes are heavy, sore, damp in the corners; I'm tempted by bed though it's the last place I wish to be, what with Derek's arms, knees, throat and everything. Kate's an enigmatic woman, breaking rules by occupying a shed at dawn. Perhaps you'll want your wicked way with her; perhaps you'll be incited to pull her aside, push her to the floor, drive some sense between her awfully soft legs. Oh! Goodness me! A man! Well I never. Since waking I've had in

60

my mind the image of a place I'd like to visit. Beneath my fingers there's a drystone wall covered in lichen, a little broken down, its fallen mossy stones cowering in nettles. Behind the wall, a tree, an ancient tree with twisted branches, gnarled green bark and sunkissed leaves. Perhaps I turn at the sound of running water to see a village pond rippled with portraits of half-timbered houses and the dancing of a blue and yellow fool. A wide ribbon of clear water drapes over the low wooden sluice. On a nest of broken reeds a third of the way across the pond, a swan stands to exercise its wings. I hear hushed voices, the tinkle of ice in a glass, the creak of a garden swing. Grass, flowers and nettlebeds bloom with butterflies. From the secluded manor house a peacock screeches. So tired, and the world continues to let you down. Hot and bothered as he is, J squeezes fingertips into my shoulders till I kneel in the grass, then relates how the blind enthusiasm of adolescence can become wide-eyed and cynical as love and ambition go wildly astray.

Though it's almost Christmas J isn't around because he has to be at his mum's to carve the lonely goose and make sure the money keeps coming. Kate slumps in her room, waiting for him where previously she'd waited for no-one. She fiddles with books for a few minutes at a time or makes mental notes to begin essays the following day, hoping for a card. A card would be fine, something to go by. At the brink of fresh companion-ship, being alone is no longer easy. She's irritated by the row of icicles hanging from the outside windowsill; can hardly be bothered to go to bed or to get up. Footsteps on the ceiling bore her to death. Kettles boil. Curries bubble. Robins peck at the frozen soil. Being alive's often a matter of waiting for next to nothing. The park's grey and preoccupied, overrun by panting labradors and screaming children. Listen hard and the heavens ring with praises of the Lord or the distant slam of doors on the unwanted choruses of carol singers. She curls in bed, wrapped in as many blankets as she can find, seeking out those fantasies which glow brightest at the edges of slumber. Her bones ache. Three drunken kings rock across open desert on the backs of melancholy camels, searching for a baby who'll later introduce Guilt to their lives. His card comes Christmas Eve. Inside he's written 'Well! Here we are then'. On the front of the card is a badly coloured print of Monet's 'Water Lilies'. She puts it on the mantelpiece and reads it several times during the day. Well! Here we are then.

On Boxing Day Catherine comes round because she's bored shitless. I don't have to say much. She throws her coat to the floor and examines my room from top to bottom as usual; pours us both continual drinks from a bottle she's brought; gazes through my curtains and talks of inconsequential things, holding the stem of her glass in one hand, rubbing the rainbowed rim with the middle finger of the other. She has a remarkable story to tell after all. On Christmas Eve she ended up in bed with a student of Town and Country Planning named Terence. Towards midnight they had an argument about South Africa and he stormed off, taking with him the box of liqueurs he'd given her as a gift, a token of his mysterious affection, a bribe towards the removal of her tight clothes.

'Don't care anyway,' she says. 'It was turning out to be the most tedious fuck I've ever had.'

Since birth, apparently, Terence had developed a number of psychological difficulties in regard to his Insurance Broking father and these had led, indirectly, to a general lack of stamina in and around the reproductive organs. So ran the tale he recounted in the unclimactic dark. Occasionally, having rested, he attacked Catherine like a Jack Russell with a bowl of mince, but then he dwindled each time into an alarming floppiness at which she could do nothing but laugh. After a few minutes' morbid self-examination, who should loom into Terence's infamous gloom, but P.W. Botha.

Apparently he liked old P.W. quite a lot.

Around the middle of the day we put on our coats and go for a walk, both dozy and nostalgic. Catherine remembers an ancient teddy bear with black buttons for eyes. The streets are empty except for puddles from the sudden thaw and mashed piles of beech leaves. Catherine's white hand swings through the pre-emptive twilight. We smell turkey, Christmas cake, schooners of sherry; hear cautious sing-songs and the shrieks of unleashed great-aunts; stamp along the damp grey dead gutters to wake ourselves up. The wind's an offensive weapon. Catherine yawns, slips her long hands into her pockets. She's been thinking of doing her hair differently, longs to be fucked on Christmas Day to spite Jesus, yet her legs are empty and her head's beset by insoluble problems. She kicks an empty yoghurt carton. Pineapple and Apricot. What will they think of next? This one has a welcome dash of the much-maligned E102. Her face is white, pointed, mysterious, unkissed, cold and, today, almost lipless. I'm grateful that she seems to have so few close friends. She doesn't particularly want to talk to me about J. I tried her out earlier but she soon brought the subject back to herself. The world's grey-green. A fat black dog sniffs at a holly bush at the edge of the park. The trees are corpse grey and will never again have leaves. In the afternoon I take a short nap while Catherine watches *Black Narcissus* and consumes more vodka. I wake up thinking I'm in his room. I can hear him whispering, but it's only Catherine singing to herself as nuns struggle on the cliff edge. I turn over to nothing. Christmas is an agony to unconnected lovers.

Slight pause there. Derek came to see me. He was still half asleep and had obviously been having bad dreams. He wanted to know if I was going back to bed with him for what he described as a 'cuddle'. I told him I might be a little while because I was trying to start my life again from scratch. He wasn't happy with this. His nose told me so. Not that he's opposed to the idea of change in principle; he just can't understand why I should need to embark on such a course at a time usually reserved for the sexual act. I protested. When you're starting your life over again, the best time to begin is when you're being urged, through force of habit, to carry on with the same old thing. He grinned. Raised his eyebrows.

'But Sunday morning is always Cuddle morning,' he said.

The netting in Miss Wintle's living-room window moved to

one side. She dislikes arguments, especially those undertaken outside the house. She strives for world peace and tranquillity and has created an old-fashioned cottage garden as a start to this ultimate goal. In summer her white head floats from back door to back fence above a sea of delphiniums and what have you.

Having argued for a few minutes, Derek changed tack. He came up with this surprise visit to a Wildlife Park he plans to take me on this afternoon, described in some detail how he's been saving up in secret for the entrance fee.

Didn't I therefore feel the slightest twinge of guilt, making such a fuss about what is, after all, a regular and somewhat pleasant aspect of a married couple's life?

He meant fucking.

Penguins Etc

It's 10.30 yesterday. Derek walks down the path whistling, a camera slung over his left shoulder, car keys waggling in his right hand. All is joy. We're not speaking to each other because Derek wanted to fuck Kate but Kate, bless her, didn't want to be fucked by Derek. Basically she'd had enough of it – things poking into things; bits of body being bitten by a bellicose bastard. The Coming and its attendant sweaty gratitude. He climbs into the driver's seat wearing his 'Humph! See if I care whether we make love or not' expression. He really is the finest of human beings, J. You and he would get along famously over Cointreau. I'm playing Dire Straits on the stereo; singing along. Derek hates a number of the tracks because he thinks the lyrics remind me of other lovers and that my soft accompaniment is some kind of hymn to lost happiness. He is, of course, perfectly correct and makes out he needs to turn the volume down because he's unable to concentrate on his driving, but you should hear how loudly he plays his *Carpenters Greatest Hits*. He's enjoyed the emaciated Karen for many years and this enjoyment has been enriched since she abandoned earth in favour of the gods.

As we drive through the gorge the sun comes out, throwing a golden light across the dark climber-dotted cliffs, picking out the railings of the suspension bridge way above us, turning the grey river into something vaguely attractive. I remember the low-water ferry just about here. It was watched over by an old man in black rags who lived in a hovel on the Somerset side.

At high tide he'd come out just to salute the many sailing ships slipping into the city from the sea. Photos of those days show large numbers of men quarrying into the rockface; the row of workers' cottages hugging the tideline; the narrow towpath frequented by visitors who'd come to gaze at the recently completed towers of Brunel's bridge. Now the various bites in the cliff are places of shade and butterflies where lovers gather on Sunday afternoons; the hovel and the ferry have long since been destroyed and the towpath has become a four-lane carriageway along which numerous Dereks drive in unconsummated silence.

At the Cumberland Basin the traffic slows down and must file past the scene of an accident. A saloon car has been crushed between two lorries. A heavy breakdown truck, directed by a black and orange policeman, is tugging the front lorry away. A man sits dead for a ducat at the wheel of the crushed car, eyes wide open, a hint of surprise amongst his eyebrows. The steering wheel seems to have penetrated his chest. Other drivers peep and waggle fists because they simply must reach the garden centre soon to avoid the afternoon rush. Derek turns off the stereo. He hates death. He's stunned by the thought that the dead man can have had no idea he was about to die as he came innocently round the corner on his way to God knows where. Probably Matilda's for gustful macaroons. We have to pull in at a tea caravan two or three miles later. Derek's plastic cup shakes.

Several other wintry families turn up at the Wildlife Park the same time as us, being shown into their parking spaces by a bent pensioner who wears a red fluorescent coat to show he's Official. The grass is soft. Derek's fancy revving as he backs in leaves an unpleasant brown gash for which he apologises. Having lost two fingers from his right hand, the toothless pensioner has no choice but to wag the stumps at Derek who pretends not to notice. We're a husband and wife as we tiptoe through the squalid field towards the entrance. J gathers acorns among the grey trees, turning to look at me every now and again. Kate's heart misses a beat. At the thought or sight

66

of him it usually does and she'd love one day to ask a surgeon about the physical processes involved. There's more to life than meets the eye. J will take the acorns home, swill them under the tap and keep them in a raffia basket on the mantelpiece for months to come.

At the turnstile Derek chooses to have a row with the woman taking the money. He wants to know why he has to pay such an exorbitant price for coming to study God's creatures. The woman is putting him down as a kind of retired hunt saboteur whose original resentment against men in black riding hats and pink jackets has festered and spread to almost everyone on earth.

'Well, Sir,' she says, 'you don't have to come in. I'm sure the animals will get along splendidly without you.'

He throws the money onto the counter without speaking further. As we walk away he's speculating what a downtrodden life her husband must lead. Out of the various pursuits possible in this world, one of his favourites is complaining of places he's chosen to visit.

The park is a landscape of grey-green ankle-deep in dead leaves. Squirrels, not known for their exotic qualities, have been driven from the area. The paths are slippery. Derek's actively engaged in not holding my hand and walks just a few paces in front of me. An obese lady in the redundant ice-cream hut snaps at everyone who comes to ask directions instead of ordering a Loganberry Ripple. I see by the pictures that they've developed a range of variously flavoured lollies in the shape of endangered species. Each one purchased guarantees five pence to a wildlife charity. The Gorillas are lemon and lime. Derek's fascinated. My hands are cold. But here's J, his pockets loaded with acorns. He squeezes me against an oak tree, puts his hands on the trunk either side of my head and kisses me, claiming that this action sends a riot of shivers through his soul. Don't be a fool, says Kate. He's leaning against me inch for inch. We're so warm with each other. With the tip of his tongue he tickles the inside of my left ear, a practice which sets me on fire. The tongue of your lover and

67

his silly words have an awful lot to answer for in terms of making the absurd truthful. I'm a magical Kate who says fuck to the world.

A range of quadrupeds mooch incongruously within their rustic enclosures. We catch up with, stumble into or are overtaken by the same ice-cream-covered old lady in a crimson hat who's chosen, much to Derek's irritation, not to follow the route suggested by the guide book, but to lead what appear to be her middle-aged children from one distant point to another ignoring all manner of disappointed wildlife in between. She avoids gravel paths, veering instead across open grassland; sneers at the coloured triangles it's possible to follow according to whether one wants the short 'must get back to the roast' route, or the long, more scientific, David Attenborough one. Facing a species at last, though more by accident than design, she stares at it as if it has no right to be there then walks away again before the bored couple accompanying her have had a chance to catch up.

J's famous occupation is waking to find I'm still beside him. Perhaps the birds are singing. His room is littered with empty milk cartons, dirty plates, record sleeves, pieces of tissue dried into awkward shapes, used joss-sticks. He's fascinated by skin against skin, the promise of further intimacy, a dozen soft white corners of my body he regards as his and the prospects they hold for the tips of his fingers, the wet squeezes of his lips, the brush of his tongue. He likes to play a record first thing then searches his bookcase for various explanatory paragraphs or nestles his head in my shoulder and whispers fantasies he expects me to remember, but the fucking elephants just pause in their interminable pacing to inspect the multicoloured Homo Sapiens walking to and fro along this path. More than anything else, the elephants love the plump, chain-smoking members of the species who, wearing tartan golf hats and supping from unpeeled beer cans, lead unsteady grandmothers from cage to cage or take time out to clout indisciplined youngsters who must throw pebbles at the pelicans.

A large notice assures members of the Animal Liberation Front that the elephants are taken for long walks around the lake each day so they are not to interpret this pacing as a manifestation of any kind of mental illness. In a cage behind us all, an eagle owl rests on its perch. The sea-lions, in defiance of the brochure, are not where they are supposed to be and yet a series of terminally ill pensioners glance into the pool and screw up their eyes, 'It must be the glare, Freda. We need some of them polar hide sunglasses.' A peacock gets edgy at the sight of Derek wielding his camera and fans out its feathers. Derek says, 'Fine. Super. Hold it there for a moment,' and clicks the button, dreaming of David Bailey. A jet roars overhead. The deer scatter in all directions yet Derek takes everything in his stride because he's a Professional. He loves to hold the camera at awkward angles to achieve a touch of Artistry, as he calls it; hates those who just point and snap with an instamatic or, worse still, gather mental families in stiff groups under the monkey puzzles and beg them to say Cheese. With this sense of the Artistic uppermost, he snaps the old lady in the crimson hat as she grips a raspberry Panda in her mouth and stoops to unwrinkle her stockings. Kate taps her feet and waits. If she were in a volume by Mr Archer she'd have had something meaty happen to her by now. There are signs everywhere telling her what a great time she'd be having if only this was summer. As an Arab approaches Derek with his hand raised it seems Kate may be on the brink of being taken hostage and held to ransom or something truly International, but the poor fellow only wishes to be directed to the Ocelots. Derek, preferring boredom to terrorism, does his best, though he admits later, with one hand on Kate's shoulder, that the directions he gave were a wild guess.

As much as she'd like to employ the phrase, Kate can't bear to write 'And time rolls across the open parkland' because it doesn't; time rolls nowhere at all, preferring to hang dismally from the cold shrubs and the tip of Derek's unremarkable nose. Love is about the only thing, J, which makes craziness socially acceptable. Let's lock the bitch up before she suffocates a nun or something. At each cage Derek reads out the name of the occupant in Latin to inspire all those not listening. He would like us to believe he knew the zoological name all along but just wanted to confirm it to everyone else. The lady in the crimson hat's unimpressed. She's slowed down a little and now leans across DO NOT FEED signs throwing crusts from a secret bag in her pocket to whatever Herbivore or Carnivore lurks within the darkened cages. The Wild Cat enjoys itself most of all. The crimson lady imagines that the wild cat is a domestic cat named Twiddles who's somehow infiltrated the cage of the wild cat who, for some reason, isn't there. In view of this travesty of justice, she throws it an extra crust. 'Poor thing must be starving,' she says. The middle-aged children turn away from her in embarrassment and pretend to be enthusiastic about the Condor. The man leans towards the bird, looks it in the eye and says, self-consciously, 'You've a tobacco named after you.' Both the Condor and the Derek chuckle.

At the hub of the park stands an uneasy house with warped windows, decorative battlements and a vicious wistaria which clings to the stonework. 'This was the house used by the BBC to make . . .' says Derek, and reels off the names of several Sunday afternoon television serials. A green and yellow board tells us visitors are NOT ALLOWED. On the large flagstone patio, a thin man in a hat, possibly the Earl himself, sits on a bamboo chair wrapped in blankets reading *The Sunday Times*, oblivious to the stream of sightseers carving muddy channels into his vast lawn. Even though linked chains underline the occupants' preference for Privacy, Derek, as an Artist, is still determined to get a photo of the Aristocracy at play. Pretending for a moment to be zooming in on the virtually barren herbacious borders, he then swivels the camera at the last moment to capture the Earl. Satisfied, he winds on, though he does display a strange mixture of Admiration For and Resentment Of the rich bastard. Meanwhile a plump woman in sepia creeps through the French windows and taps the Earl on the shoulders. Possibly the Bison à l'Orange is now ready. The Earl jumps. *The Sunday Times* slithers to the ground.

Banned visitors gasp across the chains. A scarred tourist whispers 'Oooooh' in Greek. Derek, mildly amused, consults the guide book once more, looks around him, then points to a cypress fir two hundred yards away at the edge of the lawn.

'Horatio Nelson took tea under that very tree,' he says. He is overheard by the crimson lady who turns to the couple coming up behind her.

'Did you hear that? Admiral Nelson!' she says.

Reasonably fascinated, all three cross the lawn to stand under the tree themselves, the old lady curiously non-contextual in her radiant hat, her children twisting on the spot, searching the grass with the tips of their shoes for Nelson's footprints perhaps or scraps of abandoned sea-uniform.

Kate's had enough. A band of children scream and hoot as they chase down a grassy slope into the trees. The outing sickens her. Yawning, she watches plumes of grey smoke roll from nearby woodfire. A man in a fine blue cap pushes a wheelbarrow along a gravel drive. The house itself is now surrounded by overweight post-coronary retired engineers from Rotherham. Chin raised, Derek gazes towards the misty perimeters of the park, tempted by the manmade lake which, according to the guide book, has an envied collection of waterfowl and a fully restored and operative Victorian mill. Kate's thirsty. Men are most violent when they appear as innocent as shorn lambs. Beatings wiggle in their fingertips. The waterfowl quack and hiss in the distance, but Kate persuades her husband to take tea instead.

'Oh for fuck's sake,' he says, 'why do you always have to end up in this mess whenever I take you anywhere?'

Kate moves forward. 'Who's in a mess?'

'You are. Look at you. Here five minutes and pissed off already.'

'An hour and a quarter, actually,' says Kate.

'You could at least try to enjoy yourself.'

'Would it help if I did a handstand?'

'You're just a baby, you fucking cow.'

Notwithstanding Derek's mixed similes, I'm lying on the

hearth in J's room. My hands reach back to grip the legs of the chair while warm echoes of music loom and boom from an open-air concert at the football ground. Lips touch my face. J's the red of the gas fire, the gloom of the autumnal dark. I close my eyes. Lips kiss my forehead, my nose, the corners of my mouth. A left hand rests against my thigh, a right hand in my hair. The lips move to my ear, shuffle there for a while then slide down my neck, brushing and pecking as they go. Soon they reach my breast and in response to their touch I must raise my back and moan. He's feeding like a child bringing a sweet sickness to my throat. These fingers hold the chair tightly and my pleasure pulls it forward by degrees. A tongue draws a moist trail from breast to the top of my thigh. Fingers accompany them then break away to explore.

Despite an uneasy temperature we take refreshment in the tea-room gardens which we find tucked away amongst walls of sculpted privet. The gardens comprise two dozen picnic tables around the edge of a gravelled yard dotted with occasional rockeries. At every table is a litter bin most choose to ignore. Kids everywhere wage wars with old lolly sticks and light yellow hamburger cartons, hiding under the tables from each other while parents tuck into triangles of cake and talk of the wonders they've seen.

We have tea. Derek decides now is the moment for another photo because he likes the way a watery sunlight has chosen to grace my hair. Men say the sweetest things in the process of reconstructing your personality. He asks me to act naturally. It's hard to get a really good composition because the lady in the crimson hat is sitting at a table directly in line with the angle he'd like to use. She's eating a large sandwich brought with her in a supermarket bag. Lines of tomato sauce squeeze into view each time she takes a bite.

At the familiar sensation my eyes snap open. J's proud of himself. See the faint smile around the corners of his mouth. He watches me for a while. It's a game we have. He needs to know how much time will pass before I lose control; loves to feel the rise and roll of my hips beneath his hand. Hips is a word which makes me laugh but, of course, he begs to know if my amusement is linked with the prominence of his ribs. A church bell at the top of the park rings out the hour as he twists and pushes his fingers and I watch his eyes for glints of deceit.

'I'd love someone to take a photo of us like this,' he says, introducing the moment his body slips through the firelight and squeezes partially over mine. Fingers are withdrawn.

'I'd feel much better if you told me what's the matter,' says Derek, putting down his camera. He raises his nose and sniffs unsuccessfully, preparing his excuse for a visit to the toilets and another fix of nasal decongestant. There's nothing wrong with me other than a vague discomfort deep within. I don't care where I am or what my future might be. The wooden table, gravel under my shoes, screams of a baboon, wriggle of chocolate wrappers trapped in the privet, crunch of wheel-chairs; she doesn't care. Fuck it all. The crimson lady snorts at her sandwich having related to her attendants the story of those mischievous penguins who didn't actually do a fucking thing other than waddle in misery to the edge of their prefabricated rocks and leap into the cloudy water.

At the intrepidly gay tea-rooms couples queue patiently as all good citizens should; husbands with hands feeling in pockets rise onto their toes and squeak down again; wives fiddle with tissues or yank kids back into line; young girls in blue-checked suits fuss behind the counter which is cluttered with slabs of cake and plastic domes stacked with melancholy sandwiches. One-legged survivors of the last world war reminisce about pre-war cigarette prices to babies chewing cardigans. People the world over hum from one moment to the next.

The crimson lady's hands twist wildly in front of her nose. We still have the waterfowl, the alpacas and the aardvarks to see. Kate's playing with her white polystyrene cup. The reason she can't go into great details with Derek about the state of her head has something to do with this cup, with groups of inappropriate animals and with crimson sauce-loving old ladies everywhere. Romance has fucked off. No-one will fondle those

73

cracked tomato lips again, and as for Kate herself, well, she waits and hopes and dreams too much; squeezes at her cup till it snaps. If she were a painting she'd be the one by the door people raise eyebrows at *en route* to the Mona Lisa. She's so unlike the lady with the mystic smile and will never grace the lids of Dairy Milk chocolates. Oh don't read this, Mr Burgess, if you are of a weak disposition, because her old lover's head slips between her legs. He holds her thighs and wiggles his tongue; takes a moment now and then to whisper a number of wonderful things and later they are to be found dancing round the room as nature intended to the strains of the evocative Mr Ray Charles. Derek would still like to know what her problem is and yet he's the last person she wishes to tell. One doesn't reveal secrets to husbands since secrets are probably the only treasure they can't uproot. Maybe Kate's problem has much to do with the snakes curled up in wooden boxes along the wall of the reptile house, the ragged buffalo roaming from one fence to the next, the insufferably lighthearted people streaming round this artificial countryside carrying opened packets of Haggis Crisps who chuckle as they impersonate the Orang Utan; or could it be this familiar sunshine falling weak and cool; the easy wind tugging scraps of litter across the gravel yard?

He comes back to town the Tuesday after Christmas but doesn't show up at my place till the Wednesday morning, bringing with him a bunch of dried flowers and a small bronze lion which he places on my mantelpiece. Asking me to remain silent, he shakes his head in disbelief then gives all his attention to the top button of my shirt. He's spellbound. Hands reaching through the shallow light, hands cupping my face for a moment, hands plucking at my collar. Soon each of my buttons is undone in turn. My shirt falls open and with hands can be pushed away. It falls to the floor in a tangle of blue and red squares. He sighs. Don't these breasts just beg for his mouth? As he refers in passing to a dreadful carol service he was forced to attend, his fingers draw patterns on my neck, play on my shoulders, stroke my breasts, sneak to the copper button on my jeans then tug at the zip. He managed to avoid his mum for just two hours a day by remaining in his room with Eugenie Grandet. What a fucking Christmas it's been and isn't it just as fucking from one to the next because one is always lonely for something or someone and dreams must wait their turn. On the table by the door there's an unopened tub of margarine. Kate's naked though she wishes there were other words to express this fact. Indicating that he needs me to stay perfectly still, he retreats to the far side of the room and watches me, his arms folded. My God, here's a little cracker. For a while I can't figure out what to do with my hands unless it's to lay them somewhat innocently as in the painting of that lady who stands in a seashell. 'You're beautiful,' he says. Soon he's dealing with his own clothes, unbuttoning, unbuckling, unzipping, letting them fall or throwing them aside. I have the fever in me. The dried flowers, the mirror, the lion suit one another and my room. I stare at him. He stares at me. 'It's often better to impose a delay,' he says. He seems happy though his skin is too pale and there's a blemish on his upper arm. Naked he's not the best of fellows unless we drown in the light of a coloured bulb. At the end of this period of mutual observation he strolls towards me, his arms held out. 'You'll notice I'm not so shy this week,' he whispers, sidling behind me then rolling his fingers around my body as if it were somehow his own. He hurts Kate a little, squeezing at her breasts and belly, digging deep between her legs. She breaks free, falls to the bed, spreads herself. He threatens to tickle her. Don't laugh, anyone, but I imagine he's quietly wondering what will happen to us and the world once all this has ended. For love there is often a tremendous price to pay – something like the distant nightmare of an eternal hand in your hand which you can neither touch nor see nor brush away. Reaching down he heaves my legs apart. 'Stay like that,' he says, taking a seat at the bedside. I throw back my arms. He's pleased.

Derek fidgets in his thick plastic chair, examining my hand each time it brings the second cup of polystyrene tea to my lips. If reincarnation is a fact then some poor ancient Greek has had an unlucky break amalgamating with Derek's soul. He has been to the toilets to clear his nasal passages and now, to display his fine wit, he addresses this assembly of animal lovers, asking for a Second Class Ticket to Nottingham, Please. Nottingham. Not Dottigam. Kids ignore him. The privet hedge ignores him. Enquiring after my state of mind was a token gesture now quite forgotten. Others have envied me. That Derek, they've said, why, he's quite a Dish, isn't he? A muscular Dish with a firm chin. In Dishlike fashion he now examines his camera to see how many frames he has left on his final roll of film.

'Ah, two,' he says.

'Two?' asks Kate.

'Yes,' he says, crossing his legs, 'two.'

'Oh,' says Kate.

The crimson lady tosses a piece of sandwich to someone else's dog. She could do with being sliced to· ribbons and flushed down the toilet out of harm's way.

Standing at last, J takes hold of my left hand, positions it between my legs and winks at me in the hope I'll wiggle my fingers for him. He's been fantasising this moment right through Christmas with his mum and limbs of festival goose. As yet I haven't spoken and somehow the longer I'm silent the more difficult an opening sentence becomes. Crouching down, he reorganises his fantasy a little by pushing my hand away and opening me up for his mouth and tongue, but he moves imperceptibly from joy to grief and his shoulders begin to shake as if he's crying. Biting his lower lip he climbs onto the bed, tucks himself between my legs and fiddles with my hair. His lips approach the New Year with a light kiss on the end of my nose.

'Christmas without you was like a whole winter squeezed into a few days,' he says.

Beside The Sea

The train shudders and begins to slow down as dad flops his arm around mum's shoulders and calls for one more burst of 'Ramblin' Rose'. Mum's already given him a few playful clouts, but he's made up his mind to be a barrel of laughs and nothing will stop him now, least of all Kate who crouches in the corner by the door making up sentences. Through the window she sees seagulls, timetables, ragged Bisto posters. The train stops and jumps backwards. Dad staggers against the toilet door annoying a sheepskin teddy-boy and a pair of nuns. The teddy-boy has 'Elvis' on his wrist in blue with serpents. Despite what that nice Doctor Singh said at the children's hospital, Kate has the fears and must hold on to a lucky charm in her pocket. A small brass Pixie. Mum hides her face. The man who served us pork pies at sixty miles an hour pushes and whistles his way into the next carriage waggling a pink scrap bucket. Other mums check red lips and ocean-going hats in the mirrors of their compacts. Almost everyone carries a plastic bag. Needing to be first in all things, dad opens the door, jumps to the platform and swings me down to his side. 'Now mind you remember everything about today,' he says. 'That's what going to the seaside's for, you little monkey.' He spins on his heels, squeezes his hands to his middle and breathes in deeply. This is a family day out and he's going to enjoy each moment of it like all the other dads who shuffle by with children and buckets and wives and thirsty highland terriers. 'Brought your mum here once before,' he says. 'Swore she saw Bruce Forsyth, but

I don't know. I don't reckon people like him come here. We had a few pints and some winkles, then it rained and we ended up at the bloody pictures watching old Alan Ladd in something. He was a cowpoke. D'you know what a cowpoke is, eh?' Kate doesn't or does and couldn't care less anyway. The Pixie's become damp in her palm. Meanwhile, mum's amongst the small group of people still waiting to leave the train, holding up the bag of ham sandwiches and chicken portions so they won't get squashed. She's always had a thing about Alan Ladd though he never replies to her letters. For years she's told Kate she likes men to be men and that Mr Ladd fits the bill. Elvis jumps out, lands softly on huge shoes, looks left and right, rolls his shoulders and pulls up his collar. The nuns are gazing at the blue sky, thanking God. Dad's haversack has towels, drinks, swimming costumes and a rolled-up tablecloth. Now he's knotting his hanky at the corners and putting it on his head. My feet are quite sore in the jelly sandals. Once mum catches us up Dad pulls us to the barrier pretending he has a limp then hands our tickets to the unhappy black man in blue. It's hot. The loudspeaker alarms everyone with tales of lost girls in maroon berets. From the station yard we come onto a long hill lined with coloured cottages. As he spots the saucerful of sea hanging between sky and jagged rooftops, dad begins to sing once more.

Gulls are cackling themselves to death. The tang of seaweed wraps around us in the warm wind. From the first cottage, an old lady knitting in the shade of a lilac tree raises a bony hand and waves to me. Dad bows, his arm tucked into his waist. The old lady drops the needles, slaps her hands to her cheeks and opens her mouth. Mum's embarrassed, she can't take him anywhere, she says. Kneeling down, dad pulls me onto his shoulders and suggests I rest my bum on the haversack. He explains that the sea is a vast mostly unexplored place sailors dream of and long for. 'It's in their blood,' he says. I squeeze my hands over his eyes. Elvis is following close behind us and simply must injure someone before the day's through. Mum waddles, her left knee clicking each time her foot touches the crooked pavement. There are patches of purple around her legs which she blames on too much washing up.

The shops are full of the word 'Gifts', over-coloured pictures of pink ice-cream, rubber bathing-rings with frilly fins, blown-up Mother Geese, lengths of bamboo with red or yellow nets on the end, postcards of fat ladies clouting weedy men and small chalk seafronts. Gulls swirl above the promenade, dropping to the beach in turn for pieces of bread. 'Remember when we had tea and cakes in the little café over there?' says mum to dad. 'Oh no, that's not the place,' says dad. 'Oh yes it is,' says mum. 'Don't be daft,' says dad. Mum clicks. The crowds grow thick and busy. Strangers wander this way and that, hugging one another, tossing to the sky the blue rabbits they've won at the fair or gulping from lemonade bottles. 'I'm sure it was,' says mum. 'Think again,' says dad. 'It was more over that way towards the toilets. I went, remember?' On the wall a sailor in blue and white twitches a pipe in his mouth and rubs the Kiss Me Kwik hat lying in his lap. On the sand below, a bald man with a big belly rubs the cream into his wife as she reads a pink magazine. The first page is full of Prince Philip and the headline 'Secret Anguish of a Royal Husband'.

'Head like a sieve,' says dad. He takes us to the beach huts so we can change into our swimming costumes. Mum's already wearing hers under her dress. She moans a bit while we're getting ready. 'I love your dad but he's a stubborn old bugger,' she says. When he creeps out of his hut to join us his legs are too small for the rest of him and his feet glisten with Valpeda. The sand sticks to them. Me and mum fall about while he tries to change the subject. Feet are his weak point. Mention them and his mouth turns a funny shape. At home he keeps his socks in a separate cupboard. He picks me up and spins me round. 'You're as skinny as a zip,' he says. Mum's biting her fingernail. 'The toilets you're thinking of were next to the amusement arcade. There's no café over there. I tell you the café we passed was the same one. You had a macaroon. The waitress came from Yarmouth.' 'No no,' says dad. '*that* café was in Ilfracombe.' 'Don't be daft,' says mum. 'Course it wasn't.' 'Was,' said dad. 'He'd forget his head if it wasn't screwed on,' says mum. Way ahead of us Elvis staggers through the sand trying to look cool, the donkey jacket slung over his shoulder. Other arguing mums, dads, grans, grandads and mentally ill friends of the family fill windy deckchairs, whisper in black and white or giggle into opened bottles of milk stout. A crying boy in green waterwings is led from group to group by a cheerful nurse.

Dad suddenly runs into the sea making great splashes with his hands and feet and calling out 'Tally Ho'. He's the only one of us who can swim so mum takes my hand and lets me dabble in the shallows though things aren't quite the same without the Pixie. The tideline's scattered with white bodies and damp dogs, romeos with beer bellies and unfortunate aunts in wheelchairs who can only nod and dribble at the view. The sea's grey. Clumps of weed curl in the waves. A few mums and grans lift hems and paddle in the water, screaming whenever their knees are kissed by surf. Dad's quite a way out, his head dipping through the swell. Soon he'll twist onto his back, flap forgiven feet and float for a while, shouting 'Heave to, me hearties' and 'Thar she blows'. Elvis is a thin lump unable to find anyone cheeky enough to deserve a good thumping as yet, but there's plenty of time. Swaggering to the water's edge, he slips off his brown suede shoes and white socks and rewards his toes with sips of sea water. Beyond the rocky point a cone-shaped floating bell chimes in time to the rhythm of the tide. The bloated teacher looks up from my exercise book with a glint of genius in his eyes. 'Yes, I have it now,' he says. 'It's Bournemouth, isn't it, my dear?' On the surface Kate's quite gratified that he should hazard a guess, and yet, underneath, she wants to slice him with a carving knife and dispose of the ragged fillets. His obscene grandmother doesn't care one way or the other because she's on all kinds of tablets. 'Don't for gawd's sake let yourself get cold,' says mum. 'You know what you're like with your chest.' Dad swims further and further away till he's all mixed up with the sunshine. The swing of the funfair comes and goes; dodgems shout and rumble to 'Venus in Blue Jeans'; air rifles crack. Though the nuns turn up, they're always on the move. Mum says if you love God as much as they do, it's not nice to lie down, make sandcastles or take off your clothes. She pulls a rolled-up beachball from the sandwich bag and starts to blow it up. As the nuns shuffle through the sand people turn down their radios and stub out cigarettes. Kids on lilos smirk towards the sunstruck beach. In a swift, bloated movement the teacher reaches into his inside pocket for a red pen, but I'm looking for dad. After a minute or so mum lets the beachball fall to the sand and scans the busy water. 'Now where's he got to?' she asks herself, wading in till waves and weeds swill round her waist. The bloated teacher, having scored nothing for Bournemouth tries Weymouth, but he's wrong again. 'I've a feeling it's one of those resorts down South,' he says. He's taken it into his head that he'll be able to give me another mark out of ten if he can establish the location. Teachers are forever trying to do it out of a kind of sympathy, establish the location for you. A dog floats by with a stick in its teeth. The bloated teacher hasn't a clue that just yesterday two of his favourite pupils entered the book cupboard while someone kept watch, made a rough sofa out of his precious copies of 'Bevis and Mark' and spent ten minutes fondling each other for a five-shilling dare. He considers we should all be like him and look upon Richard Jefferies or whatever his name was with hands clasped, legs crossed and eyes raised to heaven. 'I know! Bognor Regis!' he cries. Kate shakes her head and stuffs her hands in her pockets. And now Elvis holds up each set of toes in turn, waggles off the sand and replaces his socks and shoes. Time for a good murder. A blade in the guts. A rope round the Adam's apple. I'm jumping up and down, calling for dad, but my voice is drowned by radios, hooligans, excited children, the snaps of salted mongrels. Warning me to stay back, mum wades in further. 'He's a real bugger, that dad,' she shouts. To me it seems crazy that a girl should lose her dad at the seaside with everyone looking on, but then mum laughs. She's seen him climbing out of the water onto some rocks further along. Kate's mildly disappointed. He's a bugger alright, but mum doesn't particularly want to see him drown.

'That's the way it is with husbands,' she says, 'you'll learn.' He comes back cold, walking on tiptoe and shaking his hands, calling to mum for a towel. His white legs are covered in goose pimples. 'Oh no it wasn't,' he laughs. 'It bloody was,' says mum.

We have lunch close to the nuns who've come to a standstill, hands together, having a rest. Dad happily rubs my legs with his fingers and tells the loudest God jokes. Mum disowns him by laying out the picnic, putting pebbles on the corners of the tablecloth so it won't flap. Fingers make me shiver. Several other dads play cricket while mums hum on blankets or draw memories in the sand with their toes. The fingers move up and down, up and down, disturbing the nuns perhaps or making them yearn for a less solitary career. Elvis has positioned himself next to a tanned girl in a yellow polka-dot bikini and they're having an introductory argument about Buddy Holly. The bikini's rather Itsy Bitsy and Elvis must keep his drain-pipes well crossed. The thrust of his argument is directed at her yellow groin. 'That fucking Holly was the greatest of them all,' he says. Mum smacks her lips. 'The language these days,' she says. 'It's only kids,' says dad as a pair of pimply twins pull at the front of their sister's swimming costume then have a mock wrestle with the household dog. 'Yep. This is the life,' he goes on, tickling the top of my leg with one hand, holding a Senior Service in the other. Mum reckons the beach is overcrowded compared to the last time they came. She doesn't really hold with so many people. A beach should be a place where you can get away from it all. The trouble with the world is that everyone takes it in to their head to get away from everyone else at the same time so they end up in the same place making as much din as back home. Dad chews his lip. He'd give his soul for a cool pint of Double Diamond. Closing her eyes, Kate realises that a crowd of people at the seaside makes a different sound from a crowd of people anywhere else, but her reverie is broken by dad pinching her thigh. 'D'you know something? You weren't even thought of last time we were here,' he says. Mum reckons they should put gates at the end of the beach and only let so many people on at a time. The flat of dad's hand slips to the inside of my leg and rests there, getting warm.

A tremendous Thump fills the bay. A labrador races along the sand with its tail between its legs. 'What on earth's that?' whispers mum, sure that the End is here and that soon there will be Russians. Dad sighs. Tells her it was only a maroon and closes his eyes. 'A maroon what?' asks mum. 'Don't be daft,' says dad. He knows almost everything. A man in brown who's seen it all before wanders amongst the bodies clutching balloons. Elvis buys a red one for his new girlfriend but after a moment or two she lets go of it on purpose then pouts her lips. Soon a lifeboat full of men in oilskins is seen lurching through the sea towards nothing. Almost every old lady stares at the horizon with grim lips. The bloated teacher doesn't like this one bit and is about to underline it in red when Kate protests. 'I know what you mean,' he says, 'but will the Examiners? It sounds rather as if the old ladies are staring with their lips instead of their eyes.' 'Well, Sir, some do,' says Kate aloud, but inwardly she's whispering you're a fat bastard with no dreams.

After lunch the idea is for dad to be buried. For half an hour or more Kate digs with her plastic spade till she has a hole long and wide enough for him to lie in. Mum shakes out the tablecloth and folds it into a neat square then returns the crusts and chicken bones to the plastic bag. To be buried properly dad must lie flat out with his head back and his palms resting on his trunks. I scrape the sand over him till all but his face and his cigarette is covered then pat it down. Mum's head is sort of bowed. A fat man changing out of his trunks has accidentally let his towel fall and for a moment he stands like a rejected statue wondering what to do. Elvis shouts 'Watchya Cock!' 'Don't look, Kate,' says mum, using her hands as blinkers, 'it's not nice.' The man's wife turns over onto her front and pretends to be reading a book. Stray penises on the beach can cause quite a stir even though many bathers have one of their own or know of someone who does. This one wouldn't be so startling if everyone else didn't have theirs covered up. Dad begins to heave himself out of the sand. 'If it's all the same to you,' he says, 'I think it's time I was rising from the dead.' He wants to go for a walk, stretch his legs, let his lunch digest before the next swim. At the far end of the beach we find a deep warm pool surrounded by rocks. My costume is covered in frilly rubber so I feel stupid. Dad shakes his head. 'You do get in a stew,' he says, 'just like your mother.' 'I don't get in stews,' says mum, wringing her hands. 'You do,' says dad, 'you're in one now because we had to leave the bloody haversack behind. And look at the fuss you made about that café.' 'You made a fuss about it,' says mum, 'not me.' 'I didn't, did I Kate?' says dad. 'Did,' says mum. Somehow I stub my toe on a pebble. Dad hoists me in the air and runs his lips from the top of my leg all the way to my foot. 'There, there,' he says. Mum ticks her tongue. She's spotted an empty Pal tin. Dad hauls me into the clear pool, lays me out on the surface and supports me with his hand below. He floats me round and round, pushing my face into the water now and then. 'Once you get used to your head being underwater you'll be able to swim easy,' he says. In the secrecy of the pool fingers dig tight between my legs to prevent me drowning. Mum's draped across the rocks like a mermaid singing 'Shenandoah'. Part two of the exercise is dad throwing me in the air and letting me sploosh into the water. My ears ring with bubbles. Hands reach down to rescue me each time. Kate loves and hates it. Falling into the water reminds her of a dream gone by or a dream yet to come, though all the while pieces of her are terrified.

Dad must carry Kate all the way back up the long hill because she has sand in her ears and sand in her knickers and she's feeling sick with sleep. Mum's walking slowly behind us, watching the pavement wind beneath her shoes, sure Elvis is a pervert because he's been tagging along since we left the beach. 'Maybe he's just catching the same train,' says dad. Mum tells him not to keep on because she's had a long day and, besides, you can't be too careful these days. Look at that thing in the *People* last week. Really she's enjoying the last of the sun and examining her memories one by one. There are no nuns. The old lady has disappeared from the cottage garden. Elvis is all out of love and his fists have remained unscarred. He's had a so-so sort of day. A little bit of fun with the blonde bird but not a single punch in the gut. On the train mum pulls a surprise toffee-apple from her bag and holds it out to me, warning me to eat it slowly or I'll be sick. Dad laughs. 'If you're sick save the chunky bits for me,' he says. 'Oh shush,' says mum, 'I don't know what's got into you today.' I turn to the warm green trees and the soft fields slipping by, hoping to spot the sea again. Dying can't be such a bad thing after all unless there's been some mistake and you wake up one morning to find you've been laid to rest in a wooden box rather a long way underground. In surprise your head jumps and cracks against the coffin lid. Fingers rip at satin. Children play in the graveyard above in search of muffled screams. In life I'm hot and sticky. Mum must rub some cold cream into my shoulders. 'I'm going to have a little siesta,' says dad. Mum digs another blob of cream from the jar and looks at him. 'You're wrong about Ilfracombe,' she says.

Coming home the day turns grey and quiet again. The house howls uncomfy and wooden with the love-songs of ghosts. Kate gazes at the toby jugs which line the mantelpiece. Most of them are filled with old buttons, hairpins or bits of china dad will someday stick together. The one on the far left contains two-halfpennies with sailing boats on the back. The eldest of the jugs grins at Kate all evening. Its lips seem to part some more each time she looks at it. 'Oh Lord, she's getting the creeps again,' says mum. 'Give her a thrashing,' says dad. 'My old man always gave me a thrashing and it didn't do me any harm.' Maybe the jug will break into a scream. 'Come on Kate,' says mum, 'don't be a baby now.' Stockings rub together under her dress. Dad sits in his chair reading the *Mirror*. He'll be going out for a pint later on to see old Reg. 'Oh will you?' says mum. 'And what am I supposed to do if she gets the abdabs again?' Dad lowers the paper. 'Don't fuss,' he says. 'She'll be right as rain. Make her some Bournevita and stick her in bed.' Kate covers her ears with her palms and waggles her head from side to side to shut out the noise but mum clips the back of her legs and drags her up the stairs. The sheets are crisp. Rats canter round the loft. Most days Rupert ends up flying over Nutwood in some crazy machine and waves to his super chums below. Dad comes for a goodnight kiss and spares a few minutes to clamber under the blankets and play one of his games. 'Now don't be silly any more,' he says in the end, rolling out of bed again and tiptoeing to the door. He argues with mum before he leaves for the pub. Amongst the other noises in Kate's head is the sound of a cushion striking the glass partition in the living room and the slam of the front door.

Monday 7.15pm

Kate walks full of chips and wickedness from living room to shed, having chosen as her theme 'Nothing And Its Terrible Consequences'. She hasn't the energy to read a newspaper, converse with her husband or watch television. The independent channel was showing a film about the process of conception. In one romantic sequence, semen was seen ejaculating into a vagina. To which couple this moment belonged or in what sultry cove the miniature camera lay, we remained uninformed. Perhaps Derek envied those wriggling sperm since so many of his own spill into strange territories like tissues or the S-bends of water closets and must fight their way towards eggs which don't exist.

She dreams of J for a moment as a cure for these invisible sicknesses. His breath is warm against the back of her neck. Crickets ripple the garden. A piece of moon hangs in the mirror above the mantelpiece. One day she'll be great and happy. Out of love she searches for it; in love she fears for its end. After much movement and expectation a face presses into the warmth between her legs. He's kissing her goodnight. And what tickly salutations these are. One day she'll wake and want nothing more than herself and the renewed daylight, a bite or two to eat and a walk through fresh April avenues with herself, treading blossoms, nodding hello to slim young gentlemen, calling in at continental cafés to watch life as it clips by the window carrying bunches of celery or someone else's hand. Crossing arms over her breasts she falls into a great tranquillity

Occasionally words of comfort plume from the darkness or his tongue laps at her flesh. She's on the verge of tears both in her room and in her shed.

Earlier some pioneering spirit took her along the wooded hill at the back of the estate. The wind blew cruel. Her hands turned white. Through tight trees and down a long slippery path she discovered an old quarry and had half an hour's fun climbing the rocks. Behind a curtain of brambles on the left-hand side she came across a tramp crouched in a small cave. He'd been burning old *Woman's Realm*s to keep warm and had dustbin liners tied round his feet. He stared at her, rubbed grim fingers through a mass of stained whiskers then quietly asked her to leave him be. She'd imagined he'd invite her in, make a space for her beside the curling photos of women in girdles and reveal the secrets of herbs or the charms of life on the road.

Years ago the bloated teacher urged her not to use so many truncated unconnected sentences in her compositions. He had an aged grandmother made overly possessive of him by a hardening of her arteries. She often visited the school in obscene orange trews which tended to betray the structure of her bum in some detail. Kate nodded. The teacher smiled. 'Good girl,' he said. His obscene grandmother waited in the corridor, pulling spare pins from the notice board and throwing them at the small boys. Inwardly Kate whispered Fuck Off. The words thrilled her. Fuck Off. She was fifteen and pretty with breasts and blood. She often found notes in her desk asking her to discos or to the back of cricket pavilions. 'And let's not have any hints of Smut,' he said, touching her hand. 'You're too young for it, Smut.' The exercise he set for the following week was 'My Life At Home', in the hope of nipping in the bud any excessive incidents of sexual abuse. The obscene grandmother loomed into the square of glass at the door and scowled at him. A bell rang. The teacher looked at Kate in a funny way. Funny Whoops, not funny Ha Ha. Probably all men would like to start a war or fuck a little girl, but feel it would be impolite. At break-time children queued at the tuck shop to buy digestive biscuits, but Kate hung around at the top of the stairs gazing out at the rain.

The teacher adored W.B. Yeats and couldn't wait for him to come round on the syllabus. Half-way through most afternoons, as the hands of the wall-clock ground to a halt, his obscene grandmother could be seen marching down the hill beneath a chequered umbrella at which point a newcomer to the school would turn round in his chair and smile at Kate. His blazer was still neat. He didn't doodle on his book covers and he loved plays about angry young men from Yorkshire. His name was Richard and though it niggled him to bits, everyone called him Leo. If you're listening, please forgive us. At night he wrote poems about falling over before the winning-tape of life and sometimes showed them to Kate as she waited at the top of the stairs. Being Astute, he found the obscene grandmother a barrel of laughs. Many were of the opinion that he was unduly hairy for his age.

A second walk took her along the river. Usually she heads upstream, which is less muddy, but today – needing difficulty, pollution – she wandered toward the horseshoe bend where, in earlier years, bigger ships frequently came to grief. She's seen photos of a particularly grey November day when dawn broke to reveal five cargo vessels lounging diagonally against the mudbanks.

The 'Hazel' ploughed along the river on its way to the docks, throwing rolls of dark water into the narrow gullies of weeds and rotting wood. Along the line of the highest tides lay thousands of stranded plastic bottles and pieces of expanded polystyrene. Among them she discovered three beach shoes, an old baby-bath, a small broken table, the body of a dead bird, the head of a doll, a bin liner full of waste food which had been pecked open by gulls and a note in a bottle saying 'BOO' in red ink. The most weathered pieces of polystyrene were indistinguishable in appearance from lumps of rock. Around them the ugly fawn grasses were thick with mud. Her attention was finally drawn to an old condom hanging from a black branch close to the water. Kate's seen quite a few one way or another.

They slither from sewer pipes and hook themselves to other garbage, like melancholy reminders of good times now gone.

She moved to the fence where the ground was drier and watched the traffic as it ripped along the carriageway. Windy mums pushed prams in the slipstreams of careless container lorries. She made up her mind she wasn't going to care about anything any more, least of all J, but it didn't last. As she climbed the wall further down and crossed the railway line she was back in his room being entertained by words and his insatiable fingers. She wondered whether she should toss herself under the wheels of the 2.25 from Severn Harbour, but decided, on balance, that she was as yet too unspectacular to be mourned for very long. Anyway, it's no good dying to teach your old lover a lesson unless you can be around to see how he reacts. Probably he'd read the suicide report in the local paper at 4.30 in the afternoon and be grilling Bird's Eye Crispy Cod Fillets by 7.

You must forgive the unruly ways of womankind, J, because at this moment I'd love to fuck the milkman. Unlike you he's blond with curly hair, has a wife named Cheryl and once a year spends a fortnight on the Costa Del Sol.

The Old Hat

In the middle of the week after a few nights of dreams and sticky fingers mum gives in and keeps me away from school because the windows are moaning and the dark has left me with a ringing in the ears. After breakfast she grabs one of the other kids in the road and sends a note to Miss Lewis saying I have a 'rather' nasty throat. Whenever I stay away from school I have something 'rather' wrong with me except for the one time mum left dad to write the note and he put 'Double Pneumonia' as a joke. That afternoon Miss Lewis came sideways up the path carrying a bottle of Lucozade and a card signed by all the other kids. Really it was just breathlessness and nightmares which hung in my head during the day and made me want to clutch the furniture.

Kate curls the tablecloth while mum cuts up the greens, peels potatoes, rolls out floured circles of pastry. I'm wearing the speckled cardie Aunty made. It's knitted from lots of different coloured scraps. Mum says it's a very special cardie because there isn't another like it in the whole world, but I'd prefer the plain blue one I've seen in the Tolsey shop. The rolling pin thumps the surface of the table. Mum must wear her pink house-scarf to hide the marks dad made on her neck.

Following Rag, Tag and Fucking Bobtail we go to post the letter mum's finally written to a very distant cousin called Hattie who lives in America with her husband Jerome, two cars and a kid in a baseball hat. We've seen them in photos when relatives come round. Jerome's too fat and wears blue trousers.

Of course mum makes me wear my balaclava so people in the road won't think she's been telling lies about my throat. I'm finding it hard to swallow spit unless I really think about it and even then it doesn't always work. I must stroke the Pixie, remember certain songs. As we walk along I chew the bottom of the balaclava and make my lips sore. We find Mrs Jackson pretending not to pick her nose by the cemetery gate. She waves. Mum waves. She waves. The sky's blowy and grey and always has been. 'If you're a good girl we'll go and have a look at your dad's factory on the way back,' says mum. 'Yahoo,' says Kate quietly. Mr Withenshaw's flying his box kite on the green this morning. Mum warns it's best to leave him alone because he's not a happy man. He can't work much any more because of all the funny turns he's had and but for his steady Pools round would probably die or be put away. He makes kites whenever he has a spare moment and flies them above the green hoping children will come and watch. He's almost famous. Now he looks like he's holding onto thin air and praying to the sky. Some of the dirtier boys from Paradise Street have skipped school too and lark around under the lime trees. The tallest one creeps up to Mr Withenshaw and tickles him, trying to make him let go, but his nose just turns red and he holds on for grim death. Kites are his last close friends. Mum says he's never had a wife because, like Rupert, he's so much in love with flying things. Oh, rumour has it that he once walked out with an usherette from the Odeon years ago, but she soon got fed up with him working in his toolshed all hours of the day and night with glue and bits of dowelling. The story goes that he tried to win her back many times but, in the end, the promises of an empty sky were far too exciting to abandon altogether. Flight was his true romance. Mum believes he's always wanted to fly himself at heart, but has gradually come to accept second best. He has pigeons galore which roar round the houses in clumps on Saturday morning. On his day-off from kites he carries to the green a whole series of balsa-wood planes which he sends into the air with bits of elastic. Each one has a lump of lead on its nose.

There's some sick on the pavement by the edge of the green. It has dried and started to curl. Strands of it cling to wisps of grass between the paving stones. Mum says I seem to have a nose for sick and that I should shut up about it, but I find it hard not to look. There are piles of it everywhere I go.

Dad's factory is a large green place made of wood with fancy black railings at the front and double gates to one side. Inside the gates the black grass is scattered with tiny spirals of metal. We go round the building to a small door at the back which is open. We can hear men singing above the clatter of machinery. All along the outside walls are pipes hissing with steam and the bloated teacher says, Come on Kate, buck up for goodness sake, but to show the bastard she means business she just stays in the corner crouched into a ball. Through the door we can see quite a few dads playing with little wheels while long metal rods spin and rattle at the ends of the machines. Even Richard has a go, trying to ease her to her feet with a kind word here, a soft hand there, but as always she asks them to leave her alone. Dad's right over the far side. Mum must lift me up. He's wearing plastic glasses. A cigarette hangs from his lips, the white paper stained where he's been holding it in his fingers. He sees us straight away but shakes his head to warn us off. Maybe it's shame. The inside walls are covered in charts, calendars and posters of women in bikinis. To one side of the factory floor a man with a bald head and a thin cigar stares at us through his glass partition. He scoots us away with his hand.

Back home I keep my balaclava on and follow mum round the house as she hangs up shirts, hunts for lost earrings or rubs the dressing table with a yellow duster. I'm in a Wednesday mood even though it isn't. The house smells of drying socks, scorched ironing boards, soap suds, pine disinfectant. Mum has tied her hair in a bundle at the back. In the big bedroom there's a photo of a young woman and a young man holding hands in a church porch. Mum keeps pushing me out of the way, complaining I'm under her feet. My fears have almost gone so I try to find a puzzle but then there's no room on the table and I can't really be bothered to find all the side pieces.

Oh Kate, you were born infinitely exhausted. Mum suggests I move out of the road and play with my cornflake indians, using the sofa cushions as an Arizona hilltop, but then Aunty comes round and needs somewhere to sit. Today she looks a bit like the jar of pickled walnuts we've had in the pantry for as long as I can remember, yet she's brought me a tin of condensed milk which mum says I can have tomorrow. Tomorrow's the day we have everything. I sit on the carpet between the two of them while they talk of fruitcake. Aunty has strange legs and a worn gold wedding ring. She wants to know if mum uses three eggs or four, and, by the way, has she heard about old Mr Perkins who got caught in the park with a Scout?

'And you'll never guess what they were doing,' she says,

'You don't mean . . .?' says mum.

'As true as I'm sitting here,' says Aunty.

Soon mum's had enough of my fiddling with the carpet pile and sends me upstairs out of the way. Dragging a chair from the bedroom I take grandad's hat from the top of the wardrobe. It's hard and black with his name on the inside. It falls over my eyes when I try it on. Mum comes up to fetch a pair of suspenders for Aunty and catches me stumbling round the landing pretending to be blind. She snatches the hat from me as if she's going to be annoyed but then stoops down, puts her arms around me and bursts into tears.

'Your old gramps would have loved you in that hat,' she says.

The Wine Bar

Then Kate panics a little because she's brought her pages into the open air on a reasonably warm December day and feels somewhat ashamed at the curiosity of passers-by who'll barely remember her in a moment's time. She's cold and tipsy. Someone with a shrill voice screeches behind the blackened windows of the solicitor's next door. Cold and tipsy with the rest of the day free to go nowhere, J. What a lark, a hoot, a riot of imagination. Wind rolls down Effingham Street to the river yet mums, dads and kiddywinks trudge along the pavements laden with bundles of holly paper, economy fruit-hampers for invalid aunts and dark bottles of Emva Cream. The sky's overeaten with illuminated reindeer and portly angels tied to gables and streetlamps. Men and women from the University dressed as the seven dwarfs rattle collecting tins and hand out sweets to grizzling children, so whatever you do don't read Tuesday, Mr Burgess; it might take your breath away. Kate pretends to write truth at a red and white table with another glass of wine yet she aches with an unkind loneliness; she longs for a hand, a word, a touch, a purpose, a reason to move one foot in front of the other. Don't read Tuesday since this may be the degeneration – hair hanging wild around her ears, smeared lips through too much kissing; riotous nights to come with inebriated matelots; dissolute days to follow in wrecked camp beds sprinkled with rose petals. She watches the butcher's, the toy shop, the ironmonger's for signs of J. One day he'll pull up dark and unhappy to buy gifts for the friends of friends.

But our sun is warm. Your bag of secrets lies on the ground at your feet. You've ordered cocktails for a laugh. Your arms are brown. We're arguing about Class. Of course you don't believe in the concept and if you don't believe in something there's nothing a woman can do to change your mind. Some say you are firm in your resolve; others find you an opinionated bastard. Between the top of your jeans and the bottom of your tee-shirt lies a strip of brown skin. Soon I'll be kissing it and soon your stiffened spirit will squeeze into mine. The cocktails work wonders for us; we slip from the argument into a private language of touch and whispers. A few casual friends walk by and wave. Under the table your fist twists between my legs. You like to do it most as the waiter gazes at me. By now the brass band is almost level with us, thrashing out with slightly unsynchronised cornets, cymbals and drums, 'Hit The Road Jack'. Your fist twists. My head rolls back. You're grinning.

Kate couldn't stand her home any more. She watched the news for a while but turned it off as they were getting to the forbidden pictures of more blacks being beaten to death by more South African policemen. These men beat and break and thrash hoping no-one will notice it's really second nature to them. Maybe their hunger for death stems from a resentment that their wives won't fuck as much as they'd like or that for twenty years those same wives have been preparing cheese and pickle sandwiches each morning when secretly the policemen would prefer peanut butter. News is wonderful stuff. If there's none to tell, they'll make it up or else predict on the basis of what's happened before. She almost rang Derek at work, but she wasn't sure what to say. Then she took out her old address book and was going to write to everyone she hadn't seen since being married, but realised just in time the reason she hadn't seen them was because they no longer thought of her as Kate, but as some terrible amalgam of Kate and Derek. And she still wanted to fuck the milkman; imagining him so much made her wet between her legs. They'd fuck as the change in his leather bag rattled on the bed beside them. 'In return for this

96

pleasure,' he'd say, 'you can have one free pint for the whole of December excluding Sundays. Consider oral sex and I'll throw in some single cream and a dozen eggs.'

She stood at the bedroom window looking into the garden. The world lay before her somewhat cold and immovable. She deteriorated. Went to the shed. Cleared up the cigarette ends and scraps of paper. Went back to the house. Took out the photo of J. There he stood in the snow by the gabled house she couldn't trace. The Untraceable House. Call in Charles Chan Esquire. She rubbed grease and smoke stains from the window panes. They needed a good clean. Miss Wintle has often remarked how necessary it is to keep up with the household chores and thus not fall below the standards of one's neighbours. As Kate looked out she could see the lady in question stooping over her rockery, tidying its dark soil with an orange-handled trowel. The lady in question sensed this observation, forcing Kate to duck, open her drawer and return J to his hiding place amongst her oldest knickers. He loves it there, so snug, secure and intoxicated by the perfume of lavender. 'Sleep tight,' she said, yawning, rubbing her breast. She walked across the bedroom to the other window and pulled the netting aside. A pair of old ladies with sticks were tapping along the pavement. A neighbour's gate had been left open. The floor creaked beneath her shoes. She considered the possibility of taking off all her clothes and going to bed, but rejected it on the basis that she'd only wake up and have to start the day again. Hanging on the wall beside her was an enlarged photo of Derek about to drive off at the First Tee at Pennard golf club. In the distance, the glittering sea and crags of Three Cliffs Bay. Later she'd see white horses cantering through the surf. Her husband swung. Kate followed him along sandy fairways. He lost three balls to the prickly scrub. Moving to the top of the stairs she looked down. The carpet yawned for her. The front door was white. A rubber plant grew in the corner by the reproduction hatstand. Running up and down stairs to rid herself of an attack of nuclear panic, she made up her mind she'd one day drop a line to the Court of

Human Rights. Some say it's quite nice living on the threshold of extinction but Kate finds it a nusiance. In the living room the mantelpiece was tiled. Threads hung from the bottom of the sofa. Kate tapped the television and watched a kind of sunlight fall across the dead garden. She asked herself for a dance, but turned herself down, seeing no future in it.

So she came here with visions *en route* of buying gifts though she wasn't really in the mood. For Derek she'd set her heart on one of those inflatable women he could fuck in the mornings and fold away in the airing cupboard for the rest of the day. She can't think straight. Maybe it's the wine. Never sit at a table outside a wine bar if you're a woman alone: they'll put you down as a dipsomaniac or else suspect you're plying for sexual trade. Already she's had a wink from a middle-aged man in a straw hat and a couple of 'Ello Darlin's from young men with red mohican haircuts and ripped-up jeans.

She's starving to death. The idea had been to eat at home but she couldn't face the freezer even though she knew she had a cod in mushroom sauce somewhere. It's the kind of thing housewives eat in the middle of the day to stop them from keeling over during the housework. The range also includes cod in butter sauce and cod in parsley sauce and cod in cheese sauce. Housewives need plenty of cod. It comes frozen so you can just pop the plastic bag into boiling water. You hardly need pause in your dusting.

It's almost closing time. Pink-cheeked businessmen are straightening ties and pulling down waistcoats. The wind has become fresher still. She shivers. A handsome barman works his way round the table with a damp cloth. He tells her the time and points to the inch of liquid in her glass. She thanks him. From next week all the tables will be kept inside, he warns her. She doesn't really care because she's having what she would describe as a bad J day. He's everywhere, it seems – in this drink, her hands, her eyes, bag, clothes. The sunshine's crisper than ever. She writes something on a pad. The barman watches her. He adores crazy women. His dream is to live with one so his days will become less predictable. In the empty chair beside

Kate the form of another person oozes into being briefly then fades away. She seems not to notice it and continues to write. Oh he could take her home now, wrap her in blankets, make her cocoa last thing at night. Show her his photos. She's an attractive woman with fine cheekbones and an engaging smile; though there's no doubt she's one of a kind she'll soon come to resent this fucking dishcloth and be gone. She has melancholy eyes; the movements of her pen are slow, thoughtful. Perhaps she could make his barmanship more worthwhile. She sips her drink away, returns to her work. He hums a Don McLean tune in the hope that she too relates to Vincent, but she's been distracted by a tall student who passes by wearing an extraordinary top hat with a large price tag tucked into its black band. The barman pauses in his work and longs for her. Being lonesome himself, he weeps.

No Hiding Place

'And if you cry any more,' says Charmian, dragging me up the stairs, 'I'll give you a clout.' She pushes me through the door and lifts me onto the bed. While I sort through my Rupert annuals she peeks into my mirror and rearranges her hair. 'Now. Remember what I've told you,' she says to herself. 'No noise. Or else.' Having made herself as ugly as possible she taps me on the head and clumps back down the stairs bent on snooping round the kitchen for a thick sandwich of this or that. The sound of the television shakes the living-room windows. Chief Inspector Lockheart's having a troublesome episode. A bread knife rattles on the draining board, slips, and clatters into the sink. She's common as muck, Old Reg Smythe's daughter, so mum said. Wipes her nose on the sleeve of her cardigan. Hardly ever changes her skirt. Stuffs herself with cakes all day. Bites boys round the back of the Over Sixties Club. Picks and eats ear wax. Usually Aunty comes to babysit but dad's said he's fed up with her hanging about till all hours knocking back the Bristol Milk and tidying things that are none of her business.

Mum's already been into hospital twice and this is the third time. She's having a Lump removed now but dad hasn't said Of What or From Where. The old rat's busy in the loft, scampering from one side to the other then scratching at plaster. Flakes of paint fall from the ceiling to my bed. Charmian switches off the television and plays mum's favourite Roy Orbison record. Mum swoons for Roy Orbison. More than any other singer he makes her wish she hadn't married a man who keeps his hair short and wouldn't be seen dead in a pair of dark glasses.

Though the grass is green, birds sing and Tiger Lily wanders through the forest collecting herbs for her conjuring father; Bill Badger has gone missing and Rupert and his pals are frantic. In the end Rupert has to outwit several hooped villains to rescue Bill and everyone's thrilled to bits with him. Dad's late. He's taken mum some fruit and a romantic book. Old Reg Smythe's daughter wobbles when she walks. Dad loves Old Reg Smythe because he has huge muscles and can dig a trench in half the time. If dad's ever late coming home from work he usually tells mum he's been down The Swan with Old Reg Smythe. Reg Smythe, old or not, grows the longest runner beans in town, builds dry-stone walls before you can say Jack Robinson, has eight pints most dinnertimes and feeds his family with the fruits of an allotment and the accuracy of his twelve-bore.

Dad's bike clatters through the gate. Charmian takes off Roy Orbison and plumps up the cushions on the sofa where she's been lounging with a bag of Allsorts. I push Rupert under the covers and switch off the light. There's a string you can pull just above the headboard. Dad slips his bike into the coal shed. I can always tell if he's had too much to drink by the way he walks. Clearing his throat, he begins to sing, crunching to the front of the house where Charmian has opened the door for him.

'Oh Hello,' says dad. 'Everything alright?'

'Oh yes. She's been as good as gold,' says Charmian. The gold meanwhile is having a fit of giggles over her fat legs and the ridiculous name. Money rattles. Charmian says 'Right. I'd better be getting along then.'

'No no. Stay for a drink,' says dad, squeezing off his shoes and putting on his slippers.

'Better not,' says Charmian, 'mum'll wonder.'

'Oh bugger your mum,' says dad. 'Here. Let me help you off with your coat and you can come and sit down.

Charmian mumbles. Dad clears his throat. The umbrella stand falls to the floor. Claws tap the loft. Dad's saying 'Oh come on, don't be silly.'

'Dad'll go mad,' says Charmian.

Things are quiet for a while but then Roy Orbison returns. Occasionally the springs of the sofa squeak or Charmian giggles.

Sometimes as I drift off to sleep I can see the whole of my room through closed eyes. I float from the bed to the cupboard or hang from the hole in the ceiling by my toes and peer down. A pair of rough hands follow the wall. Maybe they belong to the ghost. Poor Kate squeezes her eyes together. The hands wait at the side of her bed then slither down. Fingers leap to the blankets and begin tickling her. She tries not to laugh. The blankets roll away so the fingers can touch her from ankle to hip hip hoorah, hooray. One of the rules is that she mustn't make a sound. The rat's behind me, nosing through the dark. Round and round the garden like a teddy bear. One step. Two steps. Tickle her under there. She loves nursery rhymes still. I can tell. She's pink with the effort of keeping her eyes tight. The fingers push between her legs and rub her. He put in his thumb and pulled out a plum and said what a good boy am I. Kate drifts from the ceiling, prays, finds herself in bed. The ghost cries. Its sobs fill her room, her ears. She wakes up or goes off to sleep.

One Too Many

If you asked J, he'd say that the pointless activities he pursued in his room were a form of work – spirtually rewarding, more natural work. And though you might be more inclined to classify his behaviour as 'pissing about', J would be on the look-out for individuals of a more sensitive disposition who'd think otherwise. Poor old cocked-up J. And you'll have noticed, I hope, how a certain quantity of alcohol can affect my style. Here we have a more scholarly madwoman, though we may hesitate to admit it. J would struggle from his armchair, go to the bookcase, read a page of one novel, take another to his table, make notes in its margins, then skip through several pages of a third in an effort – having studied Mr Eliot – to 'amalgamate disparate experience'. One wonders at someone of Mr Eliot's stature who must spend afternoons creating such obscure terminology while the rest of us are going to the movies or fucking one another to smithereens. No matter. Later J might colour in a little more of the mural he'd sketched onto the back wall to hide an uninteresting patch – it was a seascape looked at through an open window. In front of that window was a small table, drawn so the legs appeared to rest on the floor. Across the table, in a state of dubious perspective, lay a thick red book with a question mark as its title. J just loved enigmas. Loved his mural too and was often disturbed by the idea that one day the room might be demolished to make way for overly expensive office space. In the meantime he'd be working on the bones of his various theories by drawing a number of arrows on sheets of paper and linking those arrows with different keywords – Fear. Insincerity. Procrastination. Stuff like that.

Should these activities fail to satisfy him for the moment, he'd wander to the park and sit on his favourite bench, keeping an open book in his lap to deflect any false conclusions passers-by might reach about his character. Then he'd Observe for hours at a time while a warm sunshine filtered through the silver birch and a dozen unzipped office girls oozed in black and blouse across the soft grass. If you mentioned these girls to him, he'd proclaim with some pride that, above all, they were People. You'd marvel, of course, at his perspicacity, though you'd probably not use the word, fearing saliva and a sorrowful mispronunciation. This Observation was undoubtedly one of his favourite pastimes, though he undertook it only when all else failed. He'd study teenage girls turning on the seductive roundabout, love their white socks and brown ankles, hate the uncouth gangly boys who yelled and flapped around them with shirt-tails hanging out and inkstains on their hands. He was searching for innocence, wisdom and, above all, simplicity. It was always a shame, therefore, that those twirling girls, unfooled by books, regarded him as a weirdo, a pervert, a skinny fucker with nothing better to do.

In the company of his mother he becomes a tongue-tied boy again, full of lame excuses for his continued idleness. On my first visit, one hot, kingfisher afternoon, she abandons him and leads me on a solemn tour of her extensive gardens with their warm ornamental arches of Cotswold stone, dark lily-covered fishponds and strategic conifers. She moves unevenly because her hips have been giving her trouble and she must rest them. The precisely manicured gardens no longer hold any interest, especially to J who waits at the starting point of the tour, over-familiar with each brick and flower. With puffed and some-what embarrassed features, she takes me into an oppressive greenhouse where she presents me with a home-grown peach of which her husband, Gerald, God rest him, would have been proud. I hold it in my palm, afraid of bruising it, too charming to eat it. We mustn't have juice down the chin. She wanders up and down the narrow walkways making awkward small talk as if she's grown tired of this parade of experimental girlfriends and will only find comfort in the dim prospect of J's settling down, becoming normal.

'Oh yes,' she tells me, 'we had a lot of trouble with him as a child, but he seems almost over it now. Psychiatrists told us he was far too sensitive for his own good. His father used to say one needs to develop claws to survive this world, and I tend to agree.'

Stepping outside we peer into the green plastic water barrel. As yet she hasn't asked me any questions nor noticed her son's ghostly head between my legs. Her face quivers on the surface of the water for a moment then sinks into the gloom at the bottom.

'I was hoping he'd land himself a decent job after college,' she says, 'but I don't think he's quite sure what he wants to be. Gerald always talked of Accountancy or something good and steady in that line. I know he would have been disappointed in this idleness if he hadn't, you know, died, after paying for his college place and what have you. Still, I suppose you youngsters have a lot more time to consider these things than we ever had.'

The family mongrel hugs the paving slabs and wags itself from head to tail. The garden trembles with flowers and butterflies. I'm introduced to Padfield, the gardener, who's leaning on a hoe at the edge of the vegetable plot, rolling a cigarette and looking exactly as a gardener should from string belt to cap. I want to spring to the failed accountant's defence, but mothers on fat nostalgic afternoons are best left unchallenged. J's now slumped in a deckchair on the patio, gazing at the tiny umbrella leaning in his drink. He's crazy and hopeless, as if he's expecting his mother to talk me out of him. The tradition is that gin will make you morbid in the end but I'm finding on the way to that unpleasant state a brief period of clarity and cheerfulness. I'm there now as his mother sighs.

'Still, let's look on the bright side. If he's serious with you he may want to settle down and, you know . . .' Taking a pair of secateurs from her pocket she bends down with some difficulty and clips haphazardly at a clump of brambles threatening the footpath to the stream. Padfield always leaves her a small patch of natural vegetation to tackle. It's his way of helping her through death, boredom, the fatigue of wealth.

In the car afterwards J says, 'If I see another pink flagstone, I'll throw up,' and yet he's often confused, forced to accept the financial help of those who've settled down so that he can afford not to. He tries at all times to discover a safe course between gratitude and independence. For the moment he's a nervous, rabbity fellow ruined with guilt and he's blowed if he'll ever come here again. Most of all he's unable to connect the images of a malcontented mother and her gorgeous gardens with the more gratifying memory of my whiteness spread-eagled on his bed.

But driving from the house his other self returns and cracks jokes about the spoilt child I'd seen on the patio. His left hand jumps from the steering wheel and slides between my legs, squeezing and rolling as it achieves its ambition. No, we won't go straight back to town, he says. The afternoon's too beautiful. He's plump with dreams and the charms of romance. Fingers play and press against me as he shuffles in the driver's seat. 'This is perfect,' he says. 'To hell with mothers.' The village slips against the windscreen; a series of old mis-shapen buildings with irregular windows, carefully cleaned and pointed stone-work, low studded front doors. He wants to explain that this place was the backdrop to his life before college and before me, but he makes it more complicated than that. We move round the war memorial, just missing an elderly lady on a varicose bike. His fingers are becoming impatient, undoing the button of my jeans, pulling down the zip and slipping inside, then pushing down and down. Someone blows their horn as we swerve across the white line and turn left into Highcombe Lane. Those fingers come home to roost as we pass a large red-bricked house tucked into the trees. This is similar to the home he's dreamed of; he wants a room up there, in the left-hand gable; he'd sit at his desk by the window and look across the valley. The more he touches me, the deeper his fantasies grow. A house on the hill with Kate – or someone like Kate – who'd be throwing corn to free-range chickens in the garden below. His wrist aches, but he won't give in. To change gear he must let go of the steering wheel and reach across, losing control of the car, but never mind, his fingers are wildly happy. Parking on the broad grass verge at the top of the lane is another matter so his fingers must retreat to assist him. The engine stops. Silence envelops the car. 'Well,' says J, 'here's the country.' Kate looks out. Why, yes, so it is. J kisses me. Breaking the silence a farmer in wellingtons lumps by on a tractor. J's kind enough to pull up my zip, fasten the button. Climbing from the car he leans against the hot roof and yawns with pleasure. Kate joins him. Across the road a footpath winds into the wood. He presses me against the car and rubs my jeans with the nub of his palm. 'I want you all the time,' he says, 'even when I hate you.' 'And when do you hate me?' asks Kate. 'Oh, now and then,' he says. The tip of his tongue runs along my teeth and gums as though secretly he'd like to climb inside my body and sleep there.

Then we walk, following the path through thick humming hedgerows and pools of cool green shade. His hand's soft. I'm listening to the leaves, to the busy whispers of innumerable insects. Time and again he's overcome and must pull me aside, fill my mouth with his tongue. I end up with thorns all over the back of my shirt which he carefully picks out. He's being a romeo alright, you can see it in his eyes. The leaves, moving with the wind, sprinkle uncut diamonds of sunlight to the path. We try stepping from one to the next or catching them in our palms as a gift. He points out the number of greens and browns and sounds and moments of yellow sandstone among the saplings; unwraps, by degrees, his sense of humour though I've seen and heard it all before. I want to breathe woodland; to squeeze beneath a tree and fall asleep. J leads me by the fingers; bows with a flourish like a Shakespearean Lord; plays hide and seek in the shadow-filled hollows till I'm too weary to look for him anymore. His hands are in my hair, on my shoulders, looping around me from behind. He tickles me. Chases me when I run away. Gallops through the grass whooping like an Indian and thrashing an imaginary horse with a dead stick. At the top of a steep path lined with rocks he puts his arms around my neck to apologise.

He suddenly remembers a boyhood copse of his and takes me there. A few thin trees cling to an otherwise open slope of tall meadow grass. In a frame of more established trees we can see the whole village and the sleeping valley beyond. He stands on a moss-covered stump with his arms in the air pretending he did the same as a boy.

'This place means such a lot to me,' he says. 'It remains a firm feature of an otherwise uncertain life.' Overcome, he embarks on a paragraph which loses ground half way through. He's forced to shut up and lie in the grass, pulling me with him; begins to strip the stick of its bark, revealing the smooth creamy wood beneath. He wants me to touch it, to see if it thrills me as much. Maybe he's about to give one of those lectures which invariably begin with Walt Whitman and end up as a rationalisation of why love is the way it is. I won't listen particularly. Men have a tendency to think we're agog and will love them more if they try to explain themselves, but it's all nonsense. We either love them or we don't. If we do there's not a fat lot they can say to make a difference. From an uncertainty in the corners of his mouth I can tell the Whitman lecture diminishes as a possibility. Pointing out a small scar on his chin he tells me it was split open by a rolling quarrystone which had slipped from the hands of a boyhood friend, oh, years ago. Roger, was it? Or Colin? Roger's mum died when she was thirty-two of something long and nasty; Colin was brilliant and made everyone gasp in physics lessons because he knew the exact number of miles it was to the moon. He's often in the local papers holding silver trophies. I want to make love with J but he's too busy talking, remembering. Looking deep into the sky, the grass seems to rock beneath me. The trees seethe with birds. J plucks a buttercup, runs it down my nose and across my lips. He's now saying something about being terribly scared of wanting me so much. Spends his time making difficulties. Spends his time detailing what he'd like to do with me then forgets to carry it through. He stares at the trees, dreaming and loving and fucking in stillness, wearing himself out, leaving little energy for now. I hum. He puts the stick to his mouth and plays it like a clarinet. He has a certain fondness for soliloquies; always wanted to be Hamlet but was pipped at the post by Olivier and all kinds of other people with strange noses. It's so warm. This summer began long ago and there's not an end to it in sight. Throwing his clarinet aside, he rolls over, plays with my body. Fingers creep into my shirt, settle over my breast. His features relax for a moment till he imagines his mother may be keeping track of these activities through binoculars. The fingers, impatient with this paranoia, ignore him, slipping deeper into my shirt, squeezing the flesh around my belly button. And what's more, he's ashamed to admit he didn't bother with a shower this morning. He was in too much of a hurry. The fingers, reminded of this and not wishing to soil their intention, return from their expedition. Taking my hand they pull me to my feet. J wants to move into the wood where the wind is less brisk, though his forehead glistens and the back of his tee-shirt is damp. Really he's looking for a place where he won't be seen by himself. J hides from J. The narrow path winds beside a field of ripening corn. I want to write things down before they all fade away: the swish of his jeans, the cups of leaf-mould within raised tree-roots; the perfume of earth; the sense of expectation in my breasts. J as companion, interpreter, tourist guide. His determination to make happiness exact. I'm too dreamy by half; poems and rhymes and pieces of prose fight for supremacy in my mind. J's striding ahead, pulling me with him; looks so fed up when he's having a good time. Perhaps like me he's naturally suspicious of dreams coming true, beautiful summers, contentment. He looks best in blue. Fingers wriggle in my palm as we walk on and on; leave my hand temporarily to touch my shoulder or to press against my lips. 'This is dangerous ground we're on,' he says. A madness, a selfishness, a regrettable adventure along an off-shoot of living. Reaching a broken gate we climb over, sit down in the grass and look towards the crown of shifting corn. He can't keep still. Once more his hand moves between my legs. 'When we get back I'll have a shower and . . ' The 'and' sounds sensational. He chews a blade of grass, mentions Emily Dickinson but grinds to a halt after a few unread sentences. It turns out he probably would like her if he could get round to looking at her poems, but so far, he admits, she's only a rumour from the Simon and Garfunkel lyric which goes, 'You read your Emily Dickinson and I my Robert Frost'. Despite all he's learnt over the years of reality and the tenderness of bombs, that's really how he'd like his future to be, he says. Of course, the poets can be swopped around to suit the tastes of the protagonists. Kate slaps his leg. He stops talking, throws down his grass, lies over me, pumps his hips against mine in solemn practice. There are those hips again, by golly. Though he avoids my eyes as well as he's able, quite soon he can't help himself. 'If you don't mind, I think we'll have to do it now,' he says. He pulls me to my feet again, climbs the gate to check the path in both directions, comes back and stands before me. 'There doesn't seem to be anyone about,' he says, though Kate's not bothered either way. At first he takes great care removing items of my clothing, folding them neatly in the grass and what have you, but then, realising that such consideration is likely to use up too much time, he apologises, yanks down my jeans, lowers me into the grass, removes my shoes without undoing the laces, tugs off my jeans completely and throws them aside. They cling to a hawthorn bush. Moving against me, he kisses my breasts which tickles in the most splendid way. 'Never seen such a tickly girl,' he says, sliding his thumb under the leg of my knickers. Suddenly he becomes quite still. I can tell he wants to explain about his being on fire and what have you, but thinking better of it, shuffles his jeans half-way down, pulls up his tee-shirt for a bit of skin contact, yawns the leg of my knickers aside and – how can I put it – pokes himself into me. Soon, however, he's

110

stopping again, this time to remove his tee-shirt because he wants the whole of his chest to rest against mine. I've never known him so impatient yet he can't bear to finish, pausing at the top of each stroke to savour his pleasure, then sinking into me, his mouth wide and rather wet, sliding over mine. He nibbles my cheek, licks the downy skin beneath my ear. Kate's thinking 'And I my Robert Frost' even as she yells through the woodland. He's pleased, embarrassed, caught up in a sexual schizophrenia, wanting me to scream in ecstasy, but ever-so-quietly so no-one else hears. Stopping once more – oh when will he ever stop stopping? – he slips from me, moves onto his side and watches me, squeezing, in turn, my leg, breast and throat, beginning tales of love, fantasia, D.H. Lawrence, Madame Bovary, till, in a moment of panic, I must push my palm against his mouth. Now he's kneeling between my legs; lifts me; chews into my knickers. As ever, he needs to put what he's doing into words. 'I'm going to eat your cunt,' he says. An unexpected shiver runs through us both so he says the words again. They are only sounds yet they affect our chemistry. Only sounds. 'And then I'm going to fuck you,' he says, with just a trace of surprise about his eyebrows. Pulling down my knickers he reaches forward with his mouth to chew into me for real. 'Oh no you're not,' says Kate. The words are mere tokens. He loves me to refuse. Glory, lips and kisses. An insect hums in the grass beside my head. Glory, lips and kisses, though he hardly ever gets it right.

Derek's just come home. He of *The Desert Song* and *The Three Musketeers*. Pausing at the corner of the house he peered towards the shed, overbalanced and stepped into the herb garden. Kate managed to duck in time. Mrs Thrupp's dog is barking at him. From the upstairs window of the flat opposite an old lady watches me watching her. A pall of grey cloud has gathered and is about to envelop the sky. It's already quite dark.

Having lowered my hips, J moves to one side and, while biting a fingernail, wonders what to do next. He wants to leave nothing out just in case we are bombed and this is the last time.

111

He comes up with those devilish fingers, first one then two, removing them at intervals, licking them, playing with himself. Derek fills the kettle. J thinks again, kneels astride my breasts, lifts my head, presents his erection to my face then draws invisible circles over my cheeks and lips. Why, here's a routine rarely described on Radio Four. Seeing my mouth open, he falls back onto his hands and lifts his eyes to heaven. 'Kate, I want your cunt too much, too much,' he says. It's amusing, Kate winks. You quite often have to pretend you're in a book when you make love otherwise it's hard to take seriously and there's a danger you'll fall about laughing. He's not saying, 'Kate I want your cunt' because he wants it, but simply to hear himself say he does. I have a theory about the magic of forbidden things. J bounces up and down. I pray nuns aren't looking on. As the thighs shunt up and forward, the tip of his penis stabs to the back of my throat so by this time Kate's not so enthusiastic and feels a bit sick, though she'd love to be a heroine and bite him till it hurts. For a while, he's forgotten me, raw and blinded with a kind of rage. Bringing himself upright and taking the weight on his knees, he must lean forward, fumble amongst my lips and his pride for a sensation even greater. Now unable to look at me he supports my head with his left hand and rubs himself close to my mouth with his right. Kate wonders what expression to adopt. From the living room she can hear 'Every sha la la lah, every wow oh wow oh'. With a shortage of breath and with a timing to match the fury of his hand he says 'Maybe I'll wank all over you,' and yet this isn't the scholar or the fool with an umbrella in his drink. Another pheasant, Quentin. You may realise I hear them all over and don't you agree they make the most memorable, beautiful sound, urging a girl to curl and die among ferns and raindrops? Even J's ability to postpone the moment is beginning to fade. For his climax he'd rather be tucked inside me where maybe he belongs, cooing with his lips, smoothing my wet face with his fingers. His movement into me is so simple, so effortless, though his lip will show blood and his back will be covered in scratches. As yet he hasn't fathomed out my orgasm, wants more to show for it – a sign, a signal, a little flag, or, like him, pulses of living liquid. He kisses and kisses me saying he loves me saying I'm wonderful saying he's perfectly something or other then slumps heavily onto me, his lips still moving. With each soft thrust he slumps a little more. It's only then he realises we're mostly naked in a cornfield at the edge of a footpath. First of all, as a steady breathing returns, he wants to pull up his jeans to avoid embarrassment, but would hate to betray his haste in case I gain the impression he doesn't care two hoots about me in this calm but pointless dawn of sexual satisfaction. To banish any worries I may have in this particular direction he carefully extracts himself, turns top to toe and then, hands pulling at my thighs, kisses me long and slow between the legs, mouth widening as an initial hesitation is replaced by what could be joy; joy and his tongue drifting within me. Kate remembers the nursery rhyme Jack and Jill went up the hill to fetch a pail of water. The lid of the teapot rattles onto the draining board, accompanied by Karen Carpenter. J reminds me this is wonderful, more wonderful than anything else, so I tap tap him on the leg. He's returning to a need for words already. His squeeze is painful as my legs are opened further and he burrows into me once more. The afternoon lulls and sighs with wet symphonies. I want to write it down. Oh, not the activity, but the spiritual peace arising from it. His fingers come to assist his search for a tomb wide enough for him to slip into with his dreams. The sapling Kate has taken hold of meanwhile snaps so easily.

Salmon Sandwiches

A deathly day with rags of cloud being tumbled through the skies by fierce winds. Mums in rubber gloves run all over the estate rescuing sheets, pillow-cases and tea-towels from hedges and rosebushes then drag their kids out of the wild lime trees and thump them through the open doors. It's a ruined half-term. Mrs Jackson's in her front garden pretending to sweep the path, listening out for the strums of guitars on Waikiki beach while her husband has a hung-over day off, his boots and overall bottoms poking between the front wheels of the broken lorry. In some ways it's an ideal day for Mr Withenshaw but he's nowhere to be seen. Rumour has it that he may have tied nylon kite string round his neck and jumped into the hall from the banister.

Dad's wearing a baggy suit with turn-ups and light grey stripes. His face is red and he's flattened his hair with Brylcreem. In the middle of his cheek there's a piece of tissue clinging to a razor wound. Aunty's been up the stairs a dozen times if she's been once, warning me it's unholy to stare through the window on a day like this and isn't it time I changed into the woolly green suit hanging from the back of the door which I know will be too cold and make my legs itch. Dad's not allowed to turn on the radio. We had a Christian breakfast while she fussed from room to room with a yellow duster. Somehow she's managed to fill the creases on her upper lip with pink make-up.

Since this is a special occasion, dad's managed to borrow a

black car with red leather seats. Aunty tries hard not to sigh with contentment as we kangaroo down the road. Mrs Jackson bows her head but carries on sweeping. The Paradise kids, playing football on the green as usual, shout and jeer but I press my thumb to my nose and waggle my fingers. 'Kate!' says Aunty. 'Aunty!' says Kate. Aunty slaps me on the leg as hard as the day will allow. The tall boy with a scar on his forehead digs a handful of clay from the goalmouth and throws it after us. It slaps onto the rear window. Dad says he'll thrash the lot of them when he gets back. Aunty's terribly annoyed. Her black hat snarls.

At the church some old lady's fiddling with sad notes on the organ as dad takes my hand and leads me slowly to the front where we sit with Aunty on a long cold pew. In the window beside us a couple of lambs are being looked after by a tall bearded fellow with a golden ring above his head. It must be Jesus. He's holding a long pole with a curved handle. A choirboy hands each of us a hymn-book and an order of service. Dad flicks through both of them. Aunty's nose looks round to see Who's come and Who hasn't. Oh, there's Old Reg Smythe's daughter with ribbons in her hair and black knees. Jesus has taken a couple of paces forward next time I look at him. Good with lambs. Not so good with dying children. Three out of ten. The vicar clips in from the back, climbs into the pulpit, clears his throat, welcomes us all with a big grin on his face then makes a little speech about mum and how popular she was, glancing down at his notes whenever he gets to her name. Aunty's supervising by wringing her hands. I have a bit of a cold so dad has to lend me his hanky which is crumpled and smells of oil. Once the vicar's finished we sing a couple of hymns. Aunty's the loudest because she goes to choir practice once a week and belongs to the Bali Hai Opera Society. Dad mimes. During the second hymn mum jerks forwards once or twice before sliding neatly through a pair of purple curtains which then close after her all by themselves. Someone sobs at the back. Aunty turns round to make a note of Who it is. As if from the dead, Mr Withenshaw has appeared and settles alone in the back row. 'Oh he hasn't done it after all', whispers Aunty to dad. 'Just goes to show,' she says. Dad won't look at her yet everyone's staring at him. They can't make out whether he's laughing or crying. Aunty reaches round me to squeeze his shoulder but, shuffling sideways, he leaves the pew and walks quickly up the aisle, his head down. My heart thumps. A few members of the audience choose to mumble. Aunty turns pink as anything, brushes past me and catches him up, but he shrugs her off and disappears through the back door. The vicar raises his eyebrows at me so I raise my eyebrows at him. Aunty stands in the middle of the church wondering what to do. Her black hat's speechless.

Outside it's raining. Dad's wandering among the lopsided headstones smoking a cigarette and kicking the grass while Aunty moves from side to side behind him, wringing her hands again, beseeching him. She wouldn't normally beseech, but this is a churchyard where a great deal of beseeching is done. I try to cry but I can only make the noises. Other friends come out of the church but hang around at the door, blowing their noses, lighting their cigarettes, talking in whispers, comparing hats. One tall man in a grey suit marches sadly up to Kate and lifts her into the air, a big grin across his thick face. Aunty tells Kate later it's Old Reg Smythe. He takes Kate on a tour of the churchyard, points to the trees and makes speeches about Roots, Growth, Soil, Fruits; explains to her how Autumn and Winter come to us all but then goes on to say that God sometimes takes the nicest people in late Summer because he likes them so much. His neck is brown. Old Reg Smythe's, not God's.

Back home we have a solemn party. Aunty's made dozens of crustless tinned-salmon sandwiches cut into triangles. Putting two on a plate for me she explains she's going to stay for a couple of days and see to the Chores. 'Your dad's not himself,' she says. Strangers keep coming up to me wherever I am, messing up my hair and saying 'Hello' very seriously. Altogether I collect nearly two pounds. One fat woman with a pair of glasses nesting in her hair takes hold of my shoulders,

116

examines my face from both sides, clicks her tongue and shakes her head. 'You're the spitting image,' she says, 'the spitting image.' Aunty tells me to say Thank You. Dad has taken off his tie and wanders round with plates of sandwiches having his back slapped and, if he can find somewhere to rest the sandwiches, his hand shaken. Aunty seems to be in charge of the sherry and must turn away from the others to fill her own glass. If anyone looks in her direction she puts the bottle down and pretends to scrape crumbs from her skirt. People thank her for the spread. She says, 'Oh it was nothing really, or 'Well, it was the least I could do,' and the people nod and squeeze their lips together.

Towards the end of the party an overdose of sherry is making it difficult for some of the guests to carry on mourning; a wish to giggle creeps into the corners of their eyes and lips. To avoid being spotted by dad they must pretend to be enjoying the various plaster objets d'art from Weston-super-Mare which line the utility display cabinet. Dad gives up entertaining, flops into mum's old chair and squeezes his hands to his eyes. Having whispered amongst themselves, the guests choose a volunteer who must wander over to dad and offer him another sandwich or a nip of brandy perhaps. 'Fuck the salmon,' says dad. People sort of laugh. Each time I look at her, Aunty's leaning against a different piece of furniture explaining bits of her life to men who don't really care. Outside it rains solidly though the wind has died down. People leave in ones and twos but not before they've shaken dad's hand and bunched up my cheeks with warm palms, making my lips curl. They hate leaving but they simply must get back to the babysitter, the coal fire, the dog, the bedridden grandfather, the chicken casserole simmering in the oven.

The last to leave is Old Reg Smythe. He offers his daughter for anything that needs doing. Dad only has to say the word and she'll be round to help him out. Aunty feels her way to the kitchen to wash up leaving dad in the chair, his fingers linked, his neck sinking into his shoulders. Death has given him the chance of a lifetime to be gloomy and he's not going to give it up just yet. Kate hops from living room to kitchen. Aunty washes some of the plates two or three times without noticing. Beside her feet there's a plastic bag filling up with bread. Sitting neatly at the table, Kate has a game with the salt and pepper pots. Aunty tells her that this is a good time to be thinking about mum. 'Remember all the happy times,' she says, placing a piece of sandwich on the draining board and dropping a plate into the plastic bag.

Mum pulled up her dress and did a dance across the living room in her new black shoes. The tops of her legs shook a little and were covered in blue marks like thumbprints. It was Christmas. She tried to pull dad to his feet but he wouldn't budge. He was turning grey, playing with a cigar as mum twirled from one wall to the other pointing to the mistletoe, laughing. She had permed her hair. Her lips were deep red.

Since it's half-term I'm allowed to stay in bed till eight o'clock the next morning. When I come downstairs Aunty's standing at the stove boiling eggs. On the draining board there's a bottle of Anadin and a glass of water. Outside, kids are gathering on corners, playing football with bits of wood to pass the time. Aunty looks uglier in mum's old dressing-gown. Glancing at the wall-clock she puts an egg-cup on the table, pours a little salt onto a plate then rescues black toast from the grill and cuts it into soldiers. Using a special spoon with holes in, she then lifts the eggs from the frothy water, putting one in the egg-cup and the other on the plate with the toast. 'There,' she says. 'These'll make your hair curl.' Kate wishes she weren't so sore between the legs. Aunty smacks her for wriggling.

During the first egg Aunty tells me dad hasn't been himself for a year or more. There's been something wrong she hasn't been able to put her finger on. 'And then, well, your mum dying was really the last straw,' she says, popping two Anadin into her mouth and taking a swig of water. Anyway, during the second egg she explains dad's need to get away for a while. He'd told Aunty he was sure I wouldn't mind going to live with her in the meantime, till he'd had time to Think. For some reason the top of my second egg is undercooked. The white is

118

slimy and keeps sliding off my spoon. It would be a great kindness for a young child to have cream rubbed into those scratches and bites at the tops of her legs. Aunty still wears yesterday's make-up. Tear trails run through her face powder. 'I'm sure he'll be back one day,' she says. 'Sometimes men have to be alone to think things through.' The burnt soldiers won't bend so Kate covers them in butter hoping they'll soak it up. Aunty's glad I understand. Dads find it hard to cope, just like the rest of us and, Lord bless them, they don't have the easiest of lives.

Her council house is at 42 Winston Churchill Place, just up from the laundry. In the dark living room there's a huge piano with brass candle-holders and locked lid she polishes every day in memory of Uncle Jack who loved to play 'There's a Blue Ridge Round My Heart Virginia' and other old songs. He never took to Chopin or anyone like that. He was a bit famous once because he was asked to play for a week at 'The Moon and Stars' in Victoria Road, but for some silly reason he wasn't asked back. Above the mantelpiece six or seven seagulls fly through a lemon sky towards the ceiling. Uncle Jack now grins from the sideboard. His eyes follow me round the room. Aunty doesn't allow him to become dusty and warns me not to fiddle with him or I'll get a clip round the ear. Rule Two is that I shouldn't get sticky fingers all over the wooden arms of her three-piece suite because it's her pride and joy. Just after they were married, Uncle Jack bought it from Henderson's as a surprise and trudged all the way from Market Street with it piled up on an old cart.

The bathroom's at the bottom of two red steps which lead off the hall. It's a dirty cream bathroom with a history of large spiders and a worn lump of pumice Aunty uses to scrape her feet. A grey print of a Japanese bridge hangs on the wall next to the mirror. The bath has feet in the shape of paws and long yellow stains under the taps. Aunty warns me to check the toilet bowl throughly each time I use it because once upon a time Uncle Jack found a spider crawling on his You Know What. The medicine cabinet still contains unopened packets of

Christmas bath-cubes and a number of razorblades Uncle Jack would have used had he not died so inconveniently. Hanging through the ceiling above the bath is a nylon cord connected to a bell in Aunty's room you can pull in cases of emergency. 'Oh he loved inventing things, your Uncle Jack,' she says. A few weeks before he died he nailed a feather duster to the end of a broom and called it his 'All Purpose Cleaning Utensil' but each time Aunty swept she was tickled to death so he had to go back to the 'drawing board', which was actually an old pine bench in the garden shed.

In the kitchen Aunty cuts thick chips on a cracked marble slab and keeps Uncle Jack's army hat on a green peg behind the pantry door. On a shelf next to the hanging hat is a heavy red book with curled pages she forbids me ever to read called *The Modern Woman's Medical Guide* with many drawings of ovaries which look like ghouls hanging from a cross and, somewhere near the middle, a chapter on Intercourse. The Intercourse chapter tells you what you should do on your honeymoon, though you are warned that if you want to do it before your honeymoon, you should go hiking instead. Of course, says the book, you might feel a bit tired straight after the wedding breakfast, so it might be best to put off Intercourse till the next night. If you find yourself in a hotel room when the time comes to do it you should cover the sheets in towels to avoid embarrassment with the chambermaids. Usually your husband will lie on top of you during The Act and this might hurt a bit, though you are not to worry about this too much unless the same pain carries on for the next forty years. Remember not to be in too much of a hurry and to comfort your husband if, as a result of a suspect chicken chow mein and eight pints of Double Diamond, he flops to the side half-way through, falls asleep or throws up on the counterpane. At these moments remember him fragrant and heroic during the marriage ceremony when you and he exchanged rings and made vows to the Lord.

Christmas isn't stupendous at Aunty's because she believes toys are a waste of good money. She'll only knit me another cardigan or buy me secondhand books about Joseph and his many-coloured coat. She won't hear of decorations and refuses to have a tree because of the needles.

The first Christmas Day she makes me stay upstairs till she's tidied round and said her prayers. Then we have more boiled eggs. Sacrifice is the spirit of Christmas, she says. As soon as we've finished we go off to church where a vicar's standing in the porch shaking everybody's hand. Bending down to me, he says, 'Merry Christmas, my child, may God go with you,' then asks Aunty how she is. Aunty puts on her public smile and says she mustn't grumble, although she always does. She grumbles about the cold, grumbles when I won't sing properly and grumbles as it starts to rain on the way home. In the afternoon we have a mince pie and watch the Queen who asks us to remember those less fortunate than ourselves then pisses off for a Banquet with fat men from foreign countries.

Under the rug in my bedroom is a short piece of loose floorboard with a space beneath where a girl can hide biscuits and pages from her first diary. At one side of the space is a hole in the plaster. In the evenings, with my room in darkness, I can put my head to the floor and keep an eye on Aunty. Usually she's by the fire, her lips and ankles squeezed together. A blue something or other grows from a pair of white knitting needles. On the small table beside her chair stands a large glass of sherry. Every few minutes she rests the knitting in her lap and stares into the corner of her room, thinking of Uncle Jack and honeymoons gone by. Perhaps she likes to sip her sherry when there are people about, but alone she takes hold of the glass and drains it in one go. After another row or two she eases herself to her feet, waddles out of view to the cupboard under Uncle Jack and pours herself some more. I have a good view of her swollen ankles as she returns to her chair. Her slippers are green with woollen marigolds at the toes.

My wallpaper's roses. In the corner of the room's an old washstand with a rusty towel-rail on the side. Above my bed-end hangs an oak-framed picture of Jesus – he's moved into a clump of flowers and holds out his hand towards a fat baby

121

and a mule. The mirror on the dressing-table at the foot of my bed is tilted backwards. If I sit up and stretch my hand as high as it will go, I can just see the reflection of my fingertips. This room used to belong to Philip, Uncle Jack's older brother. Philip's hardly mentioned these days because he turned strange in his middle years and now lives on a ward full of flowers in a city miles away. There's a photo of him on the dressing-table. He's wearing khaki shorts and sits on the wing of a green and brown aeroplane with a desert and some camels in the background. He's holding a cigarette and waving to Lucy, the girl whose name he's written on the front of the photo. The noise of war was too much for him, according to Aunty. Occasionally she sends him a card but now he likes nothing better than to linger in the peace of his silver frame watching Kate come and go in the streetlight dark.

Meanwhile, Aunty guzzles and knits and frowns and hums and sucks a chicken bone.

Tidal Darkness

First of all Derek complains that Kate isn't wearing a bra then roams the china on the sideboard hoping to discover an overlooked Ming. Each piece is held upside down, examined, replaced. Unable to stop yawning tonight, he squeezes his hands into his pockets, bounces his bum against the front of the sideboard and quotes certain uninteresting facts about Lord Lucan he's learnt from a secondhand book. Kate folds her arms and gazes into space. Maybe one day she'll give him a copy of *The Awakening* to read. His bum shakes the vase of dried Love Lies Bleeding; seeds fall.

'D'you know,' he says, 'I've just realised something terrible. I'll never win the premium bonds, pick the right horse in the Grand National or be the one to discover a hoard of Roman coins in the back garden. Some other bloke will and he's a lucky bastard. Basically my life's fucked right up.'

'Yes,' says Kate, unfolding her arms and linking her fingers, 'it certainly seems that way.'

Leaving the sideboard he rocks on tiptoe by the window. Most of the china has been identified as, say, Woolworth's circa 1938. 'Tea?' he asks. Before Kate can make up her mind, the phone rings. Catherine again. Derek blows out his cheeks. Half an hour later – shortly after Derek has referred to the female sex in general as a 'mass of hormonal disasters' – Kate finds herself running down the steep path between the flats worried that she may fall headlong and make a fool of herself. She follows the stream to the old bridge then crosses onto the road, ducking her head against the wind and rain. Catherine often rings in times of inclement weather as if commanded by a wintry masochism in her soul. Kate's hands and feet are cold. She's been cozy till now with dreams of J, a hot shower, a bar of scented soap, hands. Oh no don't, she whispered to him quietly. An old man stands in the doorway of the newsagent's wrapped in duffelcoat and scarf, staring towards the dimly-lit public conveniences. Kate nods, but too slightly for him to notice. During nods her head hardly ever moves as much as it should. The tide's rolling into the creek, pushing itself against the weight of the rain-swollen stream and swirling round the bottoms of the boats lying at angles in the mud. Ghosts of white smoke drift from the aluminium chimney of the largest boat while the shadow of the retired sailor slides against the steamed-up windows. For as long as Kate has been passing by on her way to sanctuary, his boat has been moored exactly so, rising and falling twice a day with the tide. In summer he boards his dinghy and slips downriver towards a crimson sunset. In winter his shadow haunts the small cabin.

The road dwindles to a narrow track at the end of Creek View Terrace. Kate wishes she hadn't come but is glad she has, revealing an inconsistency for which she could be renowned. Crossing the railway line she comes to the Old Pilot's House where a man in oilskins pushes a wheelbarrow loaded with housebricks through the wrought-iron gate and rocks them to the edge of the creek. With a grunt he tips them into the weeds out of harm's way. For weeks he's been gutting the derelict property, day and night, in all weathers, hoping to assemble fresh dreams from the ruins of others. At the moment the house has a roof of clouds and puddles of black rainwater for a kitchen floor. He pushes the empty wheelbarrow back to the gate as Kate turns the corner and follows the path upstream. A peal of bells reaches through the darkness from St Andrew's. J loved them. Bells of all kinds. The night glugs, drips. The path squelches beneath her boots. Oh he loved bells as well as anyone. At the back of the allotments on a bench facing the river, she sits down to catch her breath. It's warmer now, daylight. J will come along one day to forgive her or ask forgiveness, though he'll have to introduce the more serious side of his speech with an appraisal of the tides or the late summer sun. On the far bank several hooded figures creep to and fro across a wooden gulley bridge, up to no good, yahooing above the sound of the rain. Below them the tide chops against the unlit low water and licks at the domes of weed-covered mud. Kate's lonely, no doubt about it. She hugs herself, lights a pre-rolled cigarette which is then extinguished by fat drops of rain, remembers and tries to hum a tune called 'Stairway To Heaven'. She loved it once. They both did.

From behind, a pair of hands take hold of Kate's shoulders. She freezes. Catherine laughs and throws back the hood of her anorak. 'Made it then,' she says. Kate's pleased enough to see her, holds those outstretched fingers and is taken further upstream through hems of wet grass, archways of hawthorn. In spring these banks will leap with white flowers; a lighter, more delicate shade of green will overrun the reed clumps. Catherine, being something of a student of life, has already sensed Kate's mood and wants to know, over and over, what's to be done about it. Kate hasn't a fucking clue and says so. Not a clue. An unsensational gloom has overtaken her. She can't have what she wants, doesn't want what's waiting for her and would stamp in the eyes of heaven if she believed in such a thing. She has a sickness simple in cause but complex and all-consuming in consequence. She wants to lie down in a quiet place where the sun is warm and have nothing more to do with this world, but Catherine says, 'Oh come come, Kate,' this being her turn for serenity. Kate wishes she'd resorted to alcohol before leaving home, but Derek advised against it. 'You're mad enough sober,' he said, scraping the tip of the scissors under his fingernail, 'don't complicate matters.'

Reaching the second set of orange steps leading from the towpath to the main road, the two dreamers sit side by side on the sea-wall, kicking their heels into the soft mud, both soaked to the skin, Catherine holding back her head to catch the raindrops on her tongue. She's been having one hell of an evening at home, she says. And bored? She could have screamed. She hates her job at the library and can't think of any reasonable way to finish it. Kate's chilled to the bone, damp from the wall having seeped through her jeans. She'd like to be flat on her back with legs open and J swooping above. The sky boils. He's an old photo wrapped in knickers. The river rises quickly, bringing its rubbish back into town: the branches of dead trees, oil cans, more expanded polystyrene, the swollen bodies of recent suicides.

'He turned up at the library today,' said Catherine, plucking a small stone from the wall and throwing it into the mud. Kate tries not to move. To a certain extent he can't turn up at the library. He's a memory, not a borrower of books. 'He was as quaint as ever,' continues Catherine. 'His hands were shaking. And his mouth wouldn't work, if you know what I mean. He came out with some story about needing a particular book on Tennyson for his "researches". I loved that bit.' But Kate's hardly listening. She's caught sight of the hooded figures again as they tiptoe through the trees, flashing in fluorescent anoraks, hands hanging in front of them at chest level like begging dogs. Though she wants to warn Catherine, her fingers won't rise from her lap. The rain comes down and down. Only once does the moon flash for an instant between the clouds. She'd love to be thrilled to bits and thanks Catherine for the news as best she can. Catherine's disappointed at Kate's lack of joie de vivre. Hoped at the very least for a hop and a smile. The hardest thing at this moment is setting down the memory of what happened since Kate has a tendency to leave out those pieces of the past which irritate her most. Catherine brightens as the weather deteriorates. Headlights of cars on the dual-carriageway search through the treetops. She takes Kate's hand, kisses it, then presses it to her breast. The wordsmith's stuck for words.

Derek goes quietly up the wall when Kate comes in. On the television — now mended, thank the Lord — an advert for Branston Pickle is superseded by a report from Afghanistan by one Sandy Gall or Gally Sand. Kate's wet through and flops to the hearth to pull off her boots. In stories married couples who find themselves indifferent to each other usually have a row at moments like these, but Kate simply studies her husband who's holding a plate piled high with bread, cheese and onions even as poor Mr Gall comes close to being fired on by a band of those nasty Afghans. Derek, bless him, is determined not to reveal his inner fury and shows Kate the *Guardian* crossword he's been working on. He hasn't solved a single clue. In one across he's tried to fit the word 'suspicious' but ran out of spaces before he reached the final 's'. 'The compiler's really cocked it up today,' he says.

And now Kate stares through the shed window. Having hidden the vodka bottle amongst the rubbish behind her, she celebrates the possibility of an early spring with a fine mugfull. It's still raining, but the sound of drops on the shed roof and greenhouse has become music to her ears.

Missing The Hoop

Meanwhile, Aunty's seeing a much older man called William because the evenings alone since Uncle Jack's death have been getting her down and have led the doctor to suggest a companion. He comes down the path one Tuesday with a bunch of catkins and an armful of library books, knocks on the door with his forehead and waits. Aunty tiptoes upstairs. She's always in but likes to pretend she's just got back from visiting friends.

'My my, what a pretty little girl,' he says as I open the door. He's still wiping his shoes on the coconut mat when Aunty floats down the stairs in a new dress and fills the hall with her smile. Telling William he's lucky to find her in, she shows him into the living room where he pretends to gasp at the splendour of the furnishings while she pours two sherries.

'Kate, this is William,' she says. William shakes my hand and then pulls from his pocket a bag of jellybabies, most of which he nibbles himself, feet first. Some parts of his body are just dying to escape from his suit. Nodding to Aunty in gratitude, he collapses into the sofa forcing puffs of dust into a stray sunbeam, then reaches forward to take his drink.

'And what have you been doing with yourself these holidays?' he asks.

'Oh, I've been playing around,' says Kate.

'Don't you mean, "Playing around, thank you, William"?' says Aunty, taking note of how much sherry William has consumed with his first sip. Kate's not sure whether she means that or not. His legs are open. He tries to open them some more but his thighs still meet a few inches above the knees. Aunty fidgets in her chair, sips sherry, spots cobwebs for the first time, then asks me if I have anything better to be getting on with. I don't think I have, so she makes me go in the kitchen with my plasticine.

'What a delightful child,' says William.

'A child she may be; delightful she certainly isn't,' says Aunty, remembering Uncle Jack and the hooting Christmases they used to share with Escalado horses racing along green canvas. 'She can be a bit of a nuisance at times. And awkward!'

'Don't worry,' says William, 'it's probably just a stage.'

Aunty notices me peeping through the crack in the door and comes to push it shut, giving me secret waggles of the fingers to warn me against anything wicked I might do in the next three years. I make a farmer with three arms and two very tall chickens. I'm trying to listen to what's being said but William mumbles too much and Aunty does nothing but squeal with laughter at his fat jokes.

Soon he's dropping by two or three times a week with more jellybabies. Usually he likes to wear the same pair of shoes with a snapped lace on the left which can't be threaded to the top of the holes. His grey trouser turn-ups are filled with purple fluff. Aunty explains that he loves God to bits despite the blue tattoo saying JENNY on the knuckles of his right hand. He likes to bring us Instructional Books to look at. It's in everyone's interest to read those volumes which cleanse the spirit, because then we'll be less inclined to wander off on Wild Goose Chases.

'The number of Goose Chases are Legion,' he says.

Then he takes us on an Historical Tour of the town centre to give us an idea of how it looked at different times. Fearing Aunty might argue with the facts, he takes along some of his old photos in a leather bag to back up his descriptions. It's drizzling. I'm down to my last Spangle. Every fifteen minutes or so we reach another Blue Plaque or come across a car park which used to be a row of Elizabethan houses. William stresses

129

the importance of imagination on a tour like this, but however much I strain mine, the car park remains a twist of concrete orange peel. Fortunately Aunty's ankles begin to play up in Lemon Street as William snoops through an alley looking for the birthplace of someone we haven't heard of, so she has to limp back to the bus station, her arm half-way round his waist for support. Back home he eases her into her favourite chair, plumps cushions for her neck and lifts her feet onto a stool. Her marigold slippers are placed side by side on the hearth to warm while he cooks tea. At one point he claims to be in the pantry searching for Spam and economy baked beans, but I catch him on a stool with his fingers in amongst the ovaries of *The Modern Woman's Medical Guide*. I'm sent away with cream to rub into Aunty while he carries on with his cubic chips or shuffles into the doorway wearing Aunty's Lakeland pinny to tell us what a wonderful time we're all having.

'Ooh. Just there. That's right. Ohh,' says Aunty.

I'm sent to bed early because I've had a long day and I must be very tired and girls my age should have their beauty sleep and if I'm good perhaps we'll all go to the zoo on Sunday and won't that be exciting? At the bottom of the stairs William pecks my cheek and warns me to take my journeys into the soul rather than round and round this unsatisfactory world. I tell him I will. His baggy jacket's covered in dust. Chip fat still glistens on his fingers. Aunty calls out from the living room, 'Don't forget to thank William for the guided tour, young lady.'

'Thank you for the guided tour,' says Kate.

'Don't mention it,' whispers Uncle William, tweaking my bum.

Lying in bed I hear the cupboard under Uncle Jack rattling time and again. Tigger's stuck up a pine tree with Roo having boasted that climbing is what Tiggers do best. Kate's books are Life with the Williams taken out. She can't sleep. Philip's knees poke like heroes from his khaki shorts. She's fairly happy because a boy called Granville left a note in her desk asking her to meet him at the corner of Isaac Crescent on Sunday if she liked him because he liked her. He's won prizes in the

Spoken English competitions, reading poems by William Wordsworth. Downstairs heavy feet, unchristian giggles, the regular rattle of Uncle Jack. An obscene chortle from Aunty is quickly muffled with a cushion. A pair of schooners kiss.

Granville wears wide grey shorts so you can see his fawn pants when he does handstands. He grew out of Tigger some time ago. Kate imagines a winding winter road, yellow shadows creeping through a tangled hedgerow, his hand holding hers. He'll be whispering, 'Kate, you're a proper Charlie.' The note says two o'clock. She falls asleep, wakes up. The clock downstairs chimes nine. One of Aunty's plates is being taken out of the china cabinet. Beside it there's a Torbay crab with a claw missing. On the shelf below a blue and white bird hovers close to Aunty's wedding photo. It's the same kind of bird as the one on the tin of toffees in the kitchen cupboard. A match is struck. William coughs. Smoking is one of the Wild Goose Chases from which he hasn't yet returned. A hand slaps on the wooden arm of the sofa. Kate's drifting round the bedroom, floating by Philip on her way to the window and back again. Flying's wonderful fun. She rolls in space above the plump eiderdown. It's a starry starry night. On her third visit to the window she sees a man in a trilby weeing into Aunty's hedge. There are some crimes it's difficult to avoid. He leans right back to see if he can reach the fishpond by clearing the hedge, but doesn't quite make it.

Granville's note says he first came to realise how much he liked me when he saw from the maths room window how regularly I missed the metal hoop during netball.

Thursday 5.03am

J, I was going to address my earliest thoughts to you this morning, but I've changed my mind; the certainties of midnight can become a comedy by five o'clock, the dimmest possibilities flare through darkness then fizzle out. Too many songs about you, I suppose. I spent an hour or two yesterday listening to them all while the sun was out. You'd have laughed at me dancing. It was with the thought running through my head that everything I do is for you, but of course that's ridiculous, isn't it? We all know about love – how it flourishes when severed in its prime. Otherwise watch it turn sour, become black and white.

Supposed to meet Catherine at seven last night but I was a bit late. Derek was in a mood and didn't want me to go. 'Just can't imagine how I'm going to keep myself occupied,' he said.

Catherine was already at the Wimpy Bar, jammed in amongst a crowd of people most of whom were waiting to see a musical at the Hippodrome. She stroked my hand, told me how pleased she was to see me. At the same time an elderly couple in matching cagoules were involved in a madness of their mutual regard for Tommy Steele. Catherine guessed Tommy was in his dressing gown, brushing his teeth, fiddling with a top hat, putting on the Ritz. She wondered whether it would be worthwhile checking to see if there were any tickets left, but I talked her out of it. I can't get used to the idea of grown, sequinned people breaking into song all over the place, especially if you're tucked into the steep dark eating a Walnut

132

Surprise with one of those flat wooden scoops. And then you're expected to leap to your feet and go crazy if someone famous comes on. A famous person is just someone you've heard of that hasn't heard of you and who wouldn't be overly perplexed if you were flattened by a bus on the way home from their show.

Catherine stroked her lips, parted them. She was gazing over my shoulder, though not at anyone or anything. She is most beautiful at the corners of her mouth and in the fathoms of her eyes. Her tongue licked the tip of her middle finger. Maybe she was contemplating the brevity of her future or making up limericks about the hamburger clientele. Her hair shone. I could have taken her head to my shoulder, held it, made myself cry.

'Perhaps we could go to the Arts Centre café,' she said. 'Come on. It'll be a laugh.'

She was making it all up as she went along. The theatregoers glanced at their watches, then, in a general mood of anticipation, began to return cups and file through the door. Some were clapping already. Occasionally Catherine smiled. The smile ran through her fingers as she ruffled my hair, asked my forgiveness. Pale and slim beyond anyone's wildest dreams, she was already a star. Yes, I said, the café sounded fine but she'd have to pay.

J's shoulder blades shift beneath his skin as he moves in his sleep; he's almost liquid. My hand finds its way from the pillow here to his neck there. He becomes quite still, as if my touch has reassured him. It's a dream I have which stubbornly refuses to repeat itself. The room's dim and warm. Still sleeping, he rolls over, holds me.

I turned up the stereo, watched the afternoon of rooftops and the strip of silver river winding through the trees. Everything I do is for you, I said. I forgot which record was playing – maybe the dangerous one by Ray Charles which can certainly ruin a girl on a Wednesday when the world's just a blank piece of paper and she's nothing in her head to put down except what's already been written too often.

J's head has at last found my pillow. On the bedside chair lie scraps of the night before.

Catherine pushed her way through the swing doors into the café and sat down at the first free table by the window so she could look out over the harbour. She didn't care who might see her or what they'd have to say for themselves. At the next table, three unlikely women were eating lasagne and laughing periodically into their palms; each of them enormously beautiful, picking at their food in continental fashion, waggling painted fingernails, tossing back their hair if the conversation called for amusement. I was examined carefully by the one facing me as I sat down. Her hair and lips unnerved me. I turned away only to see myself hanging in the window amongst the coloured lights of the quay opposite.

Catherine decided we'd have a pizza. A waiter ambled through the tables in response to her raised chin and snapping fingers. He had thick black hair, a face darkened by stubble and, with a strategic bow tie, was making the mistake of thinking himself thoroughly desirable and up to date. Catherine used her phoney Italian accent, receiving his full attention in return. Here was another Barbie Doll he might fuck some day, another legend in a list of conquests. We'd have a Mexicana and a Fiorentina with extra garlic on both, she said. If Catherine selects a pizza for you, it's best not to argue. As the waiter billowed to the counter, she sucked her finger and pushed me into the back of my seat with her eyes. Everything I do is for you, I said to the window, for goodness sake, and yet we know how much old lovers hate to be the motivation for all things. He'd prefer me to say everything I do is for myself and fuck the consequences. I'd argue that such a theory is all well and good till the moment a J comes whistling by.

'Never dabble with a waiter, my dear,' said Catherine. 'The adverts may be provocative, but the product is exceptionally bland.'

The three unlikely women heard her, as they were meant to, and giggled together. The one facing me gazed at my hair for several seconds and then, snapping back, looked at her fingers.

134

Catherine was into some mumbo-jumbo about whether to fall in love with me or not given that I was the least usual person she'd ever come across and given too that she was experiencing greater boredom and futility than at any other time in her life. She took my hand. I pulled it away. The conversation of the three women rose and fell with the tinkle of glasses, the rattle of knives and forks. Suddenly two of the three were reeling with laughter over some ticklish moment in Ibsen. Catherine raised her eyebrows then rattled at the table with the pepper pot.

I searched the whole cafe. Bruce Springsteen was singing 'I'm On Fire' through invisible speakers, driving a few of us to gestures of swooning at the thought of his neat blue thighs and sculpted face. A group of penniless male undergraduates chuckled in unison. No-one was being what they'd turned out to be first thing in the morning. A few tables away a pair of girls dressed as men lounged amongst ruins of white wine. Or perhaps they were males in limbo, dressed as men to ward off an inclination to become girls. Or women. Catherine's forever telling me off for calling women girls. She has a fixation about it, saying girls are only girls till they realise they have power at which point they toss aside poetry and a preference for pale-faced dreamers and become women. These masculine women or perplexed young men had somehow developed minimal breasts with which to suckle lovers. For a moment it seemed a good idea to be something of a minority type; break down those barriers of hello, good evening, excuse me, may I, or how are you and fuck to kingdom come regardless of any consequences. Fuck and fuck and fuck, training oneself not to feel pain at dawn or to fall into paroxysms of guilt over the betrayed, the undermined, the damaged. Bruce was over the top as usual, but to great effect. We dreamed of a time we were happier or of greater futures about to be realised. Music's the shorthand of so many shipwrecked dreams, the sketchy map of fruitful islands of paradise.

My unlikely woman looked up, looked down, played a game of hide and seek with dark latin hair. The juices ran in my

135

stomach. Maybe I'm a man, I thought. It was an emotional night. She would fly dusky-skinned to a wide warm bed, throw open her arms, her legs, her soul, stroke the length of her body with the tips of her fingers, showing Kate the way. Bruce continued to sing. Several J lookalikes had already turned out to be frauds. They were sitting awkwardly, had ridiculous voices or swooned over pointless women with black hair, black eyebrows, black lips and black fingernails who, post-coitally, would be free of their black dresses and turn out human after all, tiptoeing to the toilet in a startling flash of ivory. I looked out of the window, waiting again. In the harbour the tips of naked masts rocked lightly beneath the stars.

The waiter swung between the tables, a pizza in each hand. Dropping them in front of us, he winked at Catherine then handed her a serviette. She sighed, snatched the serviette and clicked her tongue against the roof of her mouth. The waiter took this as a sign she liked the idea of fucking too and moved away, well satisfied. She began tearing up the pizza, pressing the pieces into her mouth.

As Bruce reached the end of his song a man wearing a white dinner jacket stood up from his stool at the bar, slapped his companion on the back and walked quickly to the piano where he began to play 'Your Song', his chubby pink cheeks glistening in the light of a small candelabra. Soon he was sitting on the roof of the song and kicking off the moss. Hardly anyone wept copiously.

It's our first party, I think. A winter's night. From the outset it's all a bit of a shambles because he's been told by one of his friends at college that I'm going with someone else. And yet as I lean against the wall trying to look vaguely familiar he comes bounding up the stairs like a faithful dog, wagging his tail once he sees I'm alone. This is his great opportunity. He'll take the bull by the horns, strike while the iron is hot and numerous other clichés. He comes across, says hello, refusing to pretend he's here for any reason other than to seduce me. Catherine's in attendance, of course, sitting in the window seat, looking out as grey snow clouds cover the moon. She's quiet as death all

136

evening. Most people want to talk about the difficulties they're having over essays on old Thoreau, but she's bored to death by it all. J pursues Kate, eyes wide and fearless. Kate eludes him for minutes at a time for the look of the thing, but he roars after her, telling her his life story in tragic snatches. He's rather sensitive, he says. Good with children but not so handy at putting up shelves or wallpapering in corners. I take a handful of peanuts and move to the Discussion Area; he's behind me admitting many crazy things he's done in the past to pre-empt anyone who might start rumours. I take a seat in the perfumed gloom, drink my drink and here's J again, flopping beside me, describing my eyes and various other pieces of me. Then I'm in the beer-stained kitchen where a Political Narrative student is giving a bored girlfriend a long-winded resumé of his life's difficulties, and there is J, waiting by the sink, pretending love's a coincidence. Scattered around the work surfaces are those who'd rather talk of Marx a great deal than go into the main room and show up their loneliness. J raises his glass to me. He's brimming with confidence, and has had dreams that I'm his through some comical unravelling of destiny. 'There's absolutely no point in running away from the inevitable,' he says. 'Let's dance.' Kate gives in. We move back to the living room and Status Quo. The floorboards are sagging. Catherine's a silhouette. Someone called Janine bursts into tears because she's wanted J since the first year but, adored or not, he can't handle her passion for Mr Leavis or her souvenir photograph of Vince Hill. We dance. He won't look into my eyes. I won't look into his. He's ridiculous. Can't dance for toffee. Oh, his arms are fine, but his feet remain fixed to the carpet. 'Are you glued?' I ask. He laughs but still won't look at me. His courage has dwindled, packed up and gone home early. He's worn out by pursuit. Catherine comes over, squeezes my arm. The music pounds. He simply must tell me something I can't hear. I laugh in case it's a joke. Here comes Gladys Knight and the Fucking Pips. He wags his arms in much the same way as he did for Status Quo except they've slowed down. His wrists don't twitch quite so much. I smile. Now he looks and winks at me. Life's

137

fine. We're unlikely to be bombed tonight. Every ounce of self-pity Gladys feels, her devoted Pips reiterate. J shouts something about how nicely the room is decorated then hopes I won't notice that his arms have flopped round my neck. I like him because he starts out on the basis that everyone thinks he's a prick and works hard to change their minds. He shivers. Can it be that it was all so simple then, or has time rewritten every line? A crowd of Americans applaud in the background. Most students have stopped dancing. The remaining few squeeze waist to waist in the centre of the room, building up for Intercourse. Hardly anyone wishes to be associated with too much sentiment. J doesn't care and tells me so. He'll dance to Semprini if someone puts it on. In the corner now, Catherine occupies herself by chatting to Wilkins the Modernist Lecturer who has a reputation for taking first years back to His Place to teach them Practical Lawrence. In minutes your C's can change into A Minuses.

By the time we leave it's snowing heavily. Thick, sticky flakes fill the orange sky. J seems to be walking me home though nothing has been said. I can tell he's irritated to have Catherine along. He's been dying to repeat his dreams to me all in one go but now he's forced into dreadful small talk about areas of low pressure to the South West or George Orwell's position in English Literature.

'And what do you think his position is?' he asks Catherine, being polite.

'Standing up with his chin on his fists, I should imagine,' says Catherine.

At the corner of Ravenswood Road, having abandoned romance for the moment, he whispers 'See you' to me and gives that famous salute before walking away. Catherine and I stand in the snow and watch after him. He's trying hard not to walk like a duck – keeping an eye on his shoes, turning round every few yards to check the snowprints he's making. Catherine's tickled pink.

She chewed a piece of pizza carefully for some time then mumbled through it that she was still hoping to hear what I had to say about J turning up at the library. Girls or women everywhere were remembering themselves as the piano player caressed another love-song. Transvestites hitched skirts over lumpy knees and squeezed their high heels against the barstools. The anchovies were burning my mouth. I told her I hadn't really given the matter much thought. She knitted her brows and shook her head. The three unlikely women were still on Ibsen, two of them laughing while the third, my favourite, looked on in astonishment. It's true that if you stare at someone's head they'll eventually turn to look at you. She did. Kate tried to smile but nothing would come.

The food was making me tired. Catherine said 'Well?' Short sentences are the mark of a lazybones. Everyone says so. The sun's coming up. Kate's smoking like a madwoman. Her coffee's cold. On and on she goes. She'll never be popular, that's for sure. She doesn't write right. There's ash everywhere. All her bits and pieces sadden her. She could cry at cloud. Derek says she smells of a cigarette most of the time, but cigarettes are good to those of us insidiously into suicide. A pack of Victory Tipped, please. You smell like smoke. Derek has this compelling way with words. Birds sing. Miss Wintle cleans dawn windows. The milkman comes, comes and goes. A dog barks for the sake of it. Perhaps if the barking of all dogs could be translated into English it would mean something like, 'Actually, dear friends, Winalot's fucking awful.' When this is life it's such a relief to put a short sentence here and a short sentence there. Miss out on the Winalot humour, Kate, it doesn't suit you.

Without my noticing, the three women had somehow twisted the conversation round to Virginia Woolf, referring to suicide as if it was a natural and important part of a literary career. Slice yourself to pieces, then you'll be as famous as anything. Catherine laughed too loud. The whole café turned round. I could smile at my unlikely woman quite easily now. She smiled in return. She would make coffee at dawn somewhere and bring it back to bed. We would lie together till midday, sharing hatreds. Catherine was announcing the opinion that it's a good job we're not still at college when we're old enough to realise what garbage we've been tangled in. Me and my woman were as thick as thieves by this time. She looked at me as she sipped her drink. The latin hair fell around her cup. Following enthusiastic applause, the piano man played 'Crocodile Rock', remembering when rock was young and he and Susie had so much fun. I decided to take the world by storm if it would let me. Catherine moved off to the bar saying it was time to get pissed as parrots. A person came into the café dressed as a bear. The café, being Chic, did its level best to show no surprise. My likely unlikely woman watched me now without having to sip her drink. Oh it's so good to initiate an impossible charade.

Sometimes I expect to come across J as if we'd parted yesterday; then I find myself slipping from the house on foolish walks in anticipation of a vague reunion. Usually she ends up in a park perhaps, on a bench by herself, a faintly romantic heroine, wondering how she'll get back home now, how she'll cope with this extraordinary boredom. The sky's grey. It's drizzling. A few hardy kids play on the swings. Kate's a clown in a purple suit. Wet couples walk along the path. She dislikes them; tries to hide by looking like an ordinary woman out for a breath of fresh air, but it doesn't work; the purple dominates. She pinches the slats of her bench and remembers J's search for horsechestnuts. A plump gentleman with stick and squeaking shoes comes across the grass towards her, throwing one foot calmly in front of the other. He has seen, summed-up and become satisfied. She aches and is riddled with enquiry. He nods Good Afternoon. She feels she has responded though her lips have barely moved. She hates him, loves him, the plump gentleman, J.

Catherine came back to the table, looking away as she passed the bear. It was waiting to be served but being generally ignored. Perhaps the person within the suit was working on a thesis documenting Public Surprise. Its head was zipped on round the neck.

Setting down my glass she begged me to drink. My tongue

140

needed oiling, she said. The whole time she'd known me I hadn't said a thing worth tuppence. It was all very well claiming to be her closest friend, but I should confide in her more frequently. I'd kill myself with stagnant opinions. We drank quickly and bought another. Drank that quickly and bought several more. Catherine yawned. The evening softened. With due solemnity the piano man played 'Heartbreak Hotel'. My unlikely woman lingered this side of danger and Hallelujah. The bear hummed. We would kiss in the half light, the moonlight, in a light strewn with books and the shimmer of warm flesh, sorting things out at last.

'This J fellow', she'd say, 'describe him to me.'

When I reached his feet, she'd laugh. But Catherine had talked incessantly, became flirtatious, provocative, drew wet circles on my hand, pushed her fingers through my hair, peppered long, uninteresting critiques of the books we'd studied with brief descriptions of her more amusing encounters – the man who liked to keep his vest and spectacles on throughout, the boy 'no more than fifteen' who threw away an impatient virginity on her then sent her a card covered in sailing boats to say Thank You. She laughed, I tried to laugh with her.

The bear pulled off its right paw, took a pen from a small pouch on its chest and wrote something in a folder it had been carrying. With a flourish the piano man came to the end of his concert, bowed slightly to the applause and returned to the bar. The transvestites patted him on the back, bought him drinks. Bruce Springsteen then filled the café with greater volume than before, joining stars, night and harbour in doleful significance and a lack of love. Conversations were flagging everywhere; a veil of cigarette smoke turned the café blue. The waiter, erect by now, pulled a chair from a corner table, turned it round and sat astride the seat, passing time by cleaning his nails with a toothpick and glaring at Catherine. She really is the most glared at person on earth. The bear stopped writing for a moment, raised its arms, yawned without moving its stitched lips, then read what it had written, its ears pricked. My unlikely woman was watching me as if she knew me from somewhere but couldn't remember the exact circumstances. Gradually she was becoming alienated from the conversation of her companions which revolved tirelessly around books and literary personalities; the first had written to Doris Lessing and had received a marvellous reply; the second would like to have slept with D.H. Lawrence – the 1980s didn't really suit her, what with Mr Tebbit, the Iranians and what have you.

But my woman was a person of beauty with large hazel eyes. The bear admired her too, breaking off its writing time and again to watch her from the safety of its fur.

J's upset because I won't talk. My room's become sick with wintry indifference and he doesn't fully understand what a mood of silence and agitation can be like. He paces from one end of my room to the other, hands in pockets, top teeth biting lower lip. Music is being played in an attempt to snap me out of it. David Bowie – madness in face paint and glitter, dressed as a harlequin on the LP cover. A couple of kooks hung up on romancing. The phrase sticks in my mind, J's mind, Uncle Tom Cobbley's mind. I just want a bit of peace and quiet. A day to myself. A rest from interpretation. I can smell riversides, the winds of death and life, the spices of time.

'But there's no sense in it,' he says. 'If you want to work I'll sit in the kitchen and wait for you.' That's just it. I don't want to think of you in there fiddling with the egg-spoon, drawing faces on the steamed-up windows, tapping your fingers, passing the time of day with other tenants, waiting for me, your loved one. But I can't say so because my mouth's been sewn up since I woke to find his fingers stroking me. After breakfast I had a shower. He crept in, pulled the pink curtain aside and started fooling round with the flannel, smiling all the time. Rubbed soap over my breasts. Squeezed a flanneled finger between my legs. Became angry that I couldn't, wouldn't respond, enjoy him. He thinks the world's coming to an end because his little affair's gone crazy out of the blue. He walks up and down, up and down trying to work out exactly where he's gone wrong. Was it because he didn't say he loved me during our last ungainly fuck? 'Say something, for God's sake,' he whispers. I fiddle with the cloth on my desk. Outside at the bus stop stands a middle-aged woman with a creased neck and long legs. She's carrying an ironing board. The more he wants me to speak the less I'm capable of doing so. Taking his hands from his pockets he runs them through his hair and closes the curtains. He's scared to death.

'If you don't talk to me soon I'm going to slap you,' he says. On the carpet by my right foot there's a tea-stain. I rub at it with my toe. As I look at him he strikes me on the cheek. It stings. Now he doesn't know what to say or do because he's broken a rule, let himself down, driven words even further away, betrayed something about himself with his hand. Maybe we need a good argument to clear the air but there's nothing to argue about, things are too perfect. We eat endless crumpets in cafés and it works. We achieve a sexual climax simultaneously. As we leave supermarkets our hands automatically seek each other. Neither of us is too fond of God. We both find 'Eat Me' dates reasonably amusing. The earth coils, rattles with traffic, becomes cold, warms up again, entertains itself with cloud, with blue sky, with torrential rain, with suffocating heat, with ice, snow, darkness, songs, tickled pinks, kisses, the joys of the European Literature Mountain. We must send a wagon of books to the third world before it's too late. Tuck into a T.E. Lawrence. Sip a Solzhenitsyn. Gorge yourself on a Goethe. He opens the curtains. The woman with the ironing board is joined by a man in yellow tugging an Irish wolfhound, or was it an Irishman tugging a yellow wolfhound? The number 118 bus swings round the corner covered in advertisements for the zoo. A neighbour appears at her front door to put out milk bottles. Scouts post homesick letters to mum. I love you, he says. That's why I hit you. I love you.

'Oh,' says Kate at last.

The three unlikely women paid their bill, stood up to arrange themselves in the dark windows and started to leave, my favourite glancing at me as she passed. Often a dream becomes something less than a dream when it's seen at close

143

quarters, but, just inches from me, she was as gorgeous as she'd appeared throughout the meal except for those pale middle-class tights. Maybe I blushed. She smiled. She was creamy, dreamy, a little out of sorts, tagging along behind her certain friends. Catherine watched them go. She'd fallen into silence. For a few minutes we stared in opposite directions trying to understand why we were there. Noticing this, the waiter tumbled over to collect money from Catherine and asked her, as she handed it to him, if she was free later on.

'Drop dead.'

'Come on,' he said, 'yes or no?'

The bear struggled to its back paws as we walked to the door. It came up to us and nervously handed a leaflet to Catherine. She said, 'Why, thank you.' Nodding, the bear hobbled back to its seat. Once again coincidence hadn't acted to bring J into the same place as me at the same time. He's everywhere I'm not. The leaflet announced a West Country Lager Festival beginning in mid January. It was only when she threw it to the carpet in the foyer that we saw the message scrawled in pencil on the back. 'To Goldilocks: How about Tuesday 7.30 here? Refrain from porridge till I arrive.' Catherine laughed. 'A madman,' she said. 'The world's full of them.'

Outside in the chilled air we found ourselves more tipsy than we'd imagined and stood by the railings on the quay for maybe twenty minutes. She held my hand, examined it carefully as if she was on the verge of saying something particularly important, but seemed to be put off by a burst of song from a boat moored further along. The black water rocked. We talked on and on as people often do when they've made a decision to part. She was telling me about another collection of photos just come in at the library. A few yards from where we stood, before the main street had been built, a winding track ran all the way to the Downs. On either side were open fields and parkland. Women walked alone at their peril. One picture of an old sweep and his boy gave her the creeps, she said. J's ghost slapped through the darkness. From the warehouse shadows came a pair of drunks waggling bottles of natural dry. They moved in front of us holding each other to prevent an accidental two-step into the water. The tall Scottish one, having emptied the lime-green contents of his stomach onto the cobbles, asked us if we'd care to go back to his bed and breakfast for a few drinks. Laughing to herself, Catherine waved them away. The short one mumbled 'Fucking lesbians,' and struck out at Catherine before pulling his companion off down the quay. Reaching through the harsh light, she first stroked my hair as if in sympathy, then kissed me on the mouth. Her tongue touched my lips. My arms were on fire. She made me promise I'd go round if I had any problems with Derek then hugged me. Over her shoulder I spotted the darkened bear wandering towards the centre, head tucked under his arm. He was throwing lager leaflets in the air and watching as they flipped to the cobbles. Catherine pushed me away. Looked at me. 'I'll worry about you,' she said. I examined my shoes. Lifting my chin, she kissed me again, slipping her tongue into my mouth for an unknown dare and stroking the nape of my neck. Kate was shivering, remembering J, singing inside. She hugged me once more, pecked my ear, my mouth. Her fingers trailed over mine as she broke free and walked away towards the statue of Neptune where the bear had now stopped and was hanging in the gloom trying to light a cigarette.

By the time I came home Derek was already in bed pretending to be asleep. He'd tucked himself against the wall, hands clutching his shoulders, legs pulled up to his belly. As I climbed in he pretended to wake.

'Oh it's you,' he said.

'Princess Margaret couldn't make it,' said Kate.

Sleep wasn't easy. My feet were twisting one against the other and my heart thumped in my ears however tightly I squeezed them to the pillow. I was expecting it to stop. Maybe I'd have had time to gasp a profundity before the eternal night, who knows? The alarm clock ticked in time to tunes tripping through my head.

Living Room

Miss Wintle's in her garden singing 'My Old Man Said Follow
The Van', waiting for the Spring of Mankind when everyone
will be jolly nice to each other, but I can't find myself at all –
you know how it is, Quentin, when, turning round suddenly
you find no-one there, least of all yourself. Full of horror at
one's oddness in an even world. Time gathers momentum
wherever I hide and J won't be coming round any moment
with a bunch of something or other because he's fucked off,
leaving life's thin plot in a bit of shambles. I want to make love,
nothing else will do, though not with anyone I can think of and
none of those awful consequences such as Guilt in the face of
God knows who or this sticky business of tiptoeing home at
dawn for a bath. Besides, Derek would sniff out the Interloper
in seconds. 'You've been having Extra-Marital Relations,' he'd
say, flopping to the sofa. 'Yes, and they were smashing,' I'd
reply. He'd murmur, 'How could you?' rocking himself for
comfort. 'It was easy,' I'd explain, 'I lay on the kitchen table
while he came at me from the other side of the room.'
Recovering somewhat, he'd rear up to his full height and
shout, 'Tell me the bastard's name. Tell me before I get really
cross.'

And now I'm in a chair, J, with nothing to do, having just
seen the tail end of a children's programme in which young
girls were learning what it's like to be an African by walking
round a playground with buckets of water on their heads. Back
in the classroom the teacher asked them if anything special had

struck them about the exercise. The thin girl with ginger hair said she definitely wouldn't be taking water for granted any more. Probably it won't last; in a few days she'll be splashing around and leaving the taps running with the best of them. You can't spend your whole life treasuring water in the same way as an African if you're not an African. You can feel sorry for them, of course, having realised how much your neck aches after just one bucketful, but that's about all. The Africans probably feel sorry for those of us screwed up in tight back gardens as we sprinkle the lawn in summer. The teacher was behaving on the tentative basis that being an African isn't half as nice as having water in taps and living in Walthamstow. The Missionary Spirit still thumped in her breast. With Derek it's the Missionary Position and a faint but regular tendency to admire the third world for starving so bravely while the rest of us tuck into chicken madras or swill Chateau Le This That or the Other down our throats.

This house bores me to death, the mantelpiece especially. At the end, in a gilt frame, Derek's mum and dad stand arm in arm on the steps of Longleat House, having just witnessed first hand what it's like to be an African Lion. On the wall above them hangs a small blockboard version of Renoir's *Moulin de la Gallette*. Derek's sports socks lope over the back of my chair. Beneath the sideboard sits a black briefcase covered in dust, crammed with those old documents – unfilled-in forms, premium bonds, letters and bits of official paper – he might need some day. Kate's not a thorough housewife. Particles of skin, coal dust and carpet fluff are scattered only to fall again.

The world's exceedingly overcrowded with interesting things – Derek's Rubik's Cube, for example. It stands on William Faulkner in the bookcase. Now and then, when all else fails, he has a crack at it, screwing himself up over those yellow squares which appear in the wrong corners. The plastic joints snap for hours at a time.

Romance

Mr Withenshaw's all out of breath as he thumps across the green pulling on a piece of string and a white kite jerks into the sky. After his absence grateful mums and babies line the pavement to cheer him on with rounds of applause. It's spring and sunny but quite cold. A triangle of council-planted daffodils shiver in a chocolate-coloured bed at the centre of the green. Granville's on the corner of Isaac Street, jumping up and down to keep warm. He's probably been there hours. Because it's Sunday his mum's made him wear long grey trousers and they're all bunched up round his ankles. Grinning from ear to ear he takes a Wagon Wheel from his anorak pocket ready for the Presentation, then apologises for not wrapping it. I give him first bite. His mouth is full of fillings. He's a bit surprised when I show him the list of Rules I've made, but reckons he can manage them all quite well except Number Four which, in his opinion, takes things too far. 'Just do your best,' I tell him. He tries to change the subject, going on about how nice I am and how nice Amelia Cuthbertson, the teacher's pet who's good at everything, isn't. He went out with her once, he explains, but she had something wrong with her insides and had to take a pink medicine three times a day which made her want to wee every five minutes. He's happy to be with me instead. 'Thanks, but please excuse the coat,' I say. Aunty bought it for a shilling at a jumble sale in the church hall and there was spit or sick or something on the collar till she'd soaked it. He starts mooning around, telling me again

148

how he watches me playing netball through the maths room window. I always look very nice. He's fond of gangly legs altogether. Amelia Cuthbertson's are thick and a bit too short for his liking. He's already had one lot of lines because of me – 'I Must Confine My Attentions To The Task In Hand' five hundred times. He scuffs his shoes on the pavement. 'It was worth it, I suppose,' he says.

He has to swear he'll keep quiet about our walk because if Aunty finds out she'll go up the wall. We follow one of the narrow back-roads, hands dangling by our sides so they accidentally touch now and then. His is warm and a bit sticky. At one point he tries to hold mine but misses and has to pretend he was only adjusting his cuffs. The town disappears. Our quiet road is lined with bushes and leads steadily uphill. On the other side of the bushes are small yellow quarries and steep banks which become thick with trees. Climbing the stile, we follow a footpath criss-crossed by shadows. He's telling me he has dreams, hundreds of dreams, and that his latest dream is me. Shyness stops his throat working properly and he must keep swallowing. For years and years he's had the feeling he won't turn out to be just another boy. By the bed he keeps a book with his name on the front and every night he writes down his dreams and his strange feelings. At the back there's a map showing The Road To Happiness. At the moment he's moved only an inch from the bottom of the page.

'Love is the Answer to everything,' he says. 'I've written about it in my book.' He wants me to say I'd like to look at it some day but I get the feeling that once a girl has seen his Book, she'll be his for ever more.

Coming out of the trees we reach a steep meadow at the foot of the pointed hilltop. Being dreamy, he waits for a moment, pokes his hands to the sky and looks up at the clump of fir trees standing in a circular wall at the very top. 'To think Queen Victoria's been up there,' he says. I can't see it somehow, but he insists. 'During the Jubilee,' he says impatiently, lowering his arms.

'What Jubilee?'

He laughs and repeats to himself under his breath, 'What Jubilee! I ask you.' All around us cows are tugging at grass and flicking their tails. We follow a sandy path covered in stones which winds from the meadow and zig-zags up the hill. I can't imagine Her Majesty panting up here in thick black robes. He says they had some kind of wooden chair to carry her on. Four courtiers at the front. Four at the back. 'She was small but very fat and weighed a ton,' he says. 'I've got a Book of Facts. It's all in there.' My feet keep slipping. We have to be careful because we don't want to get dirty. His mum's forever clouting him over the state of his trousers, he says. Towards the top of the hill I fall over because I've been trying to watch the sky at the same time as climbing. Whispering a pretend 'Oh dear,' he gives me his hand. Once the danger's past he still holds on. Against the circular wall is a green bench held together by smooth iron bolts. One of the slats is missing. Just in front of the bench a shallow groove has been worn in the grass by the swing of dreamers' shoes. Here, he tells me, the Queen decreed that a special table should be set up so the poorest townsfolk could have lunch. 'Pheasant and everything,' he says. We sit down. Wind hums among the fir trees. The earth smells of glistening windows and excitable birds. Taking off his anorak he wraps it round my shoulders. His arms are white and covered in goose pimples. A town of crawling houses, redbrick chimney stacks and triangular factory roofs sprawls into the distance. And there's the laundry wriggling in weekend steam, the covered swimming-pool and the woods over the far left where he swears he once saw a Hairy Man lumbering into a cave. He reported it to the police but they wouldn't listen, so he took the Constable's name and wrote to the newspaper but they wouldn't publish it. He'd imagined headlines like 'Recently Discovered Lifeform Threatens Infant School'. Fame was one of the resting places on his Road To Happiness. Come what may, he was going to have his name splashed across a front page. He wanted people to steady themselves against a wall and say, 'Oh my God, there's Granville Whatshisname, the boy Who.' He points out how like a watercolour the sky is today and then asks me if I've ever had a really good look at the bark of a tree. 'It can be quite stunning,' he says. The cold air's making my nose run but I don't want to get out my hanky in case he goes off me. The whole time I just sniff very carefully. Suddenly he puts an arm along the bench behind me and says 'Oh well,' as it slips and hangs upon my shoulders. He's leaning heavily against me so I turn round. His chin bumps my cheek. Set into the circular wall is a plaque explaining why the fir trees were planted, but it doesn't mention Queen Victoria. His teeth are chattering. He shifts his chin till our cheeks rest together. 'This is nice,' he says, though I'm getting neckache.

'It was one of the warmest days of the year, you know. So they say, she had to lie down in a hollow for a nap.'

'You're making all this up. Queens don't sleep on hills.'

'This one did. She was Of The People,' he says. There's no point arguing with his Book of Facts.

He kisses me without asking but doesn't move his lips. I can't breathe very well because my nose is blocked up through too much sniffing. It needs a good blow. Romance is hardly worth the effort. As he pulls away he says 'Love you' without looking at me.

'Oh,' I say.

We don't go out together long. Sometimes he smells of glue because he makes Airfix planes and hangs them from his bedroom ceiling on strings so he can do The Battle Of Britain after homework. There are often little red or green paint-marks on his fingernails. His dad's quite important and used to go up and down to London to work on adverts for the television. I'm to look out for the one with a tube of Gibbs SR in a block of ice because that was something to do with him.

In their back garden an old oak tree shades the summer-house where Granville keeps the home-made spears he uses to kill the frogs which hop around a piece of marshy grass by the pond. Having made a catch he lifts the frog on the end of the spear and watches carefully as yellow stuff oozes from the hole in its back.

151

Usually Granville's mum is a busy shape the other side of the French windows. Her hair's blue. She wears cream dresses even when she's making dinner. She calls Granville's dad 'My Husband' and won't come further than the edge of the patio without her clean green wellingtons.

At half-term the three of them decide they're going off to the seaside for a few days. Granville's dad must get away from the hustle and bustle of drawing boards; his mum's had enough of the kitchen to last her lifetime and Granville himself is always happy to take his book of dreams on an expedition. He wants me to go with him but I have to say no. All the time I've been seeing him Aunty thinks I've been with a girl from school. The day after they go away Granville drowns because he's daft enough to explore the sea and floats out too far on his lilo. People in helicopters search for him but there's nothing to be found but his red plastic hat. The local paper at last runs a story about him next to the gardening column and prints extracts from his book of dreams. A photo shows him scoring for the Colts. The headmaster sweeps into the hall on the first day back to school, puts his face into a grim position and asks us to bow our heads for two minutes. One of the older boys giggles in the first few seconds and has to write out a thousand times 'I Must Not Seek Amusement In The Misfortune Of Others'. A few days later a card arrives which has been delayed in the post. There are donkeys on the front wearing straw hats. Granville has written very small to get as many Facts in as possible. Apparently Queen Victoria had a nap there too. Aunty clips me round the ear when she finds out I've been lying to her. William comes especially without jellybabies to give me a good talking to.

'Being Truthful in all things,' he says, 'is one of the first steps towards cheering up the Lord.'

Sunday, 6.22am

Begin again, this time with a little less melancholy if you don't mind. Since five she's been reaching for tea instead of her pen, using the argument that her head aches just above the temples and that this morning darkness is a thing of whispers and indefinable movement. She dreamed of being pecked, Gregory, by gulls, crows, rooks and what have you; peckity peck. And having been pecked to wakefulness she found her husband with a map on his raised knees picking a less traditional route to Lyme Regis. We'll have a day out together, he said. It'll do us the World of Good. And now he's in the kitchen transferring the route he's chosen onto twenty-mile long pieces of paper with annotations for public conveniences and roadside cafés.

He feels she shouldn't have come out to the shed, would rather she hopped from room to room having orgasms in anticipation of the trip, and yet it's memories of himself he's after; memories of a Derek he recalls with a sense of regret though in reality he's just the same now as he was then, busy in his lumberjack dressing gown, making sandwiches, filling flasks, packing hammer and plastic bags, buffing his stout walking boots. If interviewed he would gaze into the middle distance and state that this will be the second trip he and his dear wife Kate have taken to that Jewel of the South Coast. The first was a week or so after their unexpected relationship began in the park one damp, muggy afternoon. Kate had been

153

curled on a bench with tears in her eyes; he had been jogging in an attempt to stamp out the melancholy which had developed since his first wife inexplicably ran off with a Muslim. To be honest, he'd been pissed as a parakeet and took advantage of the situation by feigning to stumble at Kate's feet. She looked down in awe, or was it nausea? He looked up. Tragedy began to take shape.

At that time she was a confused, vaguely qualified girl plumped up with unwanted information about *Moby-Dick* and the use of Symbols in Literature, spending her days in hollow disbelief. It seems I'll never see him again though we were so comfortable together. His absence frightens me. It's sad that a man should have light in his eyes but take flight nevertheless. Song means nothing to me. The park's grey, unholy. It's been raining heavily and seems to have been doing so since he – no, I shan't say it, he'd only claim emotional blackmail. Clouds lie in an unbroken sheet from one horizon to the next.

Kate waited for each moment. In whatever position she sat, she had the look of a girl abandoned; around her eyes hung traces of defiance, loneliness. She saw a young man wearing a black leather coat enter the public conveniences and come out ten minutes later with a tall, slackly dressed individual with sores around his mouth. There was little hope; the world was, is, about to go Whoosh. It had taken her all this time to realise she knew nothing of any value and that dreams, far from coming true, were only there to poke her in the eye once in a while. The slackly dressed individual had a Datsun Cherry with rust around its wheel-arches and a triangular KEEP YOUR DISTANCE sticker in the back window. Though she didn't yet know his name, Kate watched as Derek jogged down the path towards her, pissed and sorry for himself. Spotting, as men train themselves to, this grief-stricken girl on a wet bench, he pretended to stumble at her feet, mumbled the rehearsed words 'Oh you're a clumsy bugger' to himself and looked up at Kate, praying she'd look down. To Kate it was immediately apparent that this man's wife had run off with a Muslim and was currently enjoying Soixante-Huit in the back of some continental hardware store.

They skipped courtship. Derek jogged. Kate followed. It's easier to stumble into a relationship without thought than it is to climb out again, even with a great deal of it. In the first instance Derek was terribly attentive, pricking his ears for hours at a time while Kate related her romantic, ex-romantic situation; indeed, so tireless was his enthusiasm for her story she began to feel she had something of a Hero on her hands. Much later it became evident he'd been trying only to gain a foothold in her expectations. Overnight he became Husband-esque, requiring a full breakfast and someone to prepare it; within a month they were having sex and watching a lot of television, often simultaneously. Kate found herself in a kitchen stirring Oxtail Soup or cutting out coupons from the tops of Daz packets; from time to time she was to be seen wearing a plastic pinafore. Derek spent his days at a shop he'd recently opened in an attempt to become bankrupt even more quickly than he'd previously anticipated. Kate wandered from room to room as if she'd just woken up, married to one man yet thinking almost continuously of another she used to know and would like to know again, though the notion was too crazy for words. She composed poems; listened to records; went to the toilet; reorganised the cupboard at the top of the stairs; looked out at the empty road on empty Wednesdays. Oh, she remembered her old lover again and again and with such commitment on her bad days, it was almost literary. Maybe J had been a man in blue and nothing more.

Derek's at the kitchen window now, filling the kettle. We'll all have tea. Lyme Regis beckons. Gazing into the garden he sees nothing but his dim dream of bumping into Meryl Streep at last.

As Kate came across the lawn on her way to the shed this morning, Miss Wintle was on her patio again, tightly wrapped in a pink padded housecoat and sporting a fine Bow Bells hat. She was pouring water into the birdbath from a plastic measuring jug. Kate turned the key and stepped into the shed, faintly relieved as usual. Soon the fan heater whined as she

155

curled in the lap of earth and birds stitched the hems of dawn. Knowing she didn't have long to herself, Kate became irritable, tense, afraid she wouldn't come back, afraid she'd be imprisoned in an unfamiliar place. Often, longing is a case of not wanting this rather than dreaming of that.

Now she writes. Her husband prepares. Heathen cats stalk neighbouring gardens. No, don't bring any more cats into this, Kate, for God's sake. Miss Wintle is back in her house. Sometimes Kate looks through her shed window and is genuinely taken aback. It's as if the world, once colourful and twirling, has ground to a black and white standstill. She dreams repeatedly both night and day. Though the dreams are vague and unscripted they have in common the theme of dissatisfaction. She'd love to love and to be loved unbearably, yet her husband takes a scouring sponge and wipes tea-stains from the stainless steel sink top. The Tamils are up in arms. Mrs Thrupp believes Tamils are a kind of hamster.

Kate will eventually abandon *The Well of Loneliness*. There have been many problems since she undertook to read it. Presently she can't come to terms with the immense number of question marks it contains. As a buffer against this imminent loss, she has taken up with 'Jill' by Mr Larkin. She spotted it in The Wise Owl and was attracted by its cover. This being Mr Larkin's first novel she thought it might be free of the complexity he was later to adopt or be accused of. The opening seemed to indicate something simple, a source of comfort. A love-story, perhaps; an antidote to the anxiety of other Literature. Sadly, she's already becoming unhappy with it; from early on it has taken great determination to turn from one page to the next. Her unhappiness has nothing to do with language or style – simple in relative terms – but springs from what she has read of the main character, the student – see! she can't even remember his name! Anyway, she would hate to share a room at any University with him, as another character – Christopher Warren – has to. Of course, Christopher is no saint, but this other fellow, the Hero if you like, really gives her the creeps.

Kate writes as if it will save her life. Her husband sips tea from a Tony Jacklin mug. Daylight begins to invade her pages. Life goes Pom Tiddly Om Pom. Around her husband's neck – as if to remind her of his eagerness to leave for Lyme – hangs the Camera.

One must photograph Life at all costs. Snapshots have a happiness about them.

The Cobb, Lyme Regis

No sign of Meryl or the divine Mr Irons. Derek's in a bad humour firstly because a metal barrier prevents access to the end of the Cobb and secondly because I don't wish to hang onto his coat while he scours the shore for fossils. Beyond the barrier a number of mud-spattered lorries stand among two cranes, a pile-driver and a clay-brown portacabin with J. O'Connor painted on the side. The Cobb's being repaired and yet how dare they embark on such a Twentieth Century exercise when Derek's pilgrimage is so ancient, so sincere! The poor sea is a transparent, restless green flecked with ribbons of seaweed. Winds are light, variable. Derek, his corduroy trousers tucked into thick blue socks, holds out his forearms for balance as he picks his way across the rocks. Look down now as these uneasy waves splash and suck at pebbles. I'm greeted by a tall bearded fellow and his beautiful companion who moons just a few feet behind him, arms folded across a plum-coloured jumper. They both nod to this young girl sitting alone with her bag of papers and cheap blue pen who waits but doesn't wait for her fossilised husband. Hammers tap. Imagine! It's like a song. A lump of rock splits beautifully in two revealing the imprint of a 1980's Derek, perfectly deline-ated. Geologists gasp as the most senior amongst them says 'Ah, now. Here we have an exceptionally fine specimen. Very common but somewhat hounded in its time. Please note the clear impression of both Nose and Camera.'

Oh Kate, you've such an imagination and yet there's no

roaring queue of Geologists to fondle your outline. Surely you should be more renowned than you are. You can't go on being well-known only to Mrs Thrupp, the postman and maybe the blackened fellow in the slag hat who delivers the coal.

The beautiful woman is bored. The last thing she had in mind today was featuring in some crazy person's diary, but I must mark time somehow; put it all down. In front of Derek lies a deserted beach ending at a point where cliff, shore and sea meet. On a bleached fallen tree just around the headland, he first lost control, pushing his hand down the front of my jeans, snapping the button. He was looking not at me but at the angry blue sky as if searching for shellfish in the depths of a rockpool.

At the barrier the beautiful woman yawns and gazes out to sea, hoping to understand what will happen next. Beyond her and beyond the portacabin stands Golden Cap, a soft curl of beige cliff draped in green. Derek took me there in the latter stages of our first visit, spent his time throwing stones into the void. Holidaymakers on the beach far below were screaming as the sea rolled in to snap at their toes, yet they were such a long way below us, it was as if the screams had been disowned by them. Golden Cap was a fine place to sit and think of all those things which might have been. Maybe I was recalling an autumn walk with J through the fringes of a beech forest while church bells rang and deeply tanned leaves swung through twigs and branches to the richly decorated earth. Perhaps J was saying, 'It'll be hard to survive if you keep watching the world through autumn-coloured glasses.' Our shoes crackled. I made a note of the moment and promised myself never to forget. From a fogbank way out to sea a mythical horn bellowed then faded away, over and over, the gathered dead of the deep moaning in unison. Derek was grotesque against the glittering water, tippytoeing forward to watch as the stones he'd thrown struck the cliff face, dislodged other fragments and bounced towards the sand. 'Why don't you have a go?' he said. 'Because I don't want to,' said Kate, 'Huh! Don't want to!' said Derek. 'Keep the stones. Throw yourself over,' said Kate, now uncomfortable with the sun.

159

'Come on, hurry up,' says the beautiful woman to the tall bearded fellow who's just popped over the barrier to examine the machinery in which he obviously has some interest. 'I'll just Do the pile-driver then I'll be back,' he shouts. A seagull twists above the beautiful woman's head. It's crying, if that's what they do, seagulls. Oh aren't words the most exquisite fun. Like you order any in them put can you.

John Kemp. That's the name of the student in 'Jill'. If the late Mr Larkin will forgive the criticism from an unlearned romantic fan, 'John Kemp' sounds just the sort of name someone would make up to use in a novel. It has no flesh to it. I can't imagine a real one on the Cobb with a mortgage and halitosis. He's drawn as a very clever person who graduates from a working-class background to reach Oxford with a number of other clever persons, many of them Spiffing. At the moment John's getting into trouble and making rather a pig's ear of himself through ill-directed hero worship of old Christopher Warren who's something of a rogue – drinking too much, borrowing money he doesn't pay back, stuff like that. You don't have to have been in wartime Oxford to appreciate the book, but it would help. At every stair you're likely to come across someone who, later in life, will have a footnote number by their right ear having written tremendous novels or made a fine contribution to the Nation. Most of them have profundities on the tips of their tongues ready for the moment you bump into them on your way to dinner. Presumably Jill will turn up soon. When she does I hope she's like the girl on the front cover. I can't see that she'll be able to fall head-over-heels for Kemp unless she's neurotic herself and needs to mother him. He has no personality. No footnotes.

Derek's a black dot moving slowly through time. Soon he'll disappear. The beautiful woman and the bearded fellow walk back along the Cobb, now arm in arm. They are close to the place Louisa Musgrove fell; the place Tennyson came to see the place Louisa Musgrove fell; the place tourists flock to see the place Tennyson came to see the place Louisa Musgrove didn't fall because, lucky creature, she was only in a book after all. The narrow steps have a history all their own based on things which didn't happen.

The first time we came we walked to the end of the Cobb hand in hand pretending to be in love. The wind was up. Green sea heaved against the stonework, thrashing us with spray. Derek took a photo. I was hoping he'd slip into the water. The hand which had snapped my button now waggled during an explanation of Ozone. Romance was in the air, but not mine or his. So many fossils, taken on as the solution to a problem, end up an even greater problem themselves. There are those whose drowning would cause much distress, and others, like Derek and certain world leaders, of whom a dozen people might say 'Oh, poor souls' for the whole of the morning and then, in the afternoon, become consoled by the ironing or the chocolate mouths of crying children.

The park's hot. It was hot. It is hot. An ice-cream van parked at the Owl Street gate plays 'In An English Country Garden' or something very much like it. Each blue figure filtering through the main entrance could be him. Behind me mums and kids splash and laugh around the cloudy dog-stick scattered paddling pool. The sun's high in the sky, removing shadows from the blue grass. We're all in love, all of us, it's something we do on a Saturday afternoon while lunch goes down. At the exercise bars a muscular, balding man in yellow heaves himself up to his chin and yet Kate's lonely. It's an unfathomable loneliness, one which doesn't depend on the number of people around her. Pensioners gather on the bowling green, some glistening with mentholathum. Pipes are lit. Broad bums stoop as eyes examine the line of the jack. Kate waits, growing restless, hungry for something, anything to happen. It doesn't. It doesn't. Spotless houses sunbathe in evergreen. She looks left, right, up, down, forward, backwards. Diagonally. In her lap lies 'The Great Gatsby'. Yobbos roar down the tarmac paths on skateboards. She hates anyone who dares to laugh. J used to sit with her just here in between fuckings. She can sense the weight of his ghost beside her. Just yards away an old man feels himself through his trouser pockets as a woman shrugs off her dress and lies under the sun. Gatsby's in a pickle over Daisy. Daisy's married to an Oil man who no longer fills the house with flowers. And Nick Carraway's just the kind of man Kate would like to share her bench with since J won't come. He won't fucking come. He won't come. She hates those who've been impersonating him all summer. They've filled bookshops, supermarkets, buses; cackled along midnight streets; trudged through the park with bags of groceries; whistled; tickled girls in the shade of the holly tree.

His songs puff the netting in open windows.

Derek's disappeared altogether now, heading for Pinhay Bay I wouldn't wonder, in search of Tyrannosaurus Rex or masochistic naturists. He'll breathe in. Out. Clamp his boots from rock to rock. Throw pebbles into the sea. Jump up and down to make echoes against the cliff. Remember the bleached tree, his hand, my snapped button. Settling down against a rock to eat his sandwich, he'll reminisce about the day he settled down against the same rock and ate a similar sandwich. Ham, perhaps, whereas this is Cheese.

And here's a rainbow woman, tucked into the arm of another while a short-legged dog paddles and pants behind. The first woman's tall, very tall, with long dark hair cascading down the back of her coat; the second's slim and curly, wrapped uneasily in a black cloak. Kate stops writing as they move close to her; she's been dreaming, worrying about Lyme, wanting to describe it for the future but lacking the energy. Probably it's old enough to resent too many strangers, small enough to retain echoes of its former tranquillity. I have an old print at home: the seas are violent, threatening cottages on the Promenade. A woman's head pokes through an upstairs window, hair blowing across her face. The sky's dark, hanging down, veiling Golden Cap. I'd love to be captured by that print, to find myself rescued from the Cobb, taken home to my brown room where I'd light an oil lamp, write my diary. And oh what a diary it would be. But now I'm tired. I can only sit on thick stonework remarking on my lack of energy. The sun shines. My husband fucks rocks. More trees fall in the rain forests. Choppity Chop. Tap tap. Derek taps and dreams of Derek. The sun warms his winter back. He'll extract an ammonite, take it home, place it on the kitchen windowsill and touch it reverently each time he passes through. Such is Derek, such the wild world.

J, I could write you so many volumes of nonsense to bristle your backbone, make you cry, Georgie Porgy Pudding and Pie. All that, in thick leather covers for your shelves of reference. I'd begin, 'My dear J,' and end with 'yours insincerely'. Crack a long joke, knowing you wouldn't laugh. Let's begin again. Here is Lyme Regis, perhaps you can smell last year's candy floss, this year's sewage or the piquant sea air. People come on Sundays to wear down excessive dinners; so many of them, determined not to be regarded in the same light as those Trippers of summer who arrive in overweight coachloads to snoop around small corners of shingle. The likes of Derek can cheat if they have a mind, buying their fossils from the Fossil Shop, so aptly named. Read these volumes, J, with Elgar in the background; read them naked and, above all, Remember Me: my hips twisting in the dark, my fingernails wealing on your skin. Cups of coffee. Plum jam sandwiches. Remember how we sat, lap upon lap, saying little but secretly connected, you into me. Your fingers explored me though they'd done the same many times; the bones, crevices, patches of damp. Here, the rainbow woman laughs her head off. It rolls unceremoniously down the sloping Cobb and plops into the sea.

Occasionally you raised yourself and then sank further into me. Soon you stiffened and whispered oh my god Kate, I'm coming. Out of control, your right foot knocked over the coffee cup and a crisp delight filled your eyes as that strange liquid poured into me, dribbled down. More plum jam sandwiches. Then ginger beer, in homage to Enid Blyton perhaps.

You stood, yawned, twisted, scratched, looked in the mirror, smiled to and at yourself. It was the smile of a Hero, of someone complete, of a scruffy young devil with jam on his lips, of an insatiable lover who must kneel down by this girl and wipe his own seed from her thighs.

Monday, 5.08am

You often told me, J, that repeated efforts in a single direction would result in success of a kind, so here I go again, praying with fingers as fog smooches round our statue of Pan and the young liquidamber. A few minutes ago the bells of St Andrews chimed five and I felt remarkably glad to be here. There, a Classical beginning. Kate's no bundle of laughs and she's hardly what you'd call a modern girl, yet she's amused each day to find her difficult world in one piece and her expectations firm though mostly inexpressible.

A mile or so beyond Crewkerne the car seemed to roll beneath us. Derek, pulling off the road, found himself striking a gatepost or, as he would have it, a gatepost striking him. For a moment he couldn't figure out what had happened and repeatedly tapped the steering wheel with his fingers. Kate, ever the source of genuis, suggested he got out and had a look. He sneered. The problem turned out to be nothing more complicated than a puncture, just as he'd finally deduced, and yet the world itself had suddenly deflated. He crouched at the front of the car, rapped the bonnet with his fist. 'It's a nasty one alright,' he shouted. Then it was to the boot for the jack. Hands rummaged through rubbish. An owl sang twit twoo as it should. 'The jack's not here, for fuck's sake,' he screamed. 'Have you had it?' 'Oh yes,' Kate told him, 'I use it all the time in my preparations for shepherd's pie.' Derek, not the sort to be amused by problems of a mechanical nature, ordered Kate to remain locked in the car while he walked into Crewkerne for help. He was going to be a teensy bit of a hero for the time being. Kate did as she was told and locked him out. Alone for half an hour she listened to her favourite music and faithfully recalled one or two awesome moonlights with J.

Towards the end of 'Telegraph Road' he returned through the gloom with a jack under his arm and asked Kate if she'd be so kind as to vacate the car while he tackled the repair. Punctures are invariably Kate's fault. She wills them on. It was very cold. Kate said 'Fine', climbed from the car, sat on the farm gate and threw gravel at an old insecticide barrel lying sideways in the ploughed field. Fucks from Derek as he wound the jack handle and repeatedly scraped his knuckles on the ground. Then he couldn't undo the wheel nuts and proceeded to curse whoever tightened them last time. Kate hummed. Stars roamed the sky. 'It's always the bloody same,' said Derek, 'we have a nice day then Boom! everything goes haywire.' 'Boom,' said Kate to herself. She disliked Derek more than she would dislike a stranger; hated the pale strip of skin between hair and jacket, the outline of bum as the corduroy trousers stretched, those long unbitten nails. Ping! She scored three out of ten. Maybe one day J would lift her onto a similar gate and subdue her with his tongue. Imagination is the finest safety valve of them all as husbands fiddle with rubber in the precise dark. J does tend to luxuriate in Kate's thighs; he's spellbound by them, easing back his mouth to trace their whiteness to the knee. The spare wheel was on. Derek wound down the jack, repeatedly scraping his knuckles on the ground. Had Kate an Elastoplast in her bag? 'Oh dozens,' she said, climbing back into the car to play Billie Holiday whose sorrow soon yawned through the immediate vicinity. Derek stomped off towards Crewkerne with the jack but returned minutes later having worked out he could now take the car. Kate clapped. Billie sang 'Oh My Man I Love Him So, You'll Never Know', driving Derek wild because she's always so coloured, so unhappy. The Plough hung upside down from the firmament. Derek had a problem. 'Everyone knows,' he said, 'that if you're trying to contact a distant spaceship by radio, the signal takes ages to get there. But what if you open the radio channel and talk continuously from the moment the ship leaves Earth? What happens to your time lag then, eh?' He grinned to himself for having cocked a snoop at Einstein, probably. Kate was in one of those moods where a sudden inexplicable release of endorphins had made her world gorgeous and the prospects of romance infinitely variable. A kissable moon loomed among the trees. Derek pulled up at the jack-owner's house in a manner prescribed by the Highway Code. The splendid man with the alsatian invited us in for coffee because we must have been frozen. Derek accepted, taking Kate's hand. She looked down in astonishment. The handsome man was a liberal with a hall full of houseplants and a dog specially trained to look as if it was about to remove one's kneecaps. Kate smiled. This man was of the type with whom one could quite easily imagine having sexual adventures on the staircase. Derek and Kate were shown into a warm living room and offered a deep, old-fashioned sofa on which to sit. A fine shedless wife lounging in an armchair opposite lit a cigarette. She was wearing a short, tight, yellow skirt. Her legs were crossed. We exchanged pleasantries about Mrs Thatcher and the hardiness of feverfew while the man made coffee. Derek twiddled his fingers and gazed at the wife. The room was thick with Encyclopedias Of Gardening. Our conversation explored Life without car-jacks, the charms of Lyme Regis and night-scented stock. Tucked up beside the sofa, Margaret, the alsatian, waited for signs of violent manoeuvre from Derek who'd become a series of straight lines veering through a given space and intersecting an inch or so from the wife's white knickers. The man came in with a tray of coffee. He was called Andrew, by the way, and he was pleased to make our acquaintance. Kate wished to further her acquaintance with him horizontally in the semi-dark. His wife's name was Nicola, but we could call her Nikki if we wanted. Derek said he was Derek and This was Kate. The alsatian growled as Derek sugared his coffee. It knew an insect when it saw one and might pounce at any time. Ignoring protests from his wife, Andrew disappeared into another room

166

and returned with an album of photos. Now these were the daffodils which came up last spring. And this was how the garden looked when he and Nicola first moved in. ('You've done a grand job,' said Derek.) Here was Andrew scything down the worst of the weeds. In between the more horticultural prints, Nicola posed topless in Corfu. ('What a fine beach,' said Derek.) And this was a friend of Nicola's cousin delivering topsoil in his truck. It had taken Andrew a week to distribute it round the garden. ('A week!' said Derek.) Nicola relaxed by the moment, her legs uncrossing, falling open. Andrew wore white trainers, clean jeans and a university sweatshirt. He was a regular charmer whose legs might have looked rather nice wrapped round Kate's naked body. And finally, here was the front lawn a month after it was sown. Look, we could just make out the zig zags of cotton designed to keep away the damn birds. Nicola laughed at this. She wore no bra. Derek's extraterrestrial vision easily penetrated her blouse and nestled therein. He's a breast man though he prefers to catch glimpses of them rather than have them thrust in his face. Kate excused the deadness of her sentences and went to the bathroom, having had adequate instructions as to its location. It overflowed with shade-loving plants and books of literary criticism. Nicola used Sure deodorant; Andrew was into Brut and certain intimate body gels. The toilet itself was of an ancient kind with its cistern high on the wall, a long chain and a porcelain handle with PULL printed on it – an altogether noisy appliance guaranteed to let everyone know exactly what you'd been up to.

J must interfere with Kate as she stands at the sink cleaning her teeth. This irritates her one day, charms her the next. Lips brush her nakedness while fingers creep round to examine her warmest domains. In the mornings she's somewhat dry-skinned and goose-pimply, but he doesn't mind; he loves to bite and nuzzle her whether she cares or not. His expert finger has found its heaven and proceeds to twiddle there till she burns and dies.

Having reached the brink and tumbled down, a pink Kate returned to the living room and raised her eyebrows at Derek who shook his head in reply. He'd been examining hollyhocks on page four, ignoring, we hope, or at least adopting a mature attitude towards, the topless Nicola beside them. The person in question sprawled even further in her chair. The hem of her skirt rode up. Not simply a piece of Derek, but the whole of him became erect. We'd all become Chums. At the conclusion of coffee Andrew shook hands with Derek and Kate while Nicola struggled to her bare feet and straightened her skirt. Derek said, 'Goodbye. It was nice to meet you,' to her blouse, then, at the front door, unwittingly picked up the car-jack and began to take it down the path. Andrew hailed him in a friendly houseplant manner. Derek gazed at the jack in disbelief and cracked a joke about his absentmindedness. Finally we left, loaded with seeds for next season. Nicola waved from the window, her blouse transparent against the living-room light. 'See you again,' shouted Derek, knowing he wouldn't then whispered to me, 'They're a cracker of a couple, aren't they?' Billie Holiday was having a terrible life and singing 'Them There Eyes' all the better for it. Derek reckoned it would have been worth losing the ability to sing if she could have been happy instead. We argued about it.

Arriving home we had a tiresome crack at the preliminaries of sexual intercourse, inspired, perhaps, by a kind of helplessness on my part and the memory of Nicola on his. She had been the very substance of his dreams, a woman of satyric insolence with brown, unfamiliar thighs. After the first few minutes of disconnected foreplay his efforts fell through. He was worried about his future, he said, though you wouldn't have guessed it at the beginning when he stomped around the bedroom without clothes, clutching an erection, delaying the moment of contact with exhilarated wife-on-bed because he was so excited with himself. Then those concerns defeated him. Had his erection been compared to a fishing-rod, he was one moment a rugged adventurer on the banks of some Canadian rapid tackling an enormous salmon, the next day a boy in short trousers on a lazy summer's day reeling in a perch. His go went. He fell on the bed, pecked at my breasts for a few

168

disinterested seconds, then twisted over and admitted, in the hyperventilating dark, that he's having cashflow difficulties. The bank's on to him. Mr James, previously a kindly manager with a quaint line in pastel shirts, has turned into a carnivorous bastard. Derek's head was half-on, half-off the pillow. He was looking at the far wall, away from me, his broad white back just inches from my eyes. Mr James has given him a good talking to about the interest payments on the loan, which starved of sufficient trading credits, have pushed things to a limit. Derek's on the brink of financial ruin and has lost something of his standing at the bank, having suggested Mr James took a very long holiday in distant lands. Oh there's nothing wrong with his stock or anything like that. People just aren't going in as much as they used to. The American customers have disappeared altogether.

The dark yawned. Kate found her hand reaching round her husband's waist. Gradually he fell silent. Soon he was asleep. She fiddled in the dark for a while then turned on the light for another go at *The Well of Loneliness*. This time she was irritated by Ms Hall's attitude to animals. According to her, they have a tendency to think in good English and have made, at some time or another, a fairly detailed study of Philosophy. They deserve a book to themselves. The dog 'David' is a particularly bright individual; Kate's surprised he can bring himself to chase sticks or sniff round the lawn when he has all the qualities necessary to sign up at the Sorbonne. Meanwhile Derek regurgitated penniless dreams and chewed them over. As far as was possible, Kate slammed the pages of the paperback together and threw it to the floor, determined not to look at it again. The cistern gurgled. Many thousands of feet above the bedroom the occupants of a Jumbo tucked into crumbling hors d'oeuvres. Mr Burgess may have been with them. Kate tried 'Jill'. John Kemp had just woken up with a hangover and was finding it difficult to carry on with his work. The book is such that one must suspect Mr Larkin of autobiography. Kate was afraid Derek would one day get hold of her diary and realise just who he's married to: 'We had a tiresome crack at the preliminaries of sexual intercourse'. She worried herself to death about it – is truth good just because it's the truth? But that's what we did – had a crack at it. He came into the bedroom with two cups of hot milk, said 'Tara!' and before a sip was taken, hurled off his dressing gown and used the sacrament and secrecy of marriage to display his primeval talents. This was grass-roots stuff. A man, a penis and a woman; the first making the second sufficiently stiff to poke into the third. The third was amused, but kept a straight face.

Kate threw 'Jill' down. She was too tired. A car door slammed. She decided she was going to think about J but this wasn't as easy as she felt it ought to be. Her memories of him were suddenly in shreds. Did he or did he not say he'd love her for all time as he handed her the toast and marmalade?

Want a thing to have happened for long enough and it slips into memory and nestles there amongst everything else.

Hide and Seek

Uncle William hooks his arms round the back of my legs and
dangles me over the stream. The silver water slips upwards to
a cloudless sky as birds with beating wings fall from the trees.
I hear him call to Aunty who's on the bank eating a peach. He
says, 'Once a chap's had something like that done there's no
going back. You'll have to take me as I am. Anyway, I don't
know why you get so worked up. It was years ago. She's
probably half-dead by now.'

'Half-dead or not,' says Aunty, 'I want you to have it
Removed.'

Blood throbs in my ears. The striped picnic dress has fallen
round my armpits. Bees, as bees will, mumble among dozens
of small pink blooms. Aunty seems to remember reading
something about a skin clinic where you can have that sort of
operation, but by now Uncle William's losing interest. My legs
are aching. He's standing on a log, pointing out that certain
death lies six feet below me and what do I think of that, eh?
He has a good view of my knickers. The ones with the giraffe.
I'm swinging slightly. The sky cups and curves. A green world
hums with wind in leaves.

'They just take slices of bum,' says Aunty, 'to replace the bits
cut away from your knuckles. Nothing could be simpler.'

Uncle William isn't convinced. 'If you think I'm having any
bum on my hand then you're mistaken,' he says.

'Well, that's where you've got most to spare,' says Aunty,
pleased with herself. 'It's quite clean and safe. After all, it's

171

your bum, nobody else's.'

William tsssks, shuffles sideways to the end of the log, then lowers me into the meadow.

'Jenny came from Singapore,' he says. 'You know how things are when you're abroad. We all did the same. Old Jimmy Pearce had an eagle on his back.'

'Never mind Old Jimmy Pearce,' says Aunty, waggling her peach, 'it's undignified.'

Uncle William looks down at me, his legs apart. It's a curiously long way from one side of him to the other. Running his hands through the grass, he gathers seeds to sprinkle in my hair. Aunty brushes them off. She can't be doing with Mess. Her chin's shining with peach juice so Uncle William chases her in a weak game of tag, hoping to have a lick or two.

'Remember my ankles, you Devil,' she squeals.

The meadow's deep with sun and buttercups. A man with white whiskers and a large gun dips behind the fat hedgerow. Aunty's repeatedly tickled by the twitter of unseen larks and kneels in the grass with a palm tucked behind her ear. Uncle William's plumpest white shirt has a frayed collar and moons of damp in the armpits. A pair of tight green and yellow braces stretch from the back of his trousers to the front, making them crease between the legs and hang above his shoes. Recently he's been clearing the fluff from his turn-ups. He drags me to my feet, wraps his arm round me and squeezes me against his shirt. It smells of fish. Those yellow fillets on the fishmonger's white slab. Thick fingers play with the lumps of bone down the middle of my back. 'She'll be quite a girl, one day,' he says, gripping my wrists and shuffling round in a tight circle. My shoes drag through the grass for a moment then rise up. The world and Aunty become a colourful streak.

'Oh stop it, for goodness sake,' she says. 'She's had cream and God knows what.'

Cream. Apricot jam. Scones. Lemonade. Cheese and Onion crisps. A lucky bag. Earlier with feet and fingers linked, we stood heads down round the tartan blanket while Uncle William said Grace. He thanked God for the food, for the warm sunshine, the skylarks, buttercups and for Aunty in particular, then moved his foot to crush a wasp crawling too near the butter.

'Got the bugger,' he said.

'William!' said Aunty, aghast.

Aghast.

'It's in such an obvious place, that's the trouble,' says Aunty, feeling her ankles.

'You must have noticed the butcher gawping at it the other day.'

Uncle William stops spinning, tells her she worries too much over nothing. Does it matter what the butcher thinks? Or anyone else for that matter?

'Well, yes, it does,' says Aunty with difficulty. She spits the peach stone into her hand and throws it away. Uncle William sighs. Romance isn't the easiest thing in the world when you once had a girl in every port. Slapping and bouncing his bum into the grass, he reaches over and takes hold of my leg just below the knee 'Get out of that,' he says.

'Look! Your hand goes nearly all the way round,' roars Aunty.

Uncle William tsssks once more. 'She's at that age,' he says.

The stream glistens and sings. Along the edges of the field stand busy hedgerows and forests of cow parsley. Uncle William suggests a game of hide and seek which he hasn't played Oh! for years and years. His chin becomes over-excited. Without waiting for anyone to agree with him, he wants to know who'll be It. Aunty tells him he should be It because it was his daft idea, so we wander off to hide while he closes his eyes and counts to a hundred. I climb the gate and run into the trees. Sometimes in summer my legs are as light as the wind and it's as if I could follow those wandering pathways for the rest of my life. Pools of shadow hang amongst the green stones and clumps of fern; the trees are old and tired; some are being smothered in thick vine. I run and run till I can hardly breathe. Birds sing out of sight high above me. I'm hoping to reach a darkness over there, but here's Uncle William crying out, feet thumping the humus and pine needles, a belly bounding with him. Catching me up, he takes me by the shoulders saying, what on earth do I think I'm doing and one of these days he's going to give me such a hiding, so help him God. His fat hand rubs the back of my leg then crawls to my knickers, squeezing and tickling as it comes. I'm a cheat. What's the point in having games if no-one follows the rules? His hand's sticky now, but cheerful in its own way as it slips with a giggle between elastic and skin. I must do just as I'm told otherwise I'll grow into a Delin Quent. Then Aunty announces herself with a snap of limping twigs. She shouts 'Yoo Hoo. Yoo Hoo,' before reminding me loudly of all she's said in the past about going too far on my own. Uncle William removes his hand and uses it to slap my leg. 'One day,' calls Aunty, 'you're going to come across one of those Devils from the *News Of The World* and it'll serve you right.'

By the time we reach the safety of the picnic blanket, she can't be bothered to play another game and takes out her knitting. She's doing Uncle William a magnificent jumper for the winter. Now and then she makes him stand to attention so she can measure what she's done so far against his curved front. There are still two or three inches to go. He's bored, wanders on his own to the trees and back, kicking off the dandelion heads. Then he stands beside us waggling his hands in his pockets till Aunty points at the grass and makes him lie down. A cloud of seagulls flying low casts a brief shadow the length of his legs and belly. He's tickled to death but soon his humour fades and he simply must have another game, Aunty or no Aunty.

'No Aunty,' says Aunty.

This time it's his turn to hide. I reach one hundred and twenty seven in my count before I'm kicked in the ribs by a marigold slipper and warned not to spoil his Fun. 'Men like to have a lark as much as little girls,' says Aunty, who then clears her throat and begins a hymn.

After a few minutes I find Uncle William crouching in a ditch at the edge of the field. As he stands I notice a damp patch on the front of his trousers. 'Look,' he says. 'I don't think we'll carry on with this game. It's too hot. I'm worn out. Tell Aunty I'm going for a stroll by myself.'

Back at the blanket, Aunty taps my hand. 'I expect he just wants a few quiet words with the Lord,' she says.

While pouring some lemonade for me, she carries on with another verse of 'Now Thank We All Our God'.

Thursday 1.08pm, The Wimpy

Then imagines herself in the department store riding escala-
tors, listening to 'Good King Wenceslas', having a grand day,
being the teeniest bit flushed, amusing. Mums all over the
place, milling and giggling at the perfume counters, dabbing
free samples of Eau De Nuit on wrists, behind ears; thumbing
through Johnny Mathis in the record department, remembering fingers, moonlit dinners, a bow tie maybe; winding
clockwork trains while bored youngsters vanish to have fun.
Hundreds of mums, and all of them fertilised at one time or
another, mums with rings, mums with more babies stuffed up
their jumpers, mums whose toddlers steal crisps from the
snack shelves. Each neat Sales Assistant has a loop of tinsel
round her hair. Father Christmas creeps scarlet and guilty
from the toilets, adjusting his belt. I'll not buy gifts for anyone,
she whispers. A brief shower crackles against the skylight while
warm Mediterranean air flows through vents in the ceiling.
Good King Wenceslas looks out, too cheery by half, and Kate
moons around with no intentions other than to imagine the
type of card she'd buy J if she knew where he lived and could
pluck up courage. There are cards of glitter, holly and robins
for unfussy grandmothers about to die; cards of semi-naked
men in tight jeans and body oil; cards composed of elephant
puns; cards of red lips, cute bottoms, impossible breasts; cards
with I Love You printed inside; cards with nothing inside so
imaginative lovers can write 'I Love You' in them.

She shivers. Dozens of dreamers stoop over the card shelves

176

to find an original message. Nowhere is there one saying 'Thanks Awfully for Screwing Up My Life', so Kate wanders from cards to electrical appliances and from electrical appliances to books. She's dying for a wee but, having been here Frequently in the course of her married life, knows for a fact there's no lock on the toilet door and hasn't the energy right now to sit there with one leg outstretched to keep it shut. Mums might giggle or anything.

Books is crowded. David Attenborough has come to sign copies of his latest creaturely volume. Mums hum, queue and wait. A chimp has been brought from the zoo to add zest. The man looking after it has ZOO stitched on his breast pocket. Kate's stuffed-up, tired, dissatisfied. She woke too late and ruined her routine; the shed snoozed in frost. She wants love and looks for a book. Now and then a loudspeaker goes Ping Pong and asks Mr Churchill to go from Menswear to Gardening or from Gardening to China and Cutlery. He's constantly required where he isn't. Each time the loudspeaker begins, the carols pause. It seems to Kate that the whole of life is geared to the idea that your lover hasn't vanished and that you're an avid fan of Useless Things. Perhaps he's here somewhere, behaving as a legend should, gazing at the card he'd send if *he* knew where *she* lived. These days mooners can simply lose track of each other in the glare of the heavens. Without doubt he'd be most attracted to the elephant puns – footprints in the butter and what have you.

Mr Attenborough is dressed for the Galapagos Islands.

Kate's wasted. A tombstone hangs between now and Glory: a simple tombstone saying 'She Would Have Come To Grips With The Whole Thing If She'd Had More Time'. Now she has this urge to wait in the Attenborough queue to see what he'll do if she hasn't bought a book. Wildlife's so expensive. He'd probably defend this on the basis that, since they've been chatting, another strain of Marmoset has become extinct. And there are balloons too: balloons tied to pushchairs, pinned in all the corners, balloons grappled with by sticky kids or hanging in posh bunches to advertise Financial Services.

Unlock your capital NOW. Kate's sad but quite enjoys it, though you've got to be careful when you're mooning that no-one from the government spots it and puts you onto a Training Scheme for those without Hope. Plumbing, most probably. If you're going to resent Mankind for a lack of opportunity, you may as well fix a few leaky taps at the same time.

She turns away, hurries through Lingerie, takes the down escalator, pushes through a door marked NO EXIT through which more mums are pushing in, and emerges onto the concourse which happens to be packed with strangers. She's developing a headache from so much concentrated Genius. The sun comes out, gilding plumes of grey cloud. She fiddles in her bag and takes a couple of Anadin. Apart from anything else they help to keep your blood thin and the idea of thin blood is always more attractive when one considers the size of the tubes through which it is pumped. The echo of shoes fills the modern complex. Here the Germans dropped bombs. Over there, beneath the fruit market, lies the site of an old burial ground. She's seen it all, on those photos of the old days. Bombs levelled drapers and trams and hat shops and men in boaters and horses and children with hoops. From the devastation, stores rose like weeds. People began to buy Do It Yourself greenhouses and bunches of plastic chrysanthemums. Now, across the sky and behind every mock-snow-covered window hang strings of coloured lights. She loves him – it's a phrase arising from the hullaballoo. By the sweet shop a man dressed as a town crier and shaking a wooden reindeer collects cash for the less fortunate children of the city while those not qualifying scream and wave from a carousel, their mums sliding by. Cold mums. Irritable mums, their children waving from fire-engines, police-cars, grounded space-shuttles. Suddenly there are an awful number of hyphens. If only he could see her searching for him he'd surely be touched or maybe he'd think she was turning into a fool all over again. She slips into the Wimpy while the going's good. Through this very spot wound a cobbled alley of ill-repute. She takes out paper. It's such a laugh, this J business; so much energy wasted on a young man's innocence, indifference. Wide-eyed children and Special K dads sneak chips and beefburgers while mum's at the British Home Stores trying on cotton nighties. A prostitute called Henrietta Thompson was hacked to death just yards away and the more sensitive listen to her moans in the darkness. Kate may buy something small for Derek after all as an apology for those aspects of herself she enjoys rather more than all the other, more predictable ones – her scrambled egg, for example, envied nationwide. She's stuck in the centre of town at a napkin-strewn table. It seemed a good idea but now she longs to be alone; longs for crazy things like the drone of biplanes through a summer sky, the whirl of lawnmowers, the scent of lilac, the perfume of grass after heavy rain.

She yawns from head to toe. Her pen can't be bothered. This coffee's cold. She would love to see him in order to ignore him; hates the cheery crowds who tumble past the window, not one of them familiar or noticing her.

Wednesday, 5.48am

Fingers, ink and an eye for the absurdities of the common-place. Dreams; a sprinkling of amours gone wrong; roadways, hedgerows, your mouth; theme tunes, cold December after-noons, rooms, your eye, eyes, whispers; your shadow in the park. Books; a glance at paragraphs, the glance returned; lovers your authors, authors your lovers; rust and yellow leaves on the shivering liquidamber. Patience; a few self-indulgent prayers to false gods; a well-polished mirror; the lunacy to begin and begin again; pain subdued, enflamed by frequent examination of the facts, the lies, the fictions, the rumours.

In the preface to his collection of old photos, a local historian claims that flowers quickly grew to beautify the ruins of those homes and holy places destroyed by warfare. Driven on by this outrage against sanctity, roots formed, shoots forced a way through rubble, charred wood and fragments of skin, finally breaking into daylight to bloom as a symbol to those wicked Huns in spotter planes who'd then know exactly what they were up against – foxgloves, pansies, rose-bay willowherb: the stubbornness of British foliage. A quiet miracle, claims the historian. Happy coincidence, says Catherine.

She ran down the library steps to meet me, almost knocking over a paperman who was leaning against the railings, counting change, yelling headlines. I was in a halfworld of sleep and shadows; the simplest movements bothered my eyes; the city had the shakes. Taking my arm, Catherine pulled me through the Norman arch into the Bishop's Courtyard. She seemed not to notice the cold or the sharp stars crackling through the sky, but hurried on ahead, skipping at intervals or taking hold of the Victorian streetlamps and swinging herself round. She was glad to be out of the library, couldn't have stood the fluorescent tubes, the dry central heating, the slither of covers or snap of pages a moment longer. As she swung, a member of the clergy crunched along the Bishop's beige drive, a bottle under his arm. Bathed in spotlights, the cathedral walls looked yellow. Hymns sounded within. Wagging her arms as if to become airborne, Catherine suddenly raced along the pavement on tiptoe, acting the goat. Lamps shone. Men you'd hardly think it of lingered in bushes or drummed fingers on walls within whistling distance of the public toilets.

At the waterfront she hung her arm round my shoulders and was daring me to parade with her through the ranks of buskers, beggers, charmers, diners, howlers. The night, in anticipation of Christmas, glowed and crooned with the scent of roasting chestnuts. A worn moon wobbled at the bottom of the harbour. Another party was in progress on the red nightclub ship. Catherine's voice was sweet, softened, comforting. At a spot she'd previously decided on, she invited me to sit at the water's edge and knelt behind me, looping her arms around my neck. Night slapped against stone, scattering cups of neon, moonlight.

'Am I in this Diary thing then?' she asked.

'Oh, hardly at all,' said Kate. In partial darkness it's easy to love hands, anyone's hands; the squeeze of a coat against your coat; the smell of hair and breath; significant insignificant silences.

'Personally, I think I should star in it. After all, where would you be without me?'

'I'll see if I can stick you in a bit more,' replied Kate, yawning.

Now a chin rested on my head. Cold hands rubbed my cheeks.

'You're freezing too,' she said.

So J leads me up the gangplank into the strobe-lit hold. It's a Gatsby night for all third years. We're the only ones not dressed in appropriate costume yet he believes I'm magical all the same and tells me so. Magical: a conjuring trick of chromosomes. He takes his time ordering the drinks because he wants to avoid the Charleston. Catherine's dolled up in a long white tennis dress and loops of gaudy beads. She's teasing a man with ginger hair who's decided to have a crack at Malcolm Lowry for his special study despite the advice he's been given by numerous tutors. He tells her Mr Lowry has become widely admired now he's dead.

'I think I'd admire you in similar circumstances,' says Catherine. The Ginger Man laughs. This is charm at its most renowned. She tells him she's tried 'Under The Volcano' more than once but has never reached page two. The man's disappointed. If she's to get anywhere at all she must persist. She says, 'Oh, must I really?' The fool hasn't caught on yet. Thinks of her as a traditional woman.

In solitude J will push me along the carpet, fucking me with his tongue, burning his knees on the nylon pile, but in the company of romantic Carraways and platinum flappers he's extraordinarily shy and polite, asking if I'd care for another drink then despairing of how far south the jet-stream has been this summer. He's a laugh and a half. Familiar faces bounce through the illuminations, hoping to attract other familiar faces bouncing adjacent to them. Degrees are discussed, rebels praised, monotonous tutors condemned for their loss of spirit. The Ginger Man has a wordprocessor because his mum has won the premium bonds and now he gets an average of five percent above his previous marks. 'Oh, how super,' says Catherine. Ginger grins. J juggles peanuts.

Her hands, slipping from my cheeks, came to rest on my legs and consoled me there. In my hair her chin was brushing from side to side. Perhaps I'd fallen into another world. She hummed. A lullaby or something. Whether she'd met the bear the night before or not, I couldn't quite decide. You never know with Catherine. She looks full-time as if there's some intrigue taking place others don't know of or understand. As much as I'd like it to be otherwise, life rarely has any meaning unless you can make up a little here and there. She kissed my neck, making me shrug. I wondered at my diary. Where on earth was the more acceptable information such as 'Met Cecelia for Canapes' or 'Don't Forget Haddock'? I shivered as her lips brushed my ear; my hands were warm and damp, my stomach turned. We seemed to be waiting for the big day; for the moment memory reaches saturation point and life begins all over again.

J helps me back onto the quay. Having had a pleasant time he's now in one of his famous good moods, bright as a button and overwhelmed by the fine histories he's creating. He looks proudly at the stars, the dark water, my face. Walks sideways. Scratches his wrist. Explains himself. Catherine has decided to stay on board with Ginger who, as we were leaving, was losing his soul to her trickery. J's footsteps are gritty because he's worn his favourite leather shoes; and though he blossoms with confidence it becomes clear that without a woman he is nothing at all. Back home we have an argument over hormones, sit naked in opposite chairs trying to score in a point of order already forgotten. If I do so-and-so he's leaving. If I don't do so-and-so he's leaving. He's had enough of the games women play and seeks simplicity. Our clothes are all over the floor. He ducks just in time to avoid being struck on the cheek by 'Catcher in the Rye'.

Catherine was in tears but wouldn't say why. Just pulled me to my feet without warning and took me to the city centre where crowds were gathering to gawp at the pantomime stars who'd been placed behind aluminium railings as a publicity stunt. Children greeted familiar television personalities. Familiar television personalities greeted children. The principal boy slapped her thighs. A dad at the back of the crowd searched anxiously for Lionel Blair. We were welcomed by the Lord Mayor to this fine occasion. Mums clapped. Those generous Norwegians had given the city yet another Christmas tree as yet another token of friendship. 'Though they can't hear us,' called the Mayor through loudspeakers, 'let's give them a hearty cheer.' The crowd, with the exception of Catherine and

183

a few drunks, did as they were asked.

One of the few solutions is to make love, drive the argument away, reinstate a sense of togetherness. Even so, there's a touch of violence involved. He attempts to destroy my body rather than bring it to life; abandons any softness inspired by Gatsby and whispers certain obscenities. His penetration of me is a punishment, his grip, an incarceration. He bites my shoulders, drawing blood. I claw his back. For half an hour or more we hate each other. He fucks me, kills me, exhausts himself. Even his I Love You's are lies, threats. He pumps, bites, slaps, examines with wet fingers the movement of himself into me and out of me. My head slides over the pillow and is squeezed against the bed-rail. Side One of Roberta Flack comes to an end. I'm to wait where I am while he turns over the fucking record. He must have a background – a melancholy voice, strings, hopefully a saxophone. Returning to the bed and having redeployed himself with his own angry fingers, he twists me round onto my knees but comes unexpectedly before he can re-introduce himself. His warmth runs down my leg. His anger fades. Remembering he has a task to complete, he wipes the semen away with his fingers and pushes them into me. Beads of sweat roll down his chest. He's sorry, so fucking sorry, as he pushes and twists his hand, but then he begins to cry. The blood on my shoulders confuses him. Tearing a sheet of tissue from a roll at the bedside, he dabs gently at my wounds, apologising again.

In the dark we lie close trying to recall the name of a particular dandy in 'Hamlet'. My shoulders sting. I'm still waiting for J to accomplish me, but he's too numb and too sorry and too finished with me for the time being. He thinks the name we're looking for sounds something like a fruit. This and other items of romance invade the scented room.

Sunday, 2.23pm, The Log, Abbot Woods

In the weak light of dawn you appeared innocent and unshakeable; knew more about life, about novels, about me than you would later on. And as your face came awake, it seemed extraordinarily beautiful. Sensing a new day, your hands would set about their task, ignoring lazy protestations on my part or yours; the first sweet touch of thigh or lip, the first reminder. The morning loomed large and though I could still feel the wriggle of the previous night's pleasure, pieces of me remained not quite satisfied. Your skin a warm brown, your hair a mess, your mouth opening to kiss me. A deeper yellow soon squeezed against the curtains; our legs would find some excuse to tangle together. Your lips were soft; mine sore, always sore. The moment you touched me I wanted you again regardless of how many reasons to do otherwise rushed to my head. The room was buoyant, fragrant with yesterday's candles. Over a cigarette we'd work to convince ourselves that all this had something to do with reality; in a brightening mood you'd come up with half-remembered poems, brief extracts of dialogue from *Midnight Cowboy* or *The Graduate* or moments of your boyhood which had signified all, like the first chapter of some turgid Russian novel. Dawn was an increase in footsteps across the ceiling, sudden radio conversations, a racing heart, the tinkles of distant music. Though we'd ceased being naked in any sense a long time before, my hand on your waist was a hand on a dream. Occasionally we'd move hands to explore another piece. Early morning dogs snapped through the park. A slither of letters slapped onto the mat upstairs. Most of all we'd enjoy the sense of body against body, softness against softness; the familiarity of movement and reaction. Stubbing out your cigarette before it was finished, you'd disappear beneath the bedclothes to begin your kissing, touching. Here were my toes in your mouth, your fingers stroking the backs of my legs, your hair pushing between my thighs. Your tongue. Here were birds; the indefinable scents of a summer morning, the journey into memory where unremarkable moments became all important; a sad loss. Here were my hands pushing into your hair, my body half-exposed to the diffused sunlight. The problem of love was having to invent so much of you; here were your words of a slightly duplicitous nature; indefinite worries on Kate's part that your travels about her rarely included her deepest opinions. Here be Tygers, more cigarettes, a cup of grateful coffee, the smell of sweat forgiven since it belonged to both of us.

It's afternoon. The wood's bone-quiet and lonely. From here many leaf-covered pathways creep round unwalked corners of naked trees. This particular fallen log is famous because we sat here, yet that's ridiculous in a world in which a woman must fight for survival against a glut of similar sentiments. This log's not famous, especially in wintertime. I'm going to sneeze – can you sense the immediacy of this outdoor piece? – No, I'm not going to sneeze. I was making it up just to show you how easy it would be to lie. I could be in a cabin in the Cairngorms for all you know. I sit here alone because I used to sit here with you. I wish we'd taken a photograph. Love's a useful thing if it can stop a person worrying about their mortality or can direct their attention from Doom to the softness or otherwise of a boiled egg, the quality of toes when tipped with pink nail-varnish. You sat right here (she slaps the wood). It was your idea, springing up in bed like a child, saying 'Let's go for a walk in Nightjar Valley.' Anyone listening would have been sick to death of us. 'When are these two going to mention The World?' they'd have asked. The World – Afghanistan, acid rain, Africans, the dwindling number of Animals? You

186

screwed up your face, not knowing the answer. The World was mostly a soft bed, an open mouth, a series of meaningless words tossed one to the other. This log, though not famous, is certainly a reference point for memories.

The whole day was yellow and very warm. You were scruffy but had stopped caring. We'd made love so often, you could hardly walk. We sat on this log and stared across the Gorge to the tree-lined streets of Clifton. You weren't really interested in my description of the gibbet at the end of Pembroke Road from which offenders used to dangle being pecked at by birds, or my tales of the highwaymen who once ruled the untamed Downs. Love's too time-consuming to make room for history.

I came here secretly because Derek had said his piece about the sickness of women and went round the back of the house with hammer, nails and tape-measure to embark on this business of being a remarkable husband. I followed the river into town then climbed the old zig-zag path up the cliff to the Downs. I'd promised myself I'd turn back at the bridge but a sense of energy had disengaged my concerns. This whole thing about time and distance and deadlines was crazy after all. From a bench by the Observatory I watched a group of clowns juggle coloured balls. There was some kind of fund-raising Carnival going on. Each clown was wearing a tall pink hat dotted with scarlet baubles. After a while I paid my fee and crossed the bridge, looking down at the cars sweeping along the dual-carriageway, wondering how bad love or lack of it has to become before you climb the rail and fall to the rocks. Stories are rife. Some suicides have taken a run-up; others have climbed into death more pensively, carefully removing their best coat or reading themselves a poem before their final act.

If you ever get it into your head to get up early or to walk into a wood just to have a go at some kind of Diary, don't give it up even for a short time because the guilt will disturb you or drive you insane. Life's like that. It runs smoothly enough till you make yourself an unreachable promise then beat yourself up for not fulfilling it. J, for example. A diary. Simple relationships. Happiness.

Since Friday night I've been completely mad. We had tea, Derek and I. Very nice it was too. He was reading the paper, eating a piece of sponge cake and rolling his toes. On the television was an American-made costume drama about the Civil War in which every soldier had blue hair and immaculate teeth. I was reading – or trying to read – a bit more of 'Jill'. Somehow I was always at the beginning of the same paragraph. The shed was a foreign land I didn't care to visit. Derek realised this and slipped into a husbandly happiness. He would conquer the cow yet, God help him. It had turned out that Jill wasn't going to be the person who came along and fell in love with John Kemp. I'd underestimated Mr Larkin. It was almost as if he'd expected my earlier reasoning and had changed everything around to teach me a lesson. Don't get comfortable with me, he kept saying. Don't get comfortable.

The room, the ornaments, the photos, the furniture, Derek – we were all fastened to the moment, frozen in time. I had nothing to say to him and nowhere to go except those places where escape is short-lived anyway. I longed for the shed yet couldn't go near it. A phrase popped into my head over and over: 'You're using up time just to be rid of it'. Derek, looking up from the paper, explained that Princess Anne had to attend a charity ball the following day and that the Queen and the Duke of Edinburgh were flying to Australia. I threw down 'Jill' and went for a bath. Using up time just to be rid of it; long, inconsequential days and nights. The mirror was steamed up. Kate took off her clothes with a sense of excitement. Why there's a remarkable body. And those legs! Oh my goodness me. The water wasn't quite hot enough. She lounged back with a cigarette, her head resting among the fronds of a fern. John Kemp made Jill up – that was the gist of the little bit she'd read, the reason she'd found herself reading it again and again. Made her up. The idea shook her. She had palpitations. The bathroom was dense with steam and smoke. She wanted something ridiculous to happen, but knew, because of her dreams, that most things would stay much the same till she died – the crack of muskets, Derek's toes, the domes of Yankee breast poking above low-cut blouses, the handsome men with broad chests, the advertisements for Mr Kipling's Exceedingly Good Cakes, Derek's mouth as it yawned to receive a hundredweight of sponge. She raised her leg to see if it looked like that of a lover. It turned out a leg, no more or less. There was another on the other side. A leg. And those, those were breasts. Rub a cold flannel over that particular part and you'd see some fireworks. Using up time, inventing rituals to help it pass less painfully. Touching herself was not quite the same as being touched. Days in, days out; the growing of plants, rooting them in spring, cutting them down in autumn then tossing blackened stems onto the compost heap. The walking and walking in uncertain sorrow, waiting for it to end or be ended. Monotonous snatches of sex. He would do this and that, kiss here, there, put that on this, waggle that, poke it in here. Using up time; the dawns and darks, the seasons, a dog yapping in the Gorge then yapping in the Gorge. Peeling potatoes. Thanking the postman. Fucking the milkman, pie-man, beggarman, thief. Glueing broken china. Answering the telephone. She rested her ankles either side of the bath. The tap dripped. A loofah rehearsed. She soaped warm folds between her baby legs, smoking all the while. His ghost pecked into her, using up time.

She was going to tell Derek. Bringing her tune to a grande finale, she dried herself quickly, dressed and wandered into the living room. Derek had finished his sponge. A clean-shaven man, home from the war, hugged a blonde wife to his wounded chest. He was called Nathaniel. Kate announced to Derek that she was using up time just to be rid of it. Her skin steamed. He peeped at her from behind the newspaper but said nothing. 'I'm committing suicide,' she explained, 'in a way no-one will ever detect.'

Then an advertisement for Sunsilk Shampoo. Derek went into the bathroom to check how many pills she had left out of the twenty-one. Finding only two he returned calm and victorious, though he understood nothing about it, nothing about women at all, nothing about Kate or anyone else, nothing about himself and nothing about the space he so unjustly occupies on earth. She wanted to drop the television out of the window; find a hammer and smash each piece of china; tip up the pine table and its four matching chairs; overthrow the fucking lot.

During the next hour or so the substance of Derek's opinion was reaffirmed. He cherishes his life and cherishes time. Cherishes the television, our ribbons of scarlet tinsel, the Christmas tree standing in its bed of green raffia, the modern gilt-framed prints of a nostalgic countryside, his slippers, the error of Kate's misfortune – cherishes it all and all.

The log's slippery with years of children clambering and lovers wasting time. Kate's too cold to do anything more. Besides, her diary's gone to pieces, lost all reason. Having been none too keen on it from the outset, she's abandoned any shred of chronology she may have had. Who needs it anyway?

Over The Hump

As a surprise for my next birthday, Uncle William chooses a
trip to the sea, but we're late leaving because he and Aunty
have been At It since dawn and she feels obliged to take a
bath.

'Sea air brings cheer to all God's creatures,' he says as we wait
in the living room. He beams, tweaks my cheek. 'Believe me,
it'll do you the world of good.' His new blue blazer with silver
buttons and cardboard hanky won't quite do up. He takes a
banana from the wooden fruitbowl, unpeels it, puts the longest
part into his mouth and offers me the rest. I shake my head.

'Fruit!' he exclaims.

'Fruit,' says Kate.

'Another of God's great gifts to Mankind. You won't go far
wrong with fruit.'

He's interrupted by an Aunty who sweeps and swoops in
from the bathroom, boasting of her new chrysanthemum
dress. Uncle William's thrilled to bits. For visits to the sea he
too likes to smarten himself up, putting aside his turned up
trousers in favour of what he calls Slacks, which are white and
even baggier. Aunty billows into the kitchen for the fishpaste
sandwiches, adjusting the photo of Uncle Jack on her way.
Uncle Jack, his pinstriped suit astride a five-bar gate in those
pre-pot belly days, smiles more broadly than for some months
as if sensing Victory's at hand.

We set off for Lady Bay. Uncle William has a grey Vauxhall

Standard by now and loves to boast of its generous leg and head room each time we climb in. He La La's the tune of 'Ten Green Bottles' hoping to get some kind of group Sing-Song going, but Aunty's embarrassed and wants to get on with her knitting. Besides, opening her mouth too much in a moving car makes her travel sick.

'Well perhaps Kate,' says Uncle William.

'Well perhaps not Kate,' says Kate.

Uncle William hides his disappointment by fiddling in his pocket for a fruit jelly. The world goes by. Have I read his copy of *The Pilgrim's Progress* yet? No, I haven't. Don't I think it's time I got round to it? Well, bits of me do and bits of me don't. Am I going to abandon this idleness in the near future? Probably not. The miles pass. There are hedgerows and people with forked walking sticks; charming little cafés where Aunty would like to stop one day on her way back from somewhere; policemen on bicycles; sheep.

Uncle William has been around. He tells us this as we wind along the lane leading to Lady Bay. Having been around, he doesn't need to fuss himself trying to park with everyone else down by the pier. He knows of this tiny cove at the end of the bay where hardly anyone goes. We drive on another mile or so, passing leafy churches and sea-dogs in bobble hats, then draw up in a lay-by beneath a copse of nut trees.

To reach the sea we have to wander in Indian file along a narrow path at the top of a low cliff, then climb down a flight of steps carved out of the rock. The last few are particularly slippery with weed so Uncle William takes Aunty's hand to guide her safely down. At the bottom she begins to mumble under her breath because the beach is covered in grey pebbles, many of them speckled with tar. Coal not Jack. Two young boys are tossing handfuls of the smaller ones into the sticky water for amusement. Traces of distress creep into the rouge on Aunty's cheeks. Trying to walk over a beach like this will do her ankles no good at all and she's sick of Uncle William not thinking these things through beforehand. Uncle William insists there weren't pebbles last time he came, just as there hadn't been a block of flats and the Lazee Dayz Gift Shop back on the clifftop.

'Someone must have put them here,' he says.

'Oh, most likely,' says Aunty at her finest. 'If I live to be a hundred I'll never understand how daft you can be sometimes.' From the name 'Lady Bay' she'd imagined a stretch of warm sand scattered with elderly ladies reading magazines and dreaming to the music of the sea. Uncle William shrugs and changes the subject by pointing out a nostalgic rock he remembers from years before. As a boy he spent long Sunday afternoons here amusing himself with a sherbet dab and a half a dozen 'Eagles'.

'I suppose,' echoes Aunty, folding her arms, 'you brought that Jenny woman here too.'

Uncle William smiles. 'Don't be silly,' he says. 'Singapore, remember?'

'   ,' says Aunty, unconvinced.

Eventually Uncle William has thought all he can about the sherbet dabs and guides us to a broad ledge at the bottom of the cliff where he wants us to eat our sandwiches. The young boys are now tipping an oil drum on its end at the tideline for target practice. Uncle William lays his hands on his knees and looks about the horizon.

'Just imagine. Coleridge came here and gazed out to sea just as we're doing.'

'Did he indeed?' says Aunty, creasing her lips. 'I don't suppose he had a tattoo.'

Uncle William begins to laugh but then his laugh trails away and is replaced by a cry of despair. Dropping from the ledge onto the pebbles and gripping a pointed rock, he takes a deep breath, stoops over and spews. Aunty slithers sideways so she won't be splashed. There's nothing worse than sick on your nylons. At a safe distance she puts down her sandwich and clenches her fist.

'What on earth's up with you now?' she asks.

Uncle William remains in his stooped position, spits the

remaining drips from his lips, then straightens up and takes another deep breath. Aunty and I lean sideways just in case. Though his chest seems to thump from the inside, Uncle William's smiling. 'Phew,' he says. As the beach begins to relax and another Ping! comes from the oil-drum, he lets go of the rock, throws back his head, wraps his arms round his belly then heaves himself forward to be sick again. This time it's a dark, evil-smelling liquid which strikes the pebbles with some force.

'Come on, give over,' says Aunty, shaking her head.

Amongst this freshest sick is a small dead fish which may have been there already. Its side has been pecked away by gulls and its eyes are missing. Uncle William straightens up once more, squeezes his fists to his ears and roars with pain.

'Perhaps he's getting one of his heads,' says Aunty. 'He gets them terrible, heads.'

Though she turns pink at the idea of creating a fuss, a man in green wellingtons who's been fishing from the headland is clambering towards us to see what's wrong. This time the dribbles of sick from Uncle William won't quite come to an end. They leave brown trails down his chin before splashing onto his new blazer. Aunty's growing angrier all the time, scooping up her half-eaten sandwich, putting it back into the plastic bag and offering me her arm so I can help her to her feet. We can say what we like about Uncle Jack, he was a smart man; put Aunty first above all things and, if he felt sick or was going to make a spectacle of himself, always found somewhere out-of-the-way to do it. Uncle William says 'Help me', or was it just a gurgle of fluid? Aunty's too busy brushing creases from her dress to pay much attention. As she steps from the ledge, Uncle William falls onto his knees moans for a moment, then bounces onto his belly amongst the pebbles, his mouth yawning and staying that way. Aunty huffs, adjusts her chest and crackles her way back to the steps. The man in boots comes to a standstill a few yards from Uncle William, leans forward on rubber toes and peers down.

'Christ,' he says.

Holding my hand he takes me back to Aunty, turning every

194

few paces to check on Uncle William, who's being mourned by an increasing number of seagulls. Aunty's tapping her fingers on a white lifebuoy, telling the pebble-boys that her husband was as right as rain when he came down these very steps just minutes before. The man in boots ruffles my hair then goes to find a telephone. Some sinful person looks at the cloud of screaming seagulls, calls out 'Congratulations, Kate,' and starts to applaud.

The Battered Wife

A car comes to an abrupt halt in the road. The engine dies. Karen Carpenter is summarily rejected in the midst of a Doo Bee Doo Bee Doo. The gate rattles. Shoes clump hurriedly from gate to back door. One's husband enters in an anguished mood once again because there have been very few customers and those who did bother to cross the shop's threshold were fiddlers, pensioners, old ladies who'd think about the dressing-table and come back next week when they'd had a word with Henry or Albert and measured the space in the alcove.

Kate's lounging around as usual, slumped at the kitchen table with coffee and a cigarette reading 'Jill'. Her husband feels it's time to dominate as, tradition says, the male of the species should. He tears the book from her hands and throws it to the floor. 'If you weren't so wrapped up in yourself and your daft books you might be able to help me,' he says. Kate, in one of those careless moods brought on by too many words and a deep fatigue, tells him that as far as she's concerned, his precious antique shop is nothing to do with her. It was his idea. He was the one who was going to make a killing and cock a snook at all those poor buggers on PAYE. Derek, fists pushed into his waist, expected this reply and tells her so. Has she ever considered who keeps her fed and watered, supplies her indirectly with tobacco, writing paper? No she hasn't and has no intention of doing so because it's evening and she's had a hard day. Besides, from the very first he's made a fuss about needing to be the breadwinner to bolster up his ego; has taken

196

pride in providing a financially secure environment in which she could pursue her own interests, such as they are. This tiny speech on Kate's part doesn't go down at all well. She should realise that circumstances have changed; should have taken some sort of initiative without being prompted. Do his tears mean nothing to her? Sensing danger, she picks up 'Jill', slips a bookmark between the pages, moves out of the kitchen and stands with her back to the fire in the living room. Enter Derek (general alarum; sound of cannon). Without thinking, she performs a curtsey then nods to an imagined audience with a single stiff finger poked to the underside of her chin. He slaps her across the face. The firelight is reflected in her eyes. Skin stings. The world has been getting the better of him for several months and the current prognosis for life in general and, more specifically, their marital relationship, isn't good. He slaps her again. She stumbles, knocking one of the pair of Staffordshire dogs from the mantelpiece. It falls slowly for some time then makes contact with the grate; a whole century of simplicity breaks into dozens of tiny pieces. Derek's shocked at himself; finally realises how it is so many Staffordshire dogs are brought into his shop without their twin. Kate follows the dog, clumps to the hearth, is pulled to her feet by a husband who'd prefer to forget he's just given a sizable donation to the cause of Women's Movement – hands on cheeks, all that – yet who continues to be verbally abusive. She's a fucking cow, a selfish bitch, oh, all kinds of animals suddenly. She slips into the kitchen for a dustpan and brush. He follows, thumping her on the back, proud and horrified, doing what he doesn't want to do, regretting every gift, every consideration, every fuck he's ever granted her. Women have come in a terrible series to castrate him. As she stoops to sweep the grate he strikes her once more. She's enjoying every moment – at least, that's what he's telling her; women love a good beating because it gives them *carte blanche* to storm off and . . . And what? He hasn't thought his sentence through, though it began really well and seemed set to reach a profound conclusion. She turns. There's blood on her lip. She can taste it. He stares at it for some time, balancing precariously at a point mid-way between pain and pleasure. Should he fetch a tissue or smack her in the teeth? 'There,' he says, 'you see what's happened now.' With difficulty he stalks towards the door, shouting, with little conviction, that he'll return when she's pulled herself together and realised just how much he does for her. She sweeps. Sweeps and beats and cleans. Offers to make sandwiches for the journey to his mum's. 'Who mentioned anything about my mother?' he asks, going out, coming in, going out. He comes in, hovers over her. As she turns with her pan of dog he holds her round the waist and – with an ease which gives due recommendation for physical fitness – picks her up, throws her to the sofa and punches her on the cheek. Of course, poor dog goes all over the place. Many hand-painted fragments here and there. Now she stings from head to toe, has time to wonder how it feels to be beaten to death because so far everything's fine – somewhat amusing. Meanwhile (exeunt Rag Tag and Bobtail) he's picking up the Victorian jug-and-basin set from the washstand. Remembering *The Perils of Pauline*, Kate raises her plump eyebrows and puts hand to mouth in surprise. With a smile of wickedness somehow manifesting itself in wavy lips, he tosses both jug and basin into the kitchen. She hears its sad disintegration on the tiled floor. Value of jug and basin: £45. Value of dogs as a pair: £90. God, what a profit we're not making here. 'And that's exactly what I think of you, my dear,' says Derek, rubbing his hands together. Now he's trying to adopt an assured caveman mood, combing his hair, putting on his coat, saluting the injured wife as he passes the sofa on his way to the door. Perhaps there's the slightest trace of panic in his eyes because he hasn't thought this through either. He hasn't packed; he's not sure whether the car keys are in his pocket or if he left them on the kitchen table; will his mum have enough spare pork chops? – he needs to find himself outside the house with everything he'll require to survive. There can be no coming back for underpants or his Rubik's Cube. He swallows. A delay at this point will mean defeat. He must hurry on his way regardless. Having crossed a certain boundary of behaviour, he decides the situation won't be made any worse if he comes over and gives Kate a hearty slap on the nose. She doesn't mind particularly. Each slap or thump or broken piece gives her a sound excuse for fantasy – J biting her breasts and suchlike. Adding a certain piquancy, her husband looms as if to say farewell, spits into her hair twice, then leaves. She can't stop laughing. She rings up Catherine who laughs with her.

Alone in bed she takes time out to think, to stretch her legs in whichever direction she chooses, to read the remainder of *The Well of Loneliness* however long it takes and regardless of how much it irritates her. After all, that's the way she's been taught. Just a dozen pages later her resolution falters. Being battered wears you out. She comes to the conclusion Radclyffe Hall's just not the kind of authoress who can console a girl last thing at night, especially if the girl has a thick lip and a photo of her ex hidden in knickers. Having, as it were, let herself down in this matter of literature, she doubts she'll ever finish it. In all probability it will join another dozen books on the special shelf where she keeps unfinished titles – *The Thief's Journal*, the omni-present *Cider With Rosie*, *The Tin Drum*, and, most unfinished of all *Under Western Eyes*.

And she misses him more and more; misses him till it becomes an illness far, far away inside her. He haunts her with his songs, his parables, his inexhaustible games and words. She misses him so completely she's sure he must lie awake himself and sense it. She loves her dream and will go on being selfish about it; will continue to nourish it. A hand or two about the head works wonders for the romantic spirit, for this sense of resolution. Fingers steal between her legs. She'd like to be with him for an hour or two to reassure herself she's not been telling lies. The bed's warm. She's as snug as a bug in a rug, remembering his hands. Hands carrying two white coffee cups from the counter in the bus-station snack bar; hands on knees as he gazes at a Sisley in the National Gallery; hands on mine, on me. She twists in bed. Then it's raining and he's making jokes about Gene Kelly, holding out the edges of his plastic cape, picking his way through mud and puddles. She's on the bank high above him. All afternoon he's been tailed by a stray dog. He throws sticks for it. Time after time the dog runs ahead, brings them back. There's fuck all in the world to bother Kate; she's a bit like the dog, chasing the sticks he throws, tail wagging. She watches from the bank as he lifts the dog over the gate and runs with it to the top of the hill. The bed's too big for her. She lies with legs and arms outstretched, grows unhappy, curls into a ball. Tomorrow she'll cast her fate to the winds, play Billie Holiday, tiptoe from kitchen to bathroom and from bathroom to bedroom without clothes.

At three she wakes to find her light still shining. She's heard or read somewhere that three's a good time to launch a war because people are at their lowest ebb and can be taken by surprise. She waits for it but there's only the wind through the trees, the growl of a solitary motorbike on the dual-carriageway and a faint continuous hum. As the moments tick by it's common to lie awake wondering how you came to be where you are and what daft things you said along the way; to examine those moments of indecision which changed things irrevocably; to regret the incapacities of spirit which others found so unmanageable but which are fine now, thank you. She hugs the pillow knowing it's just the kind of thing a fictional girl might do, but finding scraps of comfort in it anyway; a companionship, softness. She's tired but can't sleep. A genius with no audience. She considers for so long the idea of reading 'Jill' some more that on the edge of slumber she finds herself doing so, but the characters soon go haywire and she realises she's only dreaming after all. Books can drive you crazy, she decides.

Wednesday

Except for the reflections it carries, my glass is invisible. There. Started. Quite pathetically though. I couldn't decide whether to put 'Except for the reflections it carries, my glass is invisible' or 'My glass is invisible except for the reflections it carries'. Finally, I chose the first one, through tiredness rather than any grammatical pretensions. Besides, my glass *isn't* invisible except for the reflections it carries. I was making it up because I didn't want to mention the moon again. The moon must be sick to death of featuring so heavily in the diaries of those of a nervous disposition who long for Charm and other wasteful things. These days Kate's become derailed in her passions, lying on her back in a siding or on her side in a backing. Here's a toast to infidelity and to the gradual unravelling of those persons classed as highly strung. God, my hair's outrageous. Doctors once tested my palms for dampness and fiddled with cold stethoscopes between these breasts. Now, though she may pretend otherwise just for fun or in fear of seeming arrogant, Kate understands everything; can't be fooled; has her head screwed on; is sensitive to each moment, each nuance of living. This is her misfortune. No happy ignorance for her. A lack of perception would be bliss indeed. Incidentally, J, should you hear or read the word 'indeed' a great deal it indicates a certain financial superfluity or a gentle inebriation on the part of the speaker or writer. Maybe you're kissing shy girls under plastic mistletoe, regarding Kate as an undramatic paragraph in your fictional past. Snogging with them, one hand up their tickly jumpers. I'd like to rrrrip you apart, wipe you out, put an end to you, zap you – or is it double 'p'? Zapp? Batman has much to answer for. Robin's most probably gay, Tra La. At the first hint of Superheroism men must wear tights and a mask. Perhaps Batman and Robin smooch underground as Gotham City sleeps. Mast to mask. Thigh to thigh. Men are responsible for the grief of the world. They create revolution and discord, murder and restlessness, anxiety, explosive devices, pornographic films.

Yes, it's dark and I can hardly tell you're there. Having found a favourite record down the back of the cupboard, you leave the arm up on the stereo and play it over and over. St Cecilia's Mass. The air's thick with the smell of musk and fried chicken. You're an infinite friend of mine in the tickled bed. Your music celebrates God. God looks down on us in gratitude, though He's not too keen, we gather, on souls proposing for the first time an evening of nakedness and foreplay outside wedlock. He doesn't come across as the kind of person who went in for this sort of thing Himself, unless the scribes missed those bits out of the Book. We're not supposed to Do It completely because I haven't been taking the chemicals long enough. Your fingers seem to twiddle on your stomach. Wanting to Do It is almost as good as going ahead. You insisted we undressed in the dark because it's still early in our romance and you're a bit thin, you say, and haven't quite come to terms with it even now. Those gallons of Radio Malt as a child haven't done a damn thing. For years you thought it was made of melted-down radios. This joke about yourself is followed by a self-conscious chuckle. Kate's here, naked. We haven't touched. I'm feeling overweight yet I could do with a half a dozen cream cakes and I'm infinitely grateful you left off the light because I've had my end-of-week knickers on all day. You won't come any closer in case your erection reaches me before you do, poor creature. You men have no way to conceal yourselves. As soon as a tip reaches through the dark a girl can smirk to herself yet keep it a secret. Eventually you suggest you put it in without moving up and down so we can have a taste of this preoccupation without fear of pregnancy and nasty, unromantic things like that. Despite an earlier enthusiasm, Kate's not so sure it's a good idea. After all, she says, you know how resolutions can melt once it goes in. You say, Yeah, there is that I suppose. I make tea in the dark while you think about it. You're straining your eyes through the gloom to examine me. Has she fat thighs? Do her breasts droop? Are there any inconvenient birthmarks? We drink tea. St Cecilia's Mass continues to roar. There's a particular moment of it you love. Each time it comes round we must stop breathing to listen. Isn't this the finest music I've ever heard? I'm not sure. Much of my pleasure may be due to your nakedness beside me. St Cecilia probably didn't have this in mind when composing. Did she compose it by the way? Fuck knows, you whisper. Then suddenly you're rolling on top of me.

'Don't worry,' you say, 'I won't be going all the way.'

'Famous last words,' says Kate.

You're kissing my face all over very slowly. An eyebrow. A cheek. A corner of lip. A chin. An end of nose. Each time your lips slide from one spot to the next, you whisper that you love me. Quietly A slips into B. It surprises you a great deal.

'Oh God,' you say.

'Leave God out of this,' says Kate.

Once more you peck at my eyebrows. The room's beautiful, like a womb. You pretend to get comfortable but you're really moving yourself inside me.

'Careful,' says Kate.

'Who? Me?' you reply.

Maybe it's the next day. The rain's getting heavier. A light mist hangs among the thick wood with a stench of rotting leaves, wet soil. You're walking quickly, stooped against the rain in your terrifying cape, but turning quickly to check I'm still with you. We reach a muddy clearing which is used for the stripping and sawing of tree trunks. To one side there's a tumbledown shed with broken windows. Winking at me, smiling, you heave back the rotting door, pull me inside and throw me into a pile of old sacks. These are your kisses, your

203

bitings of my lips. The roof's pricked with daylight. Seized with inspiration you lift me up, bend me over the circular saw, undo my belt and pull down my jeans. It's a mad kind of day with memories of summers, rain, *Mrs Dale's Diary*. My fingers grip the rusting teeth though you're hurting me.

'Oh I'm going to ruin you at last,' you say, squeezing into me. Moments later I'm thrown to the sacks again, attacked from the front. My legs are pulled apart, my thighs bitten, my breasts pinched too hard. Maybe you regard my cries as a sign of the great fun I'm having but more than anything else I'm cold and suffering a kind of musical loneliness. Close to tears. The sacks are rough under my back. You're wicked or too passionately in love, pushing your hips to my head, pumping yourself against me, pushing your hips to my breasts, pumping yourself against me, pushing your hips between my legs and pumping yourself into me. Forcing my arms above my head, you look down to inspect what you're doing and strike home, teeth tight together, death in your eyes. A final movement, a gentle cry and you slump over me, hips pumping still. I hold your neck. It's some time before you calm down. You're breathing too heavily. Kate's frightened by it, your breathing, the rattle of rain, those fingers of cold between her legs.

Christmas Day 4.46am

Suddenly takes up her pen and begins to write without any sense of what's to come though it runs along the lines of Merry fucking Christmas, J, and a sublime New Year. Ah, now she's onto something with her inch of vodka to celebrate and her imaginary paper hat. As a gift she's just discovered her errant husband asleep in the spare room, slippers dangling from the ends of his toes. With care it's easy to spot the hallmark of a cultured man. In case you're confused, J, this is Now and I'm either prolonging the lonesome celebrations of last night or initiating new ones very early on this Christian festival. Being sober was grand, but I've come to prefer the real thing, this peaceful softening on the edges of a girl's dream, this tendency towards sweet tears, this inclination to relate the most scintillat-ing jokes — not that I can think of any right now because the podka's vissing me up — get it? No? Fuck you then.

John Kemp now writes letters to Jill knowing they'll never be delivered. Maybe he'll become completely Loopy and we'll reach the conclusion that Too Much Education Can Screw You Up. It's not easy to tell just what's going on in Mr Larkin's mind, although the reader begins to sense it's something devious intended to uproot her from the plumpness of her bed, the familiarity of her preparations for sleep on Christmas Eve. The shame is this, Mr Larkin: though there's an ample serving of Surprise in your book, joy more often comes from expectations fulfilled, especially late at night when neither reindeer nor the portly Mr Claus have bothered to call. A girl

205

needs to know what's going on; to have certain rules of Storytelling obeyed. Jumps in chronology or gratuitous tamperings with probable outcomes irritates those whose lives roll on and on through rain and Wednesdays and windy afternoons at the seaside with nothing of note to come on this page or the next or the one after that. We're mostly bored to death here on earth, Philip, and your fantasies are no consolation whatsoever. We want a boy to meet a girl or a girl to meet a Prince, not these bloodless caricatures plodding from room to room or from door to door achieving nothing, getting nowhere. Such is the case in Oak Leaze. Catherine rang late last night to inform me she'd spotted Derek leaving the wine bar in King Street with an intermittently unbalanced stranger – probably Tom or Ron. They were singing 'We Three Kings'. I underestimated him. I imagined he was at his mum's sharing disillusions by a roaring fire. And now he sleeps, poor lamb. Kate writes, noting the incompatibility of tastes between vodka and Colgate minty gel. It's as if she's torn between sense and nonsense, lunacy and vision; the present with its reminiscences, the past with its prayers for softnesses to come.

Kate remembers what's to become of her as if it were yesterday.

Dream Days

Having climbed the familiar three flights of stairs she arrives at the empty seminar room and settles in the window seat high above the college courtyard to wait. The radiators gurgle. For the moment she's bored with this aching pre-punctuality; unable to talk well, stuffed-up with books, with comparing, contrasting, annotating, nervous of her walks to and from the refectory while other, more intimate students slip to the Ski Club or argue on their way to the Debating Society. Yet as she looks through the window, it's as if she sees morning for the first time. An uneasy spring sunlight illuminates the garden, privet buds glisten, the damp rockery stones soften with moss. The old monastic buildings are beautiful. She's dreamed of this – an enervating bite to the air, ancient flecked stonework, old windows stricken in the colours of the sun, and even those same shoes walking back and forth, those white fingers round thick folders. She takes a deep breath. Maybe not liking things is just part of loving them. Disturbing its stillness, a trio of other students thump into the room, toss bags across tables and remind themselves who they're Doing today. Oh yes, it's Gatsby and next week it'll be that bloody *Day of the Locusts*. In these brave, articulate moments before the arrival of a tutor the drainpipe boy comes up with 'This Gatsby thing's a pile of elitist shit'. Later, between pulls on a limp Disque Bleu, he'll be admiring the acute sensitivity of Fitzgerald's alcoholic vision, this fine perfume of unrequited romance.

Another fortnight into spring and it's Catherine who rescues

Kate from her corner of the refectory and leads her to a soft bench beside the sunken lawn where students drape in pairs, drinking in the sunshine and drinking in the sunshine. Maybe Kate was about to bite a cheese roll or pretend to be in need of pudding, but Catherine takes her away, talks to her for hours at a time, drifting from one vague subject to another. At intervals she rests her head on Kate's shoulder or swishes blonde hair in the hope of catching the sunlight. Between them, or on Kate's lap, the college cat preens itself, ignorant that domestic animals in Radclyffe Hall's day led more constructive, thoughtful lives. Students swing through the entrance or swing through the exit, weave from the bar or thump to the grass in post-Orwellian tristesse while just the other side of the warm rooftops traffic crawls the main street, sounding horns, overheating. Should a pleasing young man happen by, Catherine hushes herself, looks him up and down, composes a dreamlike biography for him. To those more flamboyant or with an affected swagger she gives the thumbs down, having surmised they're the kind who must steal thunder in humid seminars or who will intervene now and then with snippets of information about Hesse and Masturbation.

Catherine's red trousers are famous. She wears them everywhere. Not a male goes by who doesn't surreptitiously glance at them. Kate's proud, as if in some way Catherine belongs to her; must watch as she crosses her legs or smooths the red denim with pale palms. Meanwhile geniuses gather in corduroy quartets. The sun shines. Someone's tickled pink by Honoré de Balzac. The wooden bench is warm and comfortable and we could share it all afternoon. It is necessary to rebel now and then against this amiable tranquillity. Catherine taps Kate. J's coming, blue from neck to ankle, carrying books so his hands have something to do. Waddling. His self-conscious Duckhood continues, quack. Spotting these heavenly twins at the edge of the sward, he takes a deep breath and forces his toes inwards. Between us and him a stocky tutor consoles a young man whose analysis of *Moby Dick* has finally got the better of him. The young man bows his head and stutters, 'You

see, the more I read it the more I realise it's . . . — . . . it's . . .'
The tutor wraps a fatherly arm around his shoulders. 'Yes,
don't worry, I know what you mean. It's about *everything*.' Birds
sing. On an adjacent bench the college anarchists discuss a
strike no-one will much care for. The week after, maybe they'll
halt a war somewhere. The chairperson reckons Latin America's worth looking at this year. Dinner ladies rattle cutlery.
And here's Fiona Jones handing out hurriedly photocopied
advertisements for a piano concert shortly to be given by the
silver-haired Heinrich Böll specialist. Rumours inform us
Fiona loves to be fucked as often as possible. Perhaps she'll
have it again today between *Women and War* and *Just What Are
Phonemes?* She certainly has the legs. Thus her essays are more
generously marked and thus a number of tutors become
increasingly sheepish as the term continues. Doors bang.
Sheets of paper informing us of everything other than what
we need to know dangle from every wall other than the one
we all pass on our way to nowhere.

'These are the best days of your life,' whispers a visiting
Aunt. Her nephew's been trying to hide her from the other
students all morning. Riots in Room J43C (ii) result in a chair
being thrown through the open window towards the shining
crown of a bystanding Physical Education person in white
plimsolls and maroon tracksuit who must hop to one side. A
bell rings the hour. J's unsure of what he should do next.
Having waddled from the refectory door to the wastepaper bin
he must now decide whether to bear right towards the
common-room, left towards the toilets or throw caution to the
four winds and head for this terrifying open space of the
sunken lawn. As if to witness his decision a tweed figure
appears at the office window and wrinkles its nose. Some of us
are infinitely excited because we have a famous author coming
to talk to us. He's there now, behind J, standing like a letter A,
trying to blend into the background. We must ignore him till
the allotted time in case he realises we realise he's a famous
author. He wishes to remain anonymous and acclaimed
nationwide at the same time. He'll be discussing *The Charm*

of Loneliness. Catherine yawns. J heads for these two divine companions then turns sharply to the right, having decided to look as if he's going to the common-room for high jinks, though once there he'll leave by the back door and head somewhere else. He must keep moving. Catherine yawns once more and then, with hands slipping unconsciously between them, her legs yawn. The tweed figure, snarling at the lassitude of its charges, adjusts its smart bow tie then weaves out of sight.

'Come,' says Catherine.

Opportunity Knocks

Derek's mum must have been watching for the happy couple through her husband's binoculars, for as they roll into the drive she's on the doorstep suitably Yuled, her hair permed and a circle of rouge on each cheek. Through the snowing lounge windows Kate sees four red candles, already lit, a small plastic Christmas tree wreathed in winking fairy lights, a strategic box of Walt Disney crackers and the father-in-law himself raising an early glass to his lips. Why, this is a spectacular family occasion by any definition. Vera clamps her arms to Derek, kisses him, unglues herself briefly to examine his features for signs of malnutrition, then bonds him to her breasts. The hirsute Cherub has come at last. Kate taps her feet on what should be snow. She's offered a cheek then taken to the kitchen where the son presents his mum with a gift. For some time she stands with the coloured package held at arm's length, saying, 'Oh Derek. You shouldn't have. I wonder what it is?' Kate's close at hand thinking to herself, 'Well, open the fucking thing and find out.' A rustle of robin paper, a snip of golden bow and a further addition to Vera's collection of Wedgwood china is revealed. Derek watches his toes. His mum is overcome. Weeps.

Derek leads an unenthusiastic Kate from the kitchen to the lounge where his dad presides over sherry from a brown, high-backed leather chair. A blue dog snoozes on the hearth. Whispering 'Happy Christmas, dad,' as if it's July, Derek presses into the old man's thin hands a cardboard cylinder he's been keeping silent about all the way to the house. Unbeknown to Kate, Mrs Thrupp and Tamil Separatists everywhere, the thoughtful son has written away to a place in America and had one of the countless stars in the universe named after his father. The cardboard cylinder contains a Certificate of Authenticity and a stellar map showing the star's position in the heavens. Generally speaking, it's Up. Derek's exceedingly Chuffed with himself.

'There's a star practically next door to yours called Michael Jackson,' he says. Tom's over the moon about the whole thing though he's never heard of Michael Jackson.

'He sings,' says Derek.

'Does he?' mumbles Tom. 'One of those Pop Of The Tops hooligans, I suppose.' He takes a sip of sherry, muses on the possibility that he may have planets.

Vera hugs her vase as if to suckle it, stares at Derek, a tear at the corner of each eye. Things would be perfect if he hadn't married such a Slop. As the excitement of Tom's new-found stardom wanes a little, Derek's invited to have a peep in the spare bedroom where he might be lucky enough to find something to his advantage. 'Oh mum,' he says uncontrollably. Meanwhile Vera presents Kate with a small oblong package which turns out to be another bar of Camomile Soap. Kate thanks her. All three wait anxiously. The room's too warm. The dog, having had diarrhoea for two days, must visit the vet's at the soonest opportunity. Flames from the generously banked coal fire roar into the wide chimney. Tom invites Kate to pour herself a drink. Just a small drink, mind you. None so large as would give the game away. She tips and gurgles; dreams of sharing a somnolent Christmas with J though her fantasy's interrupted by the creak of footsteps on the stair, the wading of rubber soles through deep-pile carpet and a poor impression of a fanfare made with fist on lips. Having created a certain amount of dramatic tension, Derek throws open the door and springs into the room dressed in a new scarlet tracksuit. Vera takes a deep breath. Tom almost turns round. Above Derek's breast pocket runs a tiny cotton tiger. The bubbling dog growls. Lights wink.

'This is fantastic,' says Derek, looking down at himself. As with all tracksuits, his reproductive organs have been perfectly outlined.

'Just mind you look after it,' says his mum, admiring him for a moment then leaving to attend to the dinner.

Kate's pissing it up as quickly as possible without revealing boredom or her unfathomable gloom. Hair of the dog. It begins to calm her down. Fear recedes. Derek's simply a haemorrhage clinging to the carpet by the picture windows. Since his unfortunate collision with a quantity surveyor's Porsche, Tom has developed a tendency to wag his head in times of stellar gratitude. Kate times him. Twenty-two wags per minute, decreasing steadily as he grows accustomed to official membership of the universe. Derek asks what he's bought Vera for Christmas. Tom giggles. 'Between you and me,' he says, 'I haven't let on to the old girl that I've bought her anything yet.'

Derek stiffens. 'Bit mean, isn't it?'

'Mean? Don't be daft. She knows me better than that.'

Derek unstiffens. 'Sorry, dad. I just thought . . .'

'Well don't,' says Tom.

Thrilled though she is by the subtleties of the conversation, Kate tackles the crowded silver tray for another drink. Christmas is beautiful after all. It seethes with J. Her arms bristle. A persistent drizzle falls to the grey garden; the narrow border beyond the weeping cherry is rotten with ragged marigolds. Chilly rows of grey-green wallflowers crouch in the shelter of a brick wall built by Tom in his adventurous days. Somewhere there are finer moments than this, a sense, perhaps, of tipsy tranquillity, of need, being needed. Tom has pulled a book from the shelf next to his chair. It's his gift from Vera: 'Cotswold Memories' compiled by Sir Stanley Kirkpatrick Jnr. He rubs the front cover with his palm as if the book is an old friend he's come across after many years, opens it, cracks the spine at a particular place and hands it to his congealing son.

'Read that story there,' he says, 'the one about Old Painswick Patty.'

Thanking him, Derek studies the publisher's blurb and one or two of the numerous sketches then begins to read.

Kate has finished her latest drink and now stares into the fire. Her stomach burns. Maybe she's tapping the rim of the glass with her fingernail, crushed against J on the Avon pleasure-boat. The dog stands up to stretch itself. It's having a boisterous day. Though a fine candidate for alcoholism, J didn't like to drink too much. He was a result without sufficient cause. He wanted to be conscious most of the time to ensure he didn't miss any of the perplexities he'd developed on his way to simplicity. His dreams were broad and shockingly impossible, though when confronted he'd be shy to admit more than the most innocent of them. He sang and loved and fucked and swooned.

Another drink. Vera clicks into the room carrying a leather-bound book. The leather has been ornately engraved and coloured in. A bright brass clasp locks the pages together.

'Just look at this, Derek,' she says. The dog wags. Derek puts 'Cotswold Memories' on the carpet, accepts the book from his mother's hands, unclasps it in the clumsy manner of one being minutely observed, scans the text, mumbles something akin to Oh My Goodness Me then hands it to Kate.

'It's grandad's old diary,' says Vera. 'Your Aunty Joyce found it in her attic. She thought it would be nice to have it rebound as my Christmas present. Wonderful, isn't it?'

'Fabulous,' says Derek, currently unable to open his mouth without sounding as if he's been rehearsing his lines all morning. Kate opens the diary at July 17th. 'Killed the pig at last!' it says. Life's all about time and the passing of it; time and its determination to proceed in a single direction. Families must gather tokens of what has gone before. July 23rd. 'Took Albert to skittles'.

'She cried when she first saw it,' chuckles Tom. 'Doesn't take much to turn on her waterworks.'

'Really fabulous,' says Derek.

Kate's already on August 5th, 'Mended desk', as Vera pulls the diary from her hands, refastens the clasp and returns to the kitchen.

'And how's the shop going?' says Tom to his son, who's just restarted *Cotswold Memories*. Derek does his best to look his dad in the eye and explains he's on the verge of bankruptcy.

'Oh, come on, things can't be that bad.'

"Fraid they are,' says Derek.

Tom slaps his thin legs. 'Well never mind. In business it's all swings and roundabouts. I wouldn't worry if I were you.'

Derek protests. He must worry because he is married and needs the money.

'Then you'll have to do as we did and start on the old beef-dripping sandwiches,' says Tom. 'Anyway, let's not get gloomy. It's Christmas. How are you coming along with Painswick Patty?'

Derek apologises. He's hardly started. Tom's faintly disgusted.

'Too many late nights, that's your trouble. I've always been an early bird myself. "Early to bed and early to rise", that's my motto.'

'I do jog,' says Derek.

Kate's watching the brass ornaments – most of them reproduction – which hang from the chimney breast. A pair of gunpowder flasks, a hunting horn, the nameplate of an old canal-boat called 'Druid', the flattened figure of a fox crouching in brass grass, a silhouette of Churchill. Certain well-remembered lyrics invade the festivities to at once console and intimidate her. She aches for the next drink; sees the reflections of Tom and Derek drip down the picture windows. The serving hatch slides open. Fat spits and crackles. Vera's head appears. She's asking Derek if he'll help her with the dinner. Looking up, he puffs out his cheeks, abandons *Cotswold Memories* and heads for the kitchen, patting Tom on his way past.

'Sorry about this, dad,' he says.

'Don't worry,' says Tom, 'you don't have to read it. I know the Cotswolds aren't everyone's cup of tea.'

On the front of the book a moss-covered drystone wall veers

between rugged fields. A ray of sunlight illuminates a copse of beech trees in the middle distance. And here she is again, wasting time. It becomes a theme as she abandons her charade and pours another drink.

J's coming anyway. He's been out of sight for some time at the bottom of the hill. Now he's plucking his way back, almost doubled over, out of breath. A warm wind slips across my face and hair. At my shoes the landscape stretches out and falls asleep under a haze of green sunshine. Perhaps he's doubling over on purpose to prevent me watching those aquatic footsteps. Catherine's behind him, playing with daisies. I can't do anything particularly well and it's bothering me. J's now waving and smiling. At the rim of the low-lying basin a range of hills loop and lope into a distant blue mist. I take a deep breath. The countryside's meant to enliven you. Catherine picks her way slowly upwards, turning occasionally to look back. She's so thin and white. Her face shows neither pleasure nor pain. J's a boy. He becomes a boy whenever she's around. Her loose tee-shirt flicks in the wind.

In silence we follow J through the wood to a richly shadowed glade of oak trees where he picks a suitable spot and throws a tartan blanket to the grass. Catherine sinks to her knees intending to read something by Dylan Thomas she's brought along, but after a page or two she throws it aside and lies down too, slightly apart from us. There's much to be said for having your ears close to the humming earth on a summer afternoon. Catherine shields her eyes with one hand and drapes the other at her waist, but soon she's as restless as the shadows, turning this way and that, scratching her nose or her leg, attempting to whistle. Sitting up suddenly, she pulls the tee-shirt over her head, shakes her hair, relaxes at last. Dozens of butterflies waft through the grass. She rubs sweat from her breasts with the flat of her hand, wrinkles her nose. As a signal that he's about to begin some sentimental dialogue, J sighs, plays with my hair. For years he's been looking for someone to talk to, he says. You know, really talk to. His search goes on and on. Though a woman may listen attentively to the frank opinions he has of himself, she'll invariably condemn him for the very flaws he's been most careful to include. At the end of the day he wants to be loved for himself. Every nook and cranny. Of course, he says, he's not perfect. Just an ordinary fellow with a few undeveloped talents, many, many faults and a catalogue of moods he rarely understands.

'In short,' he concludes, 'I'm a Person.'

'Wow,' says Catherine.

Trees and fields now ripple in the heat; the blue haze has crept forward bringing the horizon with it. This easy wind moves through the leaves about us. We're cocooned by the interminable hum of insects. Having rubbed the top of my head, J goes on to say how much he likes me, employing grammatical sighs of contentment in place of commas. Catherine has closed her eyes. Lying as she is, her breasts are somewhat indistinct and J's doing me a favour by declining to search for them, by taking the whole romantic afternoon in his stride. Oh, breasts aren't anything at all. Though he'd quite like to take off his tee-shirt, he's afraid Catherine might laugh at his lack of a true chest. Where others may boast proud biceps, J's lucky to muster a unicep. Catherine's even thinner, as it happens. I can count each rib. Her nipples become slightly enlarged with kisses of wind and the excitement of a naked daytime. Her belly's a soft white hollow. J turns, shuffles close to me and before long falls asleep in that innocent way he has. Old J. Wouldn't hurt a fly. Catherine seems to have been raised above the grass by those dancing leaf-shadows. Surely she's too delicate, would break if you touched her. Narrow waist. Long slender legs. Pale freckles in the sun. As the ghost places its lips against her neck, she shrugs her shoulders, tries to brush the feeling away. Intoxication, Kate decides. Halcyon days in memoriam. Catherine's fingers are now tickling back and forth across her breasts, a kind of lullaby before sleep. Several times J jumps back from the brink of dreams. Catherine's nipples become harder, darker with each touch of fingers, each squeeze of the ghost's lips against her flesh. J's hand twitches in mine. Drunkenness. Lying its head in the hollow of

217

Catherine's belly the ghost longs to reveal more of her; prays she'll run those long fingers through its hair; is haunted by the fantasy of her open thighs, a warm drink within her scented forest. There's a cuckoo somewhere. Its call comes finer than silence from the patchwork lowland. Opening her eyes, Catherine must examine these lovers while continuing to float and stroke and dream.

'Isn't he a treasure?' she says.

The fairy lights wink in time with the grandfather clock. Tick wink. Tock wink. Thank you awfully, Mary, mother of God. A bored spoon scrapes round and round the bottom of a gravy pan while the chatter of an inconsequential mother describes boredom to her bored son. Tom clicks false teeth. A further measure of vodka clings to the sides of Kate's glass. Soon her husband reappears but she doesn't recognise him; there's only a scarlet son plodding an uneasy course between birth-canal and coffin. He's beginning to see his wife as the only salvation and for this reason kisses her cheek, picks up her glass and adds more vodka. He's a dear. Partly satisfied, he returns to the floor and to *Cotswold Memories*. Just what will the remarkable Painswick Patty do next?

'You ought to try a drop of this, you know, Derek,' says Tom, waggling his sherry glass. 'There are sherries and there are sherries, but this is the Rolls-Royce of them all.'

Derek doesn't want to drink, but his dad insists. The dog creeps back into the living room having repeatedly christened the lawn. Marking his place in *Cotswold Memories* with a spill from the reproduction toby jug, Derek pours a small measure of the sherry in question and drinks it in one mouthful. Kate's a wild and restless infidel with dreams to conceal. Her husband clinks the glass back onto the silver tray and confirms that the sherry is very nice. Tom is outraged. This sherry is many things, but 'nice' isn't one of them. One doesn't use the word 'nice' in reference to drinks of quality. Besides, gulping it down in such a fashion is almost sacrilegious. He should have taken a little sip at a time; given the taste an opportunity to fully stimulate his senses.

'My God, Kate,' says Tom, 'I've brought a heathen into the world.' The fire crackles. Kate can't write and there's an end of it. She thought she could a while ago but now she's as likely to take up crochet or another of the feminine arts. She imagines riot, insurrection.

Each Christmas dinner setting comprises a vintage car table-mat, a silver-plated knife, fork and spoon, a paper hat, a cracker and a Little Something wrapped in golden paper. Vera is acutely aware that Yuletide guests may be temporarily in the doldrums through unrequited love or losing one of their Staffordshire dogs to anger. The Little Somethings are intended to minimise the grief thereof, but we mustn't open them till both dinner and pudding have been consumed. She wheels in the hostess trolley. Tom claps his hands and directs us to the table. The dog slithers under Derek's chair. As Kate floats to her place, Tom insists she should adopt her paper hat on arrival, let down her hair and have a Grand time. Derek's hat is orange and shaped like a crown. Kate's is blue. The duck makes its last flight from the hostess trolley and lands in front of Tom who must suck through his saliva and lick his lips. It's traditional that he should carve, but first he must vigorously sharpen the knife with a steel.

'Perhaps we'd better say Grace,' whispers Vera.

'Grace,' yells Tom.

Derek's hands lag in his lap. Spotting this, Tom thrusts the tip of the carving knife at him.

'Get those fingers out where we can keep an eye on them,' he says. 'Don't want any monkey business at dinner, do we, Kate?

'No. We don't want any monkey business at dinner,' says Kate.

Throughout the duck, the wine connoisseur entertains us with a history of his Christmas feasts to date; his memories as a Private, both Cotswold and otherwise; expresses disgust at those who fanatically try to ban fishing, stag-hunting, sugar and nuclear power stations and elaborates on several of the stories in his new book, taking pride in the fact that his own father used to talk of both Watercress Ethel and Old Sticky George. Though he is inclined to dissect his food rather than eat it, he does his best to compensate for this minimum of solid intake by increasing his liquid one proportionately. His appetite has indeed been severely impaired since he struck the quantity surveyor's radiator in such an unreasonable fashion. Meanwhile Kate's wishing herself to dust. Derek would probably masturbate if there weren't so many people around. He dreams that one day there will be a woman to bite his legs both before and after orgasm, or maybe he's having an Oriental day and his phantasmagorical conquests are both under-aged and indigenous to Bangkok. Pass me a glass of rice wine, my baby, and chomp your way into this.

An eighth of the way through his wing, Tom reaches across the table to take Vera's hand.

'Landed myself a great cook when I married your mother,' he says to Derek who's using knife and fork to tackle the flesh on a leg. Kate would love to cheer up but she can't because another tear is forming in the corner of Vera's eye in response to the old bastard's compliment. Derek hates sprouts. Plenty have been cooked. Christmas is a restrained face in the presence of another long winter. Ugly rain continues to fall. I can't cheer up when the traditional apple pie arrives nor when after-dinner liqueurs are poured by Tom into a set of fine glasses marked 'World Wine Fair 1978'. The crackers are damp. We're all cosy as the devil, reading jokes from the tiny rectangles of white paper, playing with our plastic giraffes, humming along with Mr Sinatra who sings carols from the stack-stereo amidst ripples of synthetic applause.

'Funny to think old Frank's still going,' says Tom. 'I always remember him as the thin gangster in a huge suit.'

'Oh yes,' says Vera, nodding to Derek to indicate he can now open his Little Something.

'This is the best bit,' says Tom, opening his. Kate follows the promptings of her husband. In life there are those who would line up against the wall and those who'd enthusiastically take aim. Except Derek, of course. He'd run back and forth, trying to shoot himself.

China and cutlery installed in the dishwasher, we return to our chairs. Vera is stoking the fire with a barley-twist poker held at arm's length while Derek pours everyone but himself another drink. The world's quite Splendid now, thank you all the same. A surfeit of waterfowl induces Kate to slumber but she's repeatedly dragged from its brink by Derek whispering words like 'impolite'. Tom's wriggly as a dying fish, reminding Derek he still has Painswick Patty to finish and commanding Vera to take the weight off her feet. As she unties her pinny and sits down, she's in tears once more. This is something we simply must forgive; every year at this time it happens in response to the memory of old friends who've passed away. She's thinking particularly of old Danny McTavish who died just a fortnight ago after a brief but painful illness. Turning to Kate she mouths the word 'Cancer'.

'Yes, poor old Danny,' says Tom, 'real character he was, if you know what I mean. I can remember him clear as day striding up the High Street with a sack of potatoes on each shoulder, no problem.'

Derek, ratty over Painswick Patty, askes Tom why anyone should want to carry that many potatoes at one time. His dad huffs. He's talking about the old days when people weren't afraid of work and took *trouble* over things. Old Danny grafted from dawn till dusk and wouldn't have help from anybody. And the meals he used to eat! God, Tom had watched him polish off a whole roast chicken by himself.

'Loony or something, was he?' asks Derek, skipping paragraphs to get Patty over with.

During the exquisite silence which follows, Tom pulls a package from under his chair and presents it to Vera.

'Bet you thought I'd forgotten,' he says.

Tucking her hanky into her sleeve, Vera sniffs, tears the paper from the package and opens her mouth in surprise. It's Trivial Pursuit. Tom goes Tara Tara. Mentally we all clap. Derek's attempting to Observe a sketch of Painswick Patty and the reality of his mother at the same time. Vodka gives Kate the giggles but she's hoping to swallow them. With luck everyone will die soon and she'll be left in peace to roam the wet countryside with a stick and a tin of dry cigarettes. Tom's certain Trivial Pursuit will prove a good game to play now he's not so capable of wooing and cooing in these dark evenings. Vera goes 'Oooooh' or perhaps it's 'Oooooooh', twisting the box as if she hasn't realised there's something inside. The fairy lights wink in rapid succession then go out altogether. Tom would like Derek to get his nose off that book for a change and give his mother a hand to set up the game. Derek throws Painswick Patty to the hearth then crawls across the carpet to his wife's feet.

'Derek will win, of course,' says Tom, looking at Kate. His son is the one with brains, although we've yet to see evidence of them in action. Deputy Head Boy and everything. Didn't the Headmaster write in his last report, 'Let Him Persevere Through To Success'? In fact Tom hasn't been able to understand why the likes of Derek and Kate can't put their heads together and think up a board-game for themselves. That's where the money is after all. He's certain the fellow who created Trivial Pursuit isn't drooping around the place with a book moaning about his cashflow.

'I wasn't moaning,' says Derek, 'just stating facts in answer to your question.'

'Facts? Facts?' says Tom. 'What do you know about Facts at your age? You've got the rest of your life in front of you.'

Vera's face melts into motherhood. She warns Tom not to go on at Derek. This is Christmas after all. We each throw the dice to see who's going first. Tom and Vera are ignorant of the rules but will learn as they go along. Derek has a six and jumps his brown plastic token straight onto Science and Nature. After a little instruction, Tom draws out a card and asks, 'Where would you find the Islets of Langerhans?'

Derek, despite his cashflow, isn't fooled for a moment.

We're driving home through the deserted village, a brown paper bag of mince pies rustling on the back seat, a crush of white and yellow stars rustling through the sky. Derek's in a good mood because we've been invited to return to his parents' in the morning. He feels generally safer in their company though they confuse and irritate him. A struggle ensues between Billie Holliday and The Carpenters as we sweep down the long hill past the farm and the unearthly silhouette of the comprehensive school. Derek wants 'It's Yesterday Once More'. Kate doesn't. Gloom splatters the windscreen. A dome of orange sky at the horizon betrays the city's existence. In the glove compartment Painswick Patty waits on her rustic rocking chair for Derek to take her up again. Kate's dreaming of a fictional countryside in this cold black night, in this world of shadow and sparkle; aches to be charmed by its more natural cycles, yet finds herself rolling on and on towards the thump of concrete, the illuminated chaos of cars on a roundabout, the shuffle of couples through frosting streets. She doesn't love her husband, whatever love is or isn't, whether he's smart for the shop; dashing, as now, in his scarlet tracksuit; or naked, too forthright, curly and naked. A satanic mill looms through trees on the right and who cares where the Islets of Langerhans are, yet people love to be asked such questions. She's planning the world's first rational nervous breakdown where psychiatrists gather round her bed mumbling, well, frankly we don't blame you at all for behaving in this way. You've a right to be Kate as far as we can ascertain. All the while Derek's saying he'll be sleeping in the spare room till things are sorted out between us. Maybe it's a threat, but Kate's thrilled to bits. One of the most common ailments of humankind is the sharing of a small mattress with someone distasteful to them on the basis that God has ordained it. Along the narrow road, over the bridge and through the County boundary without a hitch, Christmas trees twinkling in almost every window. J loves me to lay my head in his lap as we head home, his right hand holding the steering wheel, left hand playing with my hair, tickling my neck or sleeping on my breast. The open window allows summer perfumes to intoxicate and console us, especially, my goodness, the tang of wild garlic, and one day he must have a garden in which to cultivate it. On the tape now a selection of his favourites including the infamous 'Romeo And Juliet', yet he keeps a straight face as if none of this has been planned. Meanwhile Derek attempts a fancy gear-change at the bottom of Blackberry Hill and succeeds only in waking the neighbourhood.

Kate must carry the mince pies into the house. The phone is ringing. Catherine would like to wish her a Happy Christmas though she's the worse for celebration and can barely utter the words. Derek's straight off to bed if Kate doesn't mind, taking Painswick Patty with him and hoping that his sorely afflicted wife will be in a less dangerous frame of mind by the morning. Catherine must end her slippery soliloquy mid-way because there's someone at her door just as she's always dreamed.

And my voice may be as ineffectual as a candle in a cavern, but I miss you if you can ever know or care in this moonlit solitary garden coming up to midnight. Or perhaps I miss myself, it isn't always easy to tell. Memories yawn, rumble, fade away. Miss you as if winter must follow winter, night, night. So she counts sheep to keep awake; turns that corner into the realm of fairy tale and legend. One sheep, two sheep, a mixed-up girl with nowhere to go. Miss you since it's the occupation she knows best, having walked this street, that street; jumped at the sight of this car, that; miss you as a threat and as a madrigal. No eyes to confirm her reality these days, so she takes a drink to whittle herself down to the rest. Listen to this song, this symphony. The brain's melting with alcohol, Mr Burgess, so if great Literature suddenly pours out, it's not entirely my doing. I miss you as if the daffodils threw up shoots then died without blooming. I'm short of oxygen, made pointless by night, impotent by recollection. Sleeping's fine, I suppose, though it's such a waste of time, missing myself in bed, curling with cold, missing your arm as it lies around me.

Boxing Day

Dear J, it's too early even for the birds but I've been here for some time already, unwilling to speak. There are those who've said I'm going mad without you and those who prefer to believe I'm mad full stop and just choosing to blame it on you. The general opinion appears to be that madness isn't an awfully nice thing and that it should be avoided where possible, but at the moment I'm having a Super time of it. And though in the long run it would probably prove more comfortable to become the type of girl who does the fandango with a symbolic shopping trolley and a solvent Executive husband in one of those chipboard furniture stores, I have no idea how to proceed from this point to that unless by way of a scalpel and the skilled hands of an attractive surgeon.

This is one of several letters you won't be seeing, which is sad because I wish to remind you of everything you know already. Memory's a nuisance in many respects. Having traced my skin from head to foot with your lips and fingers, you begin to suck at my toes, in and out, while I lie back, shielding my eyes from the red bulb, moaning. And do you recall how malleable and inconsequential time became? I love to see you mesmerised by my body as you take my toes one by one and, between mouthfuls, whisper 'This Little Piggy'. I weigh more than I did then, though I'm still thin by some standards. My hair has changed by degrees to one of the wide range of Holy Matrimony styles though it longs to be untightened by wind and sweat. And the sexual act has slithered in importance to a point on a scale of interests between, say, televised bridge tournaments and the political speeches of Mrs Currie, or is it Curry? I'm not an adult. I'd like to stress that straight away before you start putting what I have to say in an adult context and condemn me for the result. This pre-dawn is serene and gentle and I long for you to come, though maybe you wouldn't recognise me now; married women have the chameleonic tendency to blend into wholesome backgrounds so the likes of you won't come groping for them and startle them from their long, uneasy sleep.

John Kemp no longer writes letters to Jill, by the way. He's creating fiction instead: inventing a context for her to live in; situations in which he can manipulate her as he would have liked in reality. I've given up trying to predict what Mr Larkin will do next. On the back cover there's a small photo of him. He's smirking, as well he might, having joined a somewhat revered line of smirkers who have inevitably wheedled their way into Literature syllabuses. A revered author seems to be one who induces you to say to yourself, 'now I wonder if I've understood the underlying intention here?' each time you reach the end of a page. The author enjoys it and so does the reader – after all, the only way to thoroughly confuse these days is to be straightforward. Well, J, I've just poured myself a drink which means, on the whole, that I've just poured myself a drink. The significance of this is that I'm having a crack at the truth for a change. Lying is so tiresome after a while. I've risen much too early after a rigorous Christmas Day and my plan is to Merrymake myself back to sleep, though even in bed your ghost takes advantage of my horizontal state and comes to sprinkle me with kisses or invitations to dinner. There's a Japanese restaurant opened up I'd quite like to try if it turns out you're not an invention and you manage to rouse me. The toes poking from the bed on the left at the top of the stairs are Derek's. Don't worry about them. Please note the copy of *Cotswold Memories* forming a triangle on the carpet beside him and the pair of rastafarian flip-flops tucked beneath the bedside cabinet. These, to some extent, are your rivals. Are your eyes still moist and full of questions? Could your lips still

226

tickle me into sin? Or do you laugh at a girl you once knew who has turned adhesive and alcoholic as repeated attempts to use the past as a tool of the future fail? Once upon a time, you know, there was an exceptional little thing named Kate who took years to understand she wasn't simply in rehearsal for a better life to come. This Was It – a third, maybe a half, already gone, slipped away with nothing of note to enjoy but for an extraordinary songbird she caught mid-flight then let slip away. For the rest she is fucked in a metaphorical rather than a physical way – there are few dream-inducing weapons in Oak Leaze, oh, very few. She's incapable of thinking rationally and they've all told her so; told her till she's sick of hearing it. The chronological niceties have become jumbled and unimportant. Nothing happens to her except those things she's able, once in a blue moon, to invent on paper or with intoxication. When and if she passes on, her life will have been just an anonymous sneeze from the audience at an opera. Fidelio or something. These operas have wonderful names but they're lousy to listen to, don't you think? And yet everyone in the auditorium dresses smartly, refrains from eating crisps and manages to keep a straight face. Ah, listen! The first bird! Are you still with me or has a striking maturity deafened you to pleas from the heart? Kate's a lunatic, you know, a lunatic saved from the secure ward simply because her lunacy wields no axe, dreams of but doesn't carry out death threats to those psychopathic politicians, and simply wriggles away in her beautiful head where it doesn't count. For the rest she's harmless, writing, writing, frying various reconstituted meats covered in bread-crumbs – the meat, that is, not Kate – admiring cowslips in the rockery when it is their turn, dressing, undressing, pottering around. You may have seen her Pottering. Often she Potters through town trying to appear as if she has somewhere specific to go, but it's all a game called Looking For You. She ends up wherever her energy runs out. Then you might see her limping home, eyes to the pavement. She's in love though her love has no physical object – at least, not one who could take her coat in the bar of the Japanese restaurant then show her to her chair.

Lifting me carefully onto the bed you proceed to tell me about all your unsatisfactory relationships. Maggie was a bore. Sharon a Screamer. Mary a disillusioned Freudian looking for a penis to cry on. Then there were terrible encounters with those unlikely triplets, April, May and June. Before I came along you'd been on the first leg of a journey into celibacy and intellectual Monkhood. There was really no satisfaction to be had from exhausting yourself with women to whom love was more or less a habit designed to keep the senses calm when there were so many more worthwhile pursuits.

In a series of simple manoeuvres you remove my clothes in sympathy with Elgar who's dignifying the room. We make love. An hour later, by prior appointment, Catherine arrives. We sit round your drawleaf table eating spaghetti bolognaise. You must cut up your spaghetti to avoid dribbles of sauce. Catherine sucks. All day you've been fiddling around on and off, chopping onions, unwrapping Oxo cubes, crushing cloves of garlic. Mid-meal you argue with Catherine about James Joyce. She doesn't care if she never sees another copy of *Ulysses*. In fact she's currently using her college copy as a plantstand for geraniums. The tips of your ears turn red. You're outraged, but can't put it into words. Catherine's making you look an absolute nonsense. It's as if the spectre of some huge unsentimental mother stands over you with thick arms folded. There's an almighty pause in the conversation as you change the record, put the kettle on and light another candle. Coming back to the table you pour more wine, clap your hands, but say nothing. The last inch of a piece of spaghetti waggles as it slithers through her lips. She chews and swallows.

'I suppose you two scamps have been fucking all day,' she says.

I'm exhausted. Catherine's turning wicked because this is her time. Even though you react against her audacity by changing colour, temporarily you haven't the vocabulary to deal with incongruous uses of *Ulysses*. Anyway, it's pointless to confront her. She's too sure of herself. Specks of bolognaise on the chin simply endear us to her. She embellishes your room perfectly, being bright and ephemeral as if she could dance in the wind coming through your open window – a butterfly swinging from bloom to bloom. We eat slowly now. Judy Tzuke sanctifies the night. You're wearing a white tee-shirt which I could easily peel from your skin. Your thin arms fascinate me. In dreams Catherine you and I join together and you are so fine, so brown, so compact. Could you lie with the two of us, four hands, double hunger? Could I touch you without touching her?

As you return from doing the dishes, Catherine moves away from me onto a single chair. The atmosphere thickens. You hold me tight to compensate. Catherine plays with the ends of her hair. Sprawling as she is, her jeans tuck tight against her thighs and creep into the furrow between them. Each movement she makes creates a slight twitch of breasts beneath her thin shirt. She looks away as you look at her. You change position. Catherine's enjoying herself, opening her legs a little more, making love to her glass, whispering to it, telling it what miseries she's been subjected to since birth. She and I drink like crazy while you have coffee. In a silence made more profound by the record and the hiss of the gas fire, she lifts her shirt and tickles the skin beneath. I remember your eyes as you watch her, your fingers as they play with me, your legs crossing, uncrossing. Soon she suggests going home though she doesn't relish the journey and so you say 'Sleep here', in jest more than anything but she takes you up on it and soon everything is arranged. No one moves. I drink some more. Finally she stands up, pretending to yawn. You pull me to my feet and take me to the bed, fiddle with the pillows, tissues and empty cups, delaying the crisis of your first shoelace. Catherine turns off the gas fire then gathers cushions at one end of the sofa, finding an easy retreat in candlelight. Saying Goodnight, she throws off her shoes and socks, pulls the shirt over her head, undoes her jeans and edges them down together with her knickers. I'm in a roaring, whimsical mood; Catherine's body shows grace, suppleness, is easy, rosy and boneless as she creeps naked to her chair, yawns for real, picks up her glass and drinks without pausing for breath. You and I are

229

undressing now and I'm fascinated by this quiet enthusiasm for your new game. Down to your pants, blue, with white elastic and recently purchased, thank God. Turning to smile at me, you then slip them off. Catherine, having finished her drink, pushes back her hair, takes up the blanket you've given her and climbs out of sight onto the sofa. Perhaps this moment is lost to you, but having called 'See you in the morning' to her, it isn't too long before you're making love with me again, or perhaps I should say fucking – really fucking, with muffled screams and everything. The room's too warm. Your wet skin slaps against mine. The bedclothes must be thrown back to allow more air and greater access. And there is a further audible consequence – the swish squish, swish squish of your movements into me. We're drizzling with sweat. You lick it from my breasts. Claw at my neck. It's that ol' devil called love again. The bed creaks. From several roads away in that direction comes the terrible sound of squealing brakes and then a dull thud. 'Sounds. Like. An. Accident,' you say, thumping, swish squish. Your face is red and wet as you turn top to toe, hook your arms under my knees and push your lips against me. I now have a gorgeous view of Catherine watching us, her hair and eyes sparkling in the candlelight. This is sport of a momentous nature. I'm secretly laughing to her. In her charm she swings from the sofa to extinguish the candle but before she does so she pours another drink, swallowing it in one. Maybe you've forgotten all about her, maybe you haven't, but you're turning round again, gripping the root of your erection with a certain pride then swooping into me for the last few moments. Poor Catherine's now spellbound in moonlight, as calm and poised as a mannequin but for her left hand which slips between her legs. You come with a gasp. Your head falls to the pillow. There is a seagull, a series of seagulls, weaving above the field as I tell you this, J. Listen carefully now. Catherine removes her hand but tiptoes to the window, glistening in silver, in wishes, in solitude. You breathe and breathe. Moments later we hear those warm hands clapping softly.

Doing Siegfried

All I want to do is work in a vegetable shop, preferably a small one like Whalebones in Port Street. I'm the eighth to be dragged into the office by the tweed Careers master, Mr Tubbins. I tell him I want to be the kind of girl who takes care of the vegetables. He can't understand why such a bright young thing should choose so lowly a task, so he assumes I'm being cynical and referring to geriatric nursing. I say, 'No, real vegetables. Lemons and things,' and he says, 'Aha! But lemons aren't vegetables,' and I say, 'I know, I've just been generalising.' 'Ah yes,' says Mr Tubbins, 'I see by what's written down here by your English master that you have quite a bit of trouble with your generalising.' 'Yes, I suppose I do, on the whole,' says Kate. Tubbins can't get hold of the idea that rules are for breaking. He's an unmarried cricket fanatic who rubs the ball on the front of his whites for a good deal longer than the married players and whose bum can be seen pounding towards the crease during the parent-teachers match. He says, 'Well, let's examine this vegetable mania of yours. I presume you'd like to own your own shop eventually,' and I tell him I'd rather not if he doesn't mind. I just want to serve. I have an idea I'll be able to cheer up the customers, cracking jokes about cucumbers or letting on how much Mr Whalebone is making on each pound of mushrooms. Tubbins tries to cross his legs with hysteria but they're so fat, the top one keeps slipping off. He has a black Morris Minor which he drives in first gear. Kids yell at him as he passes on the long road home. He's rather anxious because I look well placed to pass an A-Level in English Literature and he feels I'll be wasting myself. He hates those wasted girls who end up working in the laundry and having too many babies.

We've done *Murder in the Cathedral*, *Villette*, quite a lot of poems by Keats and nearly all of those ridiculous Canterbury Tales. Oh we've done all sorts of things. Wilfred Owen's another one though he had only an hour devoted to him because the teacher was away a lot with Korean 'flu. It tickles me that week after week we end up doing someone different. You walk into the toilets and there's always a friend at the washbasins who says 'And who are you Doing?' and you say 'Oh, we're Doing Keats for a bit.' And then, just to be polite, you add 'And who are you Doing?' and she replies, with a curled-down mouth, 'Oh This Chap Called Siegfried Sassoon.'

Almost forgot. We read *Great Expectations* as well. I enjoyed the marshes and Pip by the fire at suppertime with his lump of bread, but I loved Uncle Pumblechook most of all, especially when he partook of pudding. At dinnertime we all asked each other if we'd care to partake of pudding and, if so, what would we have, the semolina or the treacle tart? Uncle Pumblechook pops into my head when Mr Tubbins asks me about my expectations and I say my expectations are that I'll be working with vegetables. His arms grumble. He's surrounded by posh government leaflets and empty clipboards.

Squeezing my knee, he asks me if I've considered any alternative in case my vegetable idea (and here he smiles) fails to bear fruit. Something in the Computer line, perhaps, since Computers, like them or not, are to be the Things Of The Future. Tubbins is famous throughout the school for suggesting such a course as a preliminary to every starry-eyed career. Jenkins from the year below wanted to paint nudes in Montmartre but was given leaflets called 'Keyboard Confidence' and 'Software And YOU'. I say, no, I haven't considered any alternative. Outside, the baggy white fourth years are whacking at cricket balls in the nets while a weedy Mr Cousins tells off an unruly boy without taking the whistle out of his

mouth. There's a green-skinned fellow in my class who
picked to go to Oxford and has therefore been excuse
careers interview. Jeremy Pike. His dad's the wood
teacher with no roof to his mouth who has migraines and
strikes pupils with dowelling. Jeremy's always cracking jokes
no-one understands and has books about Plato poking from
his smart jacket. Most of the time he has bruises and there's a
rumour going round that his dad beats him up if he begins to
get fidgety about girls when he has such a wonderful future.
His green fingers are excellent on the piano and he's often
picked to Do assembly. Richard likes Jeremy because Jeremy
doesn't call Richard Leo. Jeremy calls Richard Richard. The
two sort of get together and play a lot of tennis after school.
In the sixth-form magazine, printed at the end of term, there's
a list of A-Level pupils and what they intend to do in the
future. It says PIKE: Oxford University. CHIVERS: Vegetable
Retailing.

I'm given gloves with no fingertips so I can handle potatoes
without getting too dirty and a pair of scissors hanging on a
piece of string from my belt for trimming the stems of flowers.
One moment I'm dragging bags of potting compost from a
shed round the back, the next, I'm weighing bananas. Mr
Whalebone's wife has jaundice and he must keep creeping up
the stairs to see if she Needs Anything. It seems she needs a
great deal: fruit, magazines, a radio, a tin of Nuttall's Mintoes,
a bunch of chrysanthemums, two new hairnets, a plug for her
potato-peeler, pints of Dandelion and Burdock and regular
packets of Park Drive.

Like Tubbins, Aunty's not too keen on the vegetable shop;
says I'm frittering my life away when life's too precious to be
frittered at all. She talks of Uncle William and God a lot.
Neither, it seems would glean much cheer from my employ-
ment. When I come home she's dicing potatoes, wiping down
surfaces, knitting in the living room or saying prayers to Uncle
Jack's green war hat. At seven she checks her watch, says 'Oh
well' and creeps to the cupboard for sherry, smiling at Uncle
Jack as her face looms towards him. Uncle William's on the

233

mantelpiece, leaning against a hayrick with storm clouds gathering in his background as white blossom startles a nearby blackthorn. On Sunday afternoons Aunty drags me to the cemetery. I prefer to think of it as a graveyard, but such words upset her, bring on her latest neuralgia.

The graves lie neatly along the slope of a gentle hill overlooking the town. The dead have a great fondness for scenery. Uncle Jack's in the middle somewhere, but Uncle William's almost at the back, about thirty graves from the gate. 'If people keep dying at this rate, they'll soon have to dig up the field next door,' says Aunty. Dogs aren't allowed. They might frolic or piss on your relatives. Uncle William has a marble headstone with golden lettering which says 'William. Beloved Husband Of Mary. Resting In Eternal Peace'. Uncle Jack's says 'Jack. Beloved Husband Of Mary' and then, in italics, *'He Was Gay And Indomitable To The End'*. Aunty must put a bunch of flowers on each grave then look down and say a silent prayer. She does Jack first, William second, whether chronologically or alphabetically it's not easy to tell. Most times she has to shoo the rooks from William. On the way back to the gate I always make a slight detour to look at the grave of a dead soldier with a lichen-covered headstone who's name is Tomlinson Tomlinson.

Aunty's in the kitchen cutting chips the day Kate comes in bold as brass to tell her she'll be leaving soon. Beside the pan of wet potatoes there's a bottle of Lucozade she's been drinking to aid recovery from something she's imagined is wrong with her. For some time she's unable to say a word, just puts down her knife and pretends to be dealing with the terrapins she's recently bought, shifting gravel to make a new hill and sprinkling food onto the water. The terrapins stay exactly where they've been for a week. I haven't yet seen them move. When Aunty speaks it's to say she'll probably Collapse and Die if I leave her all alone. There will be no-one to speak to, moan at, cook for. Young people these days haven't a clue what a curse it is to be getting on, lonely and cold, she says. Anyway, she doesn't see how I'll survive either because I've always been on the strange side and it doesn't look likely I'll ever find God. She sniffs, limps into the living room for a remedial sherry and comes slowly back, her glass shaking. It's Bristol Milk. The thing about Sherry Makers is that they'll go to any lengths to avoid calling their Sherry Sherry. In the course of her journey into the living room and back Aunty has thought the matter through, informs me she has been predicting this for ages and has decided, on balance, not to let me go. Thanking her for her concern, I tell her I'm leaving anyway. She sips from Uncle William's favourite glass, the one with a tiny seagull on the side. Moments later she throws it into the sink. A few slivers of glass land amongst the terrapins. Typical, isn't it? She wastes some of the best years of her life looking after me and now I just up and away without a second thought. And then there are these husbands who die just as you're getting used to them. All she ever wanted was a simple, loving life like everyone else. It's especially unfair because she's been praying for thirty years day and night without a break. She hasn't asked anything for herself yet all she receives in return is disrespect, bereavement and cruelty. She cries right through another three glasses of Bristol Milk.

Two or three days later, when Kate finally brings the two suitcases into the living room, Aunty sets to with a vigorous episode of sideboard dusting, lifting Uncle Jack, thumping him back down, her legs jigging in time with the swivels of the duster so the floorboards creak and the silver-plated cutlery rattles in the drawer. Kate stands in the doorframe waiting to say goodbye but Aunty can only remark that she's one of the cruellest girls it's been her misfortune to know.

'One day, young lady,' she says, 'I'll be found stone-dead on the floor. How will you feel then? That's what I'd like to know.'

Unable to hazard an answer to this question, Kate can only salute to Uncle Jack, pick up her suitcases, and leave.

Having The Vapours

Kate's lips are burnt with cigarettes; there are twenty-seven starlings on the lawn pecking for worms, and a grey sky falls almost to the rooftops. A sip of this, J, and a sip of that to calm a day with no beginning. You see how many sentences seem to roll down a slope and stop. However much I try, I can't always prevent this. There, I've done it again. Life's going Dee Dah Dee Dah Dee Dah Dah – it's the final 'Dah' which irritates me most. I was going to tell you, before I was so rudely interrupted by myself, that Miss Wintle has been in her garden wearing a new Yule jumper of red and white. She Cooeeee'd just now to ask me where Derek had gone in such a hurry. Proclaiming my ignorance, I ran upstairs to find a lack of both husband and *Cotswold Memories*. Gone to his mum's alone. Pissed off without his wife. Pissed off with his wife. I've heard it said that if you pray for things in the name of Jesus, you get whatever it is – new fishing tackle, a yacht, tickets for the Centre Court at Wimbledon, a cat – anything. Well, either this is a pack of lies or God's having One Of Those Days because not a scrap of my prayer has come true. Not a scrap. Or maybe God wanted you to come but you were too far away snorting into Christmas Liebfraumilch, stuffing your dreamy mouth with mince pies, dressing up as Santa to startle strawberry blondes or simply sitting alone in a room somewhere, saying 'Oh silly J' as you reviewed your past. I was going to tell you a number of things, most of them overly romantic, though not in a personal sense. There were rivers, you see, rivers, hillsides and,

236

once, the flash of a kingfisher; wet May days of thunderstorms rumbling through beech leaves; the thin green sanctuary of a stream overhung by willow, and the sharpened tiptoes of devils through a meadow at midnight. So forgive me if these things mean nothing to you. Perhaps you'd prefer to remember yourself as a grown boy, climbing the cliff in the Gorge by dangling from roots and inching your way up on footholds of limestone, standing at the top, finally, to wave.

The stories written by John Kemp about a fictional Jill now dominate the narrative, without interruption, as it were, from either Kemp himself or Mr Larkin. This appears to be one of those literary tricks which are apt to make the reader lean back and squint. The main character in a book (in this case Kemp) writes a story which becomes the temporary substance of the book itself, thus burying the original protagonist except where the characteristics of the new main character – in this case Jill – echo the original main character, Kemp. Perhaps this fictional Jill will now write a story herself which contains a fictional Kemp who, as she will discover, actually exists in a room at Oxford writing stories about her and imagining them to be fictional when in fact they are fact. If this proves to be the case let's hope John Kemp does the decent thing and commits suicide to relieve readers from the trauma of trying to work it all out. Myself, I've been reading on and on, wanting John Kemp – the real one – to return. Though he's totally unattractive, I'd somehow got used to him. Presently the fictional Jill with a Kemp-less story all her own, is idolising another fictional character, Minerva, in much the same way as Kemp idolised the unworthy Christopher Warren. It's becoming difficult to tell when one fiction ends and another begins.

Suppose I'll be condemned for having all these drinks at this time of day instead of tea. Condemned by imaginary generations who won't even know; by the television repair man; by groups of socio-historical priests out for a stroll; by penniless actors playing penguins in pantomimes. By J himself.

This is gloom, so I'll get it out of the way. It was just after Christmas in the first year. The weather was unbearable. For three weeks an arctic wind swept the country, slowing everyone down, wiping out large numbers of the elderly, decorating the trees with a lagging of frost. Barely remembered blue skies hid behind an unbroken pall of grey cloud. The period between darkness and darkness was brief, inhuman, haunted somehow. The winds howled through wires, rattled against any obstructions. Shoes scooped upwards from a world of wet glass. Femurs snapped. One unassailable morning, Catherine came to my door, white with fear, crying.

'You've got to help me,' she said.

It had begun with the essay on *Jekyll and Hyde*. She'd been having a real go at it and and read the paperback version seven times in the space of four days. At first she'd been fascinated, but then a darkness came down and threatened to engulf her. Quite soon she had a persuasive and uncharacteristic longing for sleep, deep oblivious sleep.

Every day she came round – more tears, more hugs. She was in an iced tunnel, sliding away from every familiar thing, throwing up her fingers in a vain effort to hold herself back. Physically she was exhausted, her skin dry and drawn. Her head wouldn't keep still. She must twiddle fingers in her lap or fiddle with her ears. In the evenings she drank enough to subdue the symptoms, but by morning they would have reasserted themselves. The way she described it, even the softest, most familiar things became ghouls looming in shadow, echoing with cries of the dead and dying. For a time she consulted works of cheap psychology, hoping to find a means to the end of this dread; made lists, as advised, of people, moments and places which had previously made her feel good; then she sought them out only to find she dragged the Monster with her. She took to exercise: hours of swimming, jogging, running up and down stairs, all to no avail. The symptoms returned each time she stopped moving. It was like a possession.

For most of the week we stayed together; my room became a second home to her. She lay on the sofa while I worked at the table; wrote her history down in an attempt to recognise the devil she must find a way to banish. But in form the devil turned out to be nothing, nothing at all. This fact frightened her more than anything.

For the last few nights she slept in the chair, wrapped in an overcoat, unwilling to lie down, saying to herself over and over 'I'm happy, healthy, beautiful'. I heard her through the darkness as I waited in bed. Happy, healthy, beautiful. Then the rattle of glass against bottle. J was banned. 'There must only be you,' she told me. I would have gladly taken on her fears so she needn't have suffered. Her incantation continued for hours at a time. She'd read somewhere that this was a way of re-recording the inner tapes of self-opinion which had obviously gone awry. Happy, healthy, beautiful. The weather continued to dominate the news, regarded with zealous gluttony by bored reporters everywhere. Drivers froze to death in the cabs of stricken lorries; old folk were found stuck to the floor in unheated rooms; those fortunate robins were showered with bacon-rinds and breadcrumbs; Opposition spokesmen condemned once more the Government's inability to act with speed, authority and compassion; postmen went on strike; the Thames partially froze; old politicians were struck by snowballs in Hyde Park.

Suddenly, after venturing out alone one evening, she drew breath and spiralled off in the other direction. She cleaned my room from top to bottom, arranged my dried flowers, gave me advice on my reading, my essays, my hair. Her appearance became a preoccupation. From grim inactivity she grew outrageously confident once more. The weather improved. She was soon talking of her frozen days as if they'd inflicted someone else. She returned home, came to visit me less often, telling me she had too much work to catch up on and that, as repayment for my kindness, I should be left alone to get on with mine. I said nothing. In contentment it's easier to let others go their own way, make their own mistakes.

One keepsake of the episode remained, Mr Stevenson. Your book was banished from her room then and thereafter. She wouldn't talk of it; tore up her initial attempts at the essay and chose another question. She won't entertain you now, I'm afraid. The years pass and yet she still believes those same ghouls sleep hidden amongst your pages.

And now, having said this, twinkles of nervousness begin in my hands and legs. I must gulp for life as if I'd just slithered from a womb. This could be happiness, or, more simply, alcohol. I was lying, anyway, J. You were searching for fresh blades of grass, pointing out the thick green buds and unopened bluebells. The air was cool, invigorating. Your sap was rising and you told me so. I said, Oh no, your sap has risen quite enough for one morning, thank you. 'Oh fuck,' you said, snapping your fingers. We were walking in the fringes of a spring whose quickness and sparkle gave a lie to the huge nervousness of the future. It was with due credit to your great pride that you hadn't reacted to my story of Catherine, of course. My goodness, how you hated people to think you couldn't work things out for yourself.

Silver Thread

Swallows flashing through alleyways. Secret meadows for you
and me or you and I in the boom of June, the lap and roam
of tranquil promenades, the roar of a blue cracked sky, your
voice which says now steady down as cool water splooshes
through the sluice for cows and lovers, writers of poems,
moorhens, unkissed Princes. Cowslips tinkling in the green
wind. Balls of fire towards the Vietcong and you always said
the girl was too experimental to win general respect and to be
taken seriously. She'd love to run from here through the only
remembered meadow sweeping seeds and green and hidden
wild flowers aside with her feet, naked feet, piggy toes. Soldiers
with crewcuts writing home to Mom of how they roasted a baby
today. Grilled children. Rather tasty with asparagus. Mist on
window panes; mist in your eyes; mist across the deep-running
river. Whiskers on kittens. Blisters on the cheeks of toasted
mothers. Your voice at midnight, daylight, firelight in the
wreckage of a room. Look, Kate, please try to understand this
from my point of view. It's so tough being a man, a boy,
intelligent or otherwise, wicked with dreams, wicked with
uncontrollable fingers. Lists, says the bloated teacher whose
obscene grandmother must attend an outpatients' clinic on
Tuesdays and Fridays for her gout – lists have no place in a
schoolgirl's essays. We can do without them. They tell us
nothing; serve only to confuse, irritate, aggravate, disturb,
sedate. Write out two hundred times 'Lists Tell Us Nothing'.
He's referring, of course, to Kate's fine piece on the National

241

Provincial Bank; has a bee in his bonnet, bats in his belfry, butterflies in his stomach, a frog in his throat. Perhaps he's overdrawn and we've all heard rumours of his sticky affair, with the Judy Garland lookalike from 3C whose breasts are prematurely large and who meets him for tickles and bloated kisses over the rainbow at 7.45pm, depending on the weather. My arms itch. My eyes sting. I have a chronic aching just about there. No, there. The Physics master, though not present in the room, has awfully thick legs brought on by weight training. People crack jokes about the width of his back, the circumference of his arms. He has short muscular hair and should be in films. Girls swoon if they end up in his set. The alternative is a bony man called Spoone with an E who spent his youth in India being eaten by tigers and who is unable to teach physics without instilling into his pupils a sense of atomic foreboding. Generally speaking – for which Kate's famous – his legs have amalgamated with the great bagginess of his silver suit. He smiles as we enter the class and yet his smile conceals a desire to whip boys into shape and to guide girlies inexorably towards kitchen sinks throughout England where they'll be able to combine grease-removal with speculation over the forces involved as water curls into the plughole. You can skip this bit, J. Stay with the romance. My brief history of the world isn't going too well. I was going to include the Corinthians because much of the school time-table was taken up with them, but now I can't remember for the life of me who the devil they were. All I know of them is that their regular and accurate insertion into Religious Knowledge essays almost guaranteed a pass-mark from Mrs Fyshe who owned a one-bedroomed cottage and smelt of tom cats. The naughty things will sprinkle themselves all over the place. Clout them with a broom. It used to be Fish but she changed it by deed-poll. Violins. Not a dry eye in the house as the credits roll. You and I or you and me are seen wandering towards sunset along a woodland path softened by celandine and woodruff. People whisper Thank God For That in the dark as they reach for their coats and trample the discarded Cornetto wrappers. A happy ending. At last. They were getting sick to the back teeth with the destruction in so-called Family Films where many of life's most treasured things had a tendency to explode – oh, these modern Directors, such Nihilists – Boom! Primroses, Christmas pudding, grandmothers, wardrobes, the Pope, tea with two sugars, marigolds, packets of crisps, sunglass factories, owls, fir cones. Nancy Reagan, sirloins of beef, seahorses, coathangers, mackerels, postmen, hairspray, spaceshuttles, tampons, Avon Ladies, Ascot, Muffin the Mule, tadpoles, free-range eggs, husbands, Shredded Wheat, Worzel Gummidge, premium bonds, grass, Pedigree Chum, garden gnomes, streams of consciousness, The Woolwich, Rag Tag and Bobtail, Ford Sierras, dustbinmen, mosques, the Salvation Army, Eartha Kitt, paperbacks by Graham Greene, Brighton rock, Spotty the Dog, erogenous zones, Hamlet, the Stars and Stripes, guns, golliwogs, grapefruit, alliterations, Nescafe, shortcake, Freddie and the Dreamers, hot pants, hot dogs, top cats, cat's eyes, carraway seeds, knickerbockerglories, Old Father Thames, dictionaries, the Crown Jewels, Sooty, compost, the M4, Canaletto, eiderdowns, ride a cock horse to Banbury Cross, maggots, Enid Blyton, double-glazing, loam, penguins, fragments of Marilyn Monroe, the Incas, carpets, carving knives, continental quilts, Sunset Yellow, Derek, eardrums, Old Moore's Almanack, Variegated Ivy and her sister Wild Iris, Boom! The awesome symphony of the whole lot going up.

Not to mention the shed and its inebriated but nevertheless incomparable contents.

Catherine's Room

Well, here I am, J, dozing on the sofa. Other tenants have got together in the flat above for a Boxing Day party and now they stomp on the ceiling to the music of The Who. Catherine turned down her invitation saying she'd had a tough day and was rather tired. At first she was agitated by my arrival, but then relented, fussing over my wet dufflecoat, sorting out a nightie for me to wear. I'm in it now, J. God knows where she got it from. It's not quite me; that is, some of it's me but then there are these frilly parts at the neck you'd have been unable to cope with. Kate has never been the sort to allow her nightwear to veer towards the realm of what's called Lingerie. Especially the flimsy, coloured sort. As you once said, why spend money on an article of attire designed to be seen through and hurriedly ripped off? By the way, they were all wrong about Kate. They thought she was going through an ordinary awkward patch – you know, fed up with the old man, developing a seven-year itch somewhat prematurely, longing for a romance – but they were all sure she'd soon shake off her madness and turn into a pleasant, home-loving girl – dinner on the table, pinny hanging in the cupboard, kitchen tiles clean enough to see her face in, bum regularly flattened on the bed for Sabbath spells of marital horseplay. They surmised she would save valuable pennies on Fridays by buying in bulk from the local Hypermarket; she would indulge, of course, in minor flirtations with visiting males, but commit no serious crime, toying only with the implications of a penis rather than the

244

object itself; they imagined she'd rise and wash and scrub and sit down mid-morning for a well-earned Cup-A-Soup; brush and cook and sweep and rush to the Spar before it closed; ache and dream and body-oil herself over impossible loves she'd read of in cheap novels about doctors and nurses, castle-owners and raven-haired distant cousins or oil-tycoons and their insatiable secretaries. Part Ten of her home knitting magazine would come each Thursday. She'd plant the rockery in spring; in summer, have a crack at an old-fashioned lemonade recipe unearthed from the attic; gather leaves in autumn to make nostalgic greetings cards and then, as winter loomed, bake fruit-cakes and gaze through the kitchen window at her dying garden.

Instead of that Kate they found this Kate, not knowing where to put herself, trailing along wet, cold streets towards Catherine's place on Boxing Day. She was shivering with the absurdity of moving forward or back, overwhelmed by whispers of solemnity.

Catherine sleeps. Kate shrugs off fatigue, sips vodka, writes on a piece of paper. The Who have or has been replaced by The Police. Remember 'Don't Stand So Close to Me'? Feet thump. Men tickle. The pensioner from 4a joins in for a lark, rattling her zimmer-frame each time the chorus comes round.

A memory now. Are you sitting comfortably? I follow through the frozen rain as J scurries up the steps into the theatre and waits for me at the foyer door, stamping numb feet, unzipping his plastic coat, pulling off his green hood. He's always wanted to see Van Morrison and is cock a doodle doo with both music and me. Love's a fine lark, alright. In his eyes hang traces of an unshakable pride. He needs to lead me into the foyer, help me with my coat, take it to the cloakroom, come back with a ticket tucked in his pocket; if there's time, buy me a drink, stand beside me at the bar, a prohibitive arm around my shoulders.

The MC tells us Van's late but the audience suspect he's hiding in the wings to respect a tradition and stamp their feet in protest. 'The renowned don't have to be on time,' says J, looking round the auditorium to see if he can spot anyone we know. Kate's popping peanuts. He nudges me. Look over there. Isn't that the lad from college – Harry, Larry or Barry – sitting at the far side of the Grand Circle? The one with the South African mum and a fingernail missing on his right hand? Always so weirdly dressed? Legs? Van's late some more. People eat nuts and discuss Superheroes they've seen at the NEC. J takes my hand, pretending to be a person, his soul aflame with the single idea he's in contact, actual contact, with my fingers, yet he looks here, there and everywhere as if he doesn't give a damn. Harry, Larry or Barry sits alone with a tub of ice-cream, longing to be modern but lacking the right chin and hairstyle. Suddenly the lights dim and Van struts on stage in the guise of an unemployed waiter grown plump through beef-burgers and inactivity who's inadvertently found himself in a theatre with a guitar. The audience clap. J and I refrain. The music begins. A backing group intent on growling to itself is revealed at the swish of a purple curtain. Most people stand. Van disappears behind the white neck of an effeminate insurance salesman with warts who's worn torn jeans to give himself concert credibility. J's keen to put his arm around me somehow. He's thin, unremarkable and must keep whispering in my ear but I can't hear a word because Van's got the monopoly. The thing is this – if you're a Van fan you should maintain at all times an air of respectable enthusiasm. No slashing of seats, vomiting or tossing of beer cans. These are the dope children gazing back at glory from a position of parenthood, tax-demands and the odd prize-winning chrysan- themum. In just three hours J will be in the back of a parked car on the Downs with an old schoolfriend he'll meet in the bar during the interval, his Kate having left shortly beforehand complaining of dragging pains and nausea. I'll have walked home alone, forcing him to remain behind to save wasting his money. And in that car on the Downs, beneath a canopy of stars, he'll be kissing her, believing those kisses to be a justified reaction to my strange behaviour. Later still, he'll wave goodbye to her and wander back to my place to confess Everything: how he hasn't seen her for years and how, in a moment of despair over his true love, he ended up in a wicked clinch riddled with nostalgia for the old days. He'll be enormously sorry, making love with me to compensate. Her name will be Sally – short for Salandra, or something Mexican. But for the moment I'm feeling well and he taps his feet to 'Kingdom Hall' and freely perspires. His hands are wet. He wonders what it's like to be Van himself, staring up at another few thousand unknown faces from yet another stage in whatever city this happens to be. A mild contraction grips my intestines, though, as an angel, one has a tendency to keep references to such organs to a minimum. Soon J will be shivering in the parked car with a fine view of the illuminated suspension bridge. Sally will be saying, Oh, you do remember Mr Butcher the bullfrog French teacher, making J laugh and initiating the first embrace. J will recall the mysteries of the Subjunctive, the beige desks, and the tears in Mr Butcher's eyes at the mention of Racine; soon, he'll find himself with an involuntary erection (can they be of any other kind?) excusing this to himself on the basis that when men were animals, had a great deal of body hair and made tools out of bones, an erection wasn't something to get yourself worked up about – it was simply a signal that one should get down to some copulation and so perpetuate the race that would one day create of itself persons of the magnitude of Casper Weinberger. Sally will be less philosophical than J and will clasp the offending member with gratitude. So though J will have fucked, as it were, accidentally, he will then love me in the most romantic fashion. My room will be quiet as a hush, faintly decorated by candlelight, my body forgiving him even as my mind screams insults. He'll have made no plans to see Salandra Whatshername again; the event will have been an aberration, an outrageous incongruity in the sanctity of love. He'll sedate my body with promises, wet my breast with his mouth, refrain from mentioning Van again. In the aftermath he'll be all tucked up, praying like crazy to the gods of Remorse then, at dawn, come with coffee to wake me, saying he's sorry and he's sorry and he's sorry, fucking with me all over again to shift the fact of the night before further and further away from himself, further and further into me.

Harry, Larry or Barry spent the first year at college stooped and tinkling through corridors alone, gawping and gazing at Catherine if the opportunity came along. For a while he was an entertainment, coming to seminars in whatever suit of charity-shop clothes echoed the period we were studying. There was his *Brideshead Revisited* look; the cropped, somewhat dishevelled fortnight of Solzhenitsyn. His James Joyce period included a baggy black suit and a monocle – the monocle dangled round his neck at the end of a chain and was never worn. Throughout D.H. Lawrence he came in a shabby three-piece and a cravat, a gold-plated chain looped across his waistcoat. There would frequently be the suggestion of tears in the corners of his eyes. Here was an out-of-place, emotionally flattened, terrified Romantic. In class he was a great initiator, but lacked the self-confidence to back himself up if his ideas were challenged by the tutor. He'd turn pale, bow his head and tap his pen against the table. Boy, was he crazy over Catherine. If his theories fell flat he'd be mortified, imagining – quite accurately – that she'd see him as a limp, useless fellow with everyday expectations.

I expected him to contact her like one of those bewhiskered gentlemen in restaurants who invite young ladies to dine by sending a note across with the waiter. He had come to college to find the girl of his dreams and was covering up this activity by doing his degree at the same time. A moustache drooped down the sides of his mouth in what was intended to be a Mexican fashion, but the droops were never thick enough and the left droop was always slightly longer than the right, making him look as though his head was on a tilt. Above these discordant droops stood a shiny nose with a strange bump in the middle. And those eyes! So melancholy, confused, and hungry for Catherine. Mostly he was a stiff, awkward, uncomfortable-looking fellow with farcical legs and an uneasy scowl etched into his forehead by the constant worry that female students were making him the centre of their attention and finding themselves disappointed. Sometimes he held onto his chair till his knuckles turned white or could be found skulking in the telephone booth having phantom conversations with the dialling tone. He wasn't popular. Came in through the gate in the mornings sprightly but alone; went out alone and mortified; was rarely seen in the library, common-room or bar; didn't belong to any of those enthusiastic cliques; always managed somehow to sit in the midst of large groups of students at dinner, half of whom were focusing their attention on a colleague to the left, the other half doing likewise to the right, leaving him substantially isolated with a nervous pie and chips which he'd pick at uneasily, having forgotten his knife and fork. Rumours sown by his own lips indicated that he'd spent several exhilarating years in South America having Larks with dusty-skinned wives-of-ranch-hands and had been forced to leave by husbands enraged by oddly coloured babies born with a predisposition toward Literary Criticism.

Finally he plucked up courage, decided to strike as Catherine and I were climbing the steps to the library. He made her jump by tapping her on the shoulders, then retreated to the entrance hall. We turned round. There he stood, in 'History Man' costume, fiddling with his fingernails. Would Catherine care to go to his place Thursday night as he was having an Ezra Pound evening 'with a few friends'? Catherine thought for several seconds before turning him down, using the fictional excuse that she was very busy with George Eliot and would be for some time to come. She'd been finding out about him and couldn't stand this great meal he was making out of Infatuation. His awkwardness said it all – the flushed neck rising from a buttoned-down shirt, dancing feet, shrugging shoulders. Not appearing to have understood her refusal and deciding to lay his whole hand of cards on the table, he began to recite the similarities he'd invented between himself and her – as if similarity was all she'd ever dreamt of. She – a goddess – stood on the steps in tickled awe attentive to each embarrassing fiction he came up with: he loved Literature; Flaubert was a particular favourite of his; since coming to college his whole attitude to Life had undergone a revolution, a re-evaluation;

249

in the evenings he liked to listen to music, oh, Mahler, Marley, Brahms, The Nolans; occasionally he wandered into the country-side to examine trees, catalogue flora and blow away the cobwebs. He was beginning to sound like one of those faultless people in personal columns. Catherine remained silent and unmoved. Having run out of qualities for the moment, he watched the floor in consternation then threw in his hidden Ace.

'And I'm a bit of a Writer,' he said.

Catherine laughed involuntarily. The college was full of them, writers, each one more earnest, tear-stained and anor-exic than the next, and yet Harry, Larry or Barry was the most doomed example she'd ever seen. He coughed. She slapped the banister. 'At the moment,' he said, in answer to a question she hadn't asked, 'I'm working on a little thing about the capitalist society which is intended to operate on two levels.'

'Both of them Bollocks, no doubt,' said Catherine, taking my arm and leading me on up the steps.

Harry, Larry or Barry snapped the handle of his plastic bag and called after Catherine that he didn't mind at all, though it would have been nice. It was only an idea he'd had last night. He'd thought of her on a whim, to make up the numbers. It had always been terrifically terrific listening to her theories in class. Perhaps another time. Well, he'd better go now. There was someone waiting for him in the refectory.

'Thanks for listening,' he said.

He'd been hoping to make another Daisy Buchanan out of her. She was flattered, but she'd been an unattainable dream before and it hadn't worked out. Curling round to look at him, she suggested, rather loudly, that he should hurry home and insinuate her into one of his fictional pieces. Fulfil his fantasies in that way. It would be less harmful in the long run. She was scaring him to death.

He's probably in some squalid, unheated room right now, trying to remember her as she was, wondering if she remem-bers him, smoking himself to death. He'll be a disheartened, unattractive figure, eulogising on paper, creating fiction from the scraps of a reality he has no skill with or taste for; lonely:

critical of himself for letting a dream escape so easily. What happened to his nerve, his flair, his belief in Destiny, when he needed them most? Why had he made such a hash of himself? Growing irritable with his room, he kicks over his chair and throws a handful of his papers at the wall. Now there are just cups of coffee and a few ragged memories of a girl in red trousers on the library steps, her eyes begging answers he had no questions for.

You'd find it amusing, I expect. John Kemp has put aside the story he's been writing with Jill as the central character and is now filling a diary with fictitious entries supposedly written by her. It's cheered me up no end. I wasn't too keen on the style of his previous inventions. Then Jill had far too many stock boarding-school qualities – jolly hockey sticks, What Ho!, tuck at lunchtimes – that kind of thing. In the first person she becomes more attractive, though it's still easy to tell that John Kemp himself is writing the diary. She sounds more like the idea he has of a girl rather than a real one. This is either intentional on Mr Larkin's part (remember him?) or something of a cock-up. Whatever the case, John Kemp's attempt to write such a diary at all must mean he's a little insane.

A few pages further on, during a break from the diary, Kemp wanders into a bookshop and sees the embodiment of his fictitious character! It's Jill, down to the last detail. He pursues her right through Oxford, but loses her in the suburbs. It must be heartbreaking to find such a charming dream so elusive. Maybe he'll meet up with her later in the book, get to know her. I'm wondering whether she'll turn out to be as he imagined in character, or whether he'll find himself with a stranger and be completely disappointed. I'm not sure which outcome I'd prefer. The first would be fine from a romantic point of view and I'm sure we'd all have the tips of our hankies in the corners of our eyes; but the second possibility might be better for him, might uproot his childish outlook and harden him up a bit. The outcome of this speculation relies rather heavily on the author although a girl's inclined to wish that this wasn't so.

Remembrance Day

It's some time ago in the hem of an idiotic dawn. We've been making love most of the night, the last time in a semi-dream of smells and wickedness, his wide, nightmare mouth biting me from neck to thigh. And what charming marks we shall have to remember by. When I wake he's dressing by the fire, pulling a red body into jeans and shirt, hopping and humming to himself. Ah yes, he has to see a man about a dog today and must be punctual. A damp towel hangs over the back of the sofa and his wet hair has been perfectly combed. He buttons his shirt, hiding ribs and shadows, whispers of hair. Kate's cosy with the idea that for some months she has owned almost all of him, known all of him, kissed and tasted each piece of him. Ignorant of her, he inspects his face in the mirror, smiling at what he sees. 'Good morning,' he says. 'Oh, good morning,' he replies. I vaguely remember his knees trapping my head, his hands pinching my hips, his teeth chewing between my legs. The room is just so. He Tra La La's, ties his shoes and puts on his coat. Some day he's going to be a star, I can see the certainty of it in his eyes. Having extinguished the fire and pinched out the candle, he tiptoes to the bed in darkness, raises the bedclothes, brushes and kisses each of my breasts in turn then pecks my thigh farewell. I'm pretending to be asleep because it's easier that way; besides, a girl can learn all sorts through fictions, dumb shows, pantomimes. Now he smells only of soap and promises. His lips leave me; the creak of his leather shoes crosses the room. The door is opened. Perhaps he calls 'Take

252

care'. Soon there is a rattle from the garden gate. In bed I remember many of our moments to make up for his absence, pushing them like a snowball, comforted as they grow more substantial. Then, as a snapshot, there are leaves burning on a November afternoon while a warm and somewhat weary gardener leans on his rake to view the thousands still littering the lawns and paths and rockeries. No wind, thank God, to blow them all round. For an age, it seems, I lie there quite still, drifting into sleep and out again, enjoying one reality and then the next till dreams of day invade and I must get up, sit in the chair perhaps, mid-way between slumber and activity, nursing a cup of coffee, studying my room.

At this busy time of year the neighbourhood gardens are crowded with hollyhocks, roses, limp but brilliant blades of uncut grass, the chatter of sparrows and the prowls of mousetight cats. Though Kate may thumb through one or two books, she's not really interested so she pumps her palms and sings along with the radio. Almost every lazy lyric is intended for her. He goes, then the day's a matter of patience. She follows suit, checks her face in the mirror and dabs vaseline on her lips, but soon she must move away and search her room, swinging and turning like a regular ballerina.

Now put the kettle on and make more coffee, that's the idea. It's not ten yet so there's no need to dress. Your body's rather splendid, haven't you noticed? It slips and sinks through these shafts of amber, pushes itself against the wardrobe mirror, tiptoes here and there. Waits. Now, sit on the chair like a real person sipping coffee on a real morning. Be restrained. That's fine. Now, open your legs. Close them. Open and close them very quickly to ascertain how much subcutaneous fat is set a-wobbling. Not much? Very good. Continue to avoid gateaux and pregnancy at all costs. I shall have another crack at a book. Choose one at random with a stray finger. It's a step-by-step-by-womb guide to Mr Freud, who bores me to death. Always has. Two opinions – One: the most influential thinker of the nineteenth century. Two: A Bit Of A Pervy. And here he is across the front cover in red and black, perplexed and somewhat hairy. I can get from one side of my room to the other and back again in ten large strides. I'm trying to cut it down, J, but these things take time. Let's pray for no onlookers from opposite premises. This is post-coital, post-educational and pre-employment neurosis, Prime Minister, so please take notes.

When Catherine turns up I lose my temper and throw the pork-pie she brings me at the wall. It breaks into three pieces which she picks up, brushes off and puts on a plate for me. If someone's there to retrieve your hurled pork-pie the effect is not quite the same. One feels obliged to apologise in view of the Third World, especially when the other person has just given it to you as a gift.

A week goes by, Kate would throw herself on the bed and cry, as one is supposed to, but it would be an acrobatic, melodramatic gesture and little else. Each morning the weight of his absence falls through her body. The weather's warm, uneasy and silent but for the sound of others talking, laughing. She sits in the park pretending not to wait, posts letters which remain unanswered. The bench tucked into the privet by the gardener's toolshed is her favourite. It's in the full sunlight yet out of the wind, the one with the least interrupted view of the main gate, the least lonely. A young gardener thumps back and forth in green wellingtons, pushing his wheelbarrow, pulling it, cursing, singing, clouting hooligans who leave crisp bags on the grass. At roughly the same time each day a Greek-looking man slowsteps through the gate carrying an open book in his palms, studying as he walks. Kids skate round him, shower him in weeds. He reads. Through the lunch-hour an elderly woman with a Corgi lies on the bench by the fountain and drinks a six-pack of Guinness. And here's Liana, as I've nicknamed her, drifting both nose and fingers through red and yellow rose blooms, an unhappy shoulder bag resting on the grass where she's left it; no rings on her fingers or bells on her toes, so she shall have boyfriends wherever she goes. The sunshine seems to follow her. Grandfathers hoot. She smiles in reply, hooking a spray of daisies through her hair.

Catherine does her best to comfort me; becomes therapist, physician, taskmaster; feigns annoyance as she asks me why I haven't been round to J's place to find out what's going on. The rain comes. Catherine cries too. I move indoors. Watch the sagging garden through the window, thinking to myself, now Kate, you must do something constructive here, as the pamphlets suggest. Only weak, reflected women go to pieces; only madwomen struggle against themselves in soundless rooms; sadwomen who haven't grown up.

J, I could write you such a letter this evening. Almost every single thing I've done since hasn't had any substance to it; I've had to huff them and puff them and bestow them with a passing elegance. And now my husband has just phoned. He wants to know what on earth I think I'm doing. Would I be so kind as to return to the marital home forthwith? Haven't I made things awkward enough for him already? His mum wept buckets at the empty Boxing-Day place-setting and Miss Wintle's gossiping already. I began to object. 'Don't bother to say anything,' he said,' I know what you're thinking.' And then he went on to suppose that Catherine was filling my head with more crazy ideas. She's not here now, by the way. Some dreadfully secret appointment. She woke up, fiddled with her hair, pecked me on the cheek and went out. Kate sipped or quaffed wines or spirits or anything mood-altering she could lay her hands on. It's the modern thing to do.

Derek slammed the phone down following a warning that I should be back before Dawn, whoever she is. As I said, J, I could write such a letter if I weren't so pessimistic tonight. I waste my time and waste my time over trivialities, over comings and goings, sleepings and wakings, money or the lack of it, words and words they beget.

The Immoralist

Boxing Day has gone. Harry, Larry or Barry rarely stays up so late but an unfamiliar energy moves him to light a candle next to his typewriter and set the record straight. Kate is alone in Catherine's room, waiting for her friend to return. In this brief period of isolation she has developed such a melancholy countenance that he's inclined to tear up the page and start again. Real tears don't suit her at all. It's 1.35. Catherine the Minx is God knows where. An unseen mouse scurries along the skirting board making Kate lift her feet. Her head nods. It has been so long since she had a really good night's sleep, poor lamb. Now and then both hand and pen reach up to scratch her chin. Whatever can she put next? By maintaining such independence, Catherine is apt to hold up one's plot, such as it is.

What does Rupert's father do for a living? How come he can work full time and own a nice cottage in Nutwood when so many human beings must remain on the dole?

Since yesterday, Harry, Larry or Barry has been suffering from a cold in the head, a blocked nose and watery eyes, but he fights on nevertheless. And then there's Liana who popped into his life quite suddenly to ruin his fine concentration. Oh how destructive chance encounters can be to literature. See! his imagination falters; desire steps into its place. Having paced up and down as creative persons should in moments of crisis, he summons up a scrap of self-control and, at two o'clock, brings Catherine home. She has a strange, bedraggled look about her which he hasn't created before, and which his over-congested brain isn't capable of describing. Kate's been waiting for a hug all evening, but holds back as the cold butterfly girl takes off her coat and waggles red hands in front of the fire. In the midst of indecision and perplexity, what madness can spring into being. Kate stands with her back to the mantelpiece, the room rocking a little. Warmer now, Catherine yawns, kinking herself at the waist in a most seductive manner. A chill runs through Kate. Her fingers shake. A hug would be splendid, so, to initiate reaction, she kneels down on the hearth, appeals for Catherine to follow. It is with some amusement to both that a hand reaches out of its own accord to stroke Catherine's hair. Help me, thinks Kate, her stomach in spasm as this hand traces Catherine's neck and shoulder, creeps down the arm, slinks to the knee and rests there. 'Oh you are silly,' says Catherine, gazing at the hand for a moment then idly picking at the hem of Kate's nightdress.

In nakedness Catherine is cool and beautiful. Kate's fingers tremble as they follow the white spine, soothe at the waist or run through her hair. In dread a moment is reached and given into. Catherine must assist her friend with the nightdress till she is naked too. It is no use arguing against such a moment or preparing for it logically. It just came, asserted itself, threw concentration, doubt, aside. They move close, lips to lips, Kate's hand now seeking the generous warmth between Catherine's thighs. A record should be playing. Tentative lips at first, but soon heads tilt, allowing an exploration of greater depth. Catherine has now become gorgeously wet as Kate squeezes there with all her fingers then slips the longest one into her. How strange and wonderful it is. The most insoluble problem of living is that the activities bringing finest satisfaction also create, of themselves, the most extraordinary knots to unravel. The mixture of darkness and firelight blend the two bodies till they are virtually indistinguishable. Catherine's legs have opened by degrees while Kate's finger, having finished with dipping, turns its attention to the clitoris, which is an awful word but one she mustn't miss. Rub a dub dub. Her lips too have taken control, hunting Catherine's breast, sucking there, feeding, bringing Catherine's heart to the boil. Kate has just enough time to reach the rim of perfect exhilaration before Harry, Larry or Barry, due to an imminent sneeze, is forced to abandon fiction in favour of a Kleenex. Of course while the tissue is held in place, the threat recedes and this moment of fiction dissolves. Maybe it didn't entirely suit Kate anyway. Maybe it was just a deep licentiousness on his part, indicative of the sexual obsessions of his kind.

Dragging the back of his hand across his mouth, he pulls Kate and Catherine from the typewriter and screws them up. Kate, the little monkey, squeals 'Ouch!' in jest. This tickles him. He takes a sip of cold coffee and lights a cigarette in the candle flame. Liana is just a representative of his true desire so it's no use getting strung up about her. She'd only screw him up, tie him down, make him pine for his old lonesome self – the one he gets so bored with now. Remember it's hard to assess whether a particular time and a particular state of being are Happiness till they have passed by. Just type in the meantime, that's the idea. Standing up, he crosses the room to look at the night, tears up the photo of Liana he would have had if things were different, puffs out the candle, removes his André Gide outfit and slips pimply into bed, the cigarette tip glowing in the darkness like the final ember of his genius. Despite finer intentions, his literary gifts create Liana beside him and he curls with satisfaction as she soothes and nibbles him into a comfy but unkempt sleep.

2a Chaffinch Crescent

For her first room long ago Kate buys an ivy which begins as two withered leaves in a small plastic pot. She keeps it on the table close to the wall and nurses it with cold tea till it flourishes and becomes the envy of the guests she doesn't have. With the room come several rickety pieces of varnished furniture, an odd number of bone-handled knives and forks, a set of stained beige sheets and a brown teapot with a bright yellow ring round the lid. To hide damp, the walls have been battened with flexible hardboard which thumps in and out playing Rolf Harris tunes when the wind is in the right direction, and creates an ideal hideaway for sleepless insects. The house roams a darkness busy with boiled shadows, woodworm, the creakings of feet, grim salutations and many legendary stews bubbling on the grease-covered communal cooker for a rumour called Arthur from the attic room who's later to have one of his most severe werewolf attacks at midnight and be led away by police to a psychiatric hospital.

In the middle of Kate's first day the landlady steadies herself against the banister, takes a deep breath and reiterates some of the rules. Animals are banned – they didn't used to be but one of the tenants had a great dane which shat? shitted? on the back lawn and kept Mrs Gallon awake. All Communal Items such as pots, pans, cheese-graters and the cooker itself must be thoroughly cleaned after use. Boyfriends should leave by ten o'clock. 'Morning or evening?' asks Kate, in good humour. The landlady squeezes the banister in despair. Please clean hairs from the shower plughole. Do not smoke in the kitchen or throw sanitary towels down the toilet. Parties or gatherings of friends must relate to a specific Personal or National occasion and must not include undue noise or any threatening excess of Afro-Caribbeans. Please do not slam the front door as the stained glass panel is loose.

'And for goodness sake,' she whispers, leaning forward, 'make sure you don't do what the last tenant in your room did, lazy tyke.'

Kate raises her eyebrows.

'Couldn't be bothered to come up to the bathroom, so he stored his urine in a mixing bowl till it was full then threw it out of the window. Now we just can't get that grass to grow.'

'I'll do my best,' says Kate.

Mrs Gallon is a series of limping footsteps on Kate's ceiling and lonely old whispers to the Lord. In darkness she stumbles out of bed and hisses into her chamber pot. In the mornings those bedsprings sing as she swivels herself to mumble for her slippers. Then the radio. An orchestral movement perhaps. She has medicines for a tickly cough, and an angry daughter who comes round twice a week with bags of shopping and who loves nothing more than to stand on the landing with the landlady having loud conversations about her mother's obstinacy. The story soon comes out that the old lady has a husband she doesn't like any more who lives on a geriatric ward in a mobile chair having his dinners creamed in a blender to help them go down. Pudding in with it, if the nurses are busy.

Kate's room blooms. Each day's a surprise. After a week she's invited to take sherry with the landlady and her husband Frank in their rooms on the top floor. With great pride the landlady admits she has cancer of the almost-everything but likes to thwart death by keeping puffed up and busy, hoovering the carpets in every room twice a week, giving her tenants a good ticking off if they're late for work, contract sexually transmitted diseases or come home drunk and throw up in the dustbins. She dusts the furniture and those awkward corners with a spray of feathers at the end of a bamboo cane. The ban on pets doesn't extend to her own quarters. She has an old dog which limps behind her as she cleans – poor thing has a grubby bandage round its middle to keep its tumour in. 'Still, old Spot's happy enough in his own way. You can tell by their eyes, can't you, Kate? Once that sparkle goes, we'll have him put down.' Other than Spot, she has a Siamese cat, a large tropical island fishtank, several gerbils, two talking budgies, 'and this,' she says, pointing to her husband.

Frank lingers in the living-room for most of the time working on plays he hopes will some day have an airing at the National. They are short pieces in which a number of people, usually seated and dressed in spacesuits, say 'Golly!' rather a lot and tackle the problems of Relativity. The first one he dares show Kate is a satirical piece called 'Time and Time Again'. From Kate's point of view the strange thing about Frank is that he never uses the word 'Golly' in his own conversation despite the frequency with which it appears in his drama. Frank's favourite expletive is Fucking. Whenever Kate takes up the rent and he's sitting at his desk or standing at the window, he says, 'Just drop the money on the sideboard, my love. Can't chat now. Thinking about my fucking play.' He never tells his wife he's going out till he reaches the front door, whereupon he pauses for a moment then shouts up the stairs. 'Just popping round the shop to get a fucking paper, Dot.' When strangers come to enquire after someone in the house he says, 'Hang on a mo. Think they're out. I'll just have a quick fucking look.'

Dot doesn't believe he'll ever have a play at the National and would rather he spent his time painting the ceiling, screwing the kitchen door back on or reading books to poor Mrs Gallon. For this reason it is always Kate he tells first when he completes a play, bringing it to her room, pushing it into her hands. His synopses are brief and to the point. 'There's this fucking astronaut, see. Read it. Let me know what you think.' Then he creeps up the stairs, turns at the last moment. 'And don't say anything about anything to fucking Dot, mind.'

Saturday Morning

Dry-mouthed and a touch hung over, she left Catherine to
sleep and cut through the early morning park past worn-out
hooligans and a pair of skid-rowers just rustling to wakefulness
with a raised flagon. She loved her shoes this morning;
watched them swing over dark grass and leafy tarmac paths;
listened to the thump of her heart and ears. Crossing into
Pennywise Lane from Chesterton Road she then skipped down
the narrow alley towards Montpelier, ignoring the red-bricked
mortuary, its black doors and barbed-wire wall. She came with
no expectations whatsoever, just smooched through the semi-
darkness listening to the cry of cats, the hums whistles and
rattle of milkmen. At the brow of the hill she watched for a
moment the slip of early headlights on the motorway then
heard her second milkman singing 'Oh What A Beautiful
Morning' as he criss-crossed the road from van to front doors
and back with his crate. Seeing her alone he begged her to take
care and presented her with a carton of semi-skimmed. She
thanked him. Venus was hanging heavily from a dark blue sky
adjacent to the bloom of a solemn moon which scattered its
faint decorations across violet pavements, black arrowhead
railings and the deserted Victorian schoolyard. She was looking
for him after all; oh, not in the sense that she expected a physical
form to touch, squeeze, have drinks with or wriggle beneath.
Rather, a spirit, a perfume, a glimpse through time, a quickening
of the heart. As she walked she remembered and as she
remembered, she walked, her ghost, her body, slipping through

other roads, other times; parting, meeting, parting again.

J's ever so careful on the last leg of the journey along the narrow lane, keeping in third gear, sounding his horn at corners, ducking his head as the unruly hedgerows form an arch, creep lower and lower. He's searching for his secret valley; would prefer a jalopy with a leather-belted bonnet. The car's hot, insects have splattered against the windscreen. This is a mystery tour, his excursion into a poetic past where in theory he'd like to moon with a book of Byron's poetry and an ash walking stick. He jerks his head at me. I grin at him. A line of grass and weeds runs along the middle of the lane. We're in a tunnel of greenery through which dapples of sunlight fall.

He parks at the top of a muddy track in the shade of a deserted tollhouse. This, he believes, would be his perfect home. Reaching up on tiptoe, I peer through the curtainless windows. There's an inglenook fireplace, of course, but the bare floorboards are covered in fallen plaster, chinks of red brick and the yellow dust of dry-rot. A china figurine of a woman selling flowers stands amongst debris on the opposite windowsill. Her broken left arm lies at her feet. J doesn't care. Moving behind me, he pulls one hand between my legs and pushes the other down the front of my jeans. His fingers dabble with me, but they can't quite reach. For a while we stand just so, J clutching me tight and lifting himself against me, but at the sound of a pheasant he becomes impatient to answer the call of the countryside and we must follow a soft tree-lined footpath to the fringes of a dark wood then wade through an area of fern to a wider, stone-covered track which leads, he tells me, to his secret place. His secret place calls him in the midst of busy, careworn days; reminds him of an ancient time and ancient habits now lost to us. We move towards it through a rich darkness, serenaded by the gubble of a stream, crack of twigs and rattle of insects. Reaching a gate at last, we climb over, run down a bank of springy turf and find ourselves on another overgrown track in a meadow of song and wild flowers. A moment of disappointment on his part is banished by a pretence of boyhood as he calls my name, holds me back and listens for the echo. 'Kate' it says. Dissatisfied, he moves on. 'This is the old road to London,' he says. He can hear the thunder of carriage wheels and the crack of whips. To prove his point to a sceptical Kate, he takes me to a broad tumbledown bridge, now impassable with brambles and elder saplings. 'This is where the road crossed the stream in the old days,' he says. It looks ridiculous and out of place now, but he reckons it's best to imagine the coaches racing across it – men in top hats, all that. Much of the ornate stonework has fallen into the stream below and J finds this difficult to cope with, so much history in decay. To make up for this tragedy he must kneel before me and squeeze his head to my middle. He'd cry if he could. In this predicament it's all a girl can do to look sympathetic and sure of herself. The wind comes gently through the trees, carrying with it the scent of time, the sounds of silence. After a respectable period of mourning he takes my hand and leads me along the valley to a particularly fine patch of meadow strewn with poppies and other wild flowers. We lie down within earshot of a low waterfall, and though it's a beautiful day, I'm finding it hard to be with him, really with him. It's much easier to love a romantic afternoon looking back than when you're nose to nose with a thistle, the sunlight or J. In the sky directly above us a hawk searches the meadow for prey, but J's pointing to a stone cottage about a quarter of a mile away at the edge of the trees which seems to have grown out of the beauty surrounding it, so comfy and charming it looks. The dream is confirmed. 'A poet lives there,' says J. 'A poet with three beautiful daughters, of course.' 'Of course,' says Kate.

We've brought a romantic picnic basket which squeaks and creaks as you open the lid. We eat ham, coleslaw, pâté, a soft unbroken pork-pie; J has a plastic cupful of white wine, I drink what remains from the bottle. We're almost French. He sprawls in the grass, but does it carefully, trying to achieve his finest nineteenth-century attitude as young men in a Monet might; Kate lacks a straw hat and wisps of fair hair. To avoid sleep we must cross the stream and follow the coach road further up the valley. J assures me we can leave our picnic things where they are because thieves and vandals haven't yet discovered this place. Humanity is safe; love encouraged.

At the bottom of the road by the Fancy Dress shop she turned left just to pass his old place. The curtains he bought secondhand were still in the window though the house itself, like a corpse laid out to rest, had something of the spirits, the shivers about it. The famous stone elephant in the garden was now on its side. The drive was black and silent but for the rustle of cold beech leaves; the front door, callous and immovable as if it had never been opened. From here he crept and vanished.

He's pulling off his tee-shirt both to cool himself down and to become more intimate with this secrecy. The careful tan makes his lean chest more beautiful and maybe I want to touch him at the tight dip just below his breastbone. Where those few hairs grow. The idea which suddenly obsesses him is that we should both take off our clothes and wade through the long sweet grass as if it's the sea. It's certainly a burning, memorable thing to work towards nakedness, watching each other as we perform, slivers of flimsy, unnecessary this and that falling at our feet. Knickers and pants last, a deep breath, an awkward cough, the kisses of wind, he takes my hand, pulls me splashing into the meadow then steps into the stream and encourages me to follow. The cool run of water takes my breath away, yet the contrast, the wickedness, impells us to lie down; we must allow those sun-flecked ripples to roll over us. His brown skin glistens. I wriggle my toes and drag my fingers through the soft mud. He's cupping water at my breasts, laughing as my nipples harden. The chill is a miraculous thing for devilment.

'Lie right back,' he says. 'Right back.' And his firm hand pushes me down. The stream's just deep enough to cover my ears, so though he may laugh and tease, the sound of his voice is replaced by the rumble of running water, the dim thunder of his movements. He's rising against the sun, his smile fading, those thin legs astride my waist. Then he kneels down, his weight upon me. His lips have so much to say before the inevitable begins, but I can't hear a word, not a word, fixed by the awkwardness of his mouth, the shy way his fingers dap at

265

the drops of water on his chest. Whether he realises it or not, his hips are pressing downwards in time with his words, squeezing me into the mud. He talks for some considerable time, though he's looking aside repeatedly as if what he's saying and the impatience of his wet erection embarrass him. To reassure me, between paragraphs, he stoops down to kiss my forehead or cheek. Soon we'll be making love because there's nothing to prevent or discourage us. My hands dangle in the direction of the current like tendrils of weed. Suddenly, by way of a mighty full stop to his long speech, he slips down, pushes into me, and though he grits his teeth, an expression of fatherly concern remains. This is going to be a splendid, though difficult, activity which he'll carry through with care and consideration. It's not wise to make love in water, so a memory tells me, but life's too cool, too wet, to resist. Each time his head moves a blade of sunlight penetrates and dazzles me and now he's spitting out the remnants of another, less practised monologue though his fingers play with my ears and his lips are frequently pausing to take a nipple in tenderness. Kate holds him tight, her ankles digging into the mud. Above us the hawk still searches, and Kate's crying or, at least, wanting to cry. His hips dip and splash as he fucks her and fucks her and she's plastering his back with handfuls of mud and weed. In thanks he withdraws, slides with the current till his mouth is exactly so then, taking a breath, bobs for her.

Afterwards we're sitting cross-legged in the stream. He asks me to wash the mud from his back then invents a similar soiling on my breasts and belly so he can stand me up and rub me wet with his palms. Soon he must kneel, put his head to my waist and watch as his long fingers thump into me; and though this was intended as a silly game, a thankful afterthought, he is driven to stiffness and passion once again. Falling back into the stream he asks me to sit astride him. The rumble of water seems to fill the valley. Perhaps the poet is developing a whole series of sonnets by keeping watch through binoculars as Kate lifts her hips, positions his erection, and with gluttonous care, fills herself up. He's begging her, between cries of gratitude, to remember his earlier monologue; remember it. She must lie and tell him she will. And then he needs to know if she minds what he's said and she says it's all right. Everything's all right, lifting herself, sinking down to reassure him.

We're washing ourselves off a second time. The hawk has fallen from the sky to snatch something from the grass. We lie on the bank to dry. Already I can feel the stickiness of sunburn on my shoulders. J's now a poet himself; a lean and beautiful wriggle of sinew, muscle and sentiment in the fat meadow, his limbs red from the cold water, his belly hairs black and plastered to his skin. Between his open legs poke blades of unflattened grass which he shifts and tickles himself against. And here's the poppy he must use to tickle my breasts and thighs. And here's Kate wriggling in the meadow, her legs thrown wide as excited voices at the edge of the wood precede two boys with sticks and a wet dog who suddenly run into the sunshine. The dog bounds through the grass to rout us out, wagging its tail, licking J's shoulder. Kate can't bring herself to care too much any more so she climbs to her feet and calls to the boys who gawp for a moment then run off down the track calling the dog after them. J's saying 'Shhh' and 'Shhhhh!', growing frantic, but nevertheless proud of this beautiful girl to whom he holds out his hand, glad of this day of rest from his invisible hunting and gathering. We dance in the grass, a kind of waltz, our bodies together. He's dallying – if that's the word – in my open mouth with his tongue; pushes back my wet hair to expose this infamous forehead, these ears; recites a list of the obscenities he intends to perform at some later date. As his list continues Kate feels a hardness at her belly – we don't mind 'belly', do we? It's the only word which springs to mind – so, as Guardian Angel, she invites him to lie in the grass, his arms out and his legs splayed. He's never been so compliant or glad of himself, crucified by the sun, his head flopped sideways, his eyes half-closed. The girl teases him with the tip of her tongue, slips fingers swiftly from one sensitive place to the next, tickles and pinches him then must fall from the sky and take him into her mouth. He's in agony, his hands tearing at the grass. She tastes him, swallows him till he thumps into the earth, dies for a moment, then scatters warm seed to the back of her throat. It's horror and a kind of love. Before his stiffness can completely die away she must climb over him, guide him with fingers and fill herself once more, riding out these final shreds. With difficulty he lifts his head, bites into one breast and then the other, weighing them, hurting them. She can see the two boys fiddling around the picnic so she lifts her hips, slithers onto him. It's as if each time she falls, a little of his life runs out of him, making him soft, sleepy, an invalid. Climbing from him, she wipes the droplets of semen from his belly with a handful of grass then lies across him, kissing him, the heat beating on her back, the smell of earth, water intoxicating her. Remember Billie Holliday? 'You intoxicate my soul with your eyes'? Unwilling to finish despite his exhaustion, he must die now, pulling her hips, inviting her to crouch so his tongue can reach her. A cold fire burns her thighs and breasts as he claws at her, waggles his head, makes outlandish sounds of saliva and breathlessness. He won't stop. His tongue must push into her as much as it can then move to this famous zone and wiggle tirelessly. It's a game of summer, a caveside pursuit as the words grow meaningless and the hum of a light aeroplane fills the valley. This is the gossip of water, the slither maybe of lizards and slow-worms, the rustle of mice, the slap slap of flesh. At once the mouth of loving opens wide to scream.

We gather our clothes and walk back to the picnic, J complaining of an ache in his legs, an alluring heaviness at the back of his eyes. And how ancient is this moment of a naked couple wading through the grass. The boys are standing fifty yards away, giggling one to the other, unable to move away or come any closer, flicking at the grass with their sticks. In a strange warm dream Kate throws her clothes to the blanket then walks towards the boys. She's in love, suddenly, with her own nakedness. J watches, his fists to his hips, tantalised yet faintly embarrassed at the same time now the recklessness of so much fucking has left him. The boy's won't, can't, move. Neither will they acknowledge her, but they must, they must as she stands in front of them, and, in a brief but exquisite moment, lifts her arms above her head, throws out her breasts and groin, bending at the knees. A pigeon calls. Good pigeon, wonderful pigeon. At the fall of her hands to the front of their short trousers, the two boys must run away, the taller of them calling, 'You're a crazy bitch, you are,' and of course Kate in her supreme nakedness must run after them, thrilling, with each stride, to the fire, the coming inside, as if she's never known fire or coming before.

J has remembered his body and is donning fig leaves, pants, jeans. We remain on our blanket by the stream though Kate refuses to dress, preferring to annoy him since he's dead now and has no interest in her as a physical form. As evening approaches the trees release a more suffocating scent and the sun has soon fallen sufficiently to bring a certain coolness to the valley. Kate dresses under protest, remembering, as well as she can, the postscript to his earlier monologue. 'Don't mind what?' is the question which will haunt her for the rest of the day and through the years which follow.

A thin twisting trail of wood smoke rises from the poet's cottage garden, reaches through the trees, then fades against a less luminous sky. At our shoes crickets bring the grass to life. We're walking back along the track, quiet because we've nothing left to say, hand in hand, shivering, but not from cold or from fear. J watches the earth, bites his lower lip, swings his legs like a defeated hero. What do I want with a city, with endless, pointless movement, the chatter of passers-by, the long cracked pavements, the conscience of artificial light, the kisses of brief fictional humour, the flash of food, pronounce-ments, gifts, lavish entertainment, the drip of shoes and fancy waistcoats, the charms of this awesome tomfoolery? She finds home, perhaps, and must leave it till next time. Living is unfair. She would die if she had a choice; die of tranquillity in the old-fashioned evening; die to the hollow cry of nightbirds, the hauntings of a meadow; die as the façade of the tollhouse becomes a purple silhouette in the infant dusk.

The poet saws and chops wood in his garden, hauls pruned branches across the lawn. Vigorous yellow flame snaps through the bonfire illuminating his face and hands. Those three

269

phantom daughters watch nonplussed from an old swingseat on the flagstone patio as sparks crackle the sky. With dusk too comes the perfume of wild garlic. At the memory of it, J revives. We must turn off into the wood to gather its leaves, crush them between our fingers. The melancholy fragrance is a favourite of his and signifies almost all he needs to know.

She came back through the cold park yanking at the roundabout and rocking one of the wet swings, saying well fuck you then, but quietly, without bitterness. Well fuck you then as she ran up the steps of the slide and slid down the polished surface, head back, feet in the air. Rooks were calling to one another from the tops of the beech trees. She was having an adjectival field day. Listen. I'm infinitely cold. Well fuck you then, she whispered. Having kicked at one of the largest trunks, she picked up a stick and thrashed it through the lower branches. The rooks took flight.

At the gate a tall man in a wax coat and tweed hat watched his dog scamper across the grass, its nose to the ground. As Kate abandoned her games, the man raised his hat and swept it to his waist. The long pheasant's feather poking from it bent against the path.

'And good morning to you,' he said. 'Going out or coming home?' His jaw closed with a thump, hiding blue lips beneath a dark curly beard.

'Neither one nor the other,' said Kate.

He replaced his hat, adjusting it to the favoured position. A crack appeared in his beard. Tongue and lips waggled once more.

'Then I'd hurry along if I were you. It's cold. A girl could freeze.'

Kate turned her attention from his boneless face to the carton of semi-skimmed.

'Oh yes. That's it,' she said, 'I've been out for milk.'

Drops of water vapour were clinging to his beard. A small badge on his chest indicated his profession but this didn't prevent his long hand suddenly reaching between her legs.

'Huh! Been out for milk? We know your sort,' he said.

Dangling Conversation

It's no good, J. I've been watching this paper for too long and must close an eye to concentrate. It took me several goes to throw back the bedclothes, get dressed and pour myself another drink. Though I wouldn't go so far as to say my head pounds, it certainly isn't comfortable. Sleep clings to the back of my throat and won't be washed away. Catherine left a few minutes ago having become very efficient, busy, heavy-hearted. It was hard to recognise her. Beneath her bed – in gorgeous visibility, by the way – lies a pile of memories, albums and what have you and you know how hard I find it to resist curiosity.

This morning's walk left me tired and irritable, especially since Catherine was still asleep exploring rabbit holes, eating cake, stroking Cheshire Cats. A smile lingered in one corner of the room and Kate was a wicked little monkey, undressing, slipping in beside her – for warmth, you understand, companionship. I needed to be close to someone like never before but at first I was rather tense because life had taken on a perverse, anonymous air I couldn't recognise. Then, well, you could have knocked me down with a feather if I hadn't already been recumbent. Catherine was a living figure moving round the room with a duster. I yawned and took fistfuls of blanket. She was wearing that wonderful tee-shirt she uses for sleeping. It hung to the top of her tights.

I'll try to say this seriously, J, though the mood is tongue in cheek. I was having a dream, a wakeful dream, some may say

271

a very sad dream. In my dream Catherine threw down her duster, came to the bed and squeezed me tight. Angels sang. Though the feeling may have been a simplification by the nerve endings of a complicated bodily response, my heart ached. In fact she was dusting each and every piece of china with a care which indicated resentment or fear maybe. Having finished a piece she'd hold it under the light to make sure it was spotless. I wanted to explain away my presence in her bed and wished I hadn't left my clothes on the chair in such an undeniable heap. At length Catherine came to the end of the mantelpiece and, standing on tiptoe, sighed onto the mirror and moved the rag in small circles, the tee-shirt riding over her white backside. What else shall we call it? I rolled and lit a cigarette. There was music everywhere. Kate was nauseous with wanting to fuck someone. There. Said it. My senses were all messed up or congruous at last, who can tell? When Catherine broke her silence it was to tell some cock-and-bull story about having to go to the supermarket for bread. Bread! A hand tickled the top of my leg. I love to write what I can barely bring myself to write. Manifesto. Throwing open the curtains and bending down, Catherine quickly dusted the sill, her breasts shaking. Then she made coffee, placing mine on the chair beside that pile of clothes. She was blind. I suggested she should have a drink, calm down.

'I don't need a drink,' she said. 'I need a fucking miracle.'

How typical of gods, J, to withhold their miracles when a girl needs one most. I invited her to talk with me. She mentioned the bread a second time.

New paragraph. The music was Jan Garabek, all sex and saxophones. My breasts were uncovered. Catherine was at the wardrobe. With her back to me she pulled off her tee-shirt and shook out her hair. There were bruises on her shoulders. Kate touched herself very tenderly; glimpsed Catherine's face and breasts as the mirror-door swung open; was scared a friend might notice the movement of fingers. Anyway, this is what I came to tell you. Having chosen a pair of jeans and a jumper, Catherine stooped to take knickers and socks from the drawer,

272

revealing a swollen, liquid wound between her legs. The socks were blue. Jan, Jan, the foreplay man you used to call him, J, in those innocent days. Years before, it was Barry White, but you grew up. A wound that some would ache to squeeze their lips to, ache with fingers to open further. The fine hairs at the base of her spine were glistening in the sunlight. She quickly stepped into her knickers and drew them up her legs, wriggling slightly as the cotton wrapped that succulence. Must stop drinking, J, one day soon. Oh Kate had to keep swallowing and swallowing, but heard herself say, as Catherine bunched up the jumper and pulled it over her head, 'I wish you hadn't got up so soon.' The bread was used as evidence for the third time. She sat on the floor to put on her socks. Legs are most gorgeous at the insides of the thighs within kissing distance of the white cotton. Kate's fingers were digging between hidden legs as she turned and pretended to go to sleep, wishing she could beat the pillows and go home. She heard the zip of Catherine's jeans and, moments later, the rattle of cups. An old newspaper which had been lying on the sofa was screwed up and pressed into the metal waste-bin. Jan was unceremoniously taken off. Then the door was pulled shut.

The Photograph Album

Catherine fooling around on a beach in her black bikini, arms tight round her breasts to fend off the tickles of a photographer; a grey-green sea heaving towards her, ribbons of foam, gulls posing at the waterline; scattered rocks glistening in wigs of seaweed. In the background, the hop and twirl of a seaside promenade, straw-hatted donkeys, a Punch and Judy show.

Gorgeous Catherine in a clown suit and pink hat at a fancy-dress party, about to take a sip from a rainbowed champagne glass; behind her, Mother Goose, Batman, Snow White and a Dwarf.

Catherine stretched across a black bed, breasts uncovered, knickers lowered slightly to reveal wisps of blonde hair, a tickly wicked look in her flashlight eyes.

Catherine on a ferry in rough seas, her left foot resting on tiptoe against the deck; a dim coastline centre-frame; she's trying to smile though perhaps she might be sick at any time.

Catherine on roller-skates about to topple.

Catherine curtseying to the camera from the edge of a pavement as a line of funeral cars drive by; a coffin in the back of a well-polished hearse.

And here they are in the park. Probably they've been duped

into the exercise by one of those spiv photographers who roam the city in summertime. Her arm hangs loosely round his shoulders. He's watching her lips, his forehead so crumpled it's easy to tell he's scared to death. He has an uneasy half-smile, the famous one. The wind lifts a tuft of his uncombed hair. He's wearing his beautiful blue tee-shirt and she, a cheesecloth blouse. In the background a plump gentleman waves his walking stick at someone or something out of frame. Catherine's legs are open. The tips of her fingers rest against the wooden bench. His feet are crossed at the ankles as if he hasn't a care in the world. Those red trousers are far too tight for him.

Alone this time, he's bunched up on the graveyard wall, the old church behind him yellow and delicate in an early evening haze. He's holding a balloon.

At the edge of the Downs his left foot twists in the grass as his blurred right swings to kick a football. He's wearing white trainers and blue jeans. Behind him a shirt lies crumpled on a lump of speckled stone. His ribs stand out, but he doesn't seem to mind. There's a cigarette hanging from his lips. The Downs, of course, are scattered with melancholy lovers, children with dogs, groups of students. Frisbees.

Unless they know of a perverted friend, they must have had facilities for a delayed shutter-release. Catherine lies across her bed, singularly pale and triumphant. He's on top of her though he's lifting his haunches to make clear what's going on. They're both naked. Catherine's ankles are crossed behind his back. Flesh is so white in the flash. He's brought his fingers right under her thigh and is touching her where she glistens, just half an inch from his penis which is a little way into her. He's trying in vain to turn his head far enough to be able to look directly at the camera. Catherine's left arm trails across the pillow. In her hand, a rose.

The Tower

Now finds herself high above the city on a narrow balcony looking down as families wander tarmac paths through stiff rockeries, pruned rosebeds and pastel-coloured shrubberies; wives rigid with lipstick and two charming children; husbands with cigars and a predisposition towards scarlet Christmas jumpers. A brass plaque beside Kate reads 'This Monument Was Built In Memory Of Those Who Lost Their Lives 1914 – 1918'. Someone has painted 'Fuck Off' across it in blue. These monument-makers love to use the phrase 'Lost Their Lives' rather than the truth. War's fine when it can star Robert Mitchum and when hostilities by a foreign country are regarded as an opportunity to let your tin-hat strap dangle. But remember the pieces of intestine, the liquefied brain-matter, the charcoal babies you could put your finger through. Oh, Kate hugs herself; it's so cold and she's so beautiful. Immediately below the tips of her shoes a line of benches has been set into the earth for pensioners who wish to remember the long-dead. Jaws wrinkle with boiled sweets.

She's remembering the girl from college who wrote a novel called *The Bitten Apple* which featured the tower quite heavily at the end. The draughtsman lover of the thinly disguised character 'Eve' fell or was pushed from this balcony on the last page but three. He struck the rockery with a 'sickening thud'. Eve looked on, her pale face hanging down. According to the text she was 'Aghast'. An elderly vicar and his tiny wife out walking the red setter spotted the man's body amongst the aubretia. The dog climbed the large stones to lick the man's face. Soon after publication the book was serialised by the local independent television company. The poor tower then had to endure a whole hot summer of television fans who'd come to lighten their obscurity by scratching their names upon it.

Joyce Butterborn, the authoress, had wild ginger hair and always brought her own supply of camomile teabags into the refectory with a flask of hot water. On the dust-jacket she was called J.M. Butterborn in Gothic lettering. If you have longings for success in novelism, it's a cracking good thing to have two initials. With grim mouth and big fists she frequently berated the refectory cooks for having the gall to prepare so many meals for Men.

As soon as the serialisation began there was an interview with Joyce on a tea-time magazine programme. She stood over there at the bottom of the hill, the tower rearing behind her. Before the adverts a clip from the serial was shown. Eve was running through those trees, the green-wellington'd lover in hot pursuit. He'd wanted to fuck and have babies and she'd realised what an out-and-out bastard he was. Reaching the tower, she looked up momentarily then pushed through the turnstile. Normally you have to put ten pence in a slot but this was ignored by the Director to maintain the tension. It's no good outrunning your bastard lover for half a mile only to find you haven't the right change to continue the chapter. The clip ended with a hand-held camera shot of Eve's feet stumbling up the tower steps in semi-darkness. The Interviewer obviously didn't enjoy being at the bottom of the hill with Joyce so he tried, unsuccessfully, to suppress her. Wasn't the series as a whole – and, indeed the book – detrimental to men?

Raising a freckled hand, Joyce swept the hair from her face and laughed at him. 'I certainly hope so,' she said.

For a time Kate was down there, on the third bench along, just in front of the rockery, fiddling with her fingers, not sure how to cope with herself. Then she sifted through her wad of fond papers, looked left and right, chewed the end of her pen.

A veil of mist hung over the city. The trees were winter against a blue sky. Just take the pen in these fingers and write something, for God's sake. Grass fell away in leaps and bounds to the rambling backstreets so she spent some time rolling a supply of cigarettes though most of them turned out lumpy because her fingers were cold. Oh, for Christ's sake, she said. Lumpy cigarettes and were those tears? So desperately did she wish to do some diary then but it lay just the other side of a fine intention. Over there the snakes of the Cumberland Basin slept in coils on an island between the true river and the man-made one. Cars, when they came, were on their way home from screaming days out. Kate stood up, sat down. I'll be fucked by every one of them. Then I'll leave at daybreak and giggle my way home. No cards. No anti-perspirant. No blusher. Unfortunately the only good world is the one constantly condemned. Commandments stink. Come let us be Christian and fuck up the race. No cruelty greater than righteousness. Oh you could put that down for posterity: words to prevent draughts through cracks in floorboards. Hillside Street lined with cold railings. A sign says 'Dogs Must Be Kept On Leads'. Returning the diary to its bag, Kate then walked right round the tower, touching it, realising where and when she was. Climbed up here, oh, not to throw herself off, but to find the tip of her old home; the tip of Catherine's. The tide's in. A tanker snoops down the channel towards the open sea.

Now down on the floor of the balcony. Flagstones cold as death itself. Kate's writing furiously. She'll be caught as sure as anything. Caught red-handed and uncomposed. No-one she knows writes nonsense in towers. Whether others should, she hasn't decided. Bits of her are proud to be the only one.

Cheering Down

Listen. The ratchet of the turnstile twists as someone pushes through – a man, perhaps, scuffing leather shoes on flagstones, searching the gloom for a way to proceed. Then, pulling a matchbox from his pocket, he slides open the tight tray, picks out what he prefers to call a lucifer and strikes it against the wall. Philip Marlowe comes at last, shoes tapping from one step to the next; Kate's very own Private Eye with notepad and pen, recording facts, suppositions, shadows reeling through slatted windows. Moving oh so slowly he picks his way upwards, touching the walls with both hands to combat a mild disorientation brought on by continally turning in one direction. From time to time he snaps into the scraps of sunlight streaming through the tiny windows, pauses to welcome them.

Death will mean little to Kate if she can cling to these pages as she rolls towards the celestial light but then the creep slows down, chooses to bring both feet onto each step, one two, one two, having a lark. If writing in the cold afternoon makes you shiver there's always someone who'll seek to make you shiver some more. Girl in a tower. Such a beautiful cunt; they've all wanted it, one two, one two, buckle my shoe, twenty-five steps and whistling; those wearily unshaven cheeks cracking under the strain. Let's grab that bird and fuck it, lads, eh up. Waggling her feet Kate tries to remember a favourite tune; it was something which lit up her eyes, sent shivers down her backbone. Charmed by melodies of a different kind, the man the fucker takes a dozen steps by storm and ends up panting, his whistles replaced by the howls of a wicked dad on Halloween. Put a candle in the pumpkin. Kate yawns. Time for a lullaby or two. We will rock you, rock you, rock you. That's the one. He stamps his feet. Let's fill her cunt up one by one. Slithers his fingers, squeals like a pig being greeted by a knife. Applauds himself and then, even as a fine young woman yawns her thighs, stops altogether, becomes silent. Pins drop. We have a clown, A Gollum, a Pumblechook on our hands. Kate longs for that swiftness of sentiment, that palpitation of the heart she remembers so well. He's quite close now, but takes a breather. Fancy a bit of fucking Chuck? Chook? He listens with ragged smile to the wicked promptings of an inner voice. Oh, fine word, Kate: promptings. Fine word. One deserves one's degree; one has earned one's place in the world through an exquisite sensitivity to language. He spits. It doesn't take a girl all day to realise how perversely men behave when they think themselves alone. He spits. Expectation irritates her somewhat. When there's a man in your tower you need truth; ache to peep round darkened corners; ache to put just one more semi-colon. Doctors would have cause to be concerned over the gravity of his breathing. He obviously overtaxed his lungs in the sudden charge just now, poor thing. A zip zips. His shoes haven't scraped for some time but now they clatter against the wall. The loose change in his pocket taps rhythmically. He's free at last to bite his tongue or whisper oh let's fuck her boys as his free hand waggles. He'd love to do it with young girls, plump girls, lip-glossed prostitutes, pale boys, tall boys in the scrum, boys with full lips from the choir, Shetland ponies, oh, anything at all simply to rid himself of the torment the unending desire the terrible love of violence the awesome need to fuck that he must carry with him. Then, just as his whispers are becoming too gruesome to bear, his waggling stops. This, your Majesty, could be the mighty orgasm, the sperm on the wall, the emblem of manhood. He grunts once, twice, three times, four, each grunt longer than the one before. And then he grants this lonesome pleasure a cry of gratitude.

An interval, ladies and gentlemen. He crackles sandwich wrappers or something. Sings. Songs of love, regret. Snatches of songs, his rich voice winding through the tower. Oh noble baritone. No, it wasn't sandwiches. He was preparing a makeshift handkerchief from the pages of a newspaper, blowing his nose then cleaning up.

Now he does his best to confuse us, climbing two steps, shifting down one, howling as he moves Dee Dah, Dah Dee, low to high, high to low. A mighty songster. Dee Dah, Dah Dee. A faint V of birds cuts through the darkening sky. Maybe Kate should clatter round to warn off the bastard but it's not easy to make any kind of hue and cry with soft-soled shoes and a harmless bag of papers. They're all here, J: my dreams in total; dedicated to you though with some heavy reservations. Dedicated to you. You'd laugh at him now, I bet. He's just taken another nine steps upward crying wee wee wee on every one. She prays he'll prove harmless, prays he'll turn pink, apologise, lift his hat if he has one. Prays he won't take her by the ankles, swing her over the balcony and watch as her papers fall like dead leaves to the rockery.

Here comes Johnny.

By The Rockery

The sun has now fallen away behind the softly undulating line of hills; the temperature falls even further with it. A scant succession of early-evening people curl round the slope from the houses over there, heading for the black gate, the scarlet-tinted cobbles of George Street and the neon thoroughfare beyond. Maybe their eyes seek patterns in the tarmac or grass, patterns of angels' wings or birds of prey, as we once did. Do it long enough and you'll become mesmerised, so the story goes.

Number one, a slim woman in jodhpur-style trousers, fingernails painted black to match her shoulder-bag; two, a pale girl with white ankle socks, cold legs and pigtails who won't show her anxious smile to strangers on benches; three, a plump-legged, heavy-ended man in a white dinner suit and black-and-white shoes who takes a busy short-cut through the grass. As he passes he must pull a golden watch from his waistcoat pocket and complain to himself. So much to do. So little time to do it. So far to go. Tufts of white hair poke between his large pink ears. He's so out of condition, it's as if his bum's on springs. Checking his watch a second time at the black gate, he scampers forward, in want of a hat and cane, a pair of curled black boots. It's a silly, mythical time of day. Last, and by his own admission, least, Harry, Larry or Barry, swift as a man of fictions should be, scooping through the gloom at the bottom of the hill, stopping dead with finest typing finger to his lips, then scooping in the opposite direction towards the gate. He's still brilliantly attired. A smart checked jacket with triangular lapels of enormous proportions; a blue shirt overgrown with flowers; a brown, woolly V-necked jumper; a pair of flared black corduroys with holes at the knees and out-of-shape, off-white, black-laced training shoes. Obviously his reading's a bit of a mixed bag this week. He carries a clipboard and clicks a pen in his left hand, hunting plots, themes, images, or, failing these, women; lugging behind him that familiar uncertainty. He's started to grow a beard, hoping, maybe to give his continuing unemployment a fashionable appearance. A nogood boyo, Mr Thomas, moving forward but always in reverse somehow; a sleuth seeking characters to denigrate. He'll be remembering Catherine with all his heart, seeing her in shadows, in the pools of neon, in the bristles of wind. Being, as you might say, a psychoanalytical man, he'll have worked it out that she said No to his attentions because she meant Yes. Ignored him because she wanted to sleep and have frolics with him. Disappeared from his unfurnished life because secretly she wanted to be inextricably tangled in it. Poor old Harry, Larry or Barry, famous for his inconsequence but unheard of even by himself; a man of words which whole continents will never read; in theory a great lover, someone who can make you swoon by lifting his eyebrows. Perhaps she'll be strolling in Huckleberry Street just waiting for him to chance by. This time she'll abandon those psychological barriers and allow herself to be Taken. From his lips hangs a cigarette, probably foreign. At the gate he pauses to write something down. He's probably been stricken by a sense of infinite grief and needs to remember it for subsequent unpublished works. I'd like to wave but my hand rests here, just here, unable to lift itself. For his full stop he dabs the point of the pen against the page then hurries into a side street listening for the tap of Catherine's shoes at every turn.

The tower pokes into the violet sky, its aircraft warning light already flashing. And don't go on about penises, J. I'm not into symbolism this evening. Perhaps a pair of eyes at a window, perhaps not. The rockery folds into jagged indistinction. A bird throws out a final chirp from the top of a sycamore. I can hardly see my words. Winter certainly curtails outside diary time. I have something on the tip of my mind which won't quite come. I think it would be rather sad if I could fathom it out. Now and then I shiver with simplicity and it's like the beginning all over again though this will be a most unpopular and time-consuming romance involving a great commitment to fantasy and the illogical. It's reams of paper marred by chaos; square yards of charmless blue. Kate adores full stops. She uses them at every opportunity. Her life's chopped up. She once longed to sculpt glory like F. Scott Fitzgerald but now she'd be happy with a greeting in the dark.

And here's an old man with an alastian come to lock up the tower. He calls loudly through its void several times before closing the heavy door, turning the key and walking away.

Infidel

'I feel extraordinarily good tonight,' he says. 'Don't spoil it.' As usual Royal Square is wrapped in a bracelet of parked cars and feels lonesome in the snaps of a cool wind. It's one in the morning. We've been to see *Ai No Corrida* at the small cinema club which has opened recently in the basement of an Indian restaurant. These Orientals are an insatiable crowd. Kate slips her arm through his and chatters to herself for a while about the gorgeousness of death at which point he kisses her hair and says, 'I feel extraordinarily good tonight. Don't spoil it.'

In a dark house of paper a petite but sexually dominant Oriental girl purred at her married lover then gathered his exhausted penis into her mouth. The literary audience tried to unravel this metaphor by whispering amongst itself. It turned out that one Oriental person giving oral sex to another Oriental person indicated Exactly That. An elderly man nudged his sniffly neighbour, saying, 'Oh come, come.' Most concluded their whispering by wriggling in their seats or examining grease stains on the ceiling. The odd rogan josh had been dripping through.

J's buoyant, bobbing along on the crest of his self-esteem, finding something to laugh at whenever Kate opens her mouth. Never have so many people loved him all at once, but we skip like lovers across Barbados Avenue and soon reach the main road which is lined with dustbins, skips and plastic rubbish sacks. Civilisation at last. A cat runs in front of us from under a parked car, scampers through the rubble of a demolished house then curls like a black ampersand on the wall of the abandoned electrical shop. 'Oh very good,' says J. 'Ampersand. Very good.' We decide against chips though the Chinese is still open, catering for other members of the cinema club and night owls from the homeless men's hostel next door. Though skilled at fucking, the Orientals are not so hot when it comes to the shape and required cooking time of chipped potatoes. The tang of soy sauce and a yellow light spill through the door onto the pavement.

'Well?' says J.

'Well what?' says Kate.

'The film, the film,' says J.

'Oh,' says Kate.

A group of smart but damp-skinned gangsters creep from the massage parlour, pulling up collars and lighting Eastwood cheroots. Kate's having dreams of carving knives but puts them to one side. J's graceful, confident; pulls her close in fine companionship. His eyes are full of night. A man can be an idiot when he's lost his heart, when the world's come right for him and when tomorrow will echo today and yesterday.

She remembers in technicolor. There was nothing the Oriental girl liked more than a penis and she'd go to any lengths to keep it exclusively hers. An accidental grandmother had somehow found herself in the bowels of Row G and didn't care much for Reproductive Organs, Oriental or otherwise. She took toothless bites of a choc-ice instead. In her day men didn't have penises, and a jolly good job it was too; instead they grew whiskers, wore buff-coloured suits and developed bellies as a support for the racing paper.

Perhaps it's memorable to walk with J at night, especially since his smile creates lines around his mouth and eyes. Tonight he must speculate on Infinity, pointing beyond the stars to illustrate, but Kate doesn't much care for it – and tells him so. She prefers the sense of wonder he seems to have held onto. He has hope and a curious self-affection even when the odds are stacked against him, me, us, them. Our walk home goes on and on; becomes longer the further we go. Kate recalls a day in the woods with him collecting holly; arriving like travellers at a narrow ravine of fallen trees and green, bramble-covered stones. 'This silence and natural desecration is wonderful,' he said. 'Like a Gothic novel.' He was probably wrong, but he loves to say that things are like other things. The remaining trees were being strangled by ropes of ivy and vine. A wall built long ago through the middle of the ravine had fallen down. Who went to all that trouble, he wondered. And there was a moment of understanding; a leaf-strewn vision of a death quite awesome. The air stiffened. Kate stumbled at the edge of the ravine but was saved by her lover.

Well fuck you then, she says. This area is gloomy with cut-price supermarkets and two-car driving schools. We come across a ragged black outline curled under cardboard in a loan-shark's doorway. Grey walls flap with bygone boxing or concert posters. Why, there's Van Morrison with torn trousers and, across his black belly, a purple anti-smoking slogan. Wherever J goes or whatever he does, wherever he buries himself or whenever some similar shape to his wags at a street corner, Kate has a feeling she'll be on hand, though the idea is extraordinarily cruel and difficult to bear. She's too adhesive by far. Hates herself for having to stick to so many unsuitable things.

The Oriental man fucked a grandmother who happened to be scrubbing the floor in penis-range of the bed. At first she carried on scrubbing in defiance but ended up enjoying herself. This outraged the real grandmother in the audience who excuse-me'd to a number of crossed legs in her row and walked out.

J's in love and tells Kate so. In love with who, what or for how long, he neglects to say. He's remembering the gaggle of excited servant girls who took hold of one of their companions in a bout of sexual frenzy and fucked her with a long wooden bird. In the background, still on the same old bed, the Oriental couple were having sex again. Kate wanted J to tell her in the wine-red auditorium if the people in the film were really Doing It. You know, Doing It. He squeezed her shoulders like a wise old man. 'Of course they are,' he said. 'Can't you tell?' True enough, the wooden bird slipped in for a third of its length.

And why a wooden bird? Kate wanted to know. J laughed, shuffled in his seat. 'Probably a symbol of something Eastern we don't understand,' he said. Oh. Kate had a cigarette though it wasn't allowed.

We run beneath the haunted railway arches, wander along a more prosperous rank of shops. In the toy store a pair of wooden clowns bounce between floor and ceiling on long springs. Pointing to them, J says, 'There we are. You and me,' He's proud, literary, prophetic; smells warmly of himself. Kate needs to pull up the blankets and fold against him. At the supermarket we turn right into Chestnut Lane, our shoes stamping the pavement in time with the thud of a bass guitar coming from the upstairs window of a darkened house. You'll have to forgive me for the boredom of this reminiscence for I'm too tired and I've had too much to drink. You always said I'd be a wino in the end. In the monastery window a single candle burns. J shakes his head. He's remembering the part where the oriental girl sliced off her lover's penis with a carving knife and wandered the streets with it poked inside her. In wind and grey moonlight there's something of the father in J. It makes itself known by degrees. I guess it has been his task to teach me everything he knows of the world; guide me with what he considers to be his greater insight and experience. He's a daddy. A book at bedtime. Someone to take my small hand as I clamber up the stairs. A bearer of gifts, a lexicon of wide-ranging advice. An impertinent hand reaching from the sky to keep me safe. Later on he'll be searching the gloom high and low for something similar to the wooden bird. Kate will lie back and be repeatedly charmed by the handle of a garden trowel, a fudge bar, a sponge finger, an unzipped banana, a pink candle. Articles of food amongst these splendid objects will then be consumed.

Stooping beneath the holly tree which hangs over the pavement, we hear from the park the sploosh of bricks in water and the untethered howls of toilet hooligans. Kate's of the opinion she must damage him somehow, damage him somehow, but each time she catches the moonlight in his eyes she finds herself powerless and quite awesome with grief.

Waiting for Catherine

Pours drink. Folds over the top right-hand corner of 'Jill' and puts her by the side of the armchair though a scholar should have bookmarks and be more reverential; should peruse the consumed text and attempt an understanding. Coughs instead. It's just a book. Something which stops when you close the covers. Kate could colour her lips an outrageous red, hook one of Catherine's black suspender belts round her waist, whisper herself into a see-through bra and a pair of sheer black stockings. Become something of a siren at last. Thinks about it. Decides for the time being to make a fool of herself by writing secrets on oblongs of paper which may later be hidden beneath carpets in a stranger's living room. And so she searches for sincerity; then, having become infinitely disappointed, she intoxicates herself. Oh, not with alcohol all the time; there are still one or two dreams remaining, a few few-and-far-between scraps of countryside, weeping willows, streams without bicycles, woods echoing to the grunts of ancient villagers, barren hills without steam or smoke or the roar of low-flying jets. Please forgive me, J. Surely a girl's allowed to be dreamy during her swansong, her concluding soliloquy. You called her magnificent and here she is trying to live up to it in a world of rooms in which time is measured, lives are measured, by footsteps on the floors and ceilings. Here they creep, tap, Do the Locomotion. Here they have rhythm without you. Here they proclaim by their movements the impossibility of changelessness. Here they squeeze her to this chair. Who's to say we can't have sentences which end half-way through? Who's to say? You called me a child and I. There you are – a real humdinger. And I decided to do justice to it – that's what I was going to write but I decided it sounded too squishy – the sort of sentiment one might throw up in a toilet bowl. Kate's head. Oh you'd love it now. There's such varied entertainment to be had out of it. Snatches of music including a Grieg piano concerto and whole albums by Dire Straits (albums is the modern word for records). A lecture on herbaceous perennials. Sound effects of birdsong. A red-caped hero whispering to his flimsy lover as she sneaks into his room at midnight. Reminiscences by friends and colleagues of Wynford Vaughan Thomas. The weather in French. Il pleut. Italian opera. A short story read for children by Sir Michael Hordern whom Kate's the teeniest bit in love with because of his voice and eyebrows. Fond and chuckling grandfathers. Louis Armstrong. A violent demonstration erupting into peace. The Fab Four – remember them, J? It's all in here, cluttering up the hemispheres and as I put words down here more scurry in to take their place. Majorie Anderson. Danny Kaye narrating 'The Three Billy Goats Gruff'. These days there's certainly a surfeit of Trolls, don't you think, and we could certainly do without those overcrowding the White House. Oh Kate, it's a wonder people don't parade with your photo through the streets of London. Was there ever such a Princess as this? She can hear you laughing because you're thinking to yourself, Oh here's Kate, right enough, making up nonsense in silly rooms as life passes her by; sitting in an armchair under the affluence of incohol creating amateur Dylan Thomas worlds; becoming grim as she watches the softness of her thighs go to waste; aching for repeats of the Woodentops. Why did Mummy never wear a blouse? Why wasn't Sam turned on by her wooden toplessness? You could see the wires, J. Life is so nostalgic when examined from afar. And then there was poor Mr Bolan. Once upon a time people put their feet down when they weren't happy with the world. Now they line bunkers with coins hoping to keep radiation at bay. Sorry, J. Only joking. There can be nothing more wearisome than the nuclear debate. Just remember Four Feather Falls, put your head down and carry on. She's pissed as a partridge. Oh I remember her, you say, as you dust preen press swash buckle lift slip and swoon your way to a tombstone. Let me assure you, J, there was a theme here but it has gradually disintegrated. This is one of the drawbacks of being a genius by birth rather than learning. It swoops through the brain like a seagull on the rampage and simply won't do what it's told. Each drink drives it a little wilder, makes its feathers more slippery. Hark at its squawking as her eyes grow wide and her pen begins to shake. For a while you were charm itself. Life almost came together. But then you needed to employ those long, painful objects and though her hands touched you repeatedly, they were unable to find any symbols of tenderness. So you fought with her, became turned on in that way. It was a struggle ending in penetration rather than war. And then you found splendour in throwing her to the floor and attacking her like a dog. Over and over it was necessary to strike her to achieve any workable response from your body. In those periods of calm between attacks you shook your head, saying you didn't know what had got into you. Perhaps you were worried, you said. After all, your big day was to come though you wouldn't give details. Let's just say I've got to see a man about a dog, you said. Yes, it's all in here, J, – Ella Fitzgerald, Grosvenor Square, Desperate Dan. Waking briefly in the middle of the night she found you still lying there, flat on your back, legs open, the demon sleeping with you. Oh she stroked and kissed it, determined to see it rise once more though she knew its resurrection meant nothing whatsoever. Fuck all. Demons could lie just as mouths could lie; and yet she tickled and teased, licked and rubbed till in sleep your seed came up, dribbled down, hung in warm blobs on her fingers. She drank you. You would have been so fucking proud, but she had no bird-loving servants as witnesses, no carving knife with a sharp enough blade. Now a less flamboyant celebration of the season is underway upstairs. No rock music this time.

291

Just hollow, sentimental songs of love, loss and yesterday. Neil Young. You know the sort of thing. Neil Young sailing hardships through broken harbours. And don't you think we ought to learn to put our feet down all over again? Drive our Cadillacs across middle America? Poke flowers down the barrels of ceremonial guns? It's fucking paradise here, J, waiting for Catherine. You'd love it. And what's even more amusing, reality, as far as John Kemp's concerned, has certainly taken second fiddle to his previous dreams. The old urgency of his desire, the exquisite care he used to take over his next move, and the sense of expectation he enjoyed, have all been lost. All that remains for him are these terrible facts over which he has no control. Can't even bury his head in a book because he's in one already.

And Aqua Marina. Remember her?

Going All The Way

Dear J, you've probably noticed I'm not awfully good at storytelling, but I'll do my best. It must be two or three o'clock by now, the dead of night, and it's been snowing heavily. The city's thick with it and so am I. Just before midnight Catherine tiptoes down the stairs then dangles through the door like a string puppet whose operator has been given the creeps. Her nose and hands are red with cold, so, having thrown off her coat and shoes, she collapses in front of the fire and proceeds to tell me off in that loving way she has. Oh Kate you really shouldn't spend so much time sitting down. And do you honestly think it does you any good at all writing that diary day in day out? Don't you get bored? 'Oh, crushingly,' replies Kate, reaching for the cigarettes – it's what she always does: she reaches for the cigarettes and reaches for the cigarettes. 'Now,' continues Catherine, 'make yourself useful and pour me a drink while I thaw out these fingers.' 'Well, J, you can imagine how nervous I am, wondering whether I've put everything back where I found it – the poems, souvenirs, photos. Catherine isn't able to smile because she's been out in the cold for too long. Do you get that? So cold your lips won't work? Unruly affliction on those wishing to cast Joy wherever they go. Lips won't work, well Fuck me.

At last she shuffles away from the fire and, on her knees, holds out her hands to receive the drink I've poured for her. 'Oh it's so good to be home,' she says, rubbing her chin with the rim of the glass. 'Is that Home with a capital H?' asks Kate in all innocence. Catherine sighs. 'Been at the bottle a bit, haven't you,' she says, using altogether too many B's. 'I bloody have been at the bottle a bit,' says Kate. Catherine shrugs with warmth. She's using the excuse that however much time she spends gallivanting late at night, there's nothing quite like coming home again. Would I like to put on some music? But keep the volume down because it's rather late. After a long search through her records I manage to find the track 'Vincent' by old Don McLean. She laughed and says, 'Oh Kate, you're irrepressible. You'll die of romance.' I like the bit which goes, 'I could have told you, Vincent, this world was never meant for one as beautiful as you' because it makes Mr Van Gogh sound really dreamy, though he was probably a pain in the backside. Most beautiful people are. You'd go out for a drink with him thinking here was a really poetic chap and the next day you'd get a letter through the post saying, 'Please find enclosed with these few words of love an Ear, my darling. Yours, Vince.' I pour myself another drink and sit down beside her, this slim Miss Muffet on her fucking tuffet. I tried looking 'tuffet' up, by the way, but couldn't find it anywhere. We're both dumb for a while but then I find my arm wriggling around her shoulders and my mouth thanking her for such a long and varied friendship. 'Well,' she says, 'I must admit it's nice to have unbroken connections with the past.' Gradually I realise she doesn't sound much like Catherine any more. Or perhaps I'm not like Kate. Whichever way you look at it, one of us is Up The Creek. Putting the drink on the carpet by her red toes, she curls up and lays her head in my lap. My fingers are easy then, coming to life, crawling through her hair. It must tickle because she keeps shaking her head and laughing. The record is one of those compilations and we're both amused by the weird thing which comes on next. It's the type of track where you find yourself thinking 'Oh God, I'd forgotten that,' and then smack your lips for a few minutes, only to forget it all over again. In the moment of carelessness subsequently introduced, I kiss the top of her head. Startled, she knocks over her drink and I'm racing round looking for a cloth, my heart

294

beating so fast I feel I might be sick, but on the whole it's a pleasant beating, a pleasant sickness. Of course the mood has been spoilt somewhat and she wants to climb to her feet, but I throw the cloth aside and hold her down. As you know, love of any kind can make a girl particularly strong and it's such a good feeling, strength. The thing is, I only want her to look at me, really look at me, but you know Catherine, stubborn to the last. By now her throat's a fine shade of pink through both the returning blood and the glow of the fire. It's then I notice the beautiful golden lion hanging from a chain round her neck. I try to kiss it, J, but she's not too enthusiastic, sits up and tries to push me away. As you used to say, moments of conflict are part of our daily lives and often don't mean what they appear to mean. Many pushes are actually pulls. I want her to be more reasonable, but she fights like crazy, pushing against the fire grate with her heels and forcing my chin up with the nub of her palm, trying to struggle free. Don't you find it hard loving people who keep fighting against it? Struggle is a facet of human nature about which you had many opinions, if I remember correctly. Then who begins to sing on the record but Dire Straits themselves. You'll think I'm being overly romantic again, but the words remind me so fiercely of you that I just squeeze and squeeze till she abandons her fight and slumps beside me. Dire Straits continue. In a fit of silliness I pour her another drink, sit her up, press the rim of the glass to her lips and raise it. The vodka simply runs out of her mouth and dribbles onto her jumper. The only way I can get her to take any at all is by lying her flat on her back. I apologise, but she says nothing. I'm trying to think of something comfortable to say, something that will cheer her up, but she lies wherever I put her with that silly grin on her face. My freedom's unimaginable. I kiss her eyelids, her mouth. It's both a good and a bad experience, J, if you follow me.

I undress her with scissors then spend ages dragging her over the carpet and trying to lift her onto the bed. People are much heavier when they're being uncooperative. Mind you, I'm biding my time, enjoying myself at last, though this business of sin isn't as easy as everyone makes out. I'm desperate to undress but each time I make a decision to go ahead, my heart races so dangerously, I just have to sit here in the warm and drink some more. Poor butterfly, she's thinner than ever; there's an almost painful fragility about her hips. On her white right thigh there's a single lovebite. Her breasts are small and cool, but covered in numerous tiny scratches. It's almost an hour before I can lie with her and even then she clings to a helpless innocence I'm reluctant to desecrate. In preparation I've opened her arms wide across the pillows and splayed her legs as far as they will go. She's been just so for some time, J, waiting.

I don't know if I ever told you my favourite fairy story. Once upon a time Kate's idling across the Downs, swishing her stick through the grass, listening to larks. She wishes to visit the Observatory, but isn't sure she has the energy to go all the way. In this moment of doubt her path is crossed by a Pieman, heading for the fair. She's tickled pink. Throwing her stick aside, she runs up to him as fast as her little legs will carry her.

'Excuse this interruption,' she says, catching her breath, 'but you're a living legend.'

He stops in his tracks, looks down at her with a smile, ruffles her hair. He asks her if she'd like to join him at The Goose and Bacon Rind after his rounds. It's the spirit of the age. If you so much as bat an eyelid at a pieman he'll want to wine, dine and fuck you, unless, of course, you're in love with him, in which case he won't notice your eyelids or anything else.

'I don't think you've quite understood me,' she says. 'You're a pieman, see, and you're on your way to the fair.'

He glances ahead to the mass of parked cars. Kate hears the scream of excited children. A big wheel turns softly through the sky. A waltzer twists and clatters to the sound of 'Telstar' while yobbos jeer at girls from the side. She can smell toffee apples, hot-dogs, diesel fuel. The pieman looks at her again.

'To be honest, love, I haven't a clue what you're on about,' he says, shifting the tray of pies on his shoulders. Now why don't you be a good girl and run along home.'

Monday 5.16am

It's one of the worst things in life that you can't come back to a shed after a break and expect it to feel the same. There's a damp unfamiliarity in here this morning. The ornaments, pens and scraps of paper don't belong to me any more. In this atmosphere I struggle on without making progress, as in a nightmare.

It was just after eleven o'clock when I woke. Catherine hadn't moved a muscle, of course, but continued to smile. The sun was beating against the curtains trying to break in and for a while my head thumped though I still found myself pouring another drink as soon as I was out of bed. Then I attended to Catherine, gathering blankets from the floor and tucking them round her before kissing her cheek and dressing as quickly as I could.

The softened park was blue with snow. Kate ploughed to the swings and back remembering a kind of composite day when you and she did much the same. And though it's silly, the thought of the New Year made her feel closer to you than ever and the fact of your absence even more unjust. Her aching continued, continues, you'll no doubt be pleased to hear. She listened to this jangle of memories and wanted to scream, but never mind, as you'd have said, never mind. The park was thick with squealing Edwardian children, familiar melodies coming crisp from groups of spontaneous choristers and the clang of a chilled town-crier. She took a snowball to the top of the bank and pushed it down towards the white path till she had a lump large enough to call a snowman's head, but it was then she saw you, really saw you, thumping beside the cedar in your thick gloves and sentimental dufflecoat. Probably you know how difficult it is to cry to someone when the wait seems to have been without end.

So, all told, she's had hardly any sleep. Each day it's a miracle to her that she's here at all. Surely the heart, head or lungs will give out soon and end this luxury. The snow has been thawing all night, much to Derek's relief. If you listen carefully you can hear it bubbling through the grass. The thick canopy on the greenhouse has started to slip, buckling and dripping as it reaches the gutter.

Soon the snow will have cleared. The first bright green tips of bulbs will begin to assert themselves and Kate will be aching for spring; knows she will. On her way to the shed this morning she was remembering where there'd be crocuses, daffodils, tulips. They will entice her into the garden before dawn, J; instil her with a sense of gratitude missing for the most part in this pointless, unfruitful wintertime.

Do you know, Mr Burgess, though a genius may succumb to gloom too often and spend her whole time waiting for nothing, she's unable to prevent these gorgeous words pushing up, pushing up, preparing to bloom?

Even now she loves to imagine J with this requiem in his hands.